She doesn't believe in love.
He doesn't believe in dating.

Celeste has worked her ass off to establish her freelance blog as a source of accurate crime news for the Baton Rouge area. Being a workaholic, focusing solely on her career, was her choice. Several years ago, she had a life-changing experience in a BDSM club that made it clear she is a submissive, but she believes her past makes embracing that path impossible. Then Sergeant Leland Keller walks into her life. He's the kind of Dom she's always feared and hoped she'd meet, and he recognizes her as what he wants as well. But she fights submission as much as she longs for it.

Leland always thought he was looking for a docile, sweet-natured sub, but Celeste captures his attention in a way no other submissive has. He can tell Celeste is aching for love and surrender. Having served in the military and now as a patrol sergeant in one of Baton Rouge's most dangerous districts, he doesn't shy from a challenge.

His job is to protect and serve, and he's not going to let her down.

§

Soul Rest

by Joey W. Hill

A book of the Knights of the Board Room series

Storywitch Press
Charlotte, NC

Soul Rest

A Knights of the Board Room Novel

eISBN: 978-1-942122-05-0
Print ISBN: 978-1-942122-04-3

Published by Storywitch Press
Charlotte, North Carolina, USA
http://storywitch.com

Book Design by W. Scott Hill
Cover Design by Kendra Egert
Proof Reading by Nevair Kabakian

This is a work of fiction. Names, characters, places, and incidents either are the product of the author's imagination or are used fictitiously, and any resemblance to actual persons, living or dead, business establishments, events, or locales is entirely coincidental. The publisher does not have any control over and does not assume any responsibility for author or third-party websites or their content.

Copyright © 2015 by Joey W. Hill. All rights reserved.

No part of this book may be reproduced, scanned, or distributed in any printed or electronic form without permission. Please do not participate in or encourage piracy of copyrighted materials in violation of the author's rights. Purchase only authorized editions.

Acknowledgments

To Trinity for the wonderful instruction on Ichinawa.

To author Angela Knight and her husband for the great Hearts and Handcuffs workshop and further important guidance on the behavior of cops and reporters.

To Marie for guidance on skin tones and other insights into writing interracial couples.

To NCMaster for his knowledge of whip play marks.

A very special thanks to the members of the Baton Rouge police department who took the time to point a romance author in the right direction and/or show me around, despite the many demands of their challenging jobs. Also a fond thanks to the delightful security team at the Federal Courthouse. This was the first time I'd ever had to pursue research with folks with whom I didn't have an established relationship of some kind, so all of you helped alleviate a shy person's nervousness and gave me great input for the story.

To all of the above, your help is tremendously appreciated and made Leland and Celeste's book all the better for it. Anything I screwed up is my fault entirely.

To all the fans of the Knights of the Board Room series. Since there were initially five men, we thought it would be over at five books, right? Then Max and Leland showed up on the scene, so we had two more journeys than we expected. Though the series has regrettably come to its natural end, it has been a great ride, and you all have made the journey even more wonderful with your enthusiasm and love for these characters.

Never fear...our Knights and their ladies will live on, making guest appearances in other series, and you know I'll occasionally pen a free novella or short vignette revisiting the characters. [For those who've never been to the JWH Connection forum to download these kind of vignettes, there's a blurb at the end of the book to learn more.]

Last but not least, every acknowledgment in my books should include a heartfelt thanks to the NCSF. The National Coalition for Sexual Freedom is an organization whose tireless efforts help make it possible for us to write and read books about kink, and pursue it personally in the many wonderful, consensual ways we do.

Hope you all enjoy your time with Leland and Celeste!

Author Note: The street names in Baton Rouge are intentionally fabricated so that the criminal activity in this story doesn't connect to any real businesses or specific locations. However, District 1 is actually one of the more crime-plagued areas of this otherwise great city, which just enhances my respect for the police men and women who serve in that district.

Chapter One

"Going home to watch ESPN and jack off, Sergeant Keller?"

"Not my fault, Jai. Your nachos are aphrodisiacs. Sometimes they make me feel so pretty I just can't resist myself."

Celeste bit back a snort of laughter. She was tucked in the back corner of the convenience store, studying the scant selection of frozen entrées. Even in her stiletto-heeled boots, she wasn't tall enough to see over the aisles of snack options, but she could still hear the exchange. Since her sense of humor had been stomped somewhere south of her ass since early afternoon, it was a pleasant surprise to find she could still retrieve it.

She'd walked away from the crime scene perimeter, away from the reporters fighting like starving dogs to jam their cameras and mics as close as possible to the weeping parents of Loretta Stiles. Fortunately, the uniforms had folded the grieving couple into a car, probably taking them to the home of a friend or relative. No need to go to the coroner's office to identify their teenaged daughter's body, because they'd come home from a Sunday lunch with friends and found her.

The uniforms manning the barricade hadn't had time or patience for her own questions, not that Celeste could blame them. The official statement had been that Loretta Stiles was the victim of a homicide. They hadn't said "brutally murdered," but Celeste was pretty sure that was the case. She'd also bet good money there'd been evidence of rape. From working the crime beat in New Orleans and here in Baton Rouge for the past few years, she'd learn to pick up cues from body language. Loretta's mother looked as if she needed a dose of Valium large enough to keep her catatonic for the next decade. Her father's face was pale and suffused with helpless rage, though his hunched, protective posture toward his wife suggested he was being beaten with an invisible claw hammer. Even if Celeste hadn't seen the parents, the police's behavior would have given her the nature of the crime. The uniforms manning the barrier and the detectives on scene had a more-than-usual flatness to their eyes. Their tight mouths, their general state of pissed-off, was higher than the norm, and the carrion circling the scene hadn't helped.

She would have spent the night at home to do some research and make some calls, getting as much of a jump on the prep work as possible before an official statement was made, but a lead for another story had panned out. She'd been building a series on the drug trade in the Baton Rouge and New Orleans areas, and a source had a tip for her. The one catch was she had to meet him in the crowded conditions of his favorite grunge club. Grunge being a comment on the location's hygiene, not its theme. So as not to stand out, she'd donned snug jeans, a bolero jacket and the boots that squeezed her feet like a garlic press. Big hoop earrings which made the sides of her neck itch and overdone makeup that clogged her pores completed the look. Though the outfit was a little younger generation for her, she'd been born with a youngish face, so while she was cruising into mid-thirties, she could pull off a twenty-something.

Fortunately, the aggravation had been worth it. Neil had given her a name that put her closer to the nexus of a major supplier in the area. He'd stabbed the air with his cigarette, held with surprising elegance between long, skinny fingers, and pinned her with eyes so deep in their sockets Celeste wondered that they didn't fall down his esophagus and get lost. "You talk to Stucco at the March club. You tell him Neil sent you, so he'll know you aren't trying to get him in trouble. And watch your fine ass, because he don't hang out anywhere near as nice as this."

She might need to update her tetanus shot before she met the man named after a wall paste. She'd given Neil a couple bills, resigned to the fact he'd use them on another fix rather than a healthy, nourishing meal, though she planted the suggestion to make herself feel better. She told him to take care of himself.

He'd grinned, showing rotted teeth. "I always take care of myself, reporter girl."

One day, he'd disappear, no one really remembering

how or when. Or he'd OD, probably in a toilet stall of a club like this. Celeste did short write-ups on Jane and John Does delivered to the morgue here and in New Orleans. Most weren't technically unidentified, since people on the street usually knew the deceased, but by whatever name they'd assumed out there, not what had been written on a birth certificate. She remembered one teenage hooker, LucyLou, who'd had a little gold bracelet with a teddy bear charm. Celeste included that detail in her obit, as well as her street name.

At least twice in the past few years, Celeste had discovered a person on the slab she'd used as a source. It made her think of the motto painted on the wall of a halfway house she'd visited. "God cares about everyone. God forgets no one. People forget God."

Footsteps drew her out of her thoughts. Since the only people in the store right now, besides her, were Jai and the man he'd been razzing, the other customer was headed her way. Based on his solid tread, he had to be a big man. She was going to find out, since she was where the nachos were, her hips propped against the self-serve food counter. Behind her, hot dogs glistened on metal rollers behind Plexiglas, sandwiches and salads nestled in a bed of ice, and yes, prepackaged nachos were stacked in a tower. They were placed next to sterno pans of meat, beans and cheese, everything necessary to make nachos as gooey as desired. Next to them were bins of surprisingly fresh-looking diced tomatoes, shredded lettuce and jalapeños.

She hadn't heard the telltale radio chatter that went along with a uniformed cop, but when Sergeant Keller came into view, she would have made him for one in an instant, and not just because of how Jai had addressed him.

Anyone projecting an attitude of composed vigilance like Sergeant Keller usually carried a badge. Or had a military background that included active duty in a war zone. Or both. She guessed both for this guy, because cops with an armed service background often emanated an extra dose of that watchfulness and a deeper anchor point of calm.

Baton Rouge had four police districts. This one, District 1, was the roughest, especially this part of it, where businesses kept bars on the windows and walk-in 24 hour operations like Jai's were rare or nonexistent. She was sure Jai had a panic button, handgun or both readily within reach, because his clientele could include the furtive, belligerent, or just plain up-to-no-good types. She wondered if a drug dealer with a gun tucked into his baggy jeans and an attitude as big as his perception of his genitalia was far more predictable to a police officer who'd dealt with slippery insurgents and IEDs.

She should do an article comparing police from military backgrounds to those without. What skill sets each brought to the table, what complemented or clashed with the job. The personal interest piece would be good when the crime section of her blog had a lull. She had enough friendly contacts in the districts now, it was doable. She tucked that into the back of her mind to put on her idea list, because a more immediate priority presented itself.

Aesthetic appreciation.

Whether or not he had meant it as a joke, this man *was* awfully pretty. But pretty wasn't the right term. You couldn't use the same word used to describe flowers and girls with pink ribbons to describe him. Instead, she thought of a sleek muscle sports car revving its engine, a summer lightning storm filling the air with electricity, or a single drop of water meandering down powerful biceps.

He had skin like butterscotch and golden-brown eyes, light enough to suggest mixed race somewhere in his ancestry, maybe a grandparent. He kept his hair in a close crop. The thin layer, which had a dominant color somewhere between black and brown, also had tints of gold that reminded her of a grizzly bear's coat.

She'd done a feature on a caged bear in a roadside zoo whose owner had been charged with animal cruelty. When the bear was transferred to a much more humane facility, she'd visited him to do the follow-up. It had been a pretty day, so she'd indulged herself for a couple hours, sitting on a rock outside his far more natural habitat, watching him move ponderously, sniff the air, study her. She expected if Sergeant Keller let his hair grow out, he'd have burnished curls in the same molasses-touched-by-sun tones as the bear had, particularly around his remarkable face. Celeste had characterized the animal's expression as a mix of nature's majesty and old man puzzlement with the vagaries of the human world.

Sergeant Keller's expression showed no confusion at all about human nature. The close crop made the most of his rock-strong facial features. While his street clothes said he was off duty, he wore a placket shirt embroidered on the left breast with the gold and blue Baton Rouge PD shield. The shirt outlined formidable shoulders and strained over smooth pectorals and curved biceps. When her gaze swept down to his stressed jeans, she hitched there an extra moment, no apologies for it. The strong thighs and denim creases around the groin area drew a woman's eyes like the dessert bar at a steak house buffet.

How many appalling double entendres could she pull out of that little visual?

She'd initially started her crime reporting career with a New Orleans paper and had come back to Baton Rouge as a home base in the past year. While she was getting fairly familiar with the patrol officers, sergeants tended to appear where needed for their assigned squad and weren't always at the crime scenes she visited. Even so, she was surprised she hadn't crossed paths with him yet. But if she had, she certainly would have remembered him.

Another reason she would have known he was on the job, his shirt notwithstanding, was the mental slap she could tell he gave himself for not noting her presence earlier. She didn't think he deserved bad marks for it, though, since her position wasn't an easy angle for the security cameras. On top of that, she'd been pretty motionless for the past few minutes, leaning against the counter. Those black and white monitors Jai had up front had a grainy feed.

Sergeant Keller gave her a nod and the quick once-over that told her he was evaluating who she was, what she was. Since he had a Y chromosome and she was dressed sexy, she could tell he liked what he saw, but he was also all cop. Giving her own self a final look in her mirror before she'd headed out to meet Neil, she'd wondered what the difference was between hooker wear and current club fashion. On top of that, in this part of town, she tended to keep a look on her face that said "get in my way and I will fuck you up--or call my boyfriend to do it so I don't break my nails."

So if she had to guess what was going through this officer's mind, it was probably that she had a light-handed rap sheet, punctuated by things like cat fights or sassing an officer. About twenty years ago, that would have been true. Fortunately, she'd survived her teenaged years.

The polite look on his face said she'd be treated with professional courtesy unless anything nudged him to be a little less relaxed around her. A smart cop rarely relaxed around someone they didn't know. She decided to rectify that situation. Every friend she made in the department was a potential source of information, after all.

Straightening off of the counter to give him room, she gestured to the nachos. "Never get in the way of a man and his trans-fat aphrodisiacs."

His lips twitched. The man had a good mouth. A nice full bottom lip that made a woman want to take a bite, the upper one firm, and the whole tempting shape of it a smooth mauve-brown color with hints of dark rose, suggesting velvet.

She was all too aware of the "no one is ugly at closing time" trigger. This man was far from ugly, but the mantra was a reminder that, once past midnight, human judgment was impaired by the desire not to face those lonely pre-dawn hours without company. The dingy wall clock showed them closing in on 2:30 a.m., well into that dangerous territory.

Humans were social animals, no matter how much they tried to convince themselves otherwise. She'd done one-night stands, because occasionally every single woman needed something warmer to the touch than a vibrator. Limited investment, limited chance for disappointment. But this guy was way outside the safe parameters of that kind of pickup.

Plus, she considered police, firemen, EMTs and other members of the press coworkers in a sense. She didn't shit--or fuck--where she worked. A casual fuck could turn to serious shit in no time. The sad truth was that everyone she'd dated in the past few years, pretty or not, had been a giant loser letdown.

Despite the twinge of regret about her dumb-ass ethics, she returned her attention to the frozen food case. The lasagna looked promising. It came with a side of broccoli, so she could put that with a fruit cup at home and feel like most of the food groups had been represented. She hadn't eaten since her quick late lunch, consumed in her car while waiting for an official statement from the mayor-president on budget adjustments that would impact mental health facilities in the area. The Stiles event and the grunge club had soured her appetite until now.

"The lasagna doesn't suck," he said behind her. She heard the sterno rattle, the waft of grilled meat smell telling her his selection. Then came the noise of the pump bottle as he chose his nacho cheese. "Jai has some fresh tomatoes up front. One of the ladies who lives nearby has a window garden. She barters tomatoes for cigarettes. If you cut them up over the lasagna, add a little salt, they'll give the lasagna more of a home-cooked taste. If you've got a good imagination."

She looked over her shoulder at him. Closing the lid of a sturdy cardboard container over a copious amount of meat, cheese, lettuce and tomato, he stacked two sealed packages of nachos on top of it. When he straightened and turned toward her, she found herself sandwiched between a cool refrigerated unit and a warm large male. The contrast was stimulating and the proximity...unsettling.

In her field, she dealt with a variety of alpha males. If the man in question copped an attitude, she might go balls-out aggressive with him, or shoot calm logic his way, depending on the personality or what she was trying to learn. Once a rapport was established, banter was typically the best way to go, a little on the rough side, so they grew more comfortable around her as the professional relationship progressed. Being seen as "one of the guys" also made her less of a pickup target.

However, there was one alpha personality type that could knock her off her stride. She couldn't describe it in words, because when she came up against it, her reaction was purely gut level. She'd experienced it firsthand only one night, at a BDSM club fittingly called Surreal, but since that night was stamped forever on her memory, she had a physical and emotional reaction to the quality that was all out of proportion with what it should be. It intrigued her, unbalanced her, scared her.

She was convinced the reason her dating life was the occasional meaningless hookup was because of that night. Whether it stemmed from the fear that she'd find it again and not know how to handle it, or that she'd discover it had been a fluke, she didn't know.

Yet when she met Sergeant Keller's gaze, she saw that quality there. Unmistakable Master, a sexual Dominant, whether he actively embraced it or not.

"Your clothes don't match you," he said. He had a Southern accent, but she didn't think it was from Louisiana. Baton Rouge and New Orleans were melting pots of Southern transplants. His baritone was infused with such natural authority she expected he'd be the top choice for any situation where people needed to believe that someone was in charge, in control, keeping them safe. Or to assure them they were facing someone capable of kicking their asses. Like a Daddy who knew just when a trip to the woodshed was needed to teach the offender the three most important rules about self. Self-control, self-respect, self-discipline.

Crap. It really was late, if she was letting her mind creep into that area. But instead of escaping to the front of the convenience store, she pivoted on her torturous heel so they were toe to toe.

"That's rather presumptuous," she said. There really wasn't a lot of room between the end of the counter and the freezer case.

Since she hadn't detected any suspicious looks at the grunge club, she surmised his comment showed he was exceptionally good at his job, not that she was poor at hers. What was curious was why he'd decided to confront her about it. His tone reflected curiosity, not interrogation, though a lot of cops didn't recognize there was supposed to be a difference between the two.

Keller did, even if it was after the fact. Rueful amusement crossed his expression. "Sorry. Being nosy."

She lifted a shoulder. "It's your job to take a second

look at something that doesn't quite fit. If you live around here, you watch after things. Like women who trade cigarettes for tomatoes."

As she blinked, the weight of her lashes reminded her of the excess mascara she was wearing. She regretted not washing it off before coming into the convenience store, but she reminded herself that didn't matter. Cop. Sergeant. Not a fuck buddy. It was important for a career girl to remember her priorities. Whether he had "that" quality or not was irrelevant. Besides, if she pursued it and found out her craving for submission had been a one-time occurrence, it would make that long-ago memorable night a lie. She wasn't in the mood for that kind of reality check.

She focused past that onto something more important. Being the best at her job. "You picked up on it pretty quick," she said. "What gave me away?"

"Body language. Vocabulary. The way you wear your clothes. They're a costume, not a fashion statement."

"I'm undercover," she said. "Slutty tough chick gave the source I was meeting better street cred than earnest Lois Lane with her recorder, trying to nail down details about the latest drug buys."

Some reporters tried to pretend to be someone else to get information out of cops. She'd followed such unsound advice only once, early in her career, and quickly learned whatever juicy tidbit earned was far outweighed by the permanent destruction of a potentially useful relationship. So she made a habit of letting them know as soon as possible. Best case, wary courtesy; worst case, open hostility.

She'd received plenty of reactions from both ends, so when his gaze went cool, that lush mouth tight and firm, it wasn't unexpected. But it did sting more than she'd anticipated. "I imagine so," he said. "Good night, ma'am."

Picking up his nachos, he moved toward the beverage cases. "Well, fine," she muttered. "Fuck off to you, too."

His reaction was why she'd worked her ass off to establish her own news blog, weaning herself off of working for a paper. It had taken several years and an absurd amount of hours, but now she had enough subscriptions and advertisers to give her more freedom in what kind of stories she'd write, and for whom. And she'd done it purely on faith. The faith that most people wanted news, not a selectively editorialized piece to promote sensational slants or a story released half-baked just to say she reported it first. It had been hard to do in the beginning, but typing "I'll tell you more when I know more" had paid off. Her audience knew they might have to wait a little longer, but when she wrote the story up, it would be thorough, unbiased and accurate.

It was a fierce source of pride to her, and she'd strive to keep it that way. No matter how many armpits she had to visit in the middle of the night, or how many hot-looking cops treated her like shit until they learned she was different.

She chose the lasagna and a small side salad and went up front, picking out a tomato from the basket by Jai's cash register. A reporter was only as good as her network, and the value of that network depended on creating solid relationships. She'd made a lot of those connections in this neighborhood, Jai being one of them. The middle-aged potbellied man of Asian Indian descent had been born in Chicago. He owned the store and occasionally did the late shift on the nights his wife was working her 3-day, 12-hour rotation as an ER nurse. When he worked the graveyard hours, he did it with the door unlocked, but on the nights he didn't cover that shift, he had the store rigged for window service only, to protect his employees. His two daughters were in college. One was fanatically pursuing a medical degree. The other was in her first year at LSU and majoring in partying, if his exasperated but always loving comments about her were any indication.

As she put down her choices, he gave her a considering look. "Rough day?"

"Eh." She shrugged, thought of Loretta's parents. "A lot worse for others."

He nodded. "Had the TV on and saw you in the background at that Stiles thing. You didn't ask any questions."

"No. I didn't have a chance to tag anyone useful for a quick off-the-record to start filling in the blanks. I left when the reporters started being bigger assholes than usual."

"I thought that's how they get things done." He was teasing her to get her to smile. She obliged him with a faint curve of her lips, but talking about it brought the anger back.

"They want to get the parents to talk about their daughter, cry on camera. 'How do you feel?' How do you think they feel, you fucking morons? When it was clear they weren't going to give the reporters shit, a couple of them are shouting out things like 'Don't you want people to know how much you loved your daughter?' They'll probably figure out a way to drag them on air in the next couple days and orgasm behind their cameras if they can trick Mom into blaming a public official, the Second Amendment, or the size of soft drinks for her daughter's death."

She took a breath as Jai shook his head. One of the things she liked best about the store owner was how emotionally connected he was to his community, which was reflected now by the flash of sorrow in his eyes, as well as some of the anger Mr. Stiles probably felt. Jai's youngest daughter wasn't much older than Loretta, after all.

"If I'd been Mr. Stiles," she declared, "I'd have sprayed them with buckshot."

"That would be a felony."

She started. She hadn't expected Keller to be behind her. Either he'd moved that quietly, or she'd been too caught up in what she was telling Jai.

"Or a public service," she retorted. "Just depends on your perspective."

She won an easing of that hard mouth, his eyes studying her a little differently now. "Some of my squad were doing crowd control at that circus."

"They deserve a medal for not opening fire." Taking a breath, she stuck out a hand. "Celly Lewis. Celeste."

She frowned. Even though she thought of herself as Celeste, she gave people her sassy, shorter byline name, because it went better with the image she projected. But under his steady gaze, she'd added it without thinking. "I do a news blog for the New Orleans and Baton Rouge areas. And occasionally I do freelance work for those ratings-driven fuck heads that made you dislike me on sight. The reason I do a news blog is because it lets me be a journalist, instead of a collection agent for inflammatory sound bites."

"She's smart, isn't she, Leland?" Jai said. "And pretty. Girls are pretty. Girls are good."

Leland gave him a narrow look, putting his nachos down to withdraw his wallet and hand the store owner a crisp twenty for his meal. *Sergeant Leland Keller.* Celeste made a note to look him up on the BRPD organizational chart. Maybe he had a social media page with photos of him shirtless. Hey, they were in a riverfront community, right on the Mississippi River. It was possible.

Yeah, right. He looked like the type of cop who'd jump at the chance to share personal info about himself through social media. Not. He put the change Jai handed him back into his wallet without glancing at it, because his eyes were back on her.

"What would you have asked?" he said, picking up the soda he'd bought and twisting it open with a short hiss. "If you could have asked the parents something?"

"Not a thing." She rolled her eyes. "They have enough to deal with right now, and the lead detective needs them focusing on vital details for him. He's the one I'd love to interview. Not that the detectives usually give up much of anything. You have to figure stuff out on the periphery."

"How do you do that?"

"Trade secrets, Sergeant." She gave him a bland smile. "Research. Networking. Vocabulary. Body language. That kind of thing."

He snorted at that, offered her the Dr Pepper before he took it to his own lips. "Want a sip?"

"Yeah, sure." Their fingers brushed, and she saw the flicker in his eyes as he registered the contact. His fingers had heat in them, and she bet his hands were impossibly strong. Gentle. She cleared her throat. She attributed the tingle under her breastbone to the fizz of the soda.

"But if I could ask him something, I'd want to know if it was a crime of opportunity or personal. Do they think it was someone she knew or was she just a type he preferred? Do we have enough on the suspect to put out a description so we can help catch him?"

"Are you asking me for that information?" He got that tight look again, as if he'd walked into a trap.

"No. You asked me what I would ask. I'm just answering you. I figure we've both had a long enough day." Handing the soda back to him after the quick swallow, she glanced at Jai. "How much?"

"Nothing." Jai tilted his head toward Leland. "He just paid for both of you."

Leland looked surprised at that, and Celeste suppressed a chuckle. "If your local Mini-Mart employee is matchmaking for you, you haven't had a date in a long, long, *long* time, have you?"

"One or two more 'longs' would be necessary," Jai said.

"I'm sure there are some code violations in here," Leland muttered. "Those tomatoes haven't been through a USDA inspection. Keep it up."

"Hey, I'm from Chicago. You don't scare me, copper," Jai said, beefing up the Windy City accent.

Another knot of customers arrived. Celeste guessed them to be three men carpooling from the night shift at one of the petroleum plants. From the way Jai greeted them, they were regulars, so Celeste took her cue for departure. Jai had kindly packed her dinner up in a paper bag the same way he had for Leland. While they were talking, she'd seen the store owner add extra packets of Parmesan cheese and her preferred salad dressing, as well as some crunchy roasted bell peppers. He'd dropped packets of extra sauce into Leland's bag.

Leland gave Jai a nod and followed her out, holding the door for Celeste with one long arm. "I think he has every kind of condiment or topping you could ever want behind that counter," she said as the door settled closed behind them.

"He says he keeps them there to prevent sticky fingers from grabbing more than their share, but I think he likes adding them himself. That personal touch."

She stopped in front of her car. She hadn't had to furnish her car a disguise for her visit with Neil. The battered and ancient Honda in a faded-blue color like old jeans looked exactly like what someone going to a club with a low sanitation rating would drive.

She shot Leland an amused look, though her radar was on alert. He'd stopped with her, rather than giving her a courteous *good night* and going on his way. "So you haven't had a date in an exponentially long time?" she ventured. "What's that about?"

"I haven't found what I'm looking for, and I got tired of fishing." He shifted. "You like sports?"

"That's pretty general. Are we talking baseball or curling?"

"The only sport that means anything."

"Ah. Football."

He had a breathtaking smile, especially when the golden-brown eyes warmed. She glanced around and only saw Jai's car and the one belonging to the three men. "Are you on foot?"

"I only live about a half mile that way," he said. "Good to have police living in some of the rougher spots. Makes it a little safer for folks, and shows the kids we're not the enemy."

"I did a story on that in New Orleans. It's a good idea." She hesitated, then admonished herself to get in her car. Now. "Well, I'll see you around."

"Would you like to come back to my place and watch some recaps?" he asked. "I usually tape a few game highlights and watch them or ESPN to unwind. Gives you a place to eat your salad. I have a microwave that can handle that lasagna."

"You're offering to let me use a microwave and watch dated sports news with you." She pursed her lips. "I'm starting to see the problem with your dating life."

He chuckled, and that baritone did marvelous things to it. She wondered what a full-throated laugh would sound like. Her abused toes wanted to curl.

"Any other time I'd squeal like a high school cheerleader at the chance to visit the home of a total stranger who outweighs me by a hundred pounds and is a foot taller than me," she said, "but I need to get out of these boots from hell. I don't want you to get the wrong idea when I strip them off. You might think I'm undressing for you and be overcome with lust."

"I can restrain my baser urges," he said dryly. "And in defense of my dating abilities, I might like watching sports, but I know how to focus on a woman. Though if the Tigers are playing--"

"Then you better shut the hell up so I can watch," she said. "We can talk about your feelings any old time."

He grinned. "Nice to know you care."

"About a man's feelings? One, you have to assume he has any worth considering, and two, no."

"Ouch. Okay, I'm taking my nachos and my bruised feelings and going home."

"Fine, you big pussy." This was her groove. She traded spirited trash talk with the uniforms all the time. She tried to ignore the extra kick she experienced when his eyes twinkled, but apparently her mouth hadn't caught up to her brain. "Maybe I better at least give you a ride to your place. Someone with your tender feelings won't be safe on these streets this late at night."

"Feisty."

"Most people prefer bitchy."

"Maybe they're not looking close enough."

She glanced up at that. He was looking pretty close. They were standing as near to one another as they'd been at the frozen food case, though they had plenty more room behind them to widen that space. No question that they were flirting, but the way he looked at her touched those deeper things inside her. It made her hold his gaze longer than was wise. His shoulder twitched, and she thought he was going to lift his hand, trace her mouth with one of those long fingers. She'd stay still as he did it, waiting for him to tell her what he wanted next.

She stepped back, broke the spell. "I'm not trying to assume anything here, but I don't want to be misleading, either," she said. "I don't date people who have a good chance of being a lead or source. It's late, and I know how these things can unfold. Going back to your place can lead to other stuff. We're both adults, no sense denying it."

"Okay." He pursed that distracting mouth. "Then I'll make you a couple promises. You will never use me as a lead or source. And no matter what, we won't have sex tonight. I won't take off a single item of clothing. Not even my shoes. Even if you taunt me by taking off your boots."

The man was charming, mainly because he wasn't trying to be charming. Despite the humor of the last statement, every sentence before it had been issued in a straightforward tone, with that unsettling direct eye contact. He was laying down the structure, the rules to dictate how it would be between them. Also a Dom thing. She couldn't help shifting her gaze away when he did that. She tried to snap it right back, but she saw the flicker in his gaze. He'd caught it, and she had a feeling he'd understood why she'd done it better than she did.

She tried to remain sensible, steer it away from all that. "So if I strip down naked and beg you to bang me like drum, I get nothing."

"Nada. Though you will officially be the meanest woman I've ever met. Considering some of the people I've met on the job, that's saying something." His glance slid over her. "I can't promise I won't look. You can't hold that against me."

"I'm not going to hold anything against you." She couldn't go to the home of a man she only knew from a convenience store bonding experience. Especially when that was the least dangerous thing about him. Telling herself a stern *no*, she started to backpedal toward her car.

"Looks like you're striking out, Sergeant Keller."

She jumped at the whine of the speaker Jai had mounted on the gas pump island and glanced through the window. Jai clicked the button again, smiling at her. "Despite what you've told me, apparently cops *don't* get pussy whenever they want it."

She choked on a chuckle as Leland threw a glare toward the store owner. Jai shrugged, lifting his hands in a posture of total innocence. But he looked toward Celeste again, his expression sobering as he pressed the mic control. "He's okay, Celly. He's good people. I'd trust him with my own daughters. If I'm wrong, come get me and we'll shoot him. My gun's bigger than his."

"But his aim's so bad he couldn't hit a parked car with it," Leland muttered. "Unless he threw the gun butt first."

The three men came up to the cash register to pay for their items, so Jai clicked off. Leland turned his attention back to her. "I'm good people," he repeated. "So see? You can trust my word. If you get tired, not a problem. I've got a comfortable couch where you can sack out until daylight."

She lifted a brow, blinked. "Do you usually ask strangers to sleep on your couch, Sergeant Keller?"

He glanced toward the car. "I'm not sure that's going to get you home, unless home's across the street."

"You'd be surprised. That car's a lot tougher than she looks. And I do have a cell number, Dad. I can text you when I get home safe." Which would give him her phone number, and her his. Still a mistake, but a more manageable one in the rational light of day. "It's kind of you to be concerned, but I do know this area of town."

"Which is why you should be jumping at the chance to find shelter until morning, when the worst riffraff crawl back into their holes." He crossed his arms. "I wasn't going to point this out, but you are about to be guilty of a serious code violation."

"There is nothing wrong with my vehicle. My tags and everything are up to date." At least, she thought they were.

"Not that. I bought you dinner. There's a rule that says you're at least required to eat it with me."

Swallowing the chuckle, she schooled her face into miffed indifference. She pulled the lasagna out of the bag and extended it to him. "A fair point. Jai has a microwave inside. I think it's four and a half minutes on high."

Under his bemused gaze, she settled herself gracefully on the parking curb, glad the tight jeans had spandex as she stretched her legs out in front of her, crossed her ankles and leaned back on her palms. The release of pressure on her aching arches made her want to moan. She might not get up again for a while.

"Open air dining works best for me." She smiled brightly. "And if we're talking code violations, when a man buys a woman dinner, dessert is supposed to be included. A Hershey bar should work, if you're springing for the full-course meal."

Amusement crossed his handsome face, but something else, too. Dropping to his heels, he took the frozen box from her, but not to heat it in Jai's microwave. He slid it back in her grocery bag, nudged it to the side so there was nothing between the two of them, and reached out.

Celeste went still as he cupped her cheek. His large hand cradled her face as he studied her. If he'd touched her in a more active manner, she would have drawn back, but that steady stare, the light hold, kept her still. Mostly still. Her lips had parted, her breath held in a peculiar stasis. When at last he moved, it was to slide his thumb across her bottom lip, tracing it just as she'd imagined. But then he kept going, caressing a path from the corner of her mouth, along her cheek to her jaw and lower, to her neck. The solid pressure of his thumb rested on her thudding pulse briefly before he stroked beneath her chin, making her lift it to him. She should be pulling away, saying something to break the spell. They were sitting in a convenience store parking lot, for God's sake. But she was only aware of him, the dense space between them. The way his eyes held hers as he spoke.

"You like bratting, don't you?" His voice was a quiet rumble. "If I had to make an educated guess, I'd say how much you like it scares you, because sometimes *like* is just a different word for *need*. You think you'll get in over your head, so you deny yourself."

When she was interviewing someone for a story, or cultivating a source, there was a click point. That was when the person made a step toward either trusting her enough to offer truth, or retreated behind shields and blew her off or bullshitted to establish distance, boundaries past which she wouldn't be invited if she couldn't find that pivotal instance again.

This was such an instant. All she needed to do was react the right way. She could pretend like she had no idea what he was talking about, and back that up with affront or fake laughter, an offhand comeback to take her to safer ground. But it was late, nearly three in the morning, and that damn vulnerability was affecting her more than she wanted to admit. The best she could summon to defend herself was silence.

"What I said in there, I meant," he said. His hand on her face was warm, his golden-brown eyes too kind. "Come back to my place, eat your dinner, watch some TV with me. Get to know me, and let me get to know you. That's all."

He straightened and extended the hand that had touched her, offering to help her up from the curb. As she tilted her head, she noted he was a lot of man from head to toe. She didn't see anything between those two points that helped her resist his offer.

"It's not a date," she said shortly. "It's two people who work in overlapping fields having a friendly meal and watching some TV."

"I gave up fishing, remember?" He closed his hand over hers, tugged her back up to her feet. "That's all dating is."

The stab of pain through her arches and cramped toes decided it for her. "I'll probably change my mind by the time we get to your place and kick you to the curb," she said, for form's sake.

That easy smile crossed his face once more. Picking up both their bags, he headed for the convenience store entrance.

"Where are you going?"

"To get your dessert. If I have chocolate, you won't change your mind."

Chapter Two

In the half-mile drive from the convenience store, she came up with a million good reasons she should change her mind, all of them rotating around that sudden serious exchange on the curb.

"All right?"

She jumped at a brush of fingers along her hand, which was clutched white on the wheel. She focused on Leland's concerned face. "Yeah," she said. "Fine. You know, I am really tired. I--"

"This is me, here. This next driveway."

Her attention went to his house, a box shape with wood siding. Typical for the poor neighborhood, but the simple structure was painted a clean white with green shutters. A small front porch was partially screened with lattice, attached between two posts. The tin roof looked less than five years old. The concrete steps that led up to the porch were much older, a mottled dark gray and yellow. Though they had a few small cracks, they were still serviceable. Curving around back, the gravel driveway led to a ramshackle carport with a shed built against it.

The tiny yard was mowed and edged, and the azaleas, hydrangeas and evergreens grouped around the foundation were well-tended. In short, the house looked like it had a conscientious owner, who had a few pending improvements to make.

A lawn jockey marked the short walkway connecting his driveway to the front door. The metal statue had been painted to look like a police officer, the shirt blue with a yellow BRPD badge on the breast. A wooden sign hung from the hitching ring clasped in his outstretched hand. "Po-po Place" was painted on the sign, pictures of crossed handguns serving as borders on the corners. A cheerful looking pair of wooden handcuffs, painted black, underlined the wording.

It was so whimsically irreverent, she couldn't help but chuckle. "I'm guessing you didn't do that yourself."

"I believe it was compliments of our teen graffiti artists,

since it's a little above the creative talents of the local drug dealers. God only knows where they got the lawn jockey. It's vintage, one of the heavy ones. Probably stole it off some nice lawn in the Garden District, though no one ever reported it missing. Smart-asses." But his deep voice held affection for the culprits. "I woke up one morning after my first month here and found it. My mom added the mums and brick border around it."

"It makes it easy to find you. Are the bushes your mother's plantings as well?"

"Most of it. She got me started, called and told me how to take care of them, what to add to fill it in as the seasons change. Just an excuse to talk, not that she needed one." He glanced at the front of the house, his mouth softening. It was too dark to see his eyes in the car, but she heard the love, and the loss. She deduced his mother had passed long enough ago that he could talk about her easily enough, but not so long ago that the grief didn't still slip through.

"Don't move," he said.

Her brow creased as he got out of the car. She'd lost her opportunity to make a smooth getaway. When she watched him come around the grill, she realized he'd made her wait so he could open her door. It had been a long time since a man had done that for her. While she appreciated the courtesy, she wondered if he'd done it for that reason alone or to emphasize what he'd started on the curb of the convenience store. He was taking charge of the situation.

He opened her door, held out a hand to help her from the car. As she lifted her gaze to his face, she saw patience. Calm. Much calmer than she felt.

Just TV and dinner. If that was how he was viewing this, she could do it, too. But she wasn't in the habit of lying to herself--well, not as much as she used to do--and this was a testing ground. She rationalized that she could have mistaken his meaning with the whole bratting comment. But even if she hadn't, he was likely pretty serious about keeping it platonic and easy tonight. She couldn't imagine a cop stating straight out to a reporter that he was a sexual Dominant. She sure as hell didn't want to talk about the things inside her that meshed with that, things she spent a lot of time ignoring, enough that it had pretty much killed casual dating for her.

"Celeste, would you like to know why you gave us the name Knights of the Board Room? Why you taunt us through your columns, why you goaded us by showing up at Club Surreal three times?"

She hadn't been blessed with an eidetic memory, but that night she'd been forced to see that what she needed in a relationship might be the antithesis of what she'd always thought she wanted. She'd tried to ignore it, bury it, but no detail of that evening dimmed with time. She thought about it too often. Plus, she had most of it on tape.

"There's a term for it. It's called bratting, actively seeking retribution. Asking for something you don't truly understand, but something inside you craves.

Returning to the present, she met Leland's gaze. Damn it, it was just a frozen dinner and some sports clips. Setting her jaw, she placed her hand in his.

This time the contact sent a full body shiver through her, and his grip was firmer. She wanted to jerk away, just run. While not wanting to come off like an idiot held her in place, she reminded herself that being governed by self-consciousness instead of self-preservation was the kind of thing that resulted in a woman's body being found in the woods. She wasn't worried about that with Leland, though, and it wasn't just Jai's endorsement. When Leland touched her, she knew she had nothing to fear from him in that way.

He dropped her hand once she was out, giving her some breathing room as he carried their two sacks of groceries toward the door. She paused to pull her go-bag out of the back, locked her car and followed. The man worked a pair of jeans as well from the back as he did the front. Christ, what an amazing ass. High and taut, it made a woman want to grab two handfuls and hang on as he plunged into her, his cock hammering her hard and deep, his breath against her face and neck. Her gaze slid to the pull of his shirt over the wide shoulders. She thought of those muscles rippling under the honey-gold skin as he braced himself over her. He'd tell her she'd take all of him, command her to lock her ankles higher over his ass so he could thrust so deep into her, she'd have no doubt who owned her, body and soul. He wouldn't coax or compel her surrender. He'd just demand it. He'd still the voices, so all the decisions were his. Yet weirdly, the choice to let it happen would be her ultimate decision, the one that made everything else work.

Jesus. She'd paused, her breath shortening at the power of such an image. Shoot her now before humiliation embedded itself in her brain like a permanent thorn. Which would be the end result, if she made a fool of herself in front of a man who was putting off vibes she should resist but couldn't.

In college, she'd thought herself as far from the Dom/sub world as a girl could get. Then she'd done a paper on the subjugation of women and browbeat a friend into taking her to a BDSM play party. In retrospect, the friend had probably hoped Celeste would see it differently firsthand, but Celeste had viewed it through a lens made up of self-righteous judgment and what she told herself was just a tinge of fascination, ruthlessly squelched. She'd condemned the BDSM elements in her final paper, and had kept a chip firmly on her shoulder against it for years afterward.

"Methinks the lady doth protest too much" was almost too painful a cliché, but it had fit.

Maybe if she'd had the balls to take the leap with an online relationship, or had visited Club Surreal on her own again, she'd have found a plethora of Doms to try and she wouldn't be drawn to Leland like the Pied Piper of Hamlin. Lack of options was what had her responding so strongly to him.

She stopped at the bottom of the stairs. "I should go," she said. "I am going. Let me have my lasagna. And my chocolate."

She was being stupid, acting like one of those crazy women who assumed way too much on the first date. But thanks to her job, she had highly developed intuition, and she knew what she knew. It was best not to start this.

He'd unlocked the door, gaze sweeping the interior as he deactivated a security system. Stepping back out, he held the screen door open for her with his body.

"You were right," she said, as equally as she could.

"I'm scared of this. I don't think this can go where you want it to go."

"You're the prettiest chicken I've ever seen standing on my sidewalk."

She narrowed her eyes. "You're calling me a coward. Or laughing at me."

"Neither. Being afraid isn't the same as being a coward." He pushed the door further inward with one long arm, an invitation. His gaze met hers. "Come inside, Celeste."

His voice had that gentle, inexorable note again that caressed her agitated nerves, surrounded her like a fleece blanket on a cold night. It wasn't persuasive or coaxing. It was the lack of those elements that made him irresistible to her. There were so many ways he could mess this up. Yet her anticipation of it, building to dark hope, told her how worried she was that he wouldn't mess any of it up. That would be her job.

As she stared at him, memory swam to the front of her mind. Herself as a teenager, sitting on the stoop of her mother's trailer. She'd fed her siblings and was smoking a cigarette, a habit she fortunately kicked when she reached her twenties. Two children lived in a trailer a couple lots down from hers, a girl and a boy. As Celeste had sat there, she'd heard their mother call them in for their supper. "Les, Tina, come on in. Your supper's ready."

It was the tone of voice that had dug into her gut, held her in place. Yeah, supper could be a bribe. Heaven knew, it was the way she managed to corral her two younger brothers when they were running wild. When she got them back to the trailer to eat, she had half a chance of getting them bathed, making them sit down to do homework.

But this mother hadn't called to her children in a thin tone of desperation, a cross between empty threat and whining plea. It was a loving command. *You will come when I call, because I love you and I'm in charge of your care. And I expect you to respect me.*

"Honey, do you want to come join us? There's plenty."

She'd been startled to look up and see the woman talking to her, her gaze friendly but concerned. Celeste now recognized it as how a decent human looked when they saw a person in need and wanted to help. Back then, such a look had merely made her suspicious and wary.

"No, thanks. I've eaten."

"You sure? You look hungry."

She was always hungry, never full. The body had to occasionally feel full of something, and when happiness and love weren't around to accommodate, hate, bitterness and anger were ready to step into the void if you weren't vigilant. But they weren't filling.

"I'm sure."

She wasn't sure at all, but by then she couldn't afford to show any weakness. Childhood was far away and she'd already learned not to trust adults. Their promises were worthless. She had no father, and her mother spent most her time trawling for poor substitutes, while depending on her teenage daughter to raise her other three children and figure out how to spread whatever money was thrown her way for shoes, food and the never-ending need for school supplies.

Good Christ. If this guy was making her feel this much just from a chance encounter, his impact on her senses went way beyond a late-night booty call. By saying those simple three words, he'd made the things that could surge up in her lonely heart in the dead of night overflow.

She swallowed, met his eyes. "Will you say it again?" Would it feel the same way the second time?

He nodded. "Come inside, Celeste."

The significance of her request brought additional heat to his gaze, because of course she was confirming his knowledge of what she was, what she wanted. He'd said nothing but TV tonight, but she knew enough about BSDM stuff to know how much could happen just mind to mind. It didn't have to involve sweaty sheets, getting naked or the awkward issues of protection to be over-the-top intimate, far more soul-baring than simple sex.

Yet she came up the stairs, came to him. When she was close enough, he brushed a wisp of hair from her eyes. She had a pixie cut, the hair severely short on her neck and over the ears, but long on the top so the streaked brown strands scattered across her brow and curled over her right ear. In her exposed left ear she had two diamond earring studs in addition to the big hoop. One of the studs was in the second piercing in her lobe, the other at the upper curve of her ear. He passed a fingertip over those as well, sending a tingle down her neck.

"Nothing to be scared of, darlin'. Except my microwave causing a power overload on the outdated wiring and catching the house on fire."

She smiled. "I assume you know some firemen who'll come to our rescue."

"Maybe. If they don't have a card game going. They tend to think cops are too full of themselves."

"Well, that's true." She tucked her tongue in her cheek. "But you and I both know firemen love the chance to rescue a cop, rub his nose in it. They'd be here almost as soon as you placed the 911 call."

"You're right. I'm likely to put pride first, so we'll sit on the front lawn and watch it burn. I'll salvage the nachos so we can snack by the bonfire."

She chuckled. When he dropped his hand to her hip, giving her a nudge toward the interior, she took a breath and hoped for the best. As she stepped over the threshold, she had to turn her body to navigate between him and the doorframe. He curved his hand over her lower back, an incidental embrace. Her thigh brushed his knee where he had his shoe braced on the threshold, his leg slightly bent. He had a scent like the house. Old wood, lemon and coffee, with an intriguing ripple of peppermint. She avoided meeting his gaze as she stepped inside, putting some space between them. She saw a large recliner, braided area rug, flat screen, two-seater couch and a sturdy rocking chair. The living room was so small the furniture formed an unbroken circle except for the space between the couch and rocking chair.

"If you want to change while I heat up the food, the bathroom's in the hallway there," he said.

"Excuse me?"

He pointed to her go-bag. "I assume that's carrying a change of clothes, since you were playing dress-up tonight. But go ahead and take off the boots here. Give your feet a break. Test my control."

Shooting her a quick grin at that, he went into the

kitchen to put their food down on the counter. That didn't take him very far from her. She told herself to go into the bathroom to change all of it, but instead she put her go-bag in the rocking chair and gripped the top of the chair to steady herself. She didn't look up as she unzipped the first ankle boot. Tick, tick, tick. She wasn't trying to be provocative, not consciously, but the boots had some age on them and were from a secondhand store. She didn't want the teeth to stick, so she had to lower the zipper gradually.

When the bags stopped rattling, she kept her head down as if she didn't notice, but she was keenly aware he was giving her his full attention. She was leaning over, which meant the snug jeans would be straining over her ass. If he took two steps, he could be behind her. He could put his hands on her hips, put the sizable erection that her brain conjured for him against her buttocks, against the thudding pulse between her legs, thin denim doing little to separate the heat of their two bodies.

The arch of her foot screamed in joy as she slipped the boot off her heel. It made a whisper against the knee high sheer stocking she'd worn beneath the pants. She straightened, one foot on the floor, her other knee bent since that foot was still propped up on a stiletto. When she dared a quick look over her shoulder, Leland had his arms crossed over his powerful chest, heel hooked around his ankle as he leaned in the kitchen doorway. In that position, his biceps were as big as the jumbo turkey legs they sold at festivals.

She'd learned those were mostly ham when she'd had to do a freelance piece on the horrors of fair food. The article was pointless in her opinion, since people didn't eat fair food to be healthy, any more than they went to McDonald's to eat a salad. But it had paid that month's light bill.

The kitchen light was also the entryway light, so it illuminated her but turned his face and body into a formidable silhouette. She wet her lips, intending to say something casual, but he spoke before she could.

"Now the other one."

She told herself to say something flippant to alter the

mood. Or collect her boot and hobble to the bathroom. She'd change clothes, gulp down her entrée and then head out after fifteen minutes of mindless TV watching. Instead she obeyed. She didn't acknowledge to herself that she was doing it purposefully. It was a weird subconscious, conscious thing. Leaning down, she unzipped the other boot. When she straightened he was there, reaching over her shoulder to take it from her hand. He picked up the other boot, placing them tidily by the door. She pivoted to face him and blanched.

"Holy God, you're tall."

Humor crossed his expression. "I'm not tall. You're short."

"It's a good thing you said we're not ever going to have sex. I'm not sure all our parts could align without circus contortions."

"I'm pretty flexible," he said, unperturbed. "And for a reporter, you don't have a good recollection of detail. I said we're not going to have sex *tonight*. For sex to be an impossibility between us, the world would have to end tomorrow. Which, if you have some inside knowledge about that, let me know and I'll change the rules. If the world ends tomorrow, everyone should have sex tonight. Including us."

She laughed, she couldn't help it. Had he sensed she needed that, that things were already too intense? Either way, it emphasized what was unsettling about him as much as it was attracting her. He seemed to be in control of things.

"Typical male." She picked up her go-bag and moved toward the bathroom. The top of the hallway opening was arched, a pleasing architectural feature for the modest house. As she closed the bathroom door, she heard Leland start the microwave.

The walls and floor of the bathroom had tiny golden tile likely dating from the sixties, but the space had been updated with current fixtures. Though they had been chosen to accommodate the smaller space, they were efficient and the silver gleamed. Leland Keller kept a clean house, which explained why he hadn't hesitated to invite a woman back to it. It supported her theory that he'd been in the military, and long enough that keeping his surroundings in order had taken permanent root. Former inmates from mental institutions had that tendency as well.

There was a print on the wall, the title penciled into the matting. "Sunset Over a Wake County Tobacco Field," by artist Micah Mullen. The colors were bright, the shapes geometric, the tobacco plants outlined in black. It was a vivid piece of color against the white walls and seemed to fit the man.

She washed her face. She had makeup in her go-bag, but her skin was so happy to breathe again she left it that way. She brushed her hair to release it from the brittle hold of the mousse she'd used to tease it up for a clubbing look, then feathered the long top strands over her brow. They fell in a softer framing arc along the right side of her face, the furthest tips reaching her cheekbone. Her hair would be more pleasing to the touch now, and the style enhanced her large hazel eyes, the decently thick lashes.

She wasn't a great beauty by any means, but she knew how to enhance what she had. Which she shouldn't be doing, because she shouldn't be encouraging things between them. With that thought in mind, she changed into a drawstring skirt, put a long-sleeved, cream-colored tee over it and decided to stick with bare feet, carrying her canvas sneakers in one hand and putting everything else in the go-bag. There. She didn't look sexy anymore. Just Esther Celestial Lewis, the average-looking girl whose only extraordinary feature was her middle name.

Maybe there was a time she'd felt sorry for herself and yeah, maybe she still had some dysfunctions to work out here and there, but embracing a goal and working her ass off to make it happen had gone a long way to curing the crybaby oh-woe-is-me syndrome. That and working crime stories, where she saw far worse situations, like the Stiles's today. LucyLou, the teen prostitute who'd ended up in a morgue with nothing but a teddy bear bracelet and a race track of needle marks up her arms, would trade lives with Esther Celestial Lewis in a heartbeat. More than that, she'd think herself blessed with good fortune.

Such thoughts put things in perspective, even if they didn't make her any less of a disaster when it came to relationships, or help free the things inside her she longed to offer someone. The chasm she had between desire and trust made it far more likely she'd wake up a fairy princess than in a decent relationship with a good man.

The smell of pasta and tomato sauce cooking made her stomach growl. As she left the bathroom, she caught a glimpse of the bedroom. How he'd managed to squeeze a king-sized mattress through that door was a mystery, but he had a tan quilt over it with a brace of brown, tan and green pillows. It was a bachelor's house, but her female preferences were pleased by the comfortable touches of color. Leland Keller noticed his space and liked making it home. Given what he saw every day in his job, it made sense. Ever since working in deeper, darker places on the streets, she'd paid more attention to her own home environment as well. For him, it was a colorful print on a white wall in a bathroom, or a few earth-toned throw pillows. For her, it was a patio garden of various cheerful flowers she could see from her living area, and a whimsical collection of thimble-sized glass figurines lined up on the window ledge in her kitchen.

She was tempted to step into his bedroom, see what might be out of view that would tell her more about the man, but she restrained herself. While everyone had a story, not everything in the world was put there for her to tell that story. Even so, she could see the cracked door of his closet, so she let herself imagine what was there. Uniforms, pressed with sharp creases. If she touched them, the fabric would release more of that peppermint scent. His shoes would be lined up on the floor, shiny and ready to go. He'd have a belt or two, and she'd let them slide over her palm. She'd think about him threading one through the loops of his trousers, his long fingers deftly fastening the buckle. When he donned the heavier belt with his weapon over it, he'd likely hook his thumb in the strap, bracing his hand there as he drank his morning coffee and looked down at the day's paper, spread out on the kitchen counter.

Wondering at herself, she moved back into the living room. The bedroom and bathroom seemed austere, uncluttered, but the crowded furniture in the living area still made sense. A man who enjoyed his sports wasn't going to be deterred by room dimensions when he wanted to stretch out on a recliner or couch and watch the game. She found a bowl of red-and-white mints on the coffee table. A glance into the kitchen showed he had a much larger jar of them in there. So now she knew the source of the peppermint.

The sofa did look pretty comfortable, as he'd said, with deep cushions on the back and seat. She curled up on the end of it that gave her the best view of the male enigma in the kitchen. He'd put her lasagna on a plate and her salad in a clear glass bowl and was cutting up the tomato over both. "Turn on the TV. It's already set for the sports channel. Beer, ice water or sweet tea?"

"Homemade tea?"

"Made by my neighbor, Gilly. Yeah."

"Is she sweet on you, Sergeant Keller?"

He chuckled. "You have no current competition, darlin'. She's ninety-two. She keeps threatening me with her granddaughters, but since they don't come check on her anywhere as often as they should, they don't make my A-list."

"Harsh. Just so you know, I killed my grandmother for her giant inheritance. That way I got the money and didn't have to visit the old bat. A win-win."

"Efficient."

"I thought so." She turned on the TV as he brought in the food, set it on the coffee table. Crunchy red peppers and dressing were aligned in their packets on a plate beneath the salad bowl. The Hershey bar was next to the plate. "Gotta say, the service at this restaurant is better than most, Sergeant Keller."

"Don't forget to tip the waiter."

She decided to slide onto the floor and tuck her legs under the table to eat, whereas he sat down on the couch. As he dug into the nachos and she started on the lasagna, she noticed his knee was so close that when she leaned forward to take bites of her food, her shoulder touched it. He didn't move away. Neither did she.

As dates went--if she was calling this a date--she found it was the most pleasant she'd had in quite a while. They swapped comments about play footage, traded opinions about teams and coaching tactics. From the flare of approval in his face, she knew she earned points for showing she not only understood the basics of the game but enjoyed its nuances.

"Christ. They lost to that fucking bunch of losers? Nobody loses to them. I'll be old as Gilly before the Carolina Panthers have a decent quarterback *and* coach at the same time."

Except for LSU, it was the strongest reaction he'd had to any of the pro or college teams. That, and the picture in the bathroom, helped her make an educated guess on his accent. "You're from North Carolina."

"Yeah. Came from rural tobacco country. Attended NC State after I served in the Marines." Getting up, he disappeared into the bedroom, returning with a BRPD sweatshirt. "Here you go. Gets drafty in these little old houses."

The cold had just started to penetrate the thin knit she was wearing, so his timing was pleasantly impressive. She put it on, rolling back the sleeves since the garment dwarfed her. When she tackled her food again, she was amused to see he'd put a small handful of loaded nachos on the corner of her plate. She put a forkful of salad on his and laughed at his expression.

"Those are called vegetables," she said, pointing to the carrots and broccoli. "Tomatoes don't count. They're like ketchup. All food is not meat, cheese or chip."

"Doesn't mean it shouldn't be. I'd rather have half that candy bar."

She stuck her tongue out at him but gracefully relinquished half of her dessert to him. He had cooked, after all. When she finished eating, she took her dishes back to the kitchen, then came back to the other end of the couch, curling her feet up under her again and resting her head on one of the throw pillows there. She watched him finish off the nachos and then sit back with his beer, bracing his feet on the scarred coffee table.

"You can move to your recliner," she said. "I won't think you're rude. Remember, this isn't a date. Just a meal and sports between people with overlapping career choices."

"Mmm. I like where I am, but thanks." As he lifted his

beer to his lips, he curled his other hand over her toes, warmed them with his grip. His thumb passed over her arches, began to knead. She held her breath at the sensation, wondered if she should tell him to stop.

"I assume a foot massage between people with overlapping career choices is okay," he said.

"I think it's a gray area. Keep doing it until I decide."

He smiled around the mouth of the bottle, took another swallow. The scent of the beer was pleasant, a good mix. She was watching the screen, but the food, the time of night and being off her feet were quickly having an effect. Her eyes were getting heavier. She needed to get up, thank him for a place to eat her dinner, and head home. She'd just close her eyes a second, absorb the sensations his stroking and kneading were causing.

"So what's your experience level, Celeste?" He spoke casually. "Was it too much or not enough of it that had you spooked on the steps?"

She stilled, but his fingers moved from her foot to her ankle, stroked there. Then along her calf, easy passes like a feather gliding along her skin, just the tips of his fingers. He took his time with it, not seeming to mind that she hadn't yet answered him. He moved to the front, following the line of her shin back to her ankle with his index finger. The skirt was ankle length, but it seemed acutely intimate that he had his hand underneath it. Back up to her calf again, this time going far enough to caress behind her knee, send a thrill of sensation through her thigh, tingling across her buttock. The man had long arms. He could decide to reach up further. Her legs trembled, wanting to shift, to make herself more accessible to him.

"Celeste? I'd like an answer to my question."

"I'm not sure I want to talk about that." Yet. Now. Ever. She was caught up in how he was touching her, the way her body was reacting to him. It had been so long since she'd responded to foreplay with anything more than a mix of mild interest and irritation. Her latest hookup, which had been quite some time ago, was only a lukewarm memory. She'd almost been able to hear her body sighing in resignation. *Oh, this again. Maybe I won't have to show him how to do everything.* Even then it wasn't any more earth-shattering than fantasizing with a vibrator.

They weren't all bad lovers. But she hadn't trusted any of them enough to let them be good ones. In contrast, when Leland touched her, it was as if something inside her was waiting with bated breath, immersed in what he was doing, instead of anticipating when she'd have to take control, make it work for both of them.

He'd said no sex. She needed to remind herself of that, as well as him. But he had such a confident touch. She thought of how he'd looked at her from the kitchen when he'd commanded her to take off the other boot. As well as the way he'd spoken to her in Jai's parking lot and handled things on the porch.

Plenty of good-looking men were skilled players. Self-assured, they knew how to throw out the alpha card to impress a woman. There wasn't much below the surface of that, though. An in-the-moment strategy to get between a girl's legs couldn't compare to a display of dominance that captured a woman's interest at a far deeper level.

"Still awake?"

Her lips curved at the absurdity of that, but she didn't open her eyes. His fingers slid back up her calf, past her knee, to the back of her thigh once more. He kept that easy pace as he continued to caress her legs from feet to mid-thigh and all the terrain in between, learning that part of her body. The more he ignored more intimate places, the more those places woke up, aching and throbbing for touch. She wouldn't ask for that.

"Your fingers are tight as a baby's fists. Open them up, Celeste."

She did, slowly, and was rewarded with another stroke from foot to thigh. His thumb slid down the seam between her thighs, to her knees, to her calves. He'd done nothing more than touch her legs, but she could feel the dampness between her legs against the crotch of her panties. She licked her lips and realized her breath was shortening.

"Ease this leg forward." Keeping her on her side, her upper body propped against the throw pillows between her and the arm of the couch, he adjusted her top leg forward so that knee was pressed into the wide cushion beneath her. He guided her hands so they were curled around the biggest throw pillow, big enough that she could hug it against her chest and prop her cheek on the top of it. It was a comfortable position for slumber, and the light of the TV and a dim lamp gave the room a dreamlike feel. Sleep wasn't what her body wanted. Dreaming, however, sounded awfully pleasant.

When she opened her eyes, she saw he'd left the couch, was kneeling next to it at her feet.

"Leland..."

"Mmm."

He had a way of using that one syllable to good effect. Not an interrogatory, just an acknowledgment. He bent his head, put his lips on her ankle. Then her calf. He was following the same path his hand had, though more slowly. He held his lips to her skin until the pressure of the kiss tingled through her flesh, then he moved to a new spot to do it again. He kept his hands involved, sliding them back up her calves, behind her knees, cradling her thighs. The first time she felt the tip of his tongue, tasting the delicate crease of her knee, she shuddered. As his hands climbed higher, she thought of all the reasons she shouldn't do this.

You will never use me as a lead or source.

She believed him. But that wasn't the reason she didn't stop him. He hooked her panties with his thumbs and slid the garment down her legs. The cotton pink panties weren't racy, but he removed them as if she were wearing a sexy swatch of silk. Though she had to lift the knee of her top leg an inch or two off the couch to help, as soon as he had her underwear off, he pressed her knee back down, telling her to keep her legs where he'd put them.

Maybe he'd chosen that position because it was a semifetal curl, a secure position to keep her from spooking. She was still wearing everything except her underwear. He hadn't taken off anything, even his shoes. Just as he'd promised.

While he was kissing his way along her calves, the back of her knee, he'd been pushing up the skirt, using the restless undulations of her body to free it from beneath her, so that the cloth was bunched up and held by one of his hands at the seam of her thighs, right below the curve of her ass. Now he adjusted it up to her waist, exposing her buttocks and upper thighs to the air, and to him. His sweatshirt was so big it gave him plenty of room to maneuver beneath it.

He tucked the hem of the skirt into her waistband so both his hands were free again. His mouth touched the back of her thigh and she squeezed the pillow tighter against her aching breasts. Then his mouth was cruising across and upward...

A semi-fetal position might feel secure, but he showed her how vulnerable it was as well. She made a noise as his clever lips found the folds between her legs.

With her body canted forward, her knee pressed into the couch, the lower leg stretched out, it was like she was presenting her pussy and ass for whatever he desired to do to them. Since he was leaning on the knee she had against the cushion, he'd effectively restrained her from anything but the smallest rocking movement, something she registered and responded to with one part panic and two parts *yes, God*. Her position compressed the nerve endings in her labia and clit, making them more sensitive to the wet heat of his mouth. Her fingers dug into the pillow. "Ah..."

That semi-fetal curl also gave his long arms a greater reach. He slid his hand over her skull, finding the longer hair of her pixie cut and tangling his large fingers in it, tightening his grip to draw her head back. It added to the sense of being pinned, held for his pleasure as his tongue stabbed into her pussy. She cried out, and found her writhing body couldn't budge his leaning weight as he started to fuck her with his tongue. He sucked on her labia, swirled his lips and tongue along it, just barely teasing the clit. She rocked against his mouth, yet every movement she made told her she was pitting her strength against a man who easily overpowered her, and not just physically. He simply held her still, made her feel every sensation washing through her. That thought made crazy, swirly things happen in her chest, that odd panic-pleasure mix, but her body's hungry responses wouldn't allow the panic to ruin this.

She'd been with men who thought they were being generous with the oral stuff, but in reality they only stayed down there long enough to get her lubed up before they stuffed their cock into her. It worked decently enough for good, functional sex, so she didn't push them to linger any longer down there than they wanted to do so.

This was not that. She was getting the message loud and clear that he was down there because he liked to eat pussy and that was what he wanted to do for a good, long time. He wasn't working her up to fuck her. Instead, she had the thrilling and terrifying feeling he wanted to wring every possible response out of her he could with his tongue, lips and hands, and he'd use all several hours before dawn if needed to see and feel all of them. He was also very good at driving her toward climax and keeping it just out of reach. The way he was holding her didn't allow her to adjust, to push her clit in more direct range of that amazing mouth, though that sensitive bud was feeling every bit of what he was doing to her. She was so slick that she could hear the wetness as his mouth moved over her.

Other than that, they were both silent, for the most part. She was panting, moaning, making little whimpers while he occasionally made a pleased noise, encouraging her. When he lifted his head, she was quivering, hard shakes like a nerve attack. "Leland."

He stroked her hair, tugged it again. "Do you want to come, Celeste?"

The warmth of his breath washed against her moist tissues.

God yes. Yes. But she found she couldn't speak. A paralysis was holding her tongue.

"What if I want you to come? Will you come when I tell you to do it?"

She nodded, realizing she'd closed her eyes as tightly as her hands were clenched on the pillow again. His hand slipped from her head, stroked over her white knuckles. Tracing the seams between her fingers, he gradually pried them open until they were tangled with his. He shifted their grips so her hand hooked over his, his thumb against her smallest finger.

She made a soft sound as he dipped his head and laid his lips against her cunt again, only this time when his lips parted, his spoken words sent another ripple of heat over her. "Then come now."

As he said it, his tongue slid over her labia, probing forward between her thighs, and found her clit. Just an easy stroke and tickle with the tip of his tongue, a torturously light movement, but that was all it took. She started to come, and thank God, he let her move enough to buck and give herself more friction against his teasing mouth, only now he pushed her deeper into the couch so he could also give her a more thorough lashing in that spasming area. He sucked her labia, stabbed his tongue between the folds again and nipped at her clit as his other hand shifted to hold one of her buttocks in a bruising grip. His thumb stroked her anal rim.

She screamed into the pillow at the barrage of sensations. She was shoving herself against his hold, straining for as much of that mouth and touch as she could get, and he gave her just enough leeway that she felt like an animal thrashing against restraints, his hold intended to protect her from her overwhelming hungers. She had a savage need to tear into him and take, take, take.

A scream became a shriek because he kept her going, working her through aftershock after aftershock that were more like multiple orgasms, something she'd never experienced from any man.

She knew she was coming down when the pleasure became a vise around her heart, squeezing her painfully. "Leland, stop. Please...stop."

He made a soothing noise, but eased his ministrations into caressing licks, his thumb sliding out from between her cheeks and his hand kneading instead of gripping. The way he was rubbing her ass sent little shocks of pleasure through her. Over both cheeks, a light squeeze, then more rubbing, a tracing of the creases between thighs and buttocks, a dragging, tickling stroke up the seam, then more rubbing. Wash on, wash off.

The *Karate Kid* reference brought a small, hysterical chuckle that exacerbated the hard thudding of her heart. "I..." She licked her lips. Her voice was hoarse. "I need to sit up."

"All right." He pressed a kiss to her pussy, giving it one last top to bottom stroke with his strong tongue before he eased her up to a sitting position. He stayed where he was so her legs were guided to the floor on either side of his kneeling body. The couch was a deep one, but he gave her back support, adjusting the throw pillows behind her so she was sitting up straight in front of him, her legs spread. The skirt and sweatshirt fabric were pooled together in her lap, so it wasn't like she was exposed to him, but she felt exposed by the position.

He hadn't yet said he was a Dom, but the way he used body position for restraint, how he'd taken the upper hand, how he'd commanded her orgasm, had her antenna up and receiving that message clearly enough. She'd avoided this, damn it. She'd stayed away from clubs and online chat rooms and anywhere she'd encounter people practicing BDSM. She'd met this man in a convenience store, for fuck's sake.

He twisted around, pulled a couple tissues out of a box on the table. Before she could stop him, he'd reached beneath the skirt and was cleaning her up, absorbing her climax in the tissues. She tried to bat him away, closed her hand around his thick wrist, but he wouldn't be deterred. He wiped her gently but thoroughly, making her body twitch at the stimulation, then balled up the tissues and tossed them into a waste basket beside the recliner.

She didn't want to speak, and wasn't sure what that was about, but he respected it with his own silence. It wasn't an uncomfortable, "Oh hell why did we do that and how soon can we tactfully call an end to the evening" silence. Just the opposite. It was like nothing needed to be said and he was content tending to her without there being any words. As the seconds ticked by, she realized she didn't want to talk because anything she said would just spoil it. Or inspire him to say something that would spoil it. Which unfortunately made her feel more uncomfortable with how comfortable he seemed.

"Um...where is my underwear?"

He leaned over and drew them off the floor. Instead of handing them to her, he tucked them into his jeans pocket. Before she could protest that, he'd drawn her to her feet, which let her skirt tumble back into place as he straightened the knit shirt and the sweatshirt over it. Her legs were shaking so he eased her back to the couch on her side before he got up out of his kneeling position. As he towered over her, she blinked at the evidence of an impressive arousal straining against the jeans. Holy God. She'd done that. She should do something...helpful? Quid pro quo? Was that why he was presenting it to her like that?

Maybe not. Apparently it hadn't been intentional. Before she'd had more than a tempting glance, he'd turned away and gone into his bedroom, coming back with a pillow and a fleece throw. The tiny lump of her panties in his pocket couldn't compete with the much larger impression right next to it, but the implication of the two together were disconcertingly arousing.

"Give me my underwear." She started to push up to a sitting position again, but he was already spreading the throw over her. When he eased her back down, he tucked the bed pillow under her head. They both smelled like him, a pleasant cocoon.

"Not right now," he said. "Time to sleep."

"I need to go home."

"Daylight's not far off. You might as well catch a few hours here." He went to the door, programmed the security alarm. She heard the sonorous computer voice announce "Armed... Stay."

"Trapping me here?"

"Not at all. You can open the door. It will just set off the alarm." He bent over her, kissed her forehead. A friendly gesture that he turned sensual by cupping the back of her head, mouth lingering as he murmured against her flesh. "Sleep, Celeste. It's all right. You pleased me in every way. All I want you to do is rest here so I know you're safe. All right?"

"Once my brain clears, I'm not going to let you treat me like a child."

He chuckled. "Darlin', trust me. I'm not treating you like a child. And you damn well know it. Sleep tight." He pulled back enough to meet her eye to eye. "The alarm will deactivate at 6:00 a.m. and you can slip out of here while I'm still asleep, since I'm going in mid-morning. But eventually I'll come looking for you. This isn't a one-night stand."

"What if that's what I prefer? What if I'm done?"

"Well, you can tell me that when I find you. I'll tell you you're a liar, we'll fight about it, and then we'll have makeup sex."

"There are lots of movies about cops who are psychotic stalkers," she said darkly.

"A taste of your pussy would turn any sane man into a stalker. Can't hold that against us. But I'm big enough to stay first in line."

He rose and gazed down at her, his lips flattening from a smile to serious firmness. "And you know we're not done. We're just beginning."

Chapter Three

A man who gave a woman terrified of intimacy an escape route was either making things easier on the both of them, or had lost his fucking mind. Leland heard her get up at 5:45 a.m., marked the tiny shifts as she found her shoes and slipped them on. A few more footfalls and rustlings in the front room told him she was seeking her underwear. Her panties were in his room, tucked under his pillow where the musky scent of her arousal alone had damn near compelled him several times to break all the promises he'd made. If she was brave enough to come get them, all bets would be off.

A longer pause told him she'd probably figured out where they were. He could almost hear her teeth grinding as she debated it, but then the alarm, damn it all, deactivated promptly at six with a chirp, swaying her decision. He heard the door open with a squeak then close. Leaving the bed, he padded to the living room window and watched through the crack in the curtain to be sure she made it safely into her car. Though the autumn day was likely to warm up thanks to Baton Rouge humidity, he could tell the air was chilly now from the way she moved. The bolero jacket she'd worn last night fit her slim body nicely, but when he glanced toward the couch to see she'd left his sweatshirt behind, he wished she'd taken it. He didn't like her being cold. As she turned the ignition over and pulled out onto the street, the cast of the street light through her window showed him that her eyes were locked straight ahead, her pretty mouth tight.

Since they'd met in the convenience store, he'd been intrigued by the complexity of her body language, the minute shifts in her expressions that suggested so many thoughts and emotions. He could make some good guesses at the head games she was playing with herself right now. He suspected she was a submissive who'd had a brief brush with the lifestyle, had been intrigued enough to be scared shitless by it, and had studiously avoided it ever since because of whatever was keeping her so tightly wound and self-protected.

Though he wanted to figure a way past her shields, he respected the desire to self-protect. Give a cop the choice between walking into an ugly domestic violence fight where husband and wife were armed with everything from pistols to a child's wooden building blocks--which could cause stitches if hurled with enough force, by the way--or visiting a therapist for an evaluation, each one would take the bullets and brightly colored toys without a blink.

The reporter thing had nearly been a deal breaker. Would have been, if he hadn't come up behind her and heard her saying the kind of things he and his own guys thought about the matter. If he wasn't dedicated to the code of law, he'd happily dig a giant hole, shove every media weasel right into it and bury them up to their necks. Oh, and dump a cauldron of fire ants on them. Not that he had strong feelings about it or anything.

What had cinched it, though, was her reaction to the bratting question. She'd understood exactly what he meant, and had responded in a way hard for the Dom in him to resist.

"The Dom in him" made it sound like a separate thing, rather than a vital need like the beating of his heart. He hadn't dated since he'd accepted that a submissive orientation was a must-have for whatever woman caught his attention. BDSM people respected privacy because confidentiality was critical to many of them, so he still went to a club or play party on occasion to hang out, have a drink and watch, but he hadn't found what he wanted there, either. As a result, he'd made a conscious decision to bide his time, wait and see if someone would ever ping his radar.

Celeste Lewis had, like an incoming missile.

There were people in the vanilla world who knew one another in and out, who found all the pleasure they needed in the simple intimacy of coming together in their bedroom. He guessed he was the BDSM world's version of that. He was seeking a woman with whom he could explore every corner of her submission to him in the comfort of their home. Their own private world that would never get too limited, because it was as limitless as their feelings for one another.

It made him sound like a sentimental dumb-ass, but the great thing about being built like a brick wall was he could love Hallmark movies, kittens and walking in the rain, and no one was going to say shit about it to him.

Celeste was a good-looking woman who he suspected saw herself as average-looking, despite the nicely toned body and lush breasts. If she didn't have all that fire inside her, she might have been right. But that fire gave her gold-brown-green eyes a glow, enhanced by the thick lashes. He liked a woman's hair, long or short, and hers had elements of both. The short shaved style on neck and sides let him tease the delicate bones of her nape, the sensitive shell of her ear, the erogenous occipital bone area. Yet those lustrous strands on top that tumbled over her brow and framed the right side of her face, teasing her cheek and jaw, gave him something to grip. They would let him pull her head back and expose her throat when he wanted to bite and suckle on her thundering pulse, remind her she was helpless in his hands, helpless to every crazy, nasty, over-the-top thing he wanted to do to her.

Yeah, she'd had an effect on him. Letting her leave this morning without pinning her against the wall and fucking her senseless had been difficult. He'd wanted her to leave with wobbly legs and his come slipping down those lovely thighs, because he sure as hell wouldn't give her back her underwear. But she was freaked out. Time to give her a little space, then he'd work on reeling her back in, see how that went. He was pretty sure he'd made enough of an impression to establish a tether between them. She was a submissive who'd responded to the Dominant in him, and wanted more. Needed more.

If she'd avoided the Dom/sub thing this long, though, despite her obvious craving for it, he might merely be the first one who'd gotten under her defenses in a while and been able to draw those needs back up to the surface. While he wasn't interested in being a damn gateway drug for her back into the lifestyle, that wasn't something he could control. Any more than he could stop her from leaving this morning.

Patience, timing. He usually didn't have a problem with

those things, but in truth, he'd missed her as soon as she left. When he picked up the sweatshirt and detected her scent on it, he took an extra whiff of it like a bloodhound figuring out which direction he needed to go to chase her down.

Hell, it had been a long time since he'd had this kind of reaction to a woman, that hard coil of need in the chest and the gut, a mix of pleasant anticipation and urgent need that would continue to twine together until he saw her again. As he headed toward his shower, he was grinning like a fool, just anticipating it.

§

Roll call and writing up the day's work list in his tiny cubicle started the day, but sergeants didn't spend too much time hanging around the district home base. Unless the lieutenant needed to update him or chew on his ass about something, or one of his squad needed a one-on-one, most days it wasn't too long before Leland was out on the street, monitoring the District 1 communications on his unit radio and scanning the frequencies for the other three on his portable.

He checked in on his officers, going wherever additional help or guidance was needed. Since certain resources were limited, he was one of the few who had a beanbag shotgun in his trunk, a useful aid for putting someone on the ground in a nonlethal way. Important, since the budget for more beds at the mental health facilities had been slashed. A few weeks ago, Leland had brought the weapon into play for a schizophrenic who refused to stay on his meds. The guy had secured a handful of knives to protect himself from his family members, whom he thought were invading aliens.

Leland was also trying to increase his presence in key areas for his squad because gang activity was up this month. Baton Rouge didn't really have organized gangs like the Crips out in Los Angeles or that kind of shit, but it did have loose affiliations of guys who decided they were a "gang," with drug-related crimes being their primary activity. Two had evolved enough to give themselves names, not that they'd hit the FBI's gang register anytime soon. The MoneyBoyz and the Reigning Kings. Christ, like a bunch of kids playing form-a-secret-club, which followed, since a lot of them were in high school or barely out of it.

Unfortunately, the problem with them getting an identity was it made them cockier, more aggressive. They were doing shit to intentionally step on one another's toes and that was never good for anyone.

Case in point. The crime scene he was approaching now was a laundromat robbery and assault. He expected it had been done by the Reigning Kings, probably because the owner had been brave--or foolish enough--to report that they'd set up a dealing point in the alley next to the store. The majority of violent crime in Baton Rouge surrounded drugs, so though the city was known to have a high crime rate per capita, if you weren't dealing, supplying or doing drugs, or hanging out or having to live in the places where that happened, life was little different from any other place with a far lower crime rate.

Dope dealers killing and stealing from other dope dealers wasn't something that broke his heart but, like any cop, he was all too aware of how that activity could quickly involve innocent bystanders. Like the store owner who'd been trying to do the right thing.

He'd stop in to check the scene, make sure everything was going as it should and see whether his guys needed an extra set of hands. With approval, he saw they'd secured the area properly. Billy Johnson, a rookie, was riding point on the barricade, along with a veteran, Mike Carter. Mike had been part of his district for quite a while and Leland knew he was a good man. There weren't too many people milling outside the proper range of the scene, but he made special note of at least two who were, just as he was sure Mike had.

Two Reigning King members, a pair of kids likely still earning their street cred, were lounging against a light post, smoking. If any uniform headed in their direction to question them, the kids would melt away like shadows. Or feed the cops total bullshit.

He saw one or two citizens in the doorways of

businesses across the street. The ones with creased brows and concern darkening their eyes told Leland they lived close by. All of them would know the store owner. Even so, they stayed where they were and kept their peripheral vision on the gang members. Nobody wanted to be perceived as being too sympathetic.

When he looked back toward Mike, he saw the man stiffen. Leland immediately followed his gaze back to the two kids. He blinked, sure he wasn't seeing what he was seeing, but no, he was not hallucinating.

Celeste Lewis was strolling up to the two young men with a cardboard tray full of coffee.

He was too far away to intercept her, so he made himself stay in the car, watching. Logic said they weren't going to do anything in front of a trio of cops. They also wouldn't be packing heat under their oversized shirts, because if a cop had a justifiable reason to believe they were carrying, they could get searched and hauled in. Gang members weren't exactly the types to go through the legal channels to apply for a concealed carry permit.

Even knowing all that, he didn't like her being that close to them. Let alone Goddamn chatting with them.

Whatever she said had them glancing at one another, shifting. One said something that looked a tad belligerent, and she shrugged, responded with a shake of her head. She handed them both a cup from her tray and asked a question. The shorter of the two boys stole a look at the other one and then gave a quick nod. Fishing white sugar packets out of her coat pocket, she handed them to him. When she cocked her head at the other boy, he shook his head, made a motion at her to go away, but Leland noticed he kept a firm hold on his own cup. So did Celeste. With a suppressed smile but an even look, she said something else, then stepped off the curb to cross the street.

She was wearing a snug camel-colored coat, black slacks and blunt-heeled boots. She had the lithe, athletic movements of a woman who worked out for more than her waistline. He wondered if she played any sports. She'd shown she was pretty sports-savvy last night, but that wasn't the uppermost thing in his mind as he watched her. The belted coat emphasized her generous breasts. He'd kept his attention mostly below the waist at his place, but that just made him fantasize all the more about closing his hands around those curves, snaking his tongue in the cleavage to tease and caress, moving over to suckle her nipples into swollen cherries. Her pussy would get all wet like it had on his couch. While she was gasping and arched into his mouth, he'd work his cock right into that tight fit.

The erection he was unwisely creating instantly went on hold when she approached the barrier and extended another coffee to Carter. He took it, which gave Johnson unspoken permission to do the same. The rookie leaped for the coffee like a puppy leaping on a ball. She chatted them up a few moments with the same ease she'd talked to the two boys. Then she wandered over to the curb about twenty feet away. She had a cylindrical tote slung over her shoulder which, as a football fan, he should have immediately recognized. His little Girl Scout pulled out the stadium chair, unfolded it and sat herself down, clicking open her tablet to make some notes.

She obviously was used to working the streets and talking to his men. What bugged him was their comfort with her, which suggested it was a two-way street.

Leland got out of the car, his brow drawing down, his mouth set in a thin, hard line.

They'd seen him pull up, but when Mike saw his expression, he spoke a word to Johnson. The rookie went back to his position on the perimeter with a furtive look. Leland lifted the tape and ducked under it, then gestured Carter to him.

"I wasn't aware you were our public information officer now, Mike." He spoke low, but kept his eyes pinned on his man. He was aware Celeste's head had lifted when he got out of the car, but he didn't look her way. Not yet.

"No, Sarge. It's not like that." Carter shifted uncomfortably. "Celly was approved to do some ride-alongs last year when she did an article on the BRPD, so we know her. She's at a lot of the crime scenes, because she has that blog. If you've seen it," he added lamely as Leland's expression didn't alter.

"Being approved for a fluffy PR piece doesn't give her open access to information."

Mike stiffened, the veteran cop not willing to be pushed around too much. Billy probably would have wet himself, which was why Leland was talking to Mike. "I didn't tell her anything, Sarge. You know me better than that. And she does, too. She didn't ask me anything about what's going on. She was just saying good morning, bringing us some coffee."

Yeah, and even a mature cop confronted with a pretty, smiling woman didn't always have his head on straight. A good reporter knew how to extract information without her source realizing he'd let things slip.

As if reading the direction of his thoughts, Mike sobered. "I know the routine, Leland. But she's different from the rest of them. Me and the other guys feel like when we get a reporter who treats us fair, it's okay to give her a bone now and then."

He winced as Leland gave him a fish-eye. "No, Christ. Not like that. She's not a badge bunny. Most the time she carries on as much shit with us as we do with each other. I think she was raised with brothers. Never has dated anyone on the force that we know about."

As Leland's gut eased, he realized he'd reacted more personally than expected to the idea that he'd been played a fool. Hearing that he hadn't, helped. But it also pissed him off with himself. Still, he reined back the irritation. "Why do you think she's different from the rest of them? Other than her great legs?" And the gorgeous rack. Her ass was a little on the skinny side for him, but he still didn't mind wrapping his hands around it.

"When God gives a woman those kinds of gifts and arms her with coffee, you have to show some kind of appreciation." Mike held up a hand when Leland seared him with a look. "Kidding. She doesn't pick up a piece of a story and give it the slant she wants, like most of them do. She's thorough, careful. Checks her sources. I won't say she hasn't ever managed to get some tidbit out of one of us on an off day, but it doesn't come back to bite us. Not with her."

"A cop can be written up for that kind of shit. Or lose his job." He jerked his head toward Johnson. "Maybe you know how to watch your tongue, because you have enough years and brain cells. You want to get his rookie ass fired because he sees his partner chatting up the press and thinks it's okay to do the same?"

A flare of resentment in Mike's eyes said he'd hit target, but Leland let it stand. The resentment would pass. A sergeant might be considered one of the guys on most days, but when it mattered, he'd chew their asses. It was better than one of the lieutenants doing it, and it sure as hell was better than them taking risks that could get them killed. While talking to a reporter wasn't a life-or-death situation, it was a slip in protocol that could open the door to other ones. Their lives were far more important to him than their friendship. And he valued their friendship as if they were family, because they were.

"Yeah, Sarge. Won't happen again."

"See to it. You're a hell of a good cop, Carter. Johnson will benefit from your experience. You'll help keep him on his toes."

He pivoted and strode toward Johnson. The blue-eyed rookie's military haircut didn't conceal that it was as fine as when his mother brushed it as a baby. He'd paled, telling Leland his expression was still forbidding, more in the mood to kick asses than pat them. He heard the young cop's relieved sigh as he passed him without stopping, headed for the other end of the perimeter barrier.

While he'd been grilling Mike, he'd seen Celeste leave her spot. She'd spent a few minutes talking to one of the onlookers in a store across the street. The two kids had watched her the whole time, and the store patron had noticed it as well, disappearing back inside in a matter of seconds. Shrugging, Celeste had come back to her chair. Now she was making notes and sipping the last cup of coffee in the tray. Despite that, Leland would bet his squad car she was aware of every move he'd made and the tone of the conversation he was having with Mike.

"Miss Lewis? Come here."

The formal address brought her head up, and put those hazel eyes on him. He remembered them last night, disoriented with lust, her lips parted, gasping for air as he ate her pussy, stroked her silken skin. She looked wary, but her expression had a tinge of arrogance, that public-has-the-right-to-know and I-have-the-right-to-be-here bullshit.

He could have been dead wrong about her last night. Not the Dom/sub stuff, he wasn't wrong about that, but about whether or not it was a good idea for him to be pursuing anything with her. Mike's opinion carried weight with him, but he knew he'd better stay cautious, take the same advice he'd just given his man. She'd tripped his trigger and he'd tripped hers, but she could still fuck with his head. Actually, that meant she had far more potential to do so.

As she rose and moved toward him, he saw spots of color on her fair cheeks. He'd issued her an order that he might give to anyone in the crowd. "Come here." "Stand back." "Clear this area." But she'd registered it a different way. Her responding to it with that flush didn't help settle him, so he darkened his scowl. She stopped two feet from the barrier, as if she thought he might reach across and grab her. It was an intriguing thought. Instead, he crooked a finger at her to bring her closer. She did, another step, then found her brass, because she lifted her chin and leveled eyes sparking with some fire on him.

"I have a right to be here," she said.

He almost bared his teeth in a grin. *So not the right thing to say, sweetheart.*

"You have the right to be on that side of the barrier, just like all these other good folk. As well as the not-so-good ones." He flicked a gaze toward the two gang members who were watching him with suspicious eyes.

"Darryl and Sean are in the tenth grade at the local high school," she responded. "Darryl's mother is a junkie, but Sean's mom works at the Piggly Wiggly. She doesn't know that they're hanging out here instead of being in school. Which she will know, once I stop by and see her there today to pick up some fresh tomatoes." She cocked her head. "I'm having a craving for them."

He pressed his lips together. They were far enough away from anyone that the conversation couldn't be overheard, though the intensity of their locked gazes might be interpreted myriad ways. Christ, she had delicate features.

"Neither one is sixteen yet," she continued, "so you could have them picked up for truancy and carted back to school. Then the MoneyBoyz won't have eyes on your crime scene and see who you're questioning."

He noted the pulse thudding in her throat. When she spoke, he detected the faint scent of chocolate, telling him the last coffee wasn't coffee at all. She preferred hot chocolate in the morning. He wondered if she liked whipped cream in it and thought about tasting that on her lips, teasing it away with his tongue.

Seriously, Keller?

"Did you give them hot chocolate, too?"

"Sean took hot chocolate, Darryl took the coffee, though I think he would have preferred the hot chocolate. He just didn't want to be seen as a baby." Her expression flickered. "Though they both are, more's the pity."

And either one of them might shoot her without a second thought if one of the more hardened members of the MoneyBoyz told them to do it. He kept his scowl in place. "From here forward, you don't talk to my officers, and you don't bring them coffee."

"There's no law against a reporter attempting to talk to your officers or giving them coffee. They do a tough job. I'm showing appreciation as a Baton Rouge citizen."

He pursed his lips, nodded. Then he bent so he spoke into her ear. He'd bet that little tender spot beneath it would taste sweet and smell like some kind of powder or fragrance. "I see you doing it again, I will put you over my knee and blister your ass." He drew back enough to meet her startled gaze. Shock was followed by indignation, a trace of anger, but it was the little ripple of arousal, the quick indrawn breath, that made him want to do exactly as he'd threatened.

"Are we clear, Celeste?" He kept his eyes on hers, his tone steady. He wondered what he would do if she said "Yes, sir." Probably nurse a hard-on for the rest of the morning.

He forced himself to straighten, to ease back on a couple different levels. "You should have taken the sweatshirt to stay warm this morning. I bet that car of yours doesn't heat worth shit."

She blinked in surprise again. He hadn't intended to say something stupidly intimate like that, but it was out before he could call it back. Her flush deepened. "It does well enough," she said. "Underwear would have helped, but they were stolen. I expect I should report that to local law enforcement."

"Items like that are rarely recovered. The perp has usually taken them for personal reasons, not to fence."

Her brow lifted, then her gaze swept his lower torso. "So he might be *wearing* them?"

She was not going to make him laugh, though it was a near thing. He'd just called out his man for just taking her coffee and he was flirting with her. Really fine damn example he was.

Fueled by that, he gave her a hard look. Time to put things on the right footing. His job was to protect and serve, and she was one of those he was supposed to be protecting. "Remember what we discussed, Celeste. I mean it. This neighborhood is too dangerous for you to be distracting my men. And way too damn dangerous for you to be strolling through it, chatting up high risk subjects like you know what the hell you're doing when you don't."

In a blink, her expression went from spirited sass and confused lust to hard-as-nails anger. He could handle that, just like he could handle Mike's irritation, but the quick flash of hurt dug into him. "Yes, Sergeant," she said icily. "I'll file that under 'go fuck yourself'. You don't know anything about me. My psych profile isn't tucked up inside my pussy like the prize inside a Cracker Jack box. Asshole."

She pivoted and stalked back to the curb, taking a seat once again on the chair. Though he talked to Johnson and Carter a couple more minutes before going into the store to see the demolished aisles of food, the smears of blood left by the severely beaten store owner, she didn't make eye contact with him again.

§

To any onlookers, it looked like he'd set a reporter back on her heels. In reality, she'd set him back on his. He hadn't expected her at the scene. He sure as hell hadn't expected to see her talking to the type of people responsible for most of Baton Rouge's violent crime and homicide rate. The type of people who valued life as much as they did bird shit.

There were a handful of female officers in District 1, and he was fine with that. Yeah, maybe he worried a little more about his female officers than his male ones because he was wired that way, but he put extra effort into shoving down that bias. What he'd told Mike about being an example for Billy applied just as much to him. He made sure any differences in the way he treated members of his squad had to do with their experience, not their gender. He didn't want any of his guys second-guessing or being overprotective toward an officer just because she had girl parts. The calls they faced required total concentration and trust in one another.

Logically, he knew women were competent, tough. Yet he still had a strong desire to protect them from harm. That alone didn't make him a prick. However, when he let that desire get twisted into an angry retort because he wasn't sure of his footing in a situation, then that changed things.

Expecting the unexpected was part of the job, which was why his knee-jerk reaction to her appearance irritated him. The downside of being off the dating circuit for so long was he was rusty at dealing with those edges where personal and professional overlapped. Since he was interested in a woman who was standing right on that boundary, he'd stepped right into it. She'd shown intelligence and grit, and he'd acted like what she'd called him. An asshole. In short, he needed to man up and apologize.

He'd had the two boys picked up for truancy, because that had been a good idea, no question. He'd let the detective on scene know, and Detective Allen had him send out a couple squad members to see what they could get out of the onlookers with the kids gone. After he took care of that, Leland called in an hour of personal time and went looking for her.

Celeste's car hadn't been parked on the street and she'd taken her leave on foot, so he followed a hunch. The logo on the coffee had been for a shop about two blocks away, a cheap breakfast place that cooked everything in so much grease a cardiologist could set up a chop shop right outside its doors.

Sure enough, he found the beat up little blue Honda there. Through the window, he saw her sitting at a table, tapping her tablet and scribbling in a notebook. A bagel and dish of cream cheese sat next to her.

He stepped into the shop, giving the tired-looking waitress a nod. "Just a coffee, black," he said. Then he moved toward Celeste's table.

She didn't lift her head when he stopped in front of it. "Seat's taken," she said shortly. "I'm expecting someone who isn't a jerk."

"He couldn't make it." Leland slid into the booth across from her, turned his radio down as it started to chatter. "I'm sorry."

She stopped tapping but kept her eyes on the screen. "Sorry he couldn't make it?"

"Sorry I said that. I wasn't expecting to see you there. And you talking to those guys threw me. If they aren't already, they're only a step or two away from becoming what turned that store owner into a pile of bloody meat. I had my hands on you last night, my mouth, and everything I touched was delicate, beautiful. Something I want to keep safe. That's the way I'm built, and I won't apologize for that, but I will apologize for it making me say something that stupid."

She lifted her gaze to his, her eyes thoughtful. "Wow. For a guy who just put his size fifty shoe in his mouth, that's a pretty good apology. Way more honest than I would have expected."

It was good to see those pretty multi-colored irises, the blink of her lashes, and know she was less mad at him. "I'm straight with women. What I want from them, the things I demand...clear communication is essential. You understand me?"

She swallowed, her eyes flickering. "Yes. I don't think I can go there with you. With anyone. Ever again."

"Did you have a bad experience?"

She shook her head. "No. Not exactly. Maybe one that

was too good."

"You thought it couldn't happen again. It was a one-time thing. Or it opened up things you weren't prepared to face."

"A little of all of it." Her lips curved wryly. "It was at Club Surreal. Do you go there?"

A tricky area. He lifted a noncommittal shoulder, and her face shuttered, responding to his lack of trust. She was a smart girl, she should understand his position, but then he thought of what he'd seen in her eyes last night, what she'd given him. She'd trusted him a lot more than she'd expected, and he'd left her vulnerable. Enough that his shot this morning had been more painful than it would have been if she'd been ready for the usual shit a defensive cop could dish out to a reporter.

"Yeah, I've been a couple times. Would you like to go there with me?"

She curved her fingers around her mug. She still had the paper cup containing the hot chocolate, but the mug held tea, because he smelled the light herbal scent. Soothing. "What's that?" He tapped her knuckle.

"It's chamomile. I chase the hot chocolate with it to even me out. You know, like crack after booze, only in reverse."

He smiled at her and her expression eased. He wanted to reach out again, grip her hand, but he knew that was just way too fast, far too much intimacy. Fortunately, the waitress brought his coffee and he could take hold of that instead. "Mike has a good opinion of you. Earning a cop's respect isn't an easy thing. I'll have to check out your blog."

She fished a card from her wallet, pushed it over to him. "You're welcome to post comments if you think I've got anything wrong, Sergeant. Or send me a private email. The truth is very important to me."

Her card was unexpectedly whimsical, a cartoon sketch of a harried-looking female reporter hunched over an old-fashioned typewriter, the only touch of color a pair of red sneakers tumbled next to her bare feet underneath the rickety desk. A cat was asleep on a mess of papers on the desk.

"Cute."

"It disarms people, makes them feel less threatened. Did you have Darryl and Sean picked up?"

He took a sip of his coffee in answer. "Thank you," she said. "Darryl may be too far gone, but there's still hope for Sean. He basically idolizes Darryl."

"How is it you're so involved in their lives?"

"You mean, how is it a skinny white middle-class chick knows how to handle herself in this part of town?" She shrugged. "I was born in Baton Rouge, to a poor-as-dirt family. I've lived in a trailer park where the skinheads two trailers over were burying assault weapons under their place and plotting the overthrow of the world. Not sure if they ever followed through with that, but I'm thinking it's still in the planning stages, since they liked to drink and talk about it more than anything else. Before that, I lived around here, in some really crappy apartments. Had a bullet or two go through the walls at odd hours of the night, listened to the guy next door try to beat his wife to death while his daughter screamed. Same guy would always give me hard candy when he met me on the stairs."

She lifted a shoulder. "I know this world, and since I've been back here I've reestablished a lot of contacts."

She flipped through a couple screens on her tablet. He watched the long strands of her hair slide forward to tease her lashes, the corner of her pursed mouth. "One of the people who lives near the store saw three of the MoneyBoyz leave around one o'clock, right after the attack. They had their hoods up, so you're not likely to get anything off the cameras, but when they went by her place, she heard one of them. 'Gonna tell LeRoy you punked out and hit that bitch like a girl, Dogboy.' Dogboy could have been an insult, but sounds like a nickname. LeRoy Green fancies himself the leader of the MoneyBoyz, but that part I expect you already know."

She glanced up at him. "None of that's official, and if you go ask her the same question she'll deny talking to me. Rosario has a little girl who has to walk to the bus stop alone because she works the early shift. The neighbors watch after her, but if it got back to the MoneyBoyz she told me that..."

"They won't hear it from us." Leland studied her. "I'm

not trading information, Celeste."

Her eyes cooled. "Did I ask you for anything, Sergeant?" She shut down her tablet, began to pack her stuff back into her oversized handbag. "Thanks for the apology. Guess we're done here."

The hell with it. He put his hand over hers before she could jerk back. "Celeste, you didn't answer my question." He'd go to Surreal if she was interested, if a more public venue would help her trust him enough to get back to a private one.

From the way she stilled, he knew she didn't need to be reminded of what the question had been. "You don't even trust me, Leland. Rationally, I get it, but maybe I'm too sensitive about that. Maybe I want you to trust me anyway, and that says last night was too unsettling, making me irrational. Maybe I need some time to think about the why of that."

"Okay. So maybe I want to buy you Thai takeout on Friday." He stroked her wrist with his thumb, a discreet caress of her pulse, and was pleased to feel it trip under his touch.

"Thai instead of a BDSM club?"

"Less pressure."

She gave him a half-amused, half-desperate look. "You know this is a really bad idea, right? I'm not a good bet."

"You just told me I could trust you."

"That's not what I meant. I'm broken, Leland." She waved at the tablet. "I'm damn good at this, but it's the only thing I'm good at. I suck at relationships. They fall apart when I touch them."

"All right. So I've been warned." His grip tightened on her wrist, drawing her gaze back up to him. "Celeste, let me bring you Thai food on Friday. Tell me about what happened. Why it was too good. You choose where. Totally neutral location. Let's talk about where we're going with this." He stroked her wrist again, earning more of that little flutter. "Don't hand me bullshit about it not going anywhere. You want me touching you. And I want to be touching you. So tell me where."

She set her jaw. Anticipating that she was going to dig in her heels and refuse, he moved his foot beneath the table, nudged it against her insole. When she shifted her foot slightly, he closed the gap again, nudged it once more.

Her eyes lifted to his. What could have been a tease, an innocent flirtation, wasn't that. He was giving her a direction, and he waited to see if she was aware enough to recognize it.

"You know what I want," he said.

Her fingers flexed on the table. She moistened her lips, looked out the window. He took another sip of his coffee, tried not to count the ticking seconds. Four…five…six.

She shifted her hips, adjusted. Those spots of becoming color returned to her cheeks. He slid his other foot forward. The placement of his feet inside hers, pressed against her insoles, told him where hers were. She'd adjusted her feet shoulder width, opening her legs for him. Her pulse was tripping under his touch. When he put his coffee down, it took a concerted effort to keep his grip on the mug, rather than taking a double handed one on her.

"Friday, Celeste. After I get off shift. Where do I meet you?"

"Okay. The Mall. At the carousel."

He blinked at the choice. "Pretty public. Don't trust yourself?"

Though she was unnerved by her reaction to him, she tossed him a disdainful look. "I expect you'll bring my stolen property back to me, Sergeant."

"You can expect that all you want, Miss Lewis. But District 1 has higher priorities than a woman who can't remember where she left her clothes."

She snorted and rose, dropping a tip on the table. "Asshole. Enjoy your coffee."

§

Celeste, what are you doing?

When she got into her car, she took herself away from the diner without a look back, out of range of Sergeant Leland Keller. She'd thought of Dom/sub stuff as elaborate equipment, a club setting. Safe words, paddles. Whips and chains. Leland Keller excelled at subtle gestures that took her over in a heartbeat, made all the more arousing by how he did them while they were surrounded by an oblivious world. He created a bubble for just the two of them with his direct gaze, his murmured commands, the stroke of his strong fingers.

But the maneuver at the diner was the least of it. When he'd gotten out of his car at the crime scene, her whole body went on alert. All this time, fate had kept the two of them from crossing paths, but right after she'd spent the night with him, here he was. She'd had an *oh shit* moment, because she'd snuck out of his place that morning like a thief. But right after *oh shit*, she was flooded with giddy pleasure at the sight of him, like a schoolgirl with a crush.

She remembered how she'd wanted to open his closet and look at his uniforms. Seeing one on him made every cliché about a man in uniform God's honest truth. There were plenty of cops who, due to brutal shift schedules and bad eating habits, had a gut hanging over their belts and popped blood pressure and cholesterol medicines like candy. Some of the rookies were skinny, growing into their bodies, or still nursing baby fat. Billy Johnson was one of the exceptions, with the physique of a young Marine. But Leland in a police uniform was total female fantasy material.

Baton Rouge PD uniforms had gold and blue trim, so bright it clashed with the muted tones of the dark-blue trousers and gray uniform shirts. Leland wore the uniform like dress blues. Everything ironed, spotless and fitted to his powerful torso. His belt was loaded with his Glock sidearm and nonlethal weapons such as Taser, Mace and ASP. She also glimpsed cuffs and his portable radio. On one of those skinny rookies, all that load would have looked bulky, oversized. Whereas the way Leland's hips and upper torso moved with their weight had everything inside her humming.

A vision of him cuffing her and taking her over the hood of his unit had popped into her head before she could blink. Christ. Such typical cop fantasies should have amused her, and they did, though she'd cut out her tongue before she ever said such a thing to him. He'd probably heard it from any one of the many women who'd give it up to a police officer in a heartbeat. But how many of them wanted such a fantasy, not because he was a police officer, but because of what Celeste sensed from him? The uniform and badge enhanced what was already there. Authority and protection weren't just part of the oath he'd made. They were a confirmation of what he was. She knew that because of what she herself was.

When he'd put his foot against hers under the table, her thighs had trembled, loosened. The flare of satisfaction in his eyes as he'd shifted the other foot, confirming she'd spread her legs for him, had been enough to send her into a tactical retreat. But she'd agreed to meet with him, talk about what had happened to make her so leery of getting into a Dom/sub relationship. That could lead to a lot of other things, far less subtle.

As her week continued on its normal schedule, she didn't run into him again, at least not face-to-face, but her mind kept returning to every second she'd spent with him so far. As well as mulling over what she could tell him about the pivotal event that seemed to have brought her here, personally and professionally.

The Dom at Club Surreal had cracked her hard shell. What had oozed out was banal textbook psychology. Little girl abandoned by daddy grows up into a woman who lashes out at men who are everything the male role models in her life never had been. By all rights, that Master could have rubbed her face in that, because she'd been all set to bust his balls, hoping to write a story about him and his business partners that would raise the hair of every person who read it. Instead, he'd treated her emotional state with tender care. Which was remarkable, given he was a sexual sadist who could use pain and ecstasy to take a woman far beyond her imaginings of what pleasure was. He'd done that for her too. A full-service emotional and physical ass kicking that had left her craving more.

She hadn't fallen in love with that Master, but he'd compelled a total surrender from her. The things he'd made her face weren't revelations, not by a long shot. But it was as if all her strengths and weaknesses, her memories and experiences, her dysfunctions, were presented in a different light, suggesting possibilities, not shortcomings.

At first, she'd convinced herself he was such a good Dom, he'd been able to coax a submissive reaction from her, but she wasn't really a submissive. That wasn't who she was. She'd researched BDSM with a whole new zeal afterward, though, visiting chat rooms, blogs and becoming fascinated enough with the New Orleans D/s scene to accept she was probably lying to herself. But she couldn't bring herself to go that route again. Every time she dipped a toe into it, it didn't feel right. No matter what he'd called up from the depths of her subconscious, it was a one-time thing. Since then, her persistent fantasies about it had been a secret between her and her overused vibrator.

How in the hell did she say all that in any intelligent way to Leland? And were they really at the point she could be that open with him? No way. She couldn't. Maybe they'd talk about sports instead.

She hadn't been misrepresenting herself to Leland. She was ruthlessly good at self-examination and knew she was a complete failure at all relationships, even most friendships. Thank God she was a workaholic. But that Dom had opened her eyes to the type of person she did--and didn't--want to be. She didn't want to be someone whose dubious accomplishments were built on the shaky foundation of bitterness and old angers. She'd realized it was time to grow up. While Celly the child might never be able to trust someone enough to fully love and be loved, Celeste the woman wasn't going to let that affect her decisions as a journalist.

Now when she pursued a story and hit a rich vein, she followed it to the deepest core of truth. She wrote pieces that made her feel as real and balanced as the articles themselves. She might not function well at personal relationships, but she excelled at her job and had enough challenges in it to fill a lifetime, such that most times she could ignore the personal shit she couldn't figure out.

She'd thought she was pretty comfortable and resolved with that, which made Leland more of a shock to her system. It was impossible to ignore the undercurrents between them, much stronger than anything she'd felt with a man since that night at Surreal, but too clearly similar to the vibes she'd felt with that other Dom to ignore.

Back then, she'd decided a Dom had to have something really special, akin to a super power, to silence the booming voices of her insecurities, compel her to lower her shields and help her find that still, precious balanced space inside herself like she'd found that night. Yet Leland might just have that quality. A part of her wanted to freak, bolt and run, but another part of her wanted a repeat performance too badly to let her completely break away.

Because here she was. At The Mall on Friday, and earlier than their agreed-upon time.

It hadn't helped that yesterday she'd gotten a quick glimpse of him. It had charged her up more than it should have. She'd been at the courthouse, doing some research in the clerk of court's office. After her usual fond banter with the trio of security guards who knew her well, she'd decided to sit in on a jury trial for a few minutes while she worked on her notes. It was when she'd taken a restroom break and been emerging from the side hallway that she'd seen him.

The railing at that end of the third level of the courthouse overlooked a wall of glass that descended all the way down to the lobby level. Out those windows was a peaceful view of live oaks and a small park area with benches. Leland was leaning against the rail, providing guidance to a nervous-looking rookie probably having to offer testimony for the first time. She'd stepped back into the shelter of the restroom door, but she peeked back around the corner to take another look. Leland's back was mostly toward her as he talked to the rookie, and the other officer was facing the window, so she wasn't directly in either man's view.

Lord, the man had a fine ass. Fine everything. She thought of the scent of his skin, the lemon and peppermint, the smell of old wood, and wondered how the cloth of his uniform would add to that fragrance. He'd put a hand on the young man's shoulder. The deep musical sound of his chuckle was as reassuring a sound as ever had been created. She wanted to touch his hair, the soft wool of the short crop, and trace his full bottom lip. Maybe take a nip out of it and have him growl at her, close his hands on her wrists, pull them behind her back...

God, she was acting like an idiot. Coming back to the

present, she focused on the rotation of the carousel. It was the second largest one in the world, after all. Though she wasn't entirely sure how accurate that information was, it was a premium Mall attraction, with a fairly steady flow of kids and parents taking advantage of the ride.

The carousel was in the food court, so there were a wealth of table and chair options. They'd be at a premium when Friday date night got into full swing, but right now she'd commandeered a spot, pulling two chairs and a small table away from the others, positioning it on the opposite side of one of the large indoor potted trees with its string of white lights. It gave them a bubble of privacy and still offered a good view of the carousel, as well as the opening to the first level where more large potted trees and mall decorations were touched by blocks of sunlight coming through the crisscrossed white beams of the glass ceiling above her.

Maybe it wasn't the world's most romantic venue, with the flow of people and constant noise, but with this space marked off, it would work. Public and casual enough to give her an easy escape route.

Coming here early was a mistake, though. During the past thirty minutes, she'd watched little girls get on and off the horses, helped by their mothers, a few by their fathers. As the carousel turned, flashing its hand-painted colors, her thoughts turned and her feelings played out in a different direction. She grew more uptight about the things he wanted to talk to her about. The excitement inside her, the anticipation of what was undeniably a real date, was tainted by a darkness that wanted to make it crash and burn. She wanted to burn it down so the pleasure didn't cut her with its sharp need.

When Leland set the bag down on the table, she looked up at him, startled. She'd been so lost in her head, she hadn't been watching for his approach to wave at him. Yet he'd still found her without any trouble. That made those feelings more jagged, as did his appearance. Stressed jeans, a gold knit shirt over them, a soft-shell black jacket with a stand collar over it. Casual nice, what a man wore to tell his date he'd made an effort for her. Even if he claimed not to date.

The easy greeting on his lips died as he obviously read her expression.

"I don't want to do this," she said.

"Okay." He sat down next to her, stretched an arm across the back of her chair. The length of it bracketed her body. "What do you want to do, Celeste?"

She returned her gaze to the carousel. "I want to go back to your place."

He regarded her silently. "And what do you want to do there?"

"Whatever you want."

"Hmm. My floors need cleaning. I could see you on your hands and knees doing that, Celeste. Stripped naked, scrubbing my floors."

He curved a hand over her shoulder, fingers stroking. She twitched away from him irritably and bit back a gasp as he captured the muscle between her neck and shoulder, putting enough force on that pressure point that pain resonated through her nerve endings. But it wasn't an "ouch, stop that" pain, not for her. Instead it made her breath shorter, made her straighten her upper body and tighten her thighs, absorbing the shot of sensation straight between them. Her gaze snapped to him. His brown eyes were molten gold, the planes of his face more prominent when his expression was intent, like now, registering how she reacted to the hold.

"Take a breath," he said. "A deep one."

She did, and he increased that grip incrementally, wresting a tiny whimper out of her. Her lips parted, and his gaze darkened, seeing it. "It's starting to really hurt," she managed. Yet she didn't want him to stop.

"I know. Do you like bruises, Celeste? Marks left on you by a Master?" He took it up one more notch and now she did catch a cry in her throat at the sharp bolt of pain. That was when he eased the pressure, the caressing follow-up of his fingers easing her body down the same way. He molded his palm over her shoulder once more, only this time to pull her closer so she was leaning inside the curve of his arm. With his other hand, he slid her chair over so they were frame to frame.

She didn't pull away, but she didn't know how to

answer him, so she didn't. He didn't seem to mind. His gaze touched the stubborn set of her jaw before it coursed downward. She wore a pale green shirt with a V-neck and a short black skirt, both of which clung to her curves. The black leggings beneath the skirt tucked into brown-and-gold ankle boots. She'd dressed for him, too.

He adjusted her neckline, the stretch of the fabric allowing him to pull it to the point of her shoulder. The act exposed her bra strap, but it appeared he was more interested in the impression his fingers had left beside it. Leaning across her body, he put his mouth on her bare skin there, licking it discreetly with his clever tongue. Then he bit down, sucking hard on it.

The muscle was still throbbing, but the press of his teeth coming right behind the other pain made her reach for him, her arm curling over his wide back. It was the first time she'd had the chance to touch him. Massive muscle groups shifted beneath her touch. He wasn't doing anything overtly inappropriate to her, but the erotic messages such a concentrated pain sent were enough to have her feeling as if she was spread out naked on his bed, trembling with terror and lust. Her fingers dug into that hard muscle and the heat of him beneath his shirt and jacket. Her cheek brushed his temple, his cropped hair. She closed her eyes, her body rigid with sensation as he added to that bruise with the force of his mouth. Her muscles liquefied when he released her, his tongue swirling over the mark, a balm.

As he straightened, one of her hands fell limply to his knee, the other curled in his jacket at the shoulder. He met her gaze. "I'm hungry," he said casually. "So I'm going to eat. Then I'll decide what you need."

She made herself take her hands away from him, fold them in her lap. Tried to keep her voice from shaking. "I can leave. I'm not hungry anymore."

"Yeah, you can leave. If all you want is to go back to my place and fuck each other blind, you can find that plenty of other places. That's not what you're getting with me."

She pressed her lips together. She'd known at gut level he'd respond exactly that way to her desperate attempt to turn this into only sex. He made her feel unbalanced, on edge. She should get up and walk away. But she didn't.

Once a few weighted seconds passed, he shrugged out of his jacket and folded it over the back of his chair. The knit shirt had long sleeves that followed the contours of his arms. He drew a covered takeout bowl out of the bag with packets of crunchy noodles and sauce. After opening the bowl and dumping the condiments over his food, he leaned back in his chair, one ankle braced on the opposite knee, his other knee against the side of her leg. The position stretched his trouser fabric over his thigh. Holding the bowl balanced in his hand, he began to eat, to all appearances unconcerned about her. She'd said she wasn't hungry, after all.

"What are you thinking? No, scratch that." She held up a hand. "You said you're eating. Men can't do those two things together."

He sighed, wiped his hand on a napkin on the table. "I'm thinking that you're going to be such a pain in my ass. That mouth of yours is going to make me want to do all sorts of politically incorrect things to you." He tilted his head, gave her a glance. "Want to get this on tape?"

"No," she said stiffly. "Sounds like I wouldn't want to put you to any extra effort, Sergeant."

"Ever play truth or dare, Celly?"

"Don't call me that," she snapped. She bit her lip, looked away.

Another weighted moment and he shifted, touched her knee. She saw he'd fished out the card she'd given him, was studying it. "Says right here, that's what I'm supposed to call you."

"But that's not how I introduced myself."

"No, you didn't. You said Celly, but then you corrected yourself. You want me to call you Celeste, and it makes me wonder why." His gaze came back to her face. "When you worked for the New Orleans paper, your social business column was done under the name Celeste De Mille, and the tone of those articles matched the name. Far more of a façade than Celly Lewis's articles are now. So are you playing a role with me, Celeste? It's easier to play pretend when you change names to protect the not-so-innocent?"

She picked up her light coat, got up and left. Just walked away. She left her food, which she'd really started to want, damn it, since she hadn't had any dinner. That was fine. She'd get a pretzel from Auntie Anne's. She walked past the tempting cinnamon pretzel bites, though, heading for the store closest to where she'd parked. She maintained a steady pace until she reached the door to the outside. She even made it outside. Then she pivoted. Waffled.

Cursing herself, she went back into the store. She wandered into the purse area, checked out some shoes. Her track took her back into the mall, ambling listlessly past some window displays.

When she eventually arrived back at the carousel, he was still there, though he'd finished his meal. She didn't know whether to be insulted by his presumption or relieved. That was her problem, wasn't it? When it came to approaching relationships, she was like Jekyll and Hyde. She wouldn't want to date her, so she couldn't blame anyone else for feeling the same.

That thought nearly made her turn around and leave for real. Except his arm was stretched out along the chair where she'd been, as if he was waiting for her. He took up a lot of space, so whoever sat down in that chair had to be someone okay being intimately close to him. Based on the second glances women passing by were giving him, she thought they'd be more than willing to give that a go, even if he was a total stranger.

But he wasn't looking at them. He was looking at her. Her steps slowed but they still brought her to him. She sat down. All she had to do was lean back to have his arm against her shoulders. Instead she sat straight, her gaze on the carousel.

"The night that was too good to be true," she said. "The Dom called me Celeste. The way he said it, I could tell he knew it was my real name. That the only fake part of the pen name was 'De Mille.' But it was more than that. It was the first time someone ever said my name and it felt real, like it meant a real person. Substantial, not a reflection of someone else, but who I was, soul deep. I wanted... When I introduced myself to you at Jai's, I wanted to hear how you said it. And it felt the same. Maybe better."

She took a breath. "So if you think I'm a pain in the ass, and I'm not worth any more of your time, well, fuck you. Give me my food and I'll go do better things with my day."

He lifted his arm from chair, cupped the back of her head with his big hand. As he cradled her skull, his fingers caressed the base of it, her tense neck. His thumb teased the hinge of her jaw. He used that hold to turn her toward him. She lifted her gaze, not sure what she'd see in his face, but she only had a glimpse of it before he put his mouth over hers.

The other night had been an overwhelmingly intimate evening, remarkable since they hadn't kissed once during it. That deficit made this even more potent. She'd made the barbed comment about men's inability to do more than one thing at a time, but if that was because they put all their energy and talent into that one thing, no distractions, it wasn't a bad thing. At all.

His arm slid around her waist under the coat she'd donned, turning her toward him so her right breast was against his chest as he kept his other hand cradling her head. He held her still as he coaxed her lips apart and let his tongue slide in against hers, trace and tease. His lips were a sensual pressure that she couldn't resist, so she tried to taste him as well, licking at his mouth, nipping at his tongue, her hands finding purchase on his chest, holding on to his shirt, kneading like a cat.

When he kissed her, his arms around her, holding her so securely, the world disappeared. The parts of herself that usually interfered with the feelings unfurling inside her now disappeared as well. Instead, a plea resonated through her chest and down to the very core of who she was. A core that had been asleep for so long it roused like Sleeping Beauty, with a groggy "Where the hell have you been?"

He eased back when her eyes were still closed and she was holding on to him like she wouldn't ever be able to let go. Her lashes lifted, her hands clutched hard on the front of his shirt and the man beneath, so tight a tremor was running through her arms. He made a calming noise, stroking a hand up her forearm. He closed it around her biceps.

"So what else happened that night?" he asked.

"I got angry. Really angry. Then sad. I was looking in a

mirror and it hurt worse than being cut by the glass, but afterward...I wanted to see that image again, too much. But I knew it was such a profound thing, it wasn't likely to happen ever again. If I chased it, I'd probably end up in a far worse place in my head. So it seemed better to focus on the things I knew I could attain for myself. Alone."

Her reaction to that night had always been a confusing tangle in her mind, so she was flummoxed to hear the truth spill from her mouth. She stared at his chest, not sure she could meet his gaze after saying something like that. He pried her fingers off him but left his own tangled with them on his knee. When she at last managed to look at his face, she found him studying her with an unreadable expression, but what she saw in his face didn't dismay her.

"Celeste, I want you to stand up and take off your coat."

She didn't think about anything. She just rose, shrugged out of the coat, put it on the back of the chair. As she leaned forward to do that, he slid his hand smoothly beneath her shirt. Not in an indecent way. He just took advantage of her position to slide his hand under there, fit his palm to her waist, his thumb stroking her stomach near her navel, his other fingers tracing the sensitive flesh of her lower back. The man had large hands. As she straightened, he hooked his fingers in the waistband of her skirt, gave her a little tug.

"Sit back down. You want your dinner now that you're done acting out? It's pad Thai."

She narrowed her eyes as she sat. "Acting out? You know, cops are notorious control freaks. Entirely inflexible in their opinions."

"Why change our opinion when it's the right one?" He shrugged and nudged her when she rolled her eyes. "Want crunchy noodles, too?"

"Absolutely. Carbs are best topped with more carbs."

"That's my girl." He put a packet of noodles on top of the container, handed it to her with fork and napkin. Then he fished out a bottle of water. "I figured you might be a diet cola girl, but you all tend to be picky about your brands, so I went with water."

"Water works fine."

He broke the seal for her as she opened the lid of the food and inhaled the mix of egg, peanuts, fried tofu and seasonings. When she put the first bite in her mouth, he settled back, stretching his arm behind her again. This time she leaned back against it. He moved his touch to her shoulder, his thumb sweeping along the curve of her neck to her shoulder and back again. Sometimes he went further, hooking her bra strap, tracing beneath it, then coming back again. Tendrils of sexual heat curved under her breasts, down her sternum, along her spine. Each time he passed over that place he'd pinched so mercilessly, her reaction increased.

"You're not making it easy for me to concentrate on my food."

"So women have trouble doing more than one thing at a time when sex is involved?"

"Depends on the man," she said, intending to be catty. Too late, she realized she'd complimented him. His eyes laughed at her. He threw her off her game, for certain. She'd have to work on that.

"You said I'm a pain in the ass, yet you hung around for me to come back. Why?"

"When I got here, you said you didn't want to do this. You just wanted me to take you back to my place and fuck you."

"I didn't say that last part."

"Yeah, you did." The smile disappeared, replaced by something as distracting. A piercing directness. "You have a clever mouth, Celeste. A sharp tongue. But it's what you say with your eyes that holds my attention. I could duct-tape your mouth and still find out everything I need to know about you."

What should have been offensive planted an image in her head that only made her sexual response to him worse. Irritated, she shifted forward so he'd stop touching her. Putting the lid back on the half-empty container, she resolved to eat the rest later and set it back in the bag. She tried to speak casually, as if the words didn't matter.

"So you don't want to have sex with me."

His chuckle put her back up, but when she shot a glance his way, she found she wasn't the only one with expressive eyes. His gaze told her his answer to that, even before he spoke.

"That's a no-brainer. If it wouldn't get us arrested, I'd bend you over this table and fuck you until you screamed for mercy. My cock hasn't settled since I made you come on my couch. But that's the thing, Celeste. Fucking's easy. You don't look like the type of girl who denies yourself the chance to scratch an itch, because that's functional, cause and effect, no thought required. I expect you've had a couple fuck buddies along the way."

"I'm a pain in the ass *and* a slut?" She started to get up. His hand returned to her shoulder, his grip strong enough to keep her in place.

"You're not stomping off again," he said quietly. "And no, that's not what I meant. This isn't high school. What a consenting adult does to get through the lonely hours of the night is what we do. No harm, no foul."

She thought she might grind a full layer off her teeth before the night was over. "So what is it you want, Leland?"

He considered her. "I can make a woman's cunt wet and fuck her to climax. That's mechanics. When you give me every ounce of who and what you are, because you trust me with all of it, that's the real prize. It isn't easy," he added. "Fears get in the way of need, and you tangle yourself up in all of that, so you can't tell me how to find you. And you won't trust someone to figure it out for you. With you."

She was all too aware of where he'd shifted from third person to directly referring to her. He could have chosen to be less targeted, but he'd said he was honest. Hearing it aloud still bugged her. She really did want to leave now, but as if he sensed that, he hadn't let go of her. "Sounds like I'm a lost cause."

"No. Not at all. I'm just telling you you're in for a bumpy ride. Accepting how a Master is going to touch you, handle you, in order to learn everything about you, inside and out, isn't easy for a sub like you." His gaze slid back up to hers, held. "It kind of stirs me up, thinking how tough I'm going to have to be with you."

His expression sent a little quiver through her belly, but she managed to sound dismissive. "That's your thing?

Getting rough with a woman? That's why you're looking for someone who will be a pain in your ass?"

His flash of a grin was a sensual threat. "Yeah. To keep me occupied until the sub I really want comes along. A docile little thing who keeps my house clean, sucks my dick on command and calls me sir."

"If you think that I--" she started, and then shut her mouth at the dancing light in his eyes. "Jerk," she muttered, but he'd made her smile. "Asshole," she added for good measure.

He squeezed her shoulder, then removed his hand. "You can bolt now if you want. But I'd prefer it if you stayed."

She returned her gaze to the colorful carousel. Around and around, the horses going up and down. She'd made up that rhyme the first time she'd come here as a college student. "You looked up my work history."

"Through the Internet, not through the police database."

"Good. So you don't know about my juvie record as a chronic Toys R Us shoplifter."

"I'll lock up my train sets and Star Wars action figures."

"I only go for Barbie stuff. Especially her shoe collection."

"I keep those in a safe deposit box," he said gravely. "So why did you leave the New Orleans paper?"

She was on safer ground with that and wondered if he knew it. Either way, she'd take that road in a heartbeat to get away from the less comfortable responses he was eliciting from her. "I had an opportunity to move from social business over into the crime beat. I thought it was going to be so different. Then I found out it was all about ratings and stirring up people's emotions by leaving out key facts. It wasn't about journalism anymore, giving people all the pertinent information so they could make their own informed decisions about their lives and community. It was about creating power factions, dissent. When I took the NOLA job, the person who helped me get it said he hoped my editor would appreciate the way I could tell a story. I think now he was warning me."

"I went to your blog and read some of your stories."

She glanced over her shoulder at him. She was still sitting on the edge of her chair, though she wanted to be back inside the curve of his arm. Since she wouldn't let herself do that, she turned on her hip so she was facing him. Her shoulder pressed against his forearm stretched out on the chair, a good compromise between her desires and her unwillingness to bend so soon after he'd gotten under her skin. "Thanks. I appreciate that. I did a lot more freelance work at first, until the blog started to get a following, enough that I could sell advertising. Last year, I was ahead on a couple big stories. The papers and networks released on them first, but they had the information wrong, because nowadays they don't investigate. They just do press releases, Twitter feed and people's cell phone videos. When I got it right, it was noticed. Some bloggers, concerned citizen groups, that kind of thing, started mentioning me, and my following has grown. Now I'm doing subscriptions, and people are actually paying to have access to the information."

She stopped, a little embarrassed. Though she didn't deny her job was the thing about herself that gave her the most pride, going on about it to Leland seemed as if she was trying to prove something.

"Your articles seem thorough and fair. Just like Mike told me they were. I'm one of your newest subscribers."

"I wondered who hotcop@spanksgirls.com was. Now I know."

"I think that's the chief of police's email address," he said.

"I'm going to tell him you said that. I've met him a couple times." She laughed as Leland winced. "So someone *can* intimidate Sergeant Leland Keller. I'll keep that in mind."

"Not intimidate," he said with dignity. "I just have a healthy respect for the person who decides whether or not I can pay my cable bill. Do you still do freelance?"

"Nice diversion tactic." But she smiled. "Some. Mainly because I have more control over the stories. The editors who initially cut them to give them the slant they wanted are far more light-handed now. It may sound naive, but I hope it means they might be seeing the benefit of giving people the full story."

"You obviously take a lot of pride in doing your job right. I respect that, Celeste."

She allowed herself to glow a bit. It was high praise from a man in a profession that understandably loathed the press like plague-carriers. But then she sniffed, tossed her hair out of her eyes. "You looked pretty sharp yourself Monday morning. Billy nearly wet himself when he thought you were going to chew his ass out for accepting my coffee."

"That's Officer Johnson to you, and I have a strict limit on making a rookie soil himself. Once a week, tops, and Billy already had his turn this week. I didn't look sharp at the courthouse?"

She raised a brow. "How did you know I was there? I was very stealthy."

"Saw your name on the security sign-in sheet, so I was on the lookout for you. Caught you in the corner of my eye. Would have talked to you, but Fielding was about to have a nervous breakdown. I had to be sure the kid understood judges and lawyers put on their pants the same way we do. Though the Gucci shoes lawyers wear are custom fit to cover the cloven hooves. So?" He gave her an expectant look.

"What?"

"Did I look just as sharp and irresistible at the courthouse?"

More so. She rolled her eyes, though. "I never said irresistible."

"It was implied." He nodded toward the carousel. "So why did you suggest we meet here?"

"I like it. Most people look at it and don't notice how much is there. On first look, all the color and mirrors, they think it's garish. But when you look more closely, you see how beautiful it is. All the hand-painted details, and the colors are soft, like Easter." She put her hand up over his eyes, suddenly playful. "Tell me three animals it has that you can ride, other than horses."

"None. I'm way too big."

"Everyone knows carousel animals are magical creatures. They're much stronger than they look. A detective wouldn't be dodging the question. He'd be trying to impress me with his recall of detail."

"Careful now. Those are fighting words." His lips curved under her hand, making her want to nibble on the full lower one. She didn't, but she did lean closer, such that he stilled, telling her he was aware of her breath against his face. He put his hand over hers, removed it, but when he opened his eyes, he looked straight into her eyes, no cheating.

"A tiger, an ostrich, and..." he frowned. "A rabbit."

"I love the rabbit. He's one of my favorites. Watch when the tiger goes by, though. See under his saddle? There's an eagle carved under it, or some kind of raptor. And both of the tigers are called Mike, for the LSU mascot of course. Their name is written on them." She pointed. "I never stop finding new things when I watch it turn. See how the camel has a curved knife, like a *janbiya* on the side? The cat is carrying a fish in his mouth, which you'd expect, but he also has a gold crescent moon painted on his side and a blue sash around his neck. The pig has a pink bow, because pigs always seem to wear pink. It's like whoever created it had a vision into a child's dream, where everything is whimsical, surprising, but it fits, too. Random but not."

He was watching her with a bemused fascination, and she colored a little as a result.

"Most women come here to shop."

"Well." She lifted a shoulder. "I have a limited budget. Chick-fil-A nuggets and watching the carousel works for me."

"So how many times have you ridden it?"

She shifted her gaze back to the carousel. "Never."

"You get nauseous? Afraid of horses?"

She elbowed him and he curved that arm around her again, squeezing her. "So why haven't you ridden it?"

She shrugged and he gave her a more thorough look. "You get quiet about the things that matter," he said. "If it just scares you, you shoot your mouth off, try to piss me off."

"Does it work?"

"You'll find out." He touched her mouth. "Tell me why

you haven't ever ridden it. That's a command, Celeste."

She had an interest in exploring a Dom/sub thing with him, she didn't deny it, though they hadn't really defined it further than that. Yet when he ordered her, something as simple as giving him information felt much more significant. One small step toward that place where she would want him to demand everything from her. He had dark rings around his golden-brown irises. That made his expression of authority sharper, more direct. More unsettling.

A ripple of panic went through her, but in contrast, his touch gentled, stroking her lips until they parted. "Don't get smart-mouthed and avoid it. Just tell me, darlin'."

She made a face at him, but relented. "On the carousel, everyone is with someone or being watched by someone on the ground. I've never had anyone to ride it with...or to watch me ride it. It's isolating. Like being a person in a crowded room that no one can see or hear."

"So you sit on the sidelines and watch. Which lets you feel more in control of your isolation." He didn't wait for her answer. Instead, he drew her to her feet, handed her the coat she'd folded over the back of the bench. Reaching into his coat pocket, he pulled something out in his closed hand, then put that hand over hers. After he transferred what felt like a ball of vinyl fabric and a couple marbles into her palm, he folded her fingers securely over them.

"I'm going to go put your leftovers in my truck. While I do that, go to the ladies' room and put this on. I'll meet you back here."

"What is it?" He wouldn't let her open her hand. Instead he tightened his grip.

"You said I owed you panties. I brought you some."

Chapter Four

She didn't open her hand until she was safely in a bathroom stall. Now she stared at a vinyl thong. What had felt like marbles were two bullet vibrators sewn under the slick material, positioned to stimulate a woman's anus and clit.

They must be remote-controlled or clap on, clap off, because shaking or pressing didn't result in a reaction. She waited for her mind to tell her *no way, no how*, but instead it pulled her back to the way her whole body had lifted into his hand when he pinched the muscle in her shoulder. As well as how her pulse had fluttered when he said "That's a command, Celeste."

She slid out of her leggings and underwear, tucked the latter in the pocket of her coat. The thong had adjustable Velcro fasteners on the sides, helping the bullets fit snugly right where they were supposed to go.

The idea that he could turn it on at any time, that she'd just given that control to him, should have alarmed her, and it did. But she had another reaction to it as well. As she donned the leggings again and reached inside them to adjust the panties, she couldn't resist sliding her fingers down over her pussy to stroke. Her hips twitched and she had to do it again a few more times, until she was leaning against the side of the stall, hips moving in a coital rhythm.

God, she was masturbating in a public bathroom stall. Forcing herself to stop, she readjusted her short skirt over the leggings and put the coat over her arm. When she came out of the stall, she bit her lip at the stimulation walking created. It might be easy to know where to position the bullet against a woman's clit, but how had he known which size panty to choose to ensure the other one was firmly against her rim?

She'd trained herself to think in five parts; who, what, when, where and why--or how--so her mind went straight to the other night, his hands all over her ass, his mouth between her legs.

She'd have to issue a personal retraction about a man's

inability to think while eating.

Emerging from the bathroom, she discovered him waiting for her. The hallway continued past the men's room and another twenty feet to an emergency exit, and he was leaning against the wall at that end, rather than at the end of the hallway that led back into the mall. When he remained in place, that and his expression told her he wanted her to come to him. As she walked, the bullets were rubbing against clit and rim, arousing her further. It was reflected in a more sinuous body language she couldn't help. Her hips rolled in a pendulum sway, and her nipples were stiff against the thin padding of her bra. A swift glance down confirmed it, but it wasn't necessary. The flare in his eyes as he focused on that area told her the same thing.

When she reached him, he took her hand, turned them so his body shielded her from the view of the bathrooms. He bent down, and her face was already lifting, her lips parting eagerly. He didn't have to coax her lips open this time. She met him wet heat against wet heat, and when his hand slid beneath the elastic waistbands of her skirt and leggings, he found the bullet and seated it more firmly against her anus. As he was confirming it was placed where he wanted it, his grip pressed her mound against his thigh. If there was any doubt about where that clit bullet was, her gasp into his mouth, the buck of her hips against his hold, rubbing herself against him, verified it. Her hands fell to the waistband of his jeans, hooked there through the folds of his shirt to steady herself. His erection was against her abdomen. She was a blink away from climbing up his body to bring their two sexes together.

He broke the kiss then, easing her back down to her heels. When she started to push back, wanting more, he shifted his grip to her shoulder, sending another shot of sensation right to her core with that pinch move.

"You like that, hmm?"

"I...yes." She drew a shuddering breath, realizing she'd ramped out of control. "I think this is too fast. I don't know what you're planning to do, but--"

He tipped up her chin. "I'm going to ride the carousel with you, Celeste. When we're done with that, I'm going to take you home. Your home. I'm going to have your sweet ass in your bed, on your kitchen table and then on your couch. Since I plan to take my time with all of that, when I finish, it will probably be time for the late-night sports recap."

"You're pretty serious about that."

"I try not to miss it."

"I don't know if I want you to come to my place."

"I know. It's hard, letting someone see your personal space. Let's go ride the carousel."

He took her back up the hall, one arm around her back, his hand curved over her hip, stroking. Though he was no longer touching the bullets, wherever he touched her seemed connected to them, currents of sensation running through her like water down her body in the shower.

The walk to the carousel seemed long. She didn't talk, too aroused to do more than lick her lips and bite back moans. She'd latched onto his side with her other hand and now he lifted it between them, nuzzling her skin. When he brought them to a halt a few feet away from the automated box where they would pay for their ride, he kissed her fingers, his nostrils flaring.

"Did you play with yourself in the bathroom, Celeste? Did you make yourself come?"

She flushed, realizing she'd transferred her arousal onto her fingers. "No. I just touched myself for a second."

"Have you masturbated since you saw me last, darlin'?" His low timbre vibrated through her body, all the way down to those throbbing points. The man could drawl that endearment like a threat. The kind of threat that sent a shiver through a woman and made her want him to carry it out, whatever it was.

"Yes."

"How many times?"

She flushed deeper and would have looked away, but he caught her chin, bent and put his lips over hers, then moved that wicked mouth right up to her ear. "Tell me how many times, Celeste. How many times did you rub your pussy, use your vibrator, fuck yourself with it, thinking about me? About what I'd make you do next time you saw me?"

"Twice," she lied.

His arm around her constricted. Setting his teeth below her ear, he bit, teasing her with his tongue. She jerked as the vibrators came to life, humming against her clit and sensitive rim. "I can turn these up and make you come right here," he murmured. "Hard enough you'll have to scream."

As if to prove it, they hummed at a higher frequency that accelerated her toward that peak. "Stop, please stop," she whispered, frantic. "Leland, please."

It stopped so abruptly she had to hang on to him for balance. But he was relentless. "The truth, darlin'. How many times, when and where?"

"Nine times. At bedtime every night, once when I woke up past midnight on Wednesday. Three times in the shower. And once in the park, when I was eating my lunch. I put my coat over my lap so anyone driving by wouldn't know."

"Moved your hand nice and slow to stroke your cunt?"

"Yes. Oh..." He pressed another kiss to her mouth, almost chaste, but she was so revved up, she shuddered from it. "Leland..."

"Do you know why I waited for you down the hall from the restroom? I wanted to see the way you move when you know I'm watching you. When you're thinking about all the things I'm making you do that you fight but won't refuse."

Fortunately, he didn't require a response to that. He tucked her against his side, holding her there as he removed his credit card from his wallet, swiped it to pay for two tokens. An older black woman with a name tag that said *Betty* waited at the gate counter to take the tokens. Celeste kept her face averted, sure that she looked obviously close to a climax.

"Don't get too many adults riding for their own sake." Celeste heard the smile in Betty's voice. "Wish we had more."

"I can't imagine anyone passing up the chance to ride it with their sweetheart," Leland responded. "How often do you bring yours here to do that?"

The woman chuckled. Celeste was sure Leland's warm tone had given Betty a head-to-toe tingle, the way it would a red-blooded woman of any age. It kept attention off of her, which she appreciated, but she still had to give him crap about it.

"Sweetheart?" she muttered as he guided her along the outside of the carousel.

He gave her a discreet pinch on her ass. "Which one would you like to ride?"

With arousal beating between her legs like a marching band, that question had a no-brainer answer. Pushing the hormonal response down, she pointed. "The horse between the rabbit and the cat."

The steed had the body of a blood bay, though the dark face and nose suggested a roan. He had his head tossed up in fiery defiance, the ears laid back.

"One with attitude," Leland observed. "I'm not surprised. No docile mares for my girl." He lifted her up on the platform and then steadied her as she put a foot in the stirrup, swung up and over. As she landed, she bit back a gasp. His eyes glinted with male satisfaction as he discreetly eased her forward with a hand on her hip. "Press your clit against the saddle pommel. Heels down, so your ass is pushed into the saddle. That's the way you stay."

Leland uncoiled the strap belted around the pole in front of the pommel and wrapped it around her hips. "The rules say everyone must wear a seatbelt, no exceptions." When he cinched it in one decisive movement, she swallowed a sensual noise at the provocative restraint that put her more firmly against the pommel. He hooked his thumb in the strap, his fingers curved loosely over her ass as he put his hand on the pommel again, under the coat.

"Not a twitch," he said. He spoke softly, but the look in his eye said it was a direct order. She held his gaze, not sure she dared to breathe.

Others were coming onto the carousel. Kids, teenagers, adult couples. Fortunately, none of them decided to ride the cat or the rabbit this round. The cat made sense, because Leland was standing between the cat and the horse, and there wasn't a lot of space there, such that his large body was against both animals.

"I'd like to touch the rabbit."

She bit her lip, surprised she'd spoken the desire

aloud, but when he nodded, she leaned over. Despite the hold of the belt, he shifted, putting his arm around her waist to be sure she stayed secure.

She ran her hand up one long ear, her thumb sliding along the smooth inside, down to the rabbit's brow. "I've always wanted to do that," she said. "I love his ears."

What was it about him that she'd say these childlike things aloud, things she wouldn't think of saying to a date? Maybe because he wasn't a date. He was something different, something that had her opening up in odd, disturbing ways.

She straightened, making a pretense of studying the other riders, until Leland's hand moved under the coat. His thumb glided down her pubic mound to the clit bullet. As he made it roll and twitch against her, she bore down on the stirrups as he'd directed, and the reaction was electric. God, there was no way she could stop herself from coming if he did what she was worried he would do when the ride started.

"Leland, I don't want to...be embarrassed." Though her body didn't seem to give a rat's ass what she wanted. It just wanted to release.

He stroked her back from nape to waist, then gripped the belt again, fingers caressing the upper rise of her buttocks. "I won't let that happen, Celeste. This is for me, not for anyone else. I tend to be a selfish Master and pretty damn possessive. Your pleasure belongs to me and me alone."

It was the first time he'd referred to himself as that. He'd also just stated in unequivocal terms that he saw her as his submissive. A step closer from theoretical to actual. She should be worried about that, should be thinking about limits and safe word discussions, because that was the smart thing to do, the right thing to do. Never mind that she'd felt safe around him before Jai had told her he could be trusted. She felt so safe with him, it was terrifying, because safety made surrender almost inevitable. She couldn't think of safe words when her mind was full of what he might do to her when they were behind closed doors

"We need to stop this. Stop it. I don't want this. I want to get down."

A shrill ringing like a school bell signaled the beginning of the ride. She gripped the pole as the horse started to rise. Leland adjusted for the horse's movement, but the tall horse only rose a foot or so, allowing him to keep that steadying hand on her backside and the other less steadying hand under the coat, on the pommel. When he moved the hand from her back to his pocket, she didn't have time to protest. The vibrators started humming again, the sensation rippling over her cunt and deep into her ass. She clutched the pole.

Up...up... Down...down... As she came down each time, his thumb would press against the clit bullet, work it in circles. Whenever her hips tried to jerk in coital response, the hand he'd brought back to her hip would tighten on her and the belt, keeping her still. Like roaring surf, the sensations drowned out everything else, the carousel becoming a blur of lights, sounds, childish laughter. The calliope music that could only be heard when on the carousel because of the outside mall noise played its plinking tune. She inhaled the smell of popcorn and cookies in the food court, Leland's peppermint and wood aroma, his flesh that she needed to taste. She wanted to bite him as he drove into her, leave marks on him the way he'd left on her shoulder.

"Oh...no. Oh...help..."

Her desperate whisper was lost in the noise and sound. She fought for control as the climax starting to sweep through her, her pussy and rim contracting and throbbing against the bullets. She held her forehead hard against the cool pole, her eyes shut, head down. Just as she was afraid she wasn't going to be able to stop a scream from ripping from her throat, the vibration stopped. The climax stuttered and hummed through her body. Aside from a few seizure-like twitches, it made self-control more attainable, but left her needing so much more. Her wild eyes found his face, saw how closely he was studying her. His expression was back to being unreadable. Not distant. Just in charge.

When the carousel stopped, he slid an arm around her waist, pulled her off the horse. She had to rely on his strength to guide her to the ground, because her knees were too wobbly. Her fingers trailed along the glittering rhinestones embedded in her mount's side, the purple and teal embellishments on his saddle. Leland didn't ask her where she wanted to go, didn't speak to her at all. She was barely cognizant of the time it took them to walk through the mall and head out to his vehicle. He drove a dark blue pickup truck with tinted windows. Other than that, "shiny" was the only word her keen reporter's mind could muster as he opened the passenger door and boosted her into the seat.

Whereas she would have had to use the running board to step in on her own, he was tall enough he didn't need any extra height to reach over her and fasten her seatbelt. Opening the glove compartment, he produced a pair of fleece-lined cuffs with metal links. He wrapped one around her wrist, attached the link to a clip around the seatbelt at her right hip, then did the same to her other wrist, attaching it to the left side of the seat.

He gave her knee a light squeeze, closed the door. She flexed her fingers in the cuffs, heard the rattle of the metal rings. God, she needed to come. To really come. One long, hard, lung-squeezing, full cardiovascular workout orgasm would help her find her brain again. Right now it was immersed in a boiling cauldron of her own lust. She wasn't even alarmed that the man had tied her up in his truck.

He'd circled around to get in the driver's side. After he closed the door, he put his hand against her headrest to stroke a knuckle down her cheek. "Look at you, all stirred up," he said, his eyes like molten gold. When he passed a finger pad over her lips, they parted and she teased him with her tongue. "Yeah, you're on fire, darlin'. You want to come the right way, don't you, Celeste?"

Her breath was shallow pants. "Yes."

"All right then." He put a firm hand under her ass to lift her up and pull the stretch fabric of her leggings down to her thighs. With the same economy of motion, he hiked her skirt up to her hips, leaving her sitting on a towel he fished from the back and put under her bare buttocks. He wasn't done, though. Lifting the front of her shirt, he drew it over and behind her head, tucking it back behind her neck so the sleeves constricted around her shoulders.

When he sat back to study her, his eyes slid over her

breasts quivering in lace cups, her thighs bare and spread, showing him the slick crotch of the vinyl thong. She licked her lips. "Leland, just do it. God. Make me come. Please."

As he continued to watch her, the emotions started to rise. "Damn it, don't fuck with me. Just do it."

He reached into the glove compartment again, removing a rubber ball and a sheer nylon fabric she recognized as a cut piece of sheer hosiery. Putting the ball inside the tube, he brought it up to her face.

"Don't you..."

The rest was muffled as he pushed the rubber ball into her mouth. It was large enough to hold down her tongue. She could make noise, but coherent words were out of the question. He tied it snugly behind her head, sat back and started fondling her. Calm, steady. He was just...taking over. With cool confidence, he pushed the bra cup out of the way and replaced it with his hand, thumbing a nipple. She dropped her head back, gasping at the searing sensation as he pinched her, rolled the tight peak. Then he pulled out the remote, laid it on the console and turned it on.

She came the right way, as he put it, in a couple seconds. As she bucked on the seat and screamed, her head banging against the headrest with her thrashing, he continued to stroke her breasts, pushing the cups out of the way so he could hold them in both hands, flicking his thumbs over her nipples. While he did that, he watched her as if he would never take his eyes from her. His silence was as potent as a stream of dirty comments. He absorbed her every reaction as if it was a private performance only for him. Just as he said he preferred.

"Please..." That was a word she could make him understand through her pleading gaze alone. The climax was ebbing but the vibration wasn't, and her hips were bucking at the discomfort, her pussy and clit over stimulated.

"Please, what?"

"Please, turn off...please..."

"Sir."

She managed a glare, an "in your dreams" look. He reached for the controls, turned it on maximum vibration.

"*No...no.*" She protested through the gag, called him a bastard, her hips bouncing on the seat, her lower abdomen muscles twitching. She told him to go to hell, tried to jerk away when he slid his hand from her breast to her hair. Her reward for that was him seizing a handful of it, holding her head against the headrest as he bent and took her exposed nipple in his mouth, beginning to suckle and nip with sharp teeth. The vibration, too much and vastly uncomfortable, nevertheless started her up that peak again, especially with her writhing against it, creating a stroking friction. In a matter of minutes, with him suckling her and his other hand working and playing over her clit with the vibrator, another climax tore through her.

"Please...oh God. Please...sir. Please stop." Yet some part of her didn't want him to stop. As soon as she managed to make the word "sir" understood, she wanted to retract it. Not because she wanted to disobey him, but because he'd keep doing this, forcing her out of her mind with incomprehensible pleasure so intense it was an insidious torture.

"I'm sorry, Celeste. It's hard to understand you with the gag in your mouth. What was that?"

He lifted his head, and when he did, she swung hers around, making solid contact with his cheekbone. He let out a muttered curse, followed by a snort.

"Fucking brat. All right, we do it the hard way."

She was dying, transcending, going insane. He yanked her head back against the headrest forcefully enough her throat arched and she was staring at the ceiling of the truck. Then he went after the other breast.

He turned the vibrator down, but it wasn't to give her relief. He put his hand back between her legs to play with her cunt, rub slow circles over her throbbing clit. As he did that, his other fingers slipped under the thong and pushed inside her, began to thrust. The vibration on her rim connected the three points of contact, all while he licked and bit her other nipple, suckling hard, nipping when she least expected it so she'd jerk against him.

The next climax was worse. She'd heard about forced orgasms, how they were agonizing and unforgettable at once, a way to break the mind, and she had no doubt of it after the third one crashed over her.

"Stop...stop..." It was a plea, a demand, a snarl and a curse.

Leland did stop, but he left her as she was, her breasts exposed, the bra cups pulled back, her leggings at her knees, mouth stretched over the gag, and sat back in his seat. He was revved up himself, his breath short, those golden eyes now like embers, his arm muscles bunched beneath his shirt sleeves. Her gut twisted when he fished a condom out of his console, laid it on the dash and opened his jeans. As she watched hungrily, he closed his hand over himself beneath cotton boxers and stretched out a sizable cock before her eyes. Beautiful and thick, the butterscotch-colored skin taut over its length, the slit of the broad head marked with pre-come. Her pussy, still throbbing, contracted on itself, and she felt way too empty. She wanted him inside her.

Tearing the condom open, he rolled it on and then gripped himself again, beginning to stroke. His eyes rested on her exposed breasts, her bare thighs, the small swatch of black vinyl covering her cunt. Being tied up and used as his personal pinup while he gave himself release should have been insulting, humiliating. Instead she felt anything but. She was hot, needy, angry and wanting him, even as she wanted to tear into him.

"Got to give myself some relief, darlin', because I'm not anywhere near done with you."

As he stroked himself, cupped his balls and rolled them, she imagined her mouth there, imagined him forcing her facedown in his lap to make her suck him off. Which shocked her in some distant part of her overwhelmed mind, since she hadn't given head much in her life, for plenty of good reasons. Down on her knees, helpless to a male...

Right now, though, it didn't seem to matter. She wanted her mouth on him. When she tried to lick her lips despite the gag, he chuckled.

"Oh, no. Won't tempt me with that maneuver. I can tell you're in full fight mode. I'd be taking a trip to the emergency room."

He was right. She couldn't explain it. Some part of her was ashamed, no idea why she was fighting him, trying to hurt him, why all these feelings were raging inside her, at war with her sexual response though they'd been summoned by it. Her body was still twitching from those forced climaxes, but her mind seemed to be sinking below the level of pleasure, into a darker place. She started to feel like shit about herself, about the whole situation, but he saw that, too.

"No, not going down yet." He turned the vibrator on a slow hum and when she whimpered in protest, he made a quieting noise. "If you're good, I'll take out the gag. Can you be good?"

She shook her head, and he smiled at that, though there was no humor in his gaze. He extracted the gag anyway, put it in the back. While his cock jutted between his thighs, waiting for his attention, her eyes clinging to it, he took the time to remove a handkerchief from the console, dry the corners of her mouth.

Only then did he sit back, take himself in hand again. "Make me harder, Celeste," he ordered in that stern voice, a contrast to how he'd just cosseted her. "Roll your hips, arch your back. I can smell your come soaking that towel. Nine times. You're going to come for me nine times before I get you home, because those are nine climaxes that belonged to me."

"This is just our first real date," she managed lamely. "You didn't tell me..."

"I told you I don't date. You're looking for a Master, Celeste, not a date. You want the type of Master who can handle all that fear and anger you're carrying inside you. Bring it to the surface, let you get past it to feel what you need to feel."

She refused to answer that, an answer in itself.

His breath shortened. "Don't take this as an indication of my staying power, darlin'," he said, flashing a feral grin at her. "I've been fucking steel since I sat down on that bench. I just want to get this out of the way so I can get back to playing with you. Christ, you're gorgeous, tied up and helpless, your clothes half pulled off."

Just like that, he started to come. He'd pulled his shirt up out of the way, so she saw the muscles of his lower abdomen ripple in response as come started to spray inside the tip of the condom. The tissues between her legs contracted against the low hum of the vibrator, and she found herself doing as he'd demanded, rolling her hips against it, arching her back. When he reached out to touch her breast during his climax, his hand flexing against it in involuntary response, she cried out, working her hips more furiously. Christ, it was happening again. It was short and intense, but watching him come, his mere touch on her breast while he self-pleasured, tipped her over again.

She wanted to see him naked. That large body, all muscles and honey-gold flesh, the impressive cock erect. She wanted to be lying on his bed, spread for his pleasure, trembling the way she was now, feeling overpowered not by restraints or orders, but just by his sheer size and the power of his gaze, which seemed to keep her locked in place as he stared at her. His eyes never left her throughout his release, telling her she was the center of it, the cause of it.

When he finished, her fingers were locked against the rings holding her wrists to the sides of the seat. He tucked himself back into his pants, but instead of releasing her, he chose a new way to torment her.

He turned over the ignition.

Straightening, he touched the side of her face, tucked a strand of her hair behind her ear. "Let's take the long way home."

The windows were tinted, so no one could see into the vehicle. But she still felt exposed, for he did nothing to cover her, leaving her as she was. He also bumped the vibrator up a notch or two, coupling it with an order sure to make her lose her mind.

"No fidgeting, Celeste. You just have to absorb the feeling."

She'd thought he was kidding about taking the long way home, but he wasn't. He drove downtown, past the Old State Capitol building that looked like a castle on the outside and had the sacred hush and old wood smell of a church inside, down to the riverfront where she could see the petroleum companies and other industries with their billowing white smoke in the distance. The sun was setting, moving the day into twilight.

When Leland drove through one of the poorly

maintained pay parking lots across from the river, that was where she came again, thanks to the bumps from the broken pavement. As they passed a rusted panel cut with slots, where patrons put their folded bills to pay for a parking space, she had a glazed impression of the bold message printed on it. *Parking is never free.*

He took her past the current State Capitol building, an art deco monolith that pierced the sky with its nearly thirty floors. She came again when he was driving through Spanish Town, such that she was staring at a cluster of plastic pink flamingos in someone's yard as she groaned through the waves of sensation.

Her seductive torturer was pointing out some of the houses he liked best. "If you could live in one of them, where would you live? Tell me, darlin'."

He meant it, sharpening his tone in that way that had her gasping out answers to his questions. But she also demanded he let her go. Called him a bastard once or twice. He'd just put the car back in drive and they'd move on. She hit orgasm eight when he pulled into an empty shopping center parking lot. He kissed her through it, teasing her mouth. She bit him again, only this time it was frantic, sensual little nips, not the savage tearing that had gripped her earlier.

Cupping her head, he kissed her thoroughly, his tongue lashing hers. The more ruthless he was, the more gentle his touch, the softer his kisses. She'd started to register that. It devastated her, broke her open. She pleaded with him now, noises without words. He must have seen her fear when he lifted his head, because he stroked her face, staying so close to her their foreheads almost touched.

"You're safe with me, Celeste. All of it. Everything you are."

"No more. Please."

"Ssshh." He slid his arms around her. "We're taking a little break. Just relax. Be easy."

The vibrator had stopped again. Though she didn't trust it would stay that way, his soothing touch helped steady her. Helped get her feet beneath her, pull some of her defenses together.

"We..." She coughed, tried to pull away. "We should be

talking about safe words."

He settled back, but not by much. His hand rested on her thigh, his other forearm propped on the headrest above her. "We can do that. What's your safe word, Celeste?"

"What word would make you feel safe, Celeste? You can't afford for there to be men who stand fast, who protect, who love with all they are. Who don't leave. Who take honor, commitment, and responsibility seriously. You can't afford to trust your fate to the hands of another, not for a moment."

It was like a fist reached into her chest, wrapped around her suddenly cold heart and squeezed it like a grape. She yanked herself out of the memory of that night at Club Surreal, away from the Dom with the knowing eyes, whose words had stripped her raw. He'd accurately guessed what word should have made her feel safe. A word she'd wished had represented safety, but never had.

"I don't want a safe word," she said sullenly, ignoring the fact she'd brought it up.

"Not an option," Leland responded. "I'll give you one. 'Byline.'" But here's the thing, Celeste. When you use it, everything stops. Period. We're done."

Did they read from the same playbook? The Dom at the club had set the same line in the sand. "So that's it for you and me? Game over, everything? Your way or no way?"

"No." He didn't appear to take offense at her belligerent tone. If anything, he seemed to become more patient. She wanted to hate him. Someone that made her need him this much, this fast, needed to be hated. "It means the session's over and we're on a cooldown period," he said. "The first time you do it, we won't have another session for a week. The next time you do it, it will be two weeks. Third time, three. After that, no more chances. Fourth strike is game over."

She blinked at him, sure he was joking, but she knew he wasn't. "This isn't dating," he reminded her. "There's a structure to this, and I set the framework. When a sub like you uses her safe word, typically at first it's a way to cry wolf, yank a Dom's chain, control the situation. You're trying to control your downhill slide."

"That's usually a good survival technique. Alligators could be waiting at the bottom."

"True. But maybe something else is waiting down there as well."

"What?"

"You have to trust me enough to find that out yourself. Ruins the surprise if I tell you."

Was he teasing her, trying to get her to lighten up? She wasn't biting. She sneered. "So you set all the rules, everything."

"Pretty much. And not really." He reached out and stroked those long strands of hair out of her eyes, touched her nose. "You can be a brat all day long, Celeste, whatever you need. But no crying wolf."

"What if I'm just scared?"

"Then you tell me that." His eyes did that sharpening thing, like gold struck by sunlight, and she realized he hadn't been teasing her at all. "That's what I'm trying to teach you. To trust me with what's inside."

"Will you take the cuffs off my hands now?"

"You owe me one more orgasm. Then we'll talk about that."

No. She couldn't possibly. When he reached for the vibrator controls she was prepared to beg. But he was just placing the remote control into the console. Reaching over her, under her, he unfastened the Velcro and removed the thong, carefully working it out of the clasp of her buttocks, away from her soaking wet pussy. Then he pushed her leggings all the way down to her ankles. He was folded over her lap while he did that, his chest against her bare thigh. She thought of his back, wide and strong under her palms when he was first kissing her at the mall, and she wanted to be holding on to him again.

She couldn't ask for anything right now. What was he doing? Her brain was simultaneously on overdrive and overloaded, exhausted from an array of conflicting emotions. In some distant corner, she realized she was relying on him to know where to take this next.

He straightened, gave her that penetrating look. Closing his hands on her knees, he spread them out as far as the hold of her clothing at her ankles would allow. Reaching over her, he eased the seat back, taking her down so she was gazing at the ceiling of the truck.

"Didn't have enough of eating your pussy the other night, so I'm going to enjoy another meal there."

She was so sensitive that the first touch of his mouth, the slight prickle of his evening shadow, had her crying out in protest. She fought his hold and found she couldn't match his strength, not even to move an inch. As he teased her with breath and tongue, the deliberate rasp of his beard over her clit and labia, discomfort started turning into another one of those agonizing spirals upward. He straightened when she was starting to move against his face and replaced his tongue with his fingers, holding her gaze as he slid two thick fingers inside her, pushing his thumb up under her clit hood, making her cry out as he worried that over stimulated bud.

"Drives you nuts, doesn't it? Feels terrible and good, all at once. You want me to suck on it instead, stroke it nice and slow? Rock you to climax like a baby? Take care of you the way a Master should? Like you're my baby, all mine?"

Her gaze clung to him, desperate. *Yes.* Why couldn't she form the words? Why did such things bring a jagged lump to her throat too sizable to speak around, a wall she couldn't get past? She parted her lips, swallowed. "Tell me," he said, low.

"Byline," she said.

§

It took every ounce of self-discipline Leland had to remember the rules, to draw back and do what he needed to do. The problem was, she'd given him a glimpse of what lay behind the wall. He'd only been half teasing her in the mall. When he'd considered finding his forever sub, he'd usually fantasized about someone sweet as a kitten, a woman he could cuddle and cherish as well as spank and restrain, collar. Punish her for minor infractions in a way that would be fun for both of them. But with Celeste he was realizing he wanted one he could tame, that came to him wild and fierce, who learned to trust his touch and care. Behind her angers and fears, he could see that kitten cowering and spitting in the shadows. All he wanted was for her to trust him enough to curl up in his palm. Maybe she'd hang on to it with her claws at first, thinking he'd drop her, but eventually she'd learn he never would.

He guessed a man could imagine all day long what he wanted, but Fate sent him what was needed, and laughed its ass off when a guy discovered getting what he wanted was going to be about as easy as making a touchdown across a bed of nails in bare feet.

So he pushed down his howl of protest, his knowledge that he could use her body's responses and her emotions to make her forget she'd ever said that safe word, and instead gave her a short, impassive nod. "All right."

Taking napkins from the console, he pressed them against her bare cunt. She kept herself smoothly shaved, a vision sure to torture his dreams tonight.

"What are you doing?" Her voice had a little break in it.

"Ssh." He wasn't in the mood to talk just yet. He pulled the leggings back up onto her hips and ass, lifting her up as needed to bring the skirt down over them. Her ass might be skinny by his standards, but it had a nice shape to it he was beginning to deeply appreciate. He forced himself not to linger too long with it. Adjusting the satin bra cups over her beautiful breasts, he pulled her shirt back into place. Only then did he release her cuffs.

He anticipated her reaction, fortunately, because otherwise he might have a nice shiner. He caught her thrown fist, then the other wrist when she tried to strike at him with that hand. When she struggled, snapped at him, he gave her a little shake. "Stop it," he said sternly. "It's done, Celeste. No reason to fight. Session's done. Just you and me, not Master and sub."

As it penetrated, he made his tone milder, though his heart was wrenched by her lost expression. She was definitely advanced material for a Master. He was glad for the years of experience he had. It helped him see that she could speak her safe word to protect herself and yet still be caught up in the haze of lust and emotions that had tangled her up in her submission to him, brief and sweet though it was.

When she eventually pulled back, wanting to draw in, reestablish her space, he allowed it, seeing she was back with him. She cleared her throat, cleared it again. He found the bottle of water in the takeout bag, opened it and offered it to her. Her hands were shaking so badly, he helped steady the bottle as she held it. Her hazel eyes watched him as he stroked her cheekbone.

When she lowered the bottle, he removed his hand, but only after a caress of her temple with his knuckle. "Enough water?"

She nodded.

"Okay. Hold on to it, just in case." He screwed the cap back on for her before he put the truck in drive. Thanks to the circuitous route they'd taken, they weren't far from The Mall, and it didn't take long to be back there. She told him where her car was when he asked, but beyond that they didn't speak. He was giving her time to collect herself, and himself time to think things through.

There was a space open by her car. He took it, came around to open her door. She sat there, unmoving, staring straight ahead.

"So that's it."

"For a week. If you want to continue, then we'll get together after that."

She turned her gaze to him. "So it's your way or nothing," she repeated.

"Yeah. But the point is you have to choose to give me power over you, darlin'. You called it done tonight, and I'm respecting that. Are you okay to drive? Do you need me to take you home? I don't want you driving if you don't feel up to it."

"I can drive. What if I don't want to do anything after a week?"

"That's your choice, too. I won't play mind games with you, Celeste."

"Yeah it is. It's a mind fuck," she said bitterly. "You're trying to make me feel guilty so I'll come chasing after you, like I'm some desperate badge bunny who will beg for your cock--"

She bit back a startled yelp as he closed his hand around her throat. He could damn near wrap his fingers all the way around that slender ivory column, and what got him hard as a rock all over again was her reaction. Though her hands lifted to block him, they never made it all the way up to pry at his fingers. They stopped midair, hovered, and then settled nervously in her lap as her gaze fixed on him. Her lips were parted in a way that told him his collaring her throat had silenced that harpy tongue, confusing her mind. He tightened his fingers infinitesimally, testing her and tormenting himself, and she swallowed against his hand.

"First off, eventually you will beg for my cock. That's a given. Your eyes were doing it tonight when I was jacking off in front of you, and it made me want to fuck you like it was my last act on earth. Second, you can be as much of a brat as I know you need to be, but you will not strike out at me for respecting your safe word. Respecting that respects you, protects you, allows you to protect yourself. A man who understands that, who puts you first, doesn't deserve the kind of trash talk you were just dishing out. Does he?"

She shook her head, a quick jerk. "No, sir."

It was a sub's instinctive response, no thought or taunt to it. Christ, she was trying to kill him. He withdrew, took a breath. "We're out of scene now. No need to call me that."

A ghost of a smile flirted around her mouth, at odds with her sad and confused eyes. "Could have fooled me, Sergeant."

He sighed, helped her out of the truck. As he put his hands to her waist and she slid down, her arms went around him. He gave in to her unspoken need, holding her close. She buried her face against his chest and he bent his head over her protectively as he rubbed her back. "It's all right, darlin'." He propped his chin on her head. "What is your full name, anyway? The real one. In case I want to look up that juvie record."

She snuffled a snort against his chest, though her shoulders remained tense, her body quivering with nerves. "Esther Celestial Lewis."

He blinked at that. "Precious as the stars."

She stiffened like a board and pulled away. As he watched her with a frown, she retrieved her coat. Shrugging into it, she fished out her keys to unlock her car. Her set face didn't turn his way until she was in the car and he'd closed the door for her. She rolled the window down after she started the engine.

"The stars aren't precious," she said dully. "There are millions of them and they all look the same, because they're light-years away. Too far gone to reach. Good night, Leland."

Chapter Five

"A country-western bar?" She stared at her text screen. "He wants to take me to a country-western bar."

Wednesday. Beer and line dancing.

She tapped out a return text.

I thought you said a week.

A week for our next session. This is like a date.

I haven't decided if I like you anymore. And you don't date.

Women think a guy's hotter when he's with a woman. If you go with me, I'll score some hookups with cowgirls.

You might get your testicles blown off by a .22.

That's a small caliber for such a large target. Use my Glock.

A.S.S.H.O.L.E. You and your large dick can go to a hoedown by yourselves.

I'll pick you up at eight on Wednesday.

She didn't deign to respond to that. She was aching for him. Literally. When she woke Saturday morning after that amazing climax marathon, all her muscles had tightened up, and she was barely able to walk. She discovered a text on her phone from him after she struggled into a sitting position in her bed.

Aspirin, hot shower. Massage if you have a place you go for that kind of thing.

There's one by the interstate that the truckers use. I'm sure the girls there are trained in Swiss massage and aromatherapy.

Can I watch?

She hadn't responded to that, but she wondered if her text made him smile. As she hobbled to the bathroom, all her muscle groups were screaming at her to lie down and die. Just let her body petrify, rather than suffer through movement. Nine climaxes. Thank God she hadn't told him the truth, that she'd used her vibrator or hand to get herself off several more times than that. If he'd known it had been over a dozen times instead of nine, he would have killed her with forced orgasms. When they sent him to prison, he'd have so many female groupies writing to him, rock bands would be jealous.

Once she could sit in front of her computer, she checked to see if her life had been in jeopardy. No conclusive proof of death by orgasm, but the graphic urban legends got her all worked up again. Unbelievable. Was this like the four-hour erection thing? Permanent arousal? Did she need medical help? She double-checked on that, along with death by masturbation, and found that debunked as well. If you believed the Internet.

But her worries on that score weren't why she didn't go for relief via her vibrator or the shower head. He hadn't said she couldn't masturbate, but she didn't. Because he hadn't said she could.

She'd fight him in person, tell herself she wasn't going to go out with him again when she was alone, but she was obeying his unspoken commands in absentia. It was all part of her lovely mess of contradictions. A submissive who wanted to be a submissive so badly she fought it like a trap. She'd given up trying to understand the paradox, but part of the problem was she sensed he did. It made her want to be with him as much as she didn't want to be with him.

The country western text had come in after her shower. To keep her mind off her libido and the possibility of more texts, she opened her files and went to work, since this was obviously going to be a work-at-home kind of day. She couldn't face getting out of her bathrobe.

She received feeds from a variety of news sources. As she scrolled through them, her usual routine, she frowned and stopped on one.

Tina "DeeDee" Morgan found stabbed...

"Ah, damn it." She'd bought DeeDee coffee one night, paid the price of a blow job to sit with her, get her impressions of life on the Baton Rouge streets, since Celeste was doing a series about it at that time. She remembered the woman had a wry sense of humor, very little education, a mild drug habit and pretty eyes. Plus double-D tits; hence the nickname. Celeste also remembered DeeDee was twenty-three. She'd been working the streets for six years.

The article was typically sparse, as was the police incident report. Unlike Loretta Stiles's murder, no reporters other than her would have shown up on scene for this one, and the night of the crime, Celeste had been with Leland, eating nachos and watching sports. She didn't regret that, but regretted the delay in catching the incident report. She'd been following up leads on Loretta and the drug trade series since, and DeeDee surely deserved better from her.

Something about the information niggled at her, though, telling her she'd read something else this week that was connected. Loretta's death seemed important to it as well. She read a crap ton of material every day, stuffing her head full of details, but they had a way of sorting in her head over time that had more than once led her in the right direction. So now she sifted through her thoughts and more files, trying to jog it loose. Where was it?

It wasn't until she'd made her second cup of coffee and had taken a couple more aspirin that it hit her. Despite thinking she was a little crazy, she called up the latest animal control summary report and found what she was seeking.

Animal control had been called out because a lady claimed someone had killed her dog. She'd found the dog in the same cul-de-sac where DeeDee was found a week later. Placing a call to animal control, Celeste lucked out and found her usual source working the Saturday shift. Leslie pulled the detail report and shared. It wasn't a shooting, the animal control officer had been sure of that. He'd guessed the dog was hit by a car, but when Leslie got him on the phone and she and Celeste talked to him together, he was able to recollect the extent of the wounds and the blood. Stabbing? Beating? Upon reflection, the officer and Leslie guessed it could be stabbing, but Celeste could tell she was leading them to a conclusion, which meant she had nothing.

Thanking Leslie and promising her they'd get together

soon for coffee to discuss the upcoming calendar, since Celeste offered free advertising for any animal welfare events the shelter pursued, Celeste next placed a call to the woman to whom the dog had belonged.

"I don't understand." Alana Ferrin became a little teary as she spoke to Celeste. "She was such a good dog, wouldn't hurt anyone. I had her for company, not to be a guard dog. She didn't really bark that much, except to get someone to notice and come pet her. I never had any complaints from the neighbors. She'd never gotten out, but the gate was open, like someone let her out. The police thought maybe neighbor kids did it and then she got hit by a car, but on a cul-de-sac? Who's going so fast they'd hit a dog on a cul-de-sac? Unless they did it intentionally. And it doesn't make sense. It was five miles away from my home. I wouldn't have found her at all except someone down there was nice enough to look at her collar and call."

Her voice broke. "She was just a kind, good dog. A lot of shifty characters hang out at that cul-de-sac. The graffiti and needles, all that garbage. I know one of them did it, but I don't know why, except it was just pure cruelty."

"Ms. Ferrin, I don't want to upset you more, but did she look like she'd been hit by a car?"

"It's so hard to tell. The officer said a dog can be hit by a car and not have an obvious mark on her. But she had wounds. In her side and chest. She was all bloody. Oh God."

"I'm so sorry." Celeste hated the part of the job where she had to push like that. "You sound like you were really good to her. I hope some other dog is lucky enough to be adopted by you."

"Thank you." Alana sniffled. "But it will take a while. I just feel...it's like I've been wounded down to the soul. Someone who would do that to my Lacy, they'll do that to a person. People just don't understand that. If you'd mistreat an animal that way, something's terribly wrong with you."

When Celeste ended the call, she sat back in her chair, frowning. It could be a complete coincidence, true. Yet she believed in being thorough, so she did some more digging and hit gold. The kind that sent a cold tingle up the base of her spine that told her she'd found something that didn't gel. Or that did.

Alana Ferrin lived a few doors down from the Stileses.

Scrolling through more animal control reports, she found another incident report in the Stileses' neighborhood and was back on the phone to Leslie, requesting another detail sheet. When it came through on her computer, Celeste clicked it open and frowned. A week before Loretta's death, animal control was called out to retrieve a dead dog on the street. The neighbor had insisted on animal control instead of sanitation, because the dog appeared to have been dumped in that condition, not run over. The officer who wrote the report was more detail oriented, noting that the animal had puncture wounds. He'd taken several pictures. This dog was on the thin side but not unhealthy, a shepherd mix. She didn't have tags or a chip, so she hadn't been claimed, but she did have a collar with faded pictures of dog bones on it.

Alana's dog had tags. Otherwise she likely never would have found her pet, all that distance away. What if the dog in the Stileses' neighborhood had come from another part of town...like in the area of town where DeeDee was killed? It sounded ridiculous, even to Celeste. Serial killers were far rarer than the abundance of crime dramas about them. However, the ones who existed did seem to have a tendency to establish patterns, signatures that had significance to them.

Well, it could be her dumbest hunch of all time, but she might as well check it out. Printing out the description of the dog, she put it in her to-do files for Monday and turned her attention to her other work. However, for the rest of the weekend, a part of her mind kept chewing on it. At least it gave her an alternative to thinking about Leland, though that subject kept her mind just as engaged--and was just as puzzling.

On Monday, by the time she headed for the area where DeeDee had been found, she'd about convinced herself she was looking for submarine races in the desert. But as she drove up and down the nearby streets, Celeste discovered what she was seeking. Getting out, she went to a scarred light post where a paper sign was showing the effects of an earlier rain, part of it already torn away. Pushing it up, she looked at the fuzzy picture of the lost dog noted there. Sadie. Black-and-brown shepherd mix. The description was written in a child's scrawl.

She wrote down the address, wondered if she could figure out a way to verify it without letting the young owner know Sadie hadn't fallen into kind hands. Because it was entirely possible Sadie had. Black and brown shepherd mixes weren't unique. The dog picked up from the Stileses' neighborhood would have been disposed of by now, no way except the officer's photos to tell if she was Sadie, and she sure as hell wasn't showing that to a child. Plus, a connection between two dead dogs and two murdered women, both a week apart? A lot of "ifs." She tried to scoff at the idea, but damn it, the spidey sense was tingling.

Celeste got back in her car and drove to the cul-de-sac where DeeDee had been found. A couple of working girls leaned on a broken chain-link fence in the empty lot, a trio of young men not too far away, one sitting on a bucket while two others stood around him. She recognized the subtle signs of their gang affiliation. MoneyBoyz. While they were acting like three kids with not much to do, they were waiting for customers to come by. It was a popular spot for transacting drug business.

She'd asked Alana to pinpoint as exactly as she could where the dog was found on the cul-de-sac, so she stopped her car next to that spot, which was fortunately on the opposite side. It was possible she wouldn't get any crap from the boys if she did her business quickly and acted like she had every right to be there.

The graffiti on the curb was extensive. While a lot of artists looked for vertical surfaces like the sides of buildings, most of them had a compulsive need to create, so she saw some promising artwork, despite some of it being praises of the MoneyBoyz, marking their turf. Like a colorful puzzle, it was all interlocking letters and swirling pictures. She moved along the curb, doubled back, noting the drug paraphernalia, used rubbers. She also stayed mindful of how conversation across the cul-de-sac had died off. Crouching down, she pushed some trash off the curb to get a better look at something that didn't fit.

Rough childish letters had been scrawled over a piece

of graffiti art, like a to-do list on top of a magazine ad. The letters were dark brown, nearly faded from rain. She took a picture of it with her camera phone, and then traced them on the rough ground. The first four letters could be...dead. Then...yeah. She sat back on her heels, a hard knot tying itself below her rib cage. She wasn't mistaken. Bitch. Dead Bitch.

She shouldn't be jumping to conclusions. It could be paint or a marker, done by some insensitive asshole, making a caustic comment about finding DeeDee's body here. Or a more recent spat between hookers where one had scribbled it to start a fight. If it had been left here with the dog, it could be days old, since the dog was found a week before DeeDee was killed. But with all the trash covering it since then, and the rain hadn't been a downpour...

"Yo bitch, why you hanging down here? You wantin' to suck some dick for money?"

She'd stayed too long. Slipping her phone back into her pocket, she rose and faced the two males who'd come over to see what she was doing. They weren't much older than Darryl and Sean, but the hardened looks on their faces said they were far deeper into the life than the other two boys.

She produced her card calmly. "I'm Celly Lewis. I'm a reporter. You've probably seen me around the neighborhood before. I was following up on a dog that was killed here."

The taller boy scoffed. He might not yet be a man, but he had the frame of one, nearly six feet with broad shoulders and big hands. Despite the cooler weather, he wore a wifebeater over sagging jeans and he had several tats on rippling biceps. He looked strong and mean. His companion was slim, sporting a gold earring and LSU shirt over his jeans and high tops.

"You write stories about dead bitches?" The taller one said. "You don't get much action, do you?"

Despite the curled lip and tough guy expression, he had long, thick lashes and a boy's mouth. She tended to notice such things, though it didn't ever make her foolish enough to lower her guard. Behind those thick lashes were hostile eyes. His fingers were twitching as if he had a habit...one that had to do with looking for an excuse to show how badass he could be. "Do you think someone wrote that about DeeDee or the dog?" she asked in a companionable tone, as if she considered them a valuable source for her story. That often disarmed a tense situation, because people did like to feel important. "That's what's written on the ground here. 'Dead Bitch.' Or maybe it was unrelated. A warning for someone hanging around here? Did the ladies get into a fight with one another?" She looked toward the hookers.

"We don't know no DeeDee," the tall boy said.

"Oh hell yeah, Dogboy. Remember, she had the great big titties."

Celeste's gaze snapped back to the boy as Dogboy shoved his friend. "Shut up, Bobby. You don't tell no one you know a dead person. Cops lock you up just for that. They looking for someone to pin it on."

"Aw, why do they care about dead pussy like her? She was just a ho."

Celeste glanced at Bobby but brought her gaze back to Dogboy. What she saw in his face made her increase her grip on the handgun she had tucked in a reinforced pocket holster in her coat. She knew how to shoot it with decent accuracy without having to remove the gun from its present location. She'd practiced at the range with a cheap jacket she'd bought at the Goodwill. But she always preferred to use her wits as her first defense. The gun was the last. "Wouldn't you want someone to care if someone killed you?" she asked.

"Listen to her. She's like our foster momma, Dogboy. She don't know that our real brothers watch out for us." Bobby gave her a hard grin, his eyes sparkling a little too bright. Probably pumped up on some of the product they were selling. "We take care of anyone who fucks with us," he said.

Dogboy didn't agree or disagree with that, but his unfriendly look fastened on her face, didn't waver. She was reminded of a snake watching prey. "That includes nosy reporters," he said.

"I'll keep that in mind. But a reporter can also be a friend...Dogboy, was it?" Her gaze shifted deliberately to the "Dead Bitch" impression on the ground. She was pretty certain the dark-brown remnants were some type of blood. The dog's blood? Or maybe DeeDee's, which was why enough of it was still there for her to see. What were the chances the words had been written in the approximate spot where the dog had been left seven days earlier? And possibly where DeeDee herself had been killed. If so, the crime techs would have likely combed the area and photographed that evidence. But did they know about the dog?

She needed to pull her head out of her ruminating ass, because apparently her pensiveness had been noted and hit a nerve. "Listen, bitch..." Dogboy reached under his shirt for what she was sure would be a gun or knife he could wave in her face. It wouldn't be the first time she'd had to deal with that kind of posturing. She was pretty sure he wasn't planning to shoot her in broad daylight in front of two hookers and the sparse scattering of nearby neighbors, despite their houses being dilapidated enough to suggest they were mostly inhabited by junkies and "didn't see nothin'" ostriches.

She planted her feet and prepared to defuse. But before Dogboy could follow through, his friend caught his arm. "Save it, D. Five-O."

As the boys and the hookers melted away, she stayed in place, pulling out her notebook to write a few things down. A few seconds later, the police unit pulled up next to her, now standing all alone in the circle. "Celly?"

She turned. Mike had his window down, and she could see that Billy was riding with him. District 1 sometimes had a shortage of units, causing the officers to have to double up. Though Billy had completed his obligatory four months of rotation through the districts that completed his BRPD academy training, someone had made the intelligent decision to have the rookie ride with Mike. She wondered if it had been Leland.

She bent enough to wave at Billy. "Hey, boys. Out trawling for pussy? Or donuts?"

Mike shook his head at her. "This isn't a great place for you to be hanging out."

"That's my life, Officer. Same as you."

"You don't have any on you, do you?" Billy asked.

"Donuts?"

Mike shook his head and tossed her a resigned look that said it all. *Rookies.* Though she expected he would have been happy if she had donuts as well. Sometimes she did, and it always amused her when they asked. Men did tend to think with their stomachs. "Not today. Got caught up in following some leads and didn't get past the bakery. I thought you two weren't supposed to be talking to me. Your big, bad sergeant said so."

"Hope he wasn't too rough on you," Mike said. "Leland's a good man. One of our best."

"I have a pretty tough hide. If you think good things about him, I'm on board." Too much on board, in fact. She missed him. She really did. She didn't want to wait until the next session or even freaking Wednesday. Why was she letting him set the rules?

"So why're you hanging out in a cul-de-sac with these teenage troublemakers, Celly?" Mike grinned at her. "You looking for an underage stud? I'd have to haul you in for that."

"I have all I can handle from you, Mike. I see you and my loins are all aflutter."

"Don't tell my wife. She scares the shit out of me. Says if she ever suspects my parts have been anywhere they shouldn't be, she'll cut them off."

"That woman's a keeper." Celeste considered her notes. "There was a dog killed here about ten days ago." Squatting, she pointed to the scrawled writing with her pen as Mike leaned through the window to see. "I'm think that's 'Dead Bitch,' though it's been compromised at this point. Had a lot of trash over it. Animal control thought the dog might have been hit by a car, but the owner believes the dog was murdered. Maybe beaten or stabbed."

"Christ, people who'd do that to an animal..." Billy had left his car to stand in front of Mike's grill and see what she was doing. Obviously a dog lover himself, the idea of it made his eyes and jaw much harder, showing her a face that wasn't nearly as green as she'd thought.

"Right there with you," she said. She thought about Dogboy's eyes. There was something dead there, so focused. Unlike the TV shows, sometimes a crime could be straightforward. Most criminals weren't masterminds. Usually the hardest part was finding the first couple of dots to connect. After that, the picture might draw itself, leaving the detectives only the tedious, painstaking chore of verifying every dot to build a strong case. However, all she had right now was a wacky theory. "I'm sure the techs got the blood, but I'm looking at a possible connection to DeeDee, the prostitute who was stabbed here. That one I was just talking to, Dogboy. I think he probably knows something about it, and he might also have been involved in that laundromat owner beating last Monday." She gave Mike a faint, grim smile. "Don't worry. If any of my speculations start to feel more solid than old Magnum, P.I. episodes, I'll shoot them to the lead detectives on their cases. Marquez is handling DeeDee's, right?"

"Yeah." He shook his head. "I'm glad you're not my wife, Celly. You'd give me gray hairs."

"You already have gray hairs, Mike. I think she's doing a good job all on her own."

Billy chuckled. "I like Magnum, P.I."

"Who doesn't?" She stabbed a finger at him. "Okay, what street are we on? Nope, no looking. That's cheating."

"Um..." He paused, then brightened. "Compton Court."

"Yes." She gave him a fist bump, mildly amused when he flushed a little. Christ, he was young. District 1 officers all had to learn the maze of streets by memory, because the less savory elements would take down signs or switch them to screw up the police when they had to respond to calls. She'd gotten in the habit of testing the rookies because, in truth, she felt like a protective big sister toward them. Sometimes she couldn't stop that feeling from opening the part of her that missed her two younger brothers, a part that needed to remain tidily closed.

"All right, Rook. Ass back in the car. You're lucky you got it right, or I would have made you buy our next meal." Mike shifted a similar reproving look to Celeste as Billy returned to the passenger side. "Are you about done here? We've got to keep doing our rounds, and I'm not leaving you out here by yourself."

"Yes, sir, Officer." Giving him a little salute and a wink, she tucked the notebook back into her purse. "Getting back into my car right now."

Despite the teasing, she was touched that they waited until she started her engine and pulled out before they left the cul-de-sac. When she was younger she'd had her run-ins with the police, typical for a teen with a chip on her shoulder toward authority figures. Toward anyone she perceived as trying to act like a father. Like criminal behavior, her personal shit wasn't rocket science. She didn't know why people paid a shrink to tell them the obvious.

She sighed. Damn it. She did and didn't know why she'd blurted out that safe word, but did Leland have to be such a hard-ass about it? She should just say fuck it, to hell with it, and walk away. Except she wouldn't. The same thing that had pissed her off and scared her, his steady control of all of it, his composed reaction, kept that yearning for him unabated, especially since she couldn't stop thinking about it.

Time to get her head out of her dysfunctional ass and reach out to her contact at social services. See if she could get a name on that "foster momma" of Dogboy's. As she pulled out her phone, it chirped, notifying her of a text. She received texts throughout the day from sources, editors, advertisers. Sometimes she heard from the only two women she counted as personal friends. Her siblings didn't reach out unless they needed something.

So though she told herself not to expect it would be anything other than any of the above, she still checked. Her heart leaped in that very annoying, schoolgirlish way when she saw it was Leland.

Come by my house at six if you can.

He didn't ask for a response, and she didn't give one, not for forty-five minutes. But when she did, she responded with one word.

Okay.

§

He opened the door when she reached his porch. He'd showered after his shift, because he was dressed in jeans and T-shirt. He also had that shampoo, soap and faintly damp smell a person carried when he was fresh out of the shower. She wasn't sure how to process the wave of pleasure that swept over her, seeing him framed in the doorway. "Hey there," he said.

"Hi." She didn't know what else to say, but she didn't have to say anything. He extended his hand and she placed hers in it. It was unsettling, how much that first touch did to settle her nerves. It had been that way the night at the convenience store as well. If Leland Keller had a spirit animal, it was the grizzly bear, the same animal to whom she'd compared him then. The bear's ponderous stride and the easy peace in the golden-brown eyes said that he didn't go looking for a fight. But he was calmly prepared for one, because he was the biggest and baddest of all the bears.

She thought the polar bear might be bigger, but she liked her analogy, so she left it alone. In addition to those qualities, Leland possessed a devastating sensual warmth and tenderness, such a noticeable contrast to his obvious strength, it made a woman feel protected and guided...controlled, in all the best ways.

Exercising all those traits now, he led her into the house, closing the door and taking her to the one room she hadn't yet seen, just beyond his bedroom and the one bathroom. The room was empty, no furniture, the two windows covered with thin paper shades that allowed in light but screened the view. A ceiling fan slowly turned, moving the air.

The walls were painted a cloudy blue, except for a black mark on one of them that looked like a long ribbon falling out of the sky. A mat the size of a picnic blanket was spread in the center of the room. Next to it was a braided coil of cotton rope, a brown velvet scarf arranged in a figure eight, and a fleece throw in dark blue, folded in a precise square.

He dropped to his heels at one edge of the mat. "Come sit in front of me, Celeste."

She hesitated. "Do you need me to...undress?"

"No." He looked at her from head to toe. "You look

nice."

She thought she looked okay. She'd come straight from her talk with Dogboy's foster mom, so she was still wearing her street garb of jeans and cross-trainers, her shirt a fitted button-down over a thin tank. She had pulled off on the side of the road before she arrived here to freshen her makeup and fiddle with her hair, but what would have been a polite compliment from a stranger or family member had a different, more attentive feel when it came from him. Maybe he'd missed her, too. The way he emphasized the word *nice*, the way he looked at her, made her self-conscious in a pleasant way. Under his regard, she tried not to fidget, to remember to stay in control. On top of things.

Imagining just the reverse, him on top of her, nearly locked up her mind. His body between her thighs, her heels crossed over his hips and flexing ass, his arms braced on either side of her like pillars to a building that would never fall, always sheltering her.

So much for staying in control. She couldn't even control her own mind. "Do you want to talk about what happened last time?"

He shook his head. "I know what happened last time. So do you. It's all part of this, Celeste. It's all right. You didn't do anything wrong or anything I didn't expect. You understand?"

Talking was her defense, her way of drawing people closer or driving them away, depending on what was required, but he simply took away her need to talk.

"Take off your shoes and come sit down with me," he said.

Setting down her purse, she came.

Protect, guide and control. Exercising all three of those traits now, he drew her down on the mat. He had her kneel facing away from him, and put his hands on her shoulders. He was kneeling as well, only on one knee, the other foot braced on the floor, that knee against her shoulder. He slid his hands down her arms and back up again. Up to her neck, taking a firm grip along either side of her collarbone. "Close your eyes."

With that first stroke of his hands, they were already

wanting to do that. She felt the velvet scarf feather along her neck, then her face. Her hand came up, uncertain, as he tied the scarf over her eyes.

"It's all right." He settled his large hands over the area the scarf was covering, pressing against her closed eyes beneath it, her cheeks, her forehead and lips. His fingers glided down her face, her neck, back to her shoulders and down her arms once more. Shifting so he was sitting behind her, he stretched his legs out on either side of her. He kept doing that slow, easy stroke up and down, from face to fingertips and back again.

"I missed you," she said before she could stop herself.

"I never stopped thinking about you, either, darlin'. Which is why I'm glad you came."

"I thought you said...not for a week."

"Yeah, I did. This is sort of different from a session." He gave a half chuckle. "Or I'm just rationalizing, because Friday is too damn far away."

A tiny sigh of relief spilled from her lips. Her hand curled into the denim over his thigh. "Yes."

"So we're on the same page. Good. I want you to be quiet and just listen. There's a form of bondage called Ichinawa, which means one rope. I'm sure you've done your research and seen all that fancy suspension and intricate knot work. Right? Just nod or shake your head."

She nodded. It was a peculiar relief, being told not to talk. She could listen to his voice, focus on how he continued to touch her, knead her shoulders, caress her neck. Her whole body was purring under his touch.

"Ichinawa is about the connection between Dom and sub using that one length of rope." Cradling her hand in his, he trailed the rope over her arm, across her breasts, over her shoulder, along her neck, down her spine. As he teased her with it, he kept talking in that murmuring tone. "I'll tie only one end of it to one part of you. Your wrist, your ankle, your thigh...wherever I'd like, and then wrap you up in it. Then I'll unwrap it and do it again. Different ways, the same way, over and over. Every time I wrap you in the rope and then unwrap you, it reinforces the choice. For me to take you, then let you go. For you to submit and then come back to me to submit again. It's as organic as breathing."

He went quiet then, making her aware of her breath as he stroked the rope up her thigh, back along her arm. He put his other arm around her waist, so she became aware of how he was breathing with her. When he put his lips against her throat, her breath stuttered, then caught the rhythm of his as well. There was no rush to this, no fight, no urgency. Her mind was whirling in a slow chaos, not sure what to make of it.

He shifted to kneel behind her again, his knees on either side of her hips. "Give me your hand, darlin'."

She lifted it in the air, and the rope trailed through her fingers as he spread them with his own, stroking the sensitive digits before he looped the rope around her wrist, looped it again. She felt a tightening as he inserted a finger underneath the wrap, against her pulse, then he pulled the rope through, made a knot. But it wasn't overly snug on her wrist. More like a bracelet's hold, draped over the point of her wrist and thumb joint.

"You just relax and let me play with you, darlin'. See where this takes you."

He bent her elbow so her bound hand was clasping her shoulder, and then he'd pulled the rope over it so her arm was held there. He began to wrap her in the rope, under her breasts, back up over her shoulder, across her breastbone, around her rib cage. As he did that, he rocked her back against him, eased her forward, holding her with one arm so she was like a tree swayed by the wind. His breath touched her temple, but when she turned her head in that direction, seeking him, his hand cupped her forehead and she was held back against his chest, leaning against him fully as he stroked her body. He didn't linger on her breasts or between her legs, but it didn't matter. Her body became an erogenous zone in its entirety, aware of the hold of the rope in a dozen places, of the way he stroked the outside of her breasts, her hips, along her thighs, across her stomach, up her breastbone to her face and shoulders again.

He doubled her over his arm as he unwrapped her. Once he reached that tied wrist point he began wrapping her again. A different way this time, boxing her arms behind her back and wrapping the rope around her thigh so she was held folded forward over her knees. He lifted her shirt in back, laid his lips along the delicate arch of her spine. Then she was tumbled into his arms as he unwrapped her again and eased her to her side on the mat. This time he bound her thigh to her elbow, wrapped the rope over her shoulder, under her neck, out beneath her elbow so she was in a fetal position, and he was trailing the rope over the line of her side, her hip, her thigh, down to her ankle.

Just as he'd told her, he kept doing it. Wrap, unwrap. Untie, retie to a different anchor point. Never hurried, as gradual as the flow of water in the Mississippi. The other night, the darkness within her had surged up from her soul, compelling her to fight. This had the darkness confused. Like river water, Leland simply washed over her, around her, held her up, drew her under. She became ever more malleable under his strong hands.

She was intensely aroused in a dreamlike way, no urgency to it, though moans started to break from her lips as he integrated more forceful actions into what he was doing. He brought her up on her knees again, wrapped both her hands behind her neck, the rope crisscrossed over her breasts and around her thighs. He held the two ends in his hand, which he rested with firm pressure just above her pubic mound as he curled his hand around her throat and pushed his body firmly against hers from behind. The two of them rocked and swayed together, him letting her feel how securely he held her.

On his next unwrap, he unbuttoned the shirt she had over her tank, removed it. She welcomed the tension of the rope against her bare upper arms, the compression of it over her breasts, the hold as he wrapped it around her back. Then her head fell back against his shoulder as he wrapped the rope over her mouth, parting her lips so it fitted between her teeth. He kept wrapping the rope over the scarf, over her eyes, before he settled his hands on her face as he'd done before, over both rope and cloth.

So much was surging through her. She wanted to say his name. Not Leland, but the name in her heart, poised on the cusp of all the need he was building inside her. She wanted it to be her safe word, but the literal meaning of "safe word," not the functional one. *A* safe word.

"Master."

She breathed it, barely a sound at all. He surrounded her, the focus of every sense she had--smell, touch, taste, sight and hearing. She thought he'd heard her, because his lips touched her ear.

"There's my kitten. Good girl. Good girl."

Did he realize the power of those two words? Maybe so. She thought he knew everything, understood everything. While a distant part of her mind rationalized he'd put her in some strange trance state and such unrealistic certainties wouldn't last, she'd take the respite. He unwrapped her slowly, his hand tracing the light rope marks. He left the rope knotted around her wrist, but eased her down to her side, and spread the throw over her. She was trembling. He'd left the blindfold on, and when he fitted himself behind her, holding her, she found his arms through the blanket, curled her fingers over them. The brush of his fingertips against her wrist and the tension on the rope told her he still held it, keeping her tethered to him. But it wasn't enough.

Maybe it was the blindfold making her as impetuous as a child, but she turned in his arms, following the rope past his hold by touch. It took some fumbling, and she had to sit up, splay her hands over his chest to figure out how he was lying next to her. He was lying on his hip and one elbow, propped up and probably watching her. Imagining those golden-brown eyes focused on her, she ran the rope around his back, underneath his arm. She wanted to wrap the rest around her back as well, make a full circle, but her coordination was off. She couldn't manage that without toppling over, unbalanced by the pull on her bound wrist her movements were causing. He took over, doing a second wrap around both of them as she laid her head on his chest, her bound hand against his side. She felt the pull as he tucked the end of the rope somewhere that kept their upper torsos wrapped together. He closed both arms around her and held her, spoke in a quiet voice, the bass increased by emotions the scarf allowed her to absorb without worry or question.

"All right, darlin'. All right."

He allowed them to lie together like that for a while,

tugging the blanket back over her until her shaking stopped. When one of those large hands descended to cup her ass, slide his hand into her jeans pocket to stroke and knead, she moved against him. The desire that had been flowing through her like a river immediately surged up. If the ropes hadn't been holding her, she would have tried to push him to his back, open his jeans and impale herself on his thick cock. She shuddered, imagining how it would send sensation spearing through her, catapulting her toward a climax.

"Easy. Move with me."

He was loosening the wrap from around the both of them, putting her on her back on the mat. His fingers slid over the knot on her wrist, underneath the wrap, soothing abraded flesh. But he didn't untie it. Instead, he inflated the throbbing need inside her by taking the rope over her shoulder, behind her neck and across her mouth again, fitting it between her teeth, around her scarf blindfold, then down over the other shoulder and across, wrapping the rope above and below her breasts, tucking it in so her elbows were held against her sides. Then he slipped the button of her jeans. Bending, he lifted up the tank and brought his mouth to her navel.

Her panties were the same thin cotton fabric as the tank. When he removed the jeans, he left them in place, kissing her pubic mound with that barrier between them. As he moved to the top of her thighs, she bit back a whimper. She could speak around the rope, but she understood she shouldn't. She didn't need to speak.

He'd secured the rope so it was now a binding, not just a wrap, which coaxed some of her darkness to the forefront. But he anticipated that, dispelled it. His hands returned to her waist, her arms, stroking, and then they were spread out along the sides of her face as he straddled her hips, bent and kissed her open mouth. The top lip, the bottom one. His mouth moved over her cheeks, over to her ear and the tender skin of her neck between the bands of the rope. She moved restlessly, needing him, her legs pushing against his knees, braced on the outside of her thighs.

He shifted off of her. She wanted to see him get undressed, but she didn't as well. In the darkness, her darkness stayed dormant, as if light was what pissed it off, like cancer being disturbed by a biopsy to explode, metastasize into something far worse.

She must have made a distressed noise, because he slid an arm around her, scooped her upper body against him, one knee planted between her thighs, the other foot now braced outside her hip. He was still wearing the jeans but, blissfully, he wasn't wearing a shirt. She pressed her cheek hard against bare flesh. She could feel his erection against her shoulder. She opened her mouth, tasted the ridges of muscle across his stomach, tried to wiggle lower. She wanted to wrap her lips around him.

"No. You're not ready for that yet, darlin'. But you're burning, aren't you?"

She wanted him inside her. He was right, it would probably break her like a boot stepping on glass. He was good at using his mouth or hands on her, but that wasn't what she needed, what had her aching. Which, perversely, was why everything in her was afraid again. She hated this about herself. Hated it more now than ever before. Why couldn't she just get past it? If he'd just let her go and they fucked, they'd both come and that darkness wouldn't be disturbed at all. Except she'd go home feeling hollow.

"Celeste." She'd started to strain against the bonds, was making angry noises, and he tugged her hair, bringing her focus back to him. "Hold on."

He untied the rope, unwrapped it, though she didn't want him to do that. When he tried to remove the scarf, she scrambled away from him, intending to rip it off herself, and gasped as he caught her back against his body. "Behave. Settle."

She expected he used that hard voice on his rookies. It worked on her, though she quivered with repressed resentment. She was aware it was projected self-loathing. It didn't make him any safer from the flak.

He removed the scarf, smoothed back her hair. With him behind her, she saw only the shaded windows, her folded jeans resting next to the crumpled throw. "Put those back on," he said.

He released her and she jerked away. Moving over to the pants, she yanked them on. She kept her head down, but she was aware of his gaze as she zipped and buttoned them, tucked in her tank, picked up the button-down shirt, put it on. While she did that, he moved to lean against the wall, his arms crossed over his chest. He was beside her shoes. She didn't let herself hesitate, coming over to stuff her feet in them, resisting the urge to reach out and clasp his forearm to steady herself. She used the wall instead.

"I'm not doing Wednesday or Friday," she said shortly. "I can't--"

A man she estimated at two hundred fifty pounds shouldn't be able to move like a pouncing cat, but before she could blink, he had caught her around the waist. He swung her across him and toward the wall in a swift arc. She would have face-planted into it, except he controlled her movements so she had time to put up her hands. When her palms met the wall, he'd snaked one powerful arm under her arm and behind her neck, an effective headlock as he shoved his other hand down the front of her jeans. It was a snug fit, given the size of his hand, but his fingers plunged down into her panties and found her damp pussy, began to stroke. No, stroke was the wrong word. Worry, tug, demand a response from her.

She went up on her toes, scratching the wall with her fingers as he held the clamp on her neck. "Come for me, sub." He spoke the last word in a whisper that resonated through her, shot right down between her legs.

The low simmer of response that had built during the rope wrapping turned into a geyser. She came violently against his ruthless fingers, his unshakable grip. She screamed at the intensity of it, whipping her head around to take a good chunk out of his forearm with her teeth, but the headlock didn't let her reach him. She floundered in his grip as he made sure she experienced every vibrating, excruciating second of the endless climax.

Emphasizing that he was the one in control--as if he'd left any doubt of it--he took her down at his pace, with massages and sudden squeezes of her clit and labia that had aftershocks rocking through her, drawing gasps and animal noises from her. When at last, slowly, he withdrew his hand and released her from the headlock, she kept her forehead and palms against the wall. His arm went to her waist to steady her as he tucked her tank back in, stroking the elastic of her panties before he tugged the other shirt back down over it. Then he laid a kiss on the back of her neck, her ear.

"I didn't do anything for you," she muttered.

He rubbed his steel erection against her ass. "You offering?"

Yes. "No. I have to go." She needed to go.

"All right." He stepped back, but she noticed his hands lingered until she straightened from the wall, took a couple deep breaths and made sure she could stand. Her legs were shaky, but she was all right. Mostly.

As she turned, he held on to her elbow, picked up her purse, threaded it over her arm. Guiding her out of the house the same way he'd guided her in, he walked her down the stairs. He dropped his touch as they moved onto the walkway. She thought he was establishing distance between them, but when she dared a glance at him, she saw he was watching her closely, making sure she was steady enough to drive.

It made the emotions dueling in her gut twist into a hard knot. As incredible as the orgasm she'd just had was, she knew it would be nothing to gushing around his cock when it was plunged inside her, stretching her cunt, marking her as his.

"What would you have said if I'd said yes?"

"I'd have said no." He stopped and faced her at the car. "Tempting as it would be to fuck you, Celeste, it's not yet time. You're too fragile."

She bristled at that, but he cupped her chin, lifted it. "When the time comes, and it's coming soon, Celeste, I'll use you hard. So be careful what you wish for." He leaned in, spoke against her ear. She bet if she tried to punch, kick, bite or scratch, he'd make her exceedingly sorry. Which made her want to find out if she was right. Fortunately he distracted her from the impulse.

"When the time comes, I'll fuck your cunt, your mouth, your ass. I'll jack off over you when I have you stretched out and tied, so you can't move an inch. I'll wash you off so gentle, and make sure everything that hurts, hurts less. Then I'll do it all over again, until you're screaming that word you barely spoke a while ago. And you'll be begging your Master for more."

The man didn't have to gag her to take away her ability to talk. Her stomach was rippling in an unsettling mix of trepidation and anticipation as he turned and headed back up his walkway. Twilight had moved into nighttime, so the streetlights deepened the shadows and put his powerful form in sharp relief. "I'll pick you up on Wednesday," he called over his shoulder. "You have anything to wear to a country-western bar?"

She forced herself to pull it together. She wasn't going with him. She needed to tell him that. She needed to say all sorts of vile, horrible things to him so he'd never want to see her again.

"Birkenstocks, tie-dye and my 'I Hate Country Music' button," she said instead.

His deep chuckle sent another ripple down her spine, the reaction spreading out over her buttocks and teasing her between her legs like his touch. "See you then, darlin'."

Joey W. Hill

Chapter Six

"Don't even try, Wasserman. You have as much chance with her as I do of dating a super model."

"That's because you lack basic hygiene, Foley. The day I had to ride with you, I stopped by the minute clinic for a tetanus shot."

"And the vet for a rabies update," someone else added.

Leland closed his locker door and came around the corner to the roll call room, buttoning his fresh uniform shirt. The half-sized lockers weren't intended to hold much, but they could hold an extra shirt, and experience had taught him to keep one on hand. His shift was past end, but he'd gotten hung up assisting Long on an aggressive drunk-and-disorderly. The cantankerous mechanic weighed about ninety pounds but had squirmed away from Long and decided to charge Leland with wrench in hand. Though Leland had put him down without a problem, he'd gotten splattered by the vomit when the guy had to puke mid-attack. The upside was that had taken all the fight out of him.

"Whose Wasserman got a hard-on for now?" he asked.

"His momma."

"Butch in the K-9 squad."

Leland chuckled, but he noticed Wasserman looked a little wary. A quick glance around told him the other guys were trying to distract him with the banter. They hadn't realized a sergeant was listening. He should bust their asses for not being more observant. Except for the district commander and the assistant district commander offices, there wasn't a lot of privacy to be had. The District 1 building was a converted Shopper's Fair, the cinderblock walls painted BRPD blues and grays to go with the cement floor, and had all the ambiance of a warehouse. The lieutenants had a communal office where the door could be closed, but the sergeants used open cubicles set up like a rabbit warren, only a rock toss away from the roll call area and small kitchen.

But it was home base for District 1, and they'd added

personal touches. Like the life-sized Santa Claus figure someone had picked up when it was abandoned after the holidays a year or so ago. The jolly red guy was in permanent residence on top of a bookshelf near the sergeants' cubicles. Recently someone had given him a cardboard sign that said Will Work for Food. Well, it wasn't Christmas yet. Even Santa had slow periods.

"Spit it out, Officer," he said to Wasserman. "What woman can we expect to file a restraining order against you?"

Wasserman's expression eased a little at Leland's good-natured prodding. "Aw, they're right, Sarge. We're just razzing one another. We're talking about Celly Lewis. She's hot as hell, all the more because she doesn't know it."

"And she's nice," Billy put in.

"Yeah. She thinks she might have a lead on that hooker stabbing and the assault on the laundromat manager," Mike added. He was straddling one of the metal and black vinyl chairs, sipping coffee. "She said she was going to pass it to Marquez if it panned out. Thinks Dogboy might be involved or at least know something."

Leland frowned. "He associates himself with the MoneyBoyz, and they're all about the drugs. How does he connect to the hooker?"

"Can't say. That was all she said to me, and you know Marquez can't tell us dick. But I've had some run-ins with Dogboy before." Mike's eyes went cold. "I think he's got some anger issues with girls. Even the working girls seem to give him a wide berth. When we pulled up on Celly talking to him the other day, I didn't like the way he was looking at her. There's something cooking under the surface of that one. Something nasty."

"What the hell was she doing there?" Though Leland already knew the answer to that. The damn woman didn't know how to stay out of trouble.

Mike grimaced. "What she's always doing. She knows this area almost as good as we do, Sarge. Cool as she could be. Toe-to-toe with him and looking him dead in the eye, no fear. Girl's got balls."

"Which could be why Wasserman's so interested in her…"

As the banter started again, Leland gauged whether or not it was the proper time to drop his bombshell, and then figured it was as good an opportunity as any. He waited for a pause, then let it fly.

"I'm dating her."

If he'd thrown a live grenade into roll call, he couldn't have captured their attention more effectively. In the brief silence before he was sure they were going to break into a chorus of bullshits, assuming he was messing with them, he added, "Taking her out tomorrow night, in fact. We've seen each other a couple times. Don't know how serious it's going to get, but you're right. She's pretty special. So let's keep an eye on her out there, all right?"

Mike rose. "We do, Sarge," he said seriously. "She's one of the good guys. We all know it." He cut a glance at the other guys, tucked his tongue in his cheek. "Plus, we don't want you to lose your opportunity to get some for the first time in forever. After she reports on your performance in her blog, it may be the last."

"Mike, I didn't know you were itching to take on all the domestic disturbance calls this month." Leland said. "And by your lonesome, too. We all appreciate your generosity."

The room erupted in hoots and general comments. As Leland gave the man a good-natured shove, he let out a breath. The opening had been convenient, but he was bemused by the shot of nerves that had gone through him right before taking it. Before he'd gone out on patrol, he'd talked to his lieutenant and Captain Teller, the assistant district commander, about the subject, because no way was he going to be seen dating a reporter and have any nasty speculation reflect on the district or BRPD in general. The captain had been cool about it. He'd known Leland long enough to trust him to stay within regulations on the information he'd share--or rather, not share--with Celeste.

But he'd found even the higher-ups had a good opinion of her, and that had weighed in his favor as well. Apparently her intention to send info to Marquez wasn't the first time she'd given tips that were useful. He found himself absurdly proud to hear the detectives felt she had good instincts. "She thinks like a detective," Captain Teller said. "She finds patterns, looks for things that don't fit."

Because she tried to work with the police if they asked her to hold a story until they could take the advantage her information might give them on solving the crime or apprehending the perpetrator, there were times the PIO gave her an early heads-up on statements, just to show appreciation. Respect went both ways.

It was a good thing the captain hadn't had any objections to Leland seeing her, because he wouldn't have been able to stay away from her regardless. When he'd closed his hand around himself in the shower this morning, he'd come in a matter of seconds, just by thinking of her in her thin tank, the bra beneath it doing nothing to hide the stiffness of her nipples, the generous size of her breasts. Her ass had been drum tight in her thin jeans, those tempting cheeks rubbing against him when he brought her to climax. The way she'd melted against him, letting him take her over during the flow of the Ichinawa session, had cinched it. He had her scent in his nose, the feel of her tingling against his palms. When he'd told her how many ways he planned to take her when they got to that point, she'd stopped breathing. He'd wanted to bite those lush lips, bring back that hazy, disoriented look. He wanted to hold her in his arms again.

Well, he'd have to make do holding her during a Texas waltz, because he had to keep it slow with her, at least in the sex department. As far as the emotional connection, he didn't think the two of them could go any faster if they jumped into a rocket headed for the moon. They'd seen each other twice before, yet this third time, she'd come to him, knelt on the floor at his command, trembled when he first touched her. Part of that was the Dom/sub thing, and her starting to embrace it again after her long hiatus. However, while she might not appreciate the comparison, certain breeds of dogs were known for their penchant to bond with one person only. Certain subs could be that way as well.

She was tricky, complicated, and the demons jumped right to the surface with the barest of triggers. There was no manual for dealing with that. It was all intuition, which was why the right kind of Dom had to handle her. He was determined to be that Master. Her Master. When she'd said that word to him, in a whisper that was hardly more than an exhaled breath, he'd almost missed it, but then it had hit him like a Taser in the chest.

Yeah, it was pretty soon for that reaction. Or maybe it was just in time. As Mike said, it had been a long dry run, but it had been that way for a reason. Leland knew what he wanted, and he was pretty damn sure he'd found her. The potential was there for her as well. He just had to figure out a way to convince her. Otherwise, he'd be the one with a restraining order filed against his ass. Though he expected his girl wasn't the restraining order type. She was far more likely to put a knife in him as her *keep the fuck away from me* message.

It was one of the things he liked about her. And that made him worry. He thought about her toe-to-toe with Dogboy and frowned. They were going to talk about that. Count on it.

§

It had been forty-eight hours. She shouldn't be so worked up that every phallic object in the house looked appealing. Fortunately none of them were nearly as appealing as the actual phallic object she wanted. It was her own fault. Once again she hadn't let herself touch her vibrator, though the fucking man hadn't said a fucking word about using her fucking vibrator. But she remembered those forced orgasms, so excruciating. It had been unforgettable, yet also a torment, one she didn't necessarily wanted to repeat.

She also wanted more than his cock. She wanted his warm, hard body stretched out on top of her, spreading her legs with his hips. He'd thrust deep inside her as she held on and lost herself in the look in his golden eyes. That look that said he wanted her, would have her, would keep her. It was that which would carry her to climax, as much as anything he did to her physically. It was a far cry from anything she'd ever thought she'd want from a man. Or could have, rather.

She'd sent him five texts in the past twenty-four hours.

Not going. Can't. Have conflict. We'll do it another time. Forget it.

He'd sent the same response every time.

See you at eight.

She'd fired back her typical knee-jerk answers.

Jerk. Asshole. Hard head.

He had a response for that one.

And that ain't all…

That had made her snort on a laugh. The man was impossible. But here she was, dressed to impress and coming out the door of her small rental house as he pulled up. She'd been watching for him, because she knew he was the type who would come to her door, and she hadn't had a chance to clean the disaster zone in which she lived. After seeing his military-neat domicile, no way in hell was he coming into her space until she could tackle it with a leaf blower and a sandblaster.

Confirming her suspicions about his courtly manners, he was already out of the truck and headed toward her as she was descending the stairs from the front porch. Nothing said class like a man coming to the door to escort a woman out on a date. A guy pulling up and laying down on the horn of his muscle car while swigging his first beer of the night had pretty much been the story of her teenaged dating life, such that almost twenty years later, she could still keenly appreciate the opposite.

She looked up from the stairs to give him a pleasant greeting and came to a full stop on the middle step. She didn't trust her footing, not while looking at him.

He looked like a man who planned to spend the evening at a country-western bar. He should have looked ridiculous, like he needed a loaded holster and a sheriff's star pinned to his shirt. That was what she told herself, an unsuccessful self-defense mechanism. His black shirt with pearl snap buttons was open at the throat, and his dark-blue jeans fit in a way that made her mouth go dry. His belt had one of those large silver buckles. Not rodeo award huge, like the size of a dinner plate, but big enough that when he walked, it added an intriguing twitch of motion to the roll of his hips, the long-legged stride, all of which drew her gaze to the impressively packaged groin area. It left no doubt there was plenty there to keep a woman occupied. That sexy walk was emphasized by black-and-tan cowboy boots, tucked up under the jeans. The black shirt had tan embroidery on the edges of the pockets. He was wearing an honest-to-God cowboy hat. Tan with a black braid band.

"I'm having a flashback to *Blazing Saddles*," she managed.

"'Scuse me while I whip this out?"

She burst out laughing and, just like that, it was okay. It might just be her mercurial moods, but she thought it had more to do with him. The nervousness she'd carried around with her since the Ichinawa, and all the doubts and insecurities that had crowded into her head tonight, putting her out of sorts and making her send the panicky texts, drained away. He was standing on the walkway below her, his height putting them eye level. She reached for him, curled her arms around his shoulders. He obliged, putting his foot on the step beside her and closing her in his arms, squeezing her and lifting her off her feet in a warm embrace, a hug that was sexy and reassuring at once. She pressed her cheek to his, tucking her head under the brim of the hat. When he eased back, one of those hands dropped to cover her buttock. She lifted a brow.

"Getting awful proprietary about my ass, just assuming you can handle it whenever."

"Don't see you denying it, darlin'." He grinned at her. He put her back on the step, taking both of her hands as he gave her a once-over. "Damn. I was really looking forward to seeing that tie-dye and Birkenstock combination, but I'll make do with this."

"I figured." She gave a self-conscious chuckle as he lifted one set of clasped hands, freeing his other to lay it at her waist and turn her in a circle, showing his desire to see all of her. She really didn't have any "Western" wear, but she figured what she'd put together would do. His appreciative look told her she'd succeeded. Her pale gold Planet Hollywood baby doll tee was printed with a pair of brown angel wings that ran up from her waist over her breasts and framed the vee neckline. She'd put that over a brown short skirt and a pair of ankle boots with gold tips and a decorative buckle. She wore a faux-suede choker with several bands and a seashell pendant to go with antique gold star studs in her double pierced ears. In her left ear, which had another star in the upper curve, the two lobe stars were connected by a delicate gold chain. His fingers went there, tracing it, teasing the chain. She dipped her head toward him, her hand resting on his chest.

"I'd say you're getting used to your Master's touch, Celeste. Wanting more of it, aren't you?"

"I think so." Her heart started thumping erratically when she didn't deny that possessive. *Your Master.* Tonight his eyes reminded her of desert sands, the different golds and browns on a Nevada landscape. She'd never been out to Vegas, but she'd looked at pictures on the Internet.

He scooped her off the stoop, bearing her weight on his hip to set her on her feet on the walkway. Tucking her hand into his elbow, he led her to the truck. "You have a nice place," he commented.

Nice because her rent included outdoor maintenance. Her landlord sent over a company to mow, trim, repair and pressure wash when needed. Things she was never home long enough or in daylight to do. "It's a good space to work and sleep."

"So are you in a twelve-step program for the workaholism?"

"I can stop anytime I want," she deadpanned, and pushed at him when he pinched her. "Says the cop. There's a real nine-to-five job."

"Hey, I was just checking to see if you wanted to join my support group. We can neck in the back of the room during the testimonials." He opened the door and helped her up into the truck.

A cluster of wildflowers were arranged in a vase tucked into the cup holder. She fingered them as he came around, got in the truck. "Are these for one of those cowgirls? Your booty call after you drop me off tonight?"

She expected him to continue in the same teasing vein, but instead he reached over, touched her face, skimming his knuckles along her jaw. "They're for you."

She drew back from that look in his eyes. Looked down at her hands as he closed his door. She started, not expecting it when he leaned over her. He pulled the seatbelt down over her, buckled it securely, his fingers sliding along the strap that ran between her breasts, giving her collarbone a caress before he returned to his side of the truck. She'd forgotten her seatbelt and rather than reminding her, he'd done it himself. Keeping her safe.

Or buckling her in before a bumpy ride.

"I can't stop myself from messing things up, you know," she said to her hands. "I know that sounds pathetic."

"No, it doesn't." As he pulled away from the curb, he reached over, captured her hand while he drove one-handed. "We'll talk about all that later. Right now, simple questions, simple answers. Do you like the flowers?"

"Yes."

"What's your favorite kind?"

"These." Because it was the first time anyone had given her flowers. Her eyes stayed on them because the passing city lights cut through the darkness of the cab, highlighting the colors.

Thanks to its humidity, Baton Rouge had fairly good stretches of decently warm weather in the fall, mixed with the cooler temps, but since it was closing in on November, she wondered how he'd found such a diversity of wildflowers. But she didn't ask. Magic didn't need to be explained.

When they pulled into the parking lot of Darla's Roadhouse, she saw it had an unassuming look, just a brown building covered with weathered wood siding, making it look like a run-down barn. There appeared to be a modest-sized crowd for a Wednesday night. "I expected you'd be taking me to The Texas Club," she said.

"This place is smaller and less rowdy. Here I usually don't have to break up a fight or arrest anyone."

"So you didn't bring your cuffs?"

"When I'm off duty, there's only one reason I pull those out, darlin'." The lights of the neon sign outside the bar washed his golden skin in red, flashing off his piercing eyes. Then he was out of the truck. As she reached for the handle, he made a quelling noise. "Un-unh. Stay there."

She let herself stroke the flowers as he crossed in front of the truck to come and open her door, hand her out. When he walked them toward the entrance, he had his arm around her waist, and the only logical place for her arm was around his. She hooked her thumb in his thick belt, and felt the ripple of muscle under her touch as they walked together, their hips creating a pleasurable friction.

Leaning down, he brushed her ear with his lips. "Tell me what you're wearing under your clothes, Celeste."

"A thong. Pale gold, like my bra. Lots of silk and lace, very little fabric."

He chuckled at that, nipped the chain between the gold studs, tugged on it. "Just keep teasing me, darlin'. Friday I'll have you at my mercy."

Her mouth went too dry to say anything to that, but they were in the lobby then, and he was occupied with paying the cover charge. He was obviously a regular, because the thin, tall fiftyish man in Western-style jeans and plaid shirt taking his money greeted Leland by name and gave her a speculative but friendly look.

When Leland pushed through the double doors to the main area, she saw a long polished bar with various metal and wood signs over it that fit the décor. Cow Crossing, the Bar Q Ranch, Truck Stop Ahead – Free Showers. Mounted horns from longhorn cows, photographs of Western life from the 1800s. An assortment of antique guns. Black and white framed prints of James Arness, John Wayne, Clint Eastwood. All signed.

The playbills on the door had given the schedule for weekend live music performances, but tonight there was a DJ playing popular country tunes. About fifty couples rotated on the dance floor in various set dance routines, giving her butterflies. She could gyrate properly when dancing was called for, but she didn't know any formal dances.

Leland's hand was low on her back, though, fingertips tucked into the waistband of her skirt while he stroked her hip with his thumb, making her body tingle. He leaned up against the bar and lifted two fingers, catching the attention of the bartender, a lush thirty-something with blue eyes that lighted at the sight of him. She had a riot of red and gold hair piled on her head and a generous bosom enhanced by a sparkly T-shirt. "Your usual, sugar?" she asked. Then her gaze tipped over to Celeste. "Well, sakes alive, miracles do happen, don't they? Or is this one related to you, too?"

She gave Celeste a wink as she moved in their direction. "Last time he brought a woman here, it was his sister. She didn't count."

Celeste grinned. "Until I met him, I thought I was the only one who'd given up dating for the twenty-first century."

"I hear you, honey. Ain't enough good ones out there worth leaving home most nights. You might have snagged yourself one of them, though. Hold on a second."

Tossing her towel over her shoulder, the bartender nodded to another man calling out an order. Pulling out a frosted beer mug from the well, she ran it under the beer tap and slid it to him with a deft push that took it eight feet down the polished wood. Then she closed the distance to Leland and Celeste.

"We're not related, Margie," Leland said dryly. "As if her lack of tan didn't give it away."

"I don't profile." The bartender gave him a sassy wink. "What'll you have, handsome?"

"My usual." He looked at Celeste. "What would you like?"

You. For tonight to go well. For me not to fuck everything up. I want to stop worrying that I'm going to fuck it up. "Bud Light."

As the bartender pulled their order, Celeste leaned against the bar, looked around. "You know, speaking of tanning, there aren't a lot of black people here. Like maybe none. The guy in that back corner is debatable, but I think he just hasn't had a bath in a while."

Leland nudged her with his hip. "All you need to be accepted here is an appreciation of real country. The only time they threatened to throw me out was when I sang Toby Keith on karaoke night."

"That bad?"

"No, honey." Margie slid Leland his beer from the tap and placed Celeste's bottle of Bud Light in front of her. "That good. Made a lot of girls rethink the dates they came with that night." She winked. "White boys already feel threatened by black men. You know why? They have bigger peckers and can dance."

Celeste choked on the first swallow of her beer. Leland helpfully snagged it from her hand and rubbed her back as the bartender left them to handle the next order. When Celeste could breathe, she gave Leland a look.

"Does she have firsthand experience on the non-dancing part of that statement?"

"Not from me. But it's God's honest truth. You could put it in your blog."

"It's speculation." She sniffed. "And the source isn't solid. She's hoping for a big tip."

"You keep telling yourself that. It's as much speculation as saying the sky's blue."

She rolled her eyes at him, then gestured with her beer at the whole scene. "I don't get it. Why you like this."

"What, you think all of us like rap? Racist."

She punched him in the side and he caught her fist, laughing as he squeezed it. Then he opened her fingers, caressed her palm. As her eyes fastened on what he was doing and her body vibrated under the attention, his expression grew more serious. Guiding her hand to his waist, he let her have the decision of letting it rest there as he shifted closer. Leaning against the bar so his elbow was braced in front of her, he tipped her chin up, bent and kissed her. The brim of the hat shadowed them on the bar side, closing them into their own world. Her fingers clutched his waist, the belt, and she sighed her need into his mouth as his lips parted, his tongue stroking hers so that she came closer, lifting her mouth to take him deeper. A moan caught in her throat as his hand moved to her jaw and settled on her shoulder, thumb tracing her sternum, a small path up and down that sent tingles straight through her.

He lifted his head, their faces so close. "I'm going to teach you that you have nothing to fear when you're with me, Celeste."

She stared up at him. She wanted that. God, she did. But she had no faith or trust in such a thing, so she drew back, went back to holding her beer with one hand and the side of her chair with the other, keeping her hand to herself. For his part, he turned so his arm was hooked behind her, his hip against hers as they watched the dancers on the floor. He liked surprising her with those mind-numbing kisses, offering them at unexpected moments. He seemed to realize it took her a couple minutes to unscramble her brain after them, because he had a tendency not to talk right away. Very considerate of him. It made her want to punch him again.

"So what is your story?" she asked. "Your background." She slipped into the mode she knew, daring him to object, since the only one nosier than a reporter was a cop. It was second nature to both of them to ask questions.

He gave her a look that said she hadn't gotten away with anything, but he answered her question. "My daddy was a tobacco farmer. Not a really great one, but it was what his father did, and my father didn't have a lot of education. We were dirt-poor growing up." He gestured with his beer. "So a lot of the things they sing about in classic country songs are things I know about. The only reason I'm here instead of on the same track as my dad is that way of life died out and Mama stayed on my ass to make sure I graduated high school. My dad died when I was a high school freshman. Lung cancer. We had to move to Baton Rouge to live with my mother's sister, and that's how I got here. I was good at football, but not scholarship material, so right after I graduated, Mama marched me down to the Marine recruiting office so I could get a college education when I finished my tour. Entered the academy out of college."

"The picture in your bathroom, the tobacco fields? Is that similar to where you grew up?"

"Yeah. Liv, my mom's sister, gave me that as a graduation gift, to remind me of my roots. No chance I'd forget. It was hard, but it was good, too, if that makes sense. My dad wasn't really smart enough to make a better life for himself or his family, but there was never any question that he loved us. We had a picnic every Sunday after church together, and he'd play ball and fish with us, listen while Mama had us tell him what we were learning in school. Other men like him would ignore their families, go out and drink to escape a life they knew they'd never leave, but he saw his blessings."

He took a swallow of his beer, studying the dancers. "You know, when we came to Baton Rouge, I worried that the other kids would laugh at my old, patched hand-me-down clothes, but I still have one of those shirts. Doesn't fit anymore," he acknowledged with a wry smile. "But I wanted to keep something Mama had mended. She had the tiniest stitches, could make it look almost like new. We were always clean. She made us scrub ourselves pink before we headed off to school. We came to Baton Rouge in the summer before I entered tenth grade. That first morning of school when I was getting dressed, she came into my room. She could tell I was worrying. She fixed my collar, smoothed her hands down over my chest and then gave me this smile. She was always tired. Always. But when she looked at us, you could tell that didn't matter. She loved us. All of it was worth it to her."

Celeste glanced up at him. He'd put the bottle down behind her, had his hand clasped on it. His eyes hadn't left the dance floor, but his expression said that wasn't what he was seeing at all.

"When she smoothed my shirt and stepped back, I said, 'Mama, why do you always look at me like I'm dressed in a fancy suit?' She said, 'Because I see your soul, Leland Keller. Your soul is as a spick-and-span and sharp as a man in his church suit. That's what's important in life. Make sure your soul is dressed right, always in its church clothes. That's the only thing that matters to God.'"

He picked up the beer, took another swallow.

"I'm sorry," Celeste said, her throat tight. "When did she pass?"

"Fourteen months ago. A minute ago." He took a breath, turned so he was facing her again. "Your turn. Tell me about Esther Celestial Lewis."

She shook her head. "Let's not, okay? Not tonight." No way could she follow that kind of story up with her own. She was dealing with enough raw feelings around him. She wanted him to kiss her again, help her lose herself in that feeling, but she could already tell the riot of feelings inside her would turn that sour.

"All right," he said. "So we dance instead."

"What? No. I don't do this kind of--"

He was already pulling her toward the floor, lifting her off the stool in one smooth movement. "I wasn't finished with my beer," she protested.

"It'll be there when you come back. Or I'll buy you another."

"Just because you're big enough to push people around, doesn't mean you should."

"I've heard that a lot. Usually from people I'm cuffing." Grinning at her flush, he swung her onto the dance floor. Surprisingly, she picked up on the steps fast, thanks to his guidance. Before she knew it, she was doing what he called the Texas two-step, and then from there he had her doing a couple line dances. Once she was comfortable with those, he snagged his beer. Watching him out of the corner of her eye, she found herself absurdly captivated. He held the beer loosely in one hand, his thumb tucked into his belt as he did the footwork of the line dance beside her, and then in front of her as they turned. Which provided her a fine view of his backside working the denim of his jeans, the shirt pulling across his wide shoulders. As they made the turn and she gave him a similar opportunity, she felt his gaze sliding over her.

When the song came to a finish, he moved up behind her, slid an arm over her shoulder and down between her breasts, fingers hooking in the waistband of her skirt to hold her against him as they swayed together, his pelvis against her ass. The DJ mentioned a few of the drink specials, but the words blurred for her as Leland bent and pressed his mouth against the side of her throat, arm tightening over her body. She rotated her hips discreetly against him, unable to stop herself from taunting, asking for what his mouth was promising her.

"Well, well... Margie tells me our local sergeant has brought a date tonight." The DJ, a balding middle-aged man with a great radio voice, spoke into the mic. "Since this is such a rare occurrence, seems only neighborly that we should help him out. It's been a while since we let him show off his Barry White magic, but come on up here, Sergeant. Do us some Toby Keith. That way we'll know you'll get lucky tonight."

Leland cursed against Celeste's ear as she giggled. "I'm going to kill that woman," he promised.

Celeste propped herself against the impressive mound of his biceps so she could drop her head back against his shoulder and bat her eyes at him. "C'mon, Sergeant. Don't you want to get lucky tonight?"

"I already got lucky, darlin'. I went into Jai's at just the right time."

The look in his eyes took her breath, then he gave her a squeeze and a wink. With a wave toward the DJ and a dark look toward the smirking bartender, he headed toward the stage. As Celeste backed up to the bar, reclaiming her beer, Leland stepped straight up on the stage, no need to use the short set of steps on the side. The DJ handed him the microphone, leaning over to say something in Leland's ear that had her date laughing and giving the man a friendly clap on the shoulder before he turned his attention to the audience.

"Now y'all remember you applauded for this," Leland drawled. "I don't want to hear no catcalls. I'm trying to impress the lady, after all."

"She can't drink enough alcohol for that to happen, Sarge," a man called from the back.

Leland snorted. "Too true, John. But we'll give it a try. Let's do a fun one." He spoke to the DJ, and the man gave him a thumbs-up, turning on the karaoke machine.

Leland had no stage fright. He started with "How Do You Like Me Now", a fast tune that had them twirling and circling the floor in an energy-raising rhythm that rolled through the bar. As for Celeste, she stood rooted at the bar and tried not to let her jaw drop.

Holy crap. She'd thought Margie was exaggerating, but Leland's baritone, the resonance and depth of it, pulled off a great Toby Keith. On top of that, the man didn't need formal dance steps to move well. He worked his hips, shoulders and hands with the song in a way that claimed her attention fully. She slid a hip onto one of the stools, one hand closed over the back of it as if she was holding on to him. His voice and the music resonated through her, a continuous vibration like a generator.

He kept glancing toward her, and she realized she had a light smile on her face, one that refused to go away. It became as much a part of her as the clothes she'd worn for him, as the breath that shortened as he shouted "how do you like me now" with the crowd, singing the chorus along with him.

When he finished, cheers, applause and affectionate catcalls showered him from the audience. He answered the catcalls good-naturedly. Then he turned and consulted the DJ once more. At his nod, Leland glanced back at his audience.

"Since you liked that one, I'm going to make you suffer through one more. This one's for my girl there at the bar. And no, I don't mean you, Margie. Troublemaker. No tip for you, woman."

Another wave of comments came, including Margie's exaggerated sniff and rude gesture that sent the small crowd laughing again. When they settled, Leland gave the DJ the go ahead.

Celeste knew the ballad. "You Shouldn't Kiss Me Like This" put every couple on the floor, many of them rotating in a country waltz, holding one another close in the dim light. This time Leland's eyes were entirely on her. As he told her if she meant that kiss the way she shouldn't, then baby, kiss me again, she was rising, moving toward him. She wasn't much for being center stage in any aspect of her life, let alone literally, but as she held his gaze, she was only distantly aware that he was standing on a stage. The important thing was she wanted to be with him. When she got there, he reached a hand down and she put hers in it. As he lifted her up to join him, she closed her eyes. What was it about the man holding her hand? If the only way he'd ever touched her was that, she thought she'd still feel like this about him. Her heart tipped over whenever his fingers closed over hers.

Maybe it was because his grip alone told her what he kept saying in a variety of ways. She was okay with him. She could trust him.

She was up on stage, but she didn't feel that way. It was just the two of them. He kept singing the song, but he folded her against him, holding her close to his side as she slid her arms up under his, laid her cheek on his chest, closing her eyes again as he swayed with her. His heart beat under her cheek, his body vibrating as he sang, as the music came through the speakers. She internalized every word and, when he nudged her face up at the end of the song to put his mouth on hers, she melted into him, holding on, unaware of the crowd applauding and whistling once again.

§

After the performance, he found them a table in a back corner and ordered another couple of drinks. For a while they listened to the music, made casual conversation, and traded comments about the dancers. He kept his arm around her, their chairs pulled close together. She expected that cozy position was what kept anyone from wandering up to engage him in conversation. In some ways she was glad of that. But having him so close and thinking about her reaction to the way he'd sung to her made her wonder if being joined by some other couples might have been better, to help keep her mind out of bad places. Her hand lay on his thigh, tracing meaningless doodles when he asked her things about herself. Nothing too personal, just about her work, which should be easy for her.

"We're different," she said abruptly.

"How so?"

"You came from a poor background, but it wasn't a shit background. You weren't pulling yourself out of shit. Your mom tells you that wearing poor clothes isn't a reflection of your soul, who you are, because she's right. But when you are shit, you have to make up an image different from who you are, and keep at it until the past starts not to matter. You become that image and leave the crap, who you are, *were*, behind. It's different."

"Hmm." He'd moved his hand to the back of her head, was cradling it in that way that she found distracting, especially when he was caressing her nape, the tension there. "What music do you like, Celeste?"

Automatically, she rattled off some popular groups and

song titles. He listened, asked her about some of them and placed a few. The discussion put her more at ease, thinking that he'd overlooked the sudden outburst, the discomfiting vomit of emotion.

"What's been your proudest moment so far, with the articles you've written?"

Safer ground for her, though she was less comfortable bragging on herself. She changed the focus by explaining her answer. "Every story has more than one side. Sometimes more than two. I think when you give a balanced account of a story, it's easier for people to understand one another and work together. Doing it the other way, all you do is polarize people, create destructive factions, which is the point of most media reporting these days. Conflict generates ratings."

She lifted a shoulder. "When I was at a New Orleans City Council meeting, one of the members pulled me aside and told me that the article I wrote on redistricting had helped her understand the motivations of everyone who had a stake in it. She told me it had helped the council figure out the best solution. Before that, they were drawing lines in the sand, seeing one another as the enemy and hedging their decision against their next election run."

She was on a roll and couldn't seem to stop herself. He seemed so interested in what she was saying, his attention on her in that way that made her self-conscious and unable to stop talking at once. "That really felt good to hear, because that's what I want to do as a reporter. It's one of those jobs that can't be about ego, because doing it right means simply doing the job. Nothing less, nothing more. Give people all the pertinent information, not just pieces to create a slant, and let them decide what to do with it. People can be manipulated really easily, that's true enough. But that doesn't make it right to do it. If you don't manipulate them, if you let them make up their own mind, things might just go the way you hope anyway. And even if it doesn't, that's not my judgment to make."

"Just do the job." Leland nodded. "That's what I tell my guys. Don't get caught up in the end game, the politics or bullshit, people's bad attitudes about the police. Or even the good ones, the overinflated kind."

"All police are either saints or sinners."

"Exactly. We're just guys doing a job 100 percent. Protect and serve. From rookies to retirement."

"Speaking of which, that was a good idea, putting Mike and Billy together."

"Yeah. Billy's already got a good head on his shoulders. Mike will help him keep it there. Mike's not only a good cop, but one with a good attitude about being on the job, despite being a veteran of the bullshit politics and red tape. No need to squash a rookie's enthusiasm or burn him out too fast by sticking him with a grumpy complainer."

Leland touched his beer to hers. "That's damn impressive about the city council, Celeste. Most times, I just want to line up all of those election-fixated, image-obsessed, special interest assholes and use them for target practice. Not that I'd say that out loud. Especially not to a nosy reporter."

She sniffed. "I'll be sure to post it on my blog tonight. Let me see. That was 'election-fixated, image-obsessed...' what was that last thing, Sergeant Keller? Keller with two l's?"

He snorted. "So what kind of music do you really like, darlin'? What's on the playlist you pull up when no one's around and you aren't worried about denting your Celly Lewis persona?"

She looked up at him. He was leaning back against the wall, one booted foot propped against the slat of an empty chair pulled up to their table. His pose was relaxed, but his gaze speared right to her heart. When she started to move, his grip on her neck increased, keeping her in place. "I asked you a question, Celeste. Answer me."

Two of his fingers were stroking the juncture between neck and shoulder. Their presence reminded her of that centering pinch, which closed down her mind in a way that made it easier to speak her true feelings. But he wasn't doing that right now.

"That wasn't fair," she accused. "You caught me off guard. And I don't appreciate being compared to those kind of politicians. I'm not like them."

"No, you're not. You just gave me the opening, and I won't let you bullshit me on anything. So tell me."

"I can't. I don't want to." She set her jaw stubbornly.

"Three songs. First three that come to mind."

"It's dumb." When his fingers began to tighten again, she drew in a breath. "'Simple Love.' Alison Krauss."

"Another."

"'Heaven.' Bryan Adams."

"One more." This time he did shift his grip and compress the muscle in that way that hurt and pleasured at once. She gripped his leg. His other hand covered hers, tangled with her fingers. He kept his eyes locked on hers, his mouth firm.

"'Angel of the Morning.' Juice Newton."

"Good." He eased his touch, both a relief and a disappointment. He guided her legs over his so she was half on his lap, her butt on her chair but the rest of her leaned into him, held by him. He slid his lips over her brow. "You know, Alison Krauss does bluegrass. Not far from country. And Juice Newton has done some country, I'm sure. You may be a closet country fan, struggling to break free."

"The same way you'll embrace rap music tomorrow, Cowboy Troy." She curled her fingers against his shirt, played with one of the pearl snaps and flattened her palm to feel the man beneath the cloth. He'd said she'd have to wait for their next session another couple of days. She didn't want to go home alone, and she wanted to be with him, as a sub. Tonight.

Staring at the wall, she wondered if she had the courage to do what she wanted to do. She gripped his collar, leaned in closer so she didn't have to talk over the noise. "I know you said Friday. But is there anything that would make you reconsider that…sir?"

"Sincerity," he said after a long pause. He'd dipped his head to hear her low words, his eyes trained on her thighs until he shifted his attention to her face. "What will be different if I take you home tonight, Celeste?"

He'd left his hat on the table, and her nervous hand had wandered over to it, was playing with the felt brim. "I'll tell you…if I'm scared. I won't use my safe word unless I want to be done…"

"For two weeks. Second strike."

"For two weeks." She took a breath. "Leland, I…"

"If you're talking to me as your Master right now, address me properly." Tracing a line up her arm to her collarbone, he skimmed his knuckles along her sternum and the rise of her breasts over the vee neckline of the angel wing shirt.

"Okay. Sir." She kept hesitating over calling him Master, though it wasn't because she didn't want to call him that. It was because she really wanted to do so, and that need made it seem like such a huge word, so portentous. "What happened the other night... When things start getting crazy, I go crazy. Something dark takes over in my head. Dark and angry and... I can't explain it. It's me but not me. You say I'm bratting, but when I looked up bratting, there are some bad definitions for that, like I'm deliberately trying to manipulate you. A brat misbehaves to force a Dom to punish her, because that's what gets her off."

"In BDSM, terms can mean a lot of different things," he responded. "It depends on the Dom and sub. You do brat, and yes, you do it to try and control the situation. But you're motivated by fear and uncertainty, not by a calculated desire to manipulate me. There's a big difference."

He said it so calm and easy, like it wasn't really so bad. But she thought of spending two weeks without him, without his touch. Crazy as it sounded, because that really wasn't a long time, she wasn't prepared to risk that. She had to be entirely honest and hope he understood.

"I can't control that reaction. It doesn't seem like I can. I fight it, Leland. I want it, but I fight it. I'm afraid I'll use the safe word because of that, and I won't want to."

"You don't want to do without your Master for a couple weeks?"

She wasn't sure she could do without him for the less than two days between tonight and Friday. The energy around them had heat and weight, his gold eyes so penetrating she couldn't move. "No, sir."

"All right." He stroked her hair, curved one of those longer strands behind her ear. "You fight because you have to fight. Because you need the punishment, a firm hand, to get you past the need to fight. But think about this. You didn't fight it the first night."

"Because it was different." She trailed off uncertainly. Was it? He hadn't used restraints or punishment, but he'd restrained her with his voice, his touch. She'd felt totally under his command.

"Like this?" He gestured to the dance floor. "The vanilla sex, dating stuff. Maybe you fight because you don't want the overt Dom stuff."

She thought of how often she'd dreamed of the night at Club Surreal, how she'd responded to the Dom side of Leland the first time they'd met, the way he'd touched her in Jai's parking lot.

"Is it okay to want both?"

"Hell yeah." He smiled, showing his pleasure with her answer. "It's not 24/7 for most of us, Celeste. Being your Master isn't at odds with me taking you to a country bar to romance you some."

His expression changed, transforming from affable warmth to a hard stare that startled her. "Just like romancing you at a country bar doesn't change the fact I'm going to punish you good for calling yourself shit. When I look at you, I see a woman who wants to improve something already good at the core, not someone creating an image to cover or replace shit. You want me to stripe your ass for something, tearing yourself down like that would top the list."

His tone brimmed with a sensual menace that sent her scrambling for her defenses even as a part of her hoped he would jerk them out of reach before she got there. "I'm not tearing myself down," she managed. "It's just the truth."

She didn't want him messing with that reality. It had taken too long for her to accept it, build everything on it. Including the walls that surrounded her as a result. She set her jaw, plowed forward, hoping they could just skip over all that. "So I guess that's a no, right? About tonight."

"Not up to you to draw the lines in the sand, darlin'. You've asked. Now it's up to me to decide."

She fidgeted at that, resenting but understanding at the same time. He nudged her shoulder, making her look at him. His expression was easy again. He could be so matter-of-fact and straightforward about things. Dancing, singing to her, threatening to beat her ass.

"You have a decision of your own to make," he said. "I want to take you to a wedding."

"What?"

"I have some friends in New Orleans getting married this month. I RSVPed single, but I'm sure they won't mind if I bring a plus one. They aren't likely to run out of food if a few extra folks show up. I figured I'd go to NOLA for the wedding on Saturday, stay overnight, make a trip of it. It'd be nice to have female company."

"I've lived in NOLA. Finding female company isn't difficult, even on a cop's bank account. Long as you use protection and have all your shots up to date."

She yelped as he pinched her thigh, then locked his arm down over her shins when she tried to scramble back in self-defense. The restraint meant she had to keep her legs over his lap and do nothing but squeal as he kept pinching her, tickling her. She struggled, but he had his arm securely around her back, holding her to him.

"Stop, stop. Mercy."

He paused, eyed her. She dropped her head back on his shoulder and gave him an exasperated look. "Didn't we talk about the using-your-size thing?"

"This wedding is a classy affair," he said, ignoring that. "Something a little above the twenty-five dollar hooker range, which hits the ceiling of my illegal sex budget. So have pity on me and go as my classy date. You can wear a slinky dress to make the bride mad, and I'll be all puffed up and territorial around the other guys."

She looked away, toward the dance floor. "Seems a little soon."

"We're going to watch them get married. Not get married ourselves."

"You know what I mean. To go off together like that."

He touched her face, guided it back toward his. "You know it's not too soon, Celeste."

"Yes, it is. It's too fast. It's all too fast." She started to get up, not playing this time, and he wouldn't let her go.

"Easy," he said. "Talk to me, Celeste."

"Can we just... I want to take it a step at a time. All I wanted was to have you take me home tonight. See how that goes. All I've been doing is thinking about that, and wondering if it's real or...hell, I haven't been thinking about it, as in *thinking* about it, because if I was really doing that, I probably would have cancelled our date altogether. I've just been wanting it."

Realizing how that sounded, she shook her head, her cheeks warming. "I don't mean that. I'm not looking for a desperation hookup." But she was desperate, she realized with a hopeless surge of disgust with herself. "I'm done. I need to go."

She thrust herself out of his grip with a sudden burst of temper and energy, and underestimated the propulsion of both. The table wobbled, her empty beer bottle toppling as she snagged the adjacent chair and tangled up her feet so she had to catch herself on the chair back or fall over it. She felt his hands at her waist, steadying her, but she pushed away.

"I'm going to the ladies room. You don't need to take me home. I'll just catch a cab."

She was already walking away swiftly, making a beeline for the bathroom. She wasn't sure if he'd heard her or not. The faces she passed were a blur, and when she got to the restroom, she shut herself into one of the stalls. A mural of wild horses was running along the cinderblock wall across from them. She could see it through the cracks. What the hell was wrong with her?

Same thing that was always wrong with her, and she always tried to bolt. It was so fucking tedious. It was one thing to push someone away when they were getting close. Classic abandonment issues, do it to them before they could do it to you. But Leland seemed to trigger it in her randomly. She couldn't predict anything with him, so she was unable to protect him from her fallout. Dragging him into her train wreck wasn't fair to him.

She'd go back to making do with her solitary Dom/sub fantasies with her vibrator. Or just focus on the functional, 'apply electronic device to responsive part, turn on full power, have quick orgasm and then move on with the evening's blog notes and research.' Yet even when she tried to do that, her imagination would sneak into it. She'd find herself hearing an authoritative male voice, commanding her to spread her legs. She'd see the shadow of that Master holding the vibrator in his hand as he whispered wicked things in her ears. *When you come without permission--*which was going to happen, since he was the one making sure she would fail--*I'll spank you, then fuck you.*

She'd hold the vibrator trapped between her thighs and tuck her hands under her ass. Cupping her buttocks, she'd imagine her arms were tied behind her back, her breasts thrust up shamelessly, so she was unable to hide their aroused state. She'd bite into her pillow so her screams were muffled.

Up until Leland, she'd come harder during those solitary sessions than she'd ever come during vanilla sex with a living, breathing person.

She could say the Dom at Club Surreal had corrupted her, ruined her, but he'd only taken her to the door. She'd chosen to open it, and discovered a part of her identity that made her feel less miserable about the other parts of who she was. But she'd closed the door before she could get more than a taste, hadn't she? She hadn't gone within a foot of a BDSM club since. She hadn't encouraged her blind dates or one-night hookups toward topping her, because none of them had that vibe that made her want to test that boundary.

Okay, well...maybe that wasn't entirely true. During sex, she'd found herself pushing them, taunting them in passive-aggressive ways, and some overtly aggressive ones. One guy had evacuated the hotel bed as soon as the sex was done, put on his clothes and left her with the terse farewell of "Nobody wants to be in bed with a total bitch." Another had suggested, not too subtly, that she was too mean, too aggressive. She challenged a bed partner to the point it was exhausting, not pleasurable.

With a sigh, she came out of the stall, washed her hands, looked at herself in the mirror. Her eyes were guarded, her mouth firm, her body set in tense lines. Time to get a grip and apologize. Go home and resume her life. Forget the throbbing, screaming need that told her he'd been about to agree to another session tonight. He'd have taken her back to his place and made wonderful, amazing things happen to her. But that was that bad definition of a brat, wasn't it? Misbehaving to get exactly what she wanted. Well, she wasn't going to reward her own bad behavior. Leland might be kind enough to do so, but she had enough honor not to put him through that.

"Christ, you are fucked up," she told her reflection. "Get back to what you do best." If she was home within the hour, she could work off her nervous energy with some writing until she found exhaustion and sleep.

But first, time to swallow pride and offer her date a heartfelt apology. He was a great guy. He deserved way better things than putting up with her shit.

Chapter Seven

When she came out, she wasn't surprised to find him leaning against the wall, waiting on her. But he had that rock carved look to his face that suggested she should retreat behind the deceptive safety of the door that said Cowgirls Only.

"Listen," she said, forcing the words free. "I'm sorry. I know I'm not worth all this. I--"

He straightened, took her elbow. "Come with me."

His tone was probably the one he used when he escorted suspects to the car. A tone that said everything would be all right, as long as they didn't do anything that would compel him to totally kick their asses. He guided her out the door, back into the parking lot. She parted her lips, but found she didn't know what to say. His set expression didn't encourage conversation anyway. Opening the passenger door of the truck, he lifted her into the seat, guided the seatbelt over her and buckled it at her hip. She wanted to lay her palms on his broad back, inhale his scent off his neck and shoulder. She knew she shouldn't touch him now, no matter how much she wished to do so. He was probably taking her home as fast as he could be done with this.

An ache rose in her throat. When he circled around and got into the truck, she turned her face toward the window, her hands clutched in a knot in her lap. When his hand covered them, squeezed, she looked toward him.

"Your fingers are cold." He released her to fiddle with the vents, direct them toward her lap before turning it on low. "It starts out cold, but heats up pretty fast." Turning over the ignition, he twisted around to back the truck out of the cramped parking area that was little more than a narrow gravel perimeter around the bar. His hand was on the headrest behind her as he navigated the vehicle. When he removed it to put the truck in drive, he touched her shoulder briefly before pulling out of the parking lot.

He wasn't mad at her at all. She'd acted like a bitch and an idiot, and he was concerned that her fingers were cold. She turned her face away again, stared sightlessly out the window at the passing scenery. The ache had moved down, like a heavy padlock in her chest, making it hard to breathe. Her mind went away a little bit, because thought and awareness were just too difficult. She only surfaced when the truck came to a stop. They were in his driveway.

"Celeste."

She wouldn't look at him. She'd locked her neck in this position, denying herself the sight of him. She ascribed it to her usual perversity. A ruggedly handsome, patient, good man. What woman would want to look at that, right?

Every single one of them, unless the woman in question was certifiably insane.

He left the truck, came around to open her door. When she met his gaze, she realized why she hadn't wanted to look at him. He was blurry around the edges, which was what happened when her eyes were filled with tears, spilling silently down her cheeks. She didn't believe in crying. He cupped her face, his brows drawing down over his kind eyes as he followed the damp tracks with his thumbs. "C'mon darlin'. I know what you need."

He unbuckled her seatbelt, put his arm around her and slid her out of the truck against his side, holding her suspended that way before letting her feet touch. He locked the doors, kept the arm around her as he took her up to the porch, again holding her close. She felt like she could have tucked herself against him, lifted her feet, and he would have carried her forward without a hitch in his step.

He didn't turn on any lights in the house. He held on to her elbow as he closed and locked the door after them, set the security code, and then took her around the circle of furniture in the living room to the short hallway. He brought her to the empty room where he'd wrapped her in rope, that incredible session that had made her long for more connections with him like that.

A table had been set up in the shadows in the far corner. As her eyes adjusted to the dimness, a street light filtering through the window shade showed her the picnic blanket-size mat was still in the center of the floor, but it had been folded over into a rectangle and there was something else arranged at the four corners, a small pile of glinting chains and gleaming silver cuffs.

She jumped as the door closed behind her. Leland's hands had slipped from her, and she turned to see him leaning against the door.

"Stays warmer in here with the door shut. Can you see well enough to go to the corner of the room, darlin'? By the window."

"Y-yes."

"Go there now. To the card table."

She complied. The top third of the windows were visible above the shades, showing a sky lit with a scattering of pinpoint stars, competing with the rose glow of the city. Looking down, she saw a cluster of candles and a long-necked lighter in front of her.

"When you light the candles, your session will start. When you light them, you're telling me that I'm your Master, in charge of everything that happens in this room."

"And if I don't light them?"

"That wasn't multiple choice, Celeste. I'll stand here as long as you need to wrap your mind around it, but the plain fact is I am your Master. You lighting the candles tells me only that you know that. That you accept it for tonight."

"I'm afraid of what I'll do. I'll ruin it. I thought I already had."

"No," he said. "As long as you try to be as honest with me as you can, Celeste, you can't ruin anything. I can tell you're trying really hard to be honest. But sometimes you're brutal and honest. Honest with me, brutal with yourself. We're going to handle that."

She looked over her shoulder at him, at his silhouette. He had a thumb hooked in his jeans, his other leg straightened to brace himself as he leaned against the door. "I'm in charge of everything that happens in this room," he repeated. "Including your behavior and how to handle it. Light the candles, darlin'."

She looked back down at the candles. Somehow she had the lighter in her hand, but she held it for a couple seconds, listening to her breath, loud in her head, feeling light-headed as she contemplated what she might be about to do. No, what she was *going* to do, because he'd ordered it. She wouldn't refuse him. Not a Master's command.

She flicked on the lighter, bent and lit the candles, one by one. There were thirteen of them, different sizes and colors, all sitting on a big tray. When they were lit, her gaze was drawn to what else lay on the table, lined up in a neat arrangement.

A thin, flexible rod whose length shone in the reflection of the flickering light. A flogger with black rosebuds at the tips. A paddle with a cushioned, satiny-looking business side in a rich purple. Another whip that looked like a coiled piece of cloth attached to a handle. Six condoms. A gag with a short, thick phallic mouthpiece attached to a large rectangle that would cover the mouth completely. A collar with a two-inch wide strap and a ring attached to it. The collar was lined inside with a cushion of purple velvet. Her fingers were on it, caressing the plush, before she realized what she was doing. She drew back.

"Celeste, turn around and face me."

She did, wondering if he could hear her heart thudding in her chest. In this dim light his eyes were dark, burning coal. "Take off all of your clothes. Fold them neatly on the end of the table. Then bring me the collar and the gag."

The candles' scent was a mix of cinnamon and vanilla, with a trace of something muskier, like a man's desire. She was in an erotic dream, one from which she didn't want to wake. Her tears were still drying on her cheeks, her throat still ached and her stomach hurt a little, but it was feeling better. He'd touched her face in the truck, wiped away her tears, and what she saw in his expression told her he might know things about herself she didn't know. When to soothe and when to demand, like now.

"That's a pretty outfit," he said casually. "If it's not off in the next two minutes, I'll be the one taking it off. You'll wear one of my shirts and no panties home because I'll cut it all up for cleaning rags."

The hard gleam from those dark eyes told her he meant it. She bent and unzipped the boots, holding on to the table to pull them off her feet, remove the thin ankle stockings beneath. Then she unzipped the brown skirt, wiggled out of it. Pulled the angel wing shirt over her head. Reached behind her with fumbling fingers to unhook the gold lace bra. With a brief hesitation, she shimmied out of the matching panties. The warming air of the room touched her skin.

"Jewelry, too."

The shell choker and five earrings followed. He'd stayed at the door, silent and watching. She put her clothes on the end of the table. He didn't need to remind her of the rest of his command. It was what had made her fumble through the removal of her clothes. She wasn't sure how neatly she'd managed to fold them, but they were in a reasonably symmetrical pile. She closed her hand over the stiff strap of the collar and the rectangular part of the ball gag. Her fingers split onto either side of the thick rubber phallus that he would put in her mouth, taking away her ability to speak.

The wood floor was worn smooth under her bare feet. It was less than fifteen feet to cross, but it felt much longer, though he straightened and closed the distance between them, so she came to a stop on the cushioned mat.

"On your knees, darlin'."

A shiver went through her knees, her lower abdomen, and she swayed. He put his hand on her shoulder, her elbow, the pressure taking her safely to the floor. Once there, she stared at the shiny buckle of his belt, the way the strap defined his waist, the powerful upper torso above it, the straight lines of his hips below, the impressive shape of his genitals under straining denim, emphasized by the pressure of his thighs on either side of them.

"First this." He stroked her lips then parted them, guiding the phallus into her mouth. Fitting the rectangle over it, he buckled the strap behind her head. She let out a needy sound as he cinched it so it molded over her lips, the straight edges pressing against her cheek and jaw on either side. Unlike a regular ball gag, it rendered her incapable of any kind of speech. Her gaze lifted to him, a pleading look in her eyes she didn't know how to explain. He cupped her chin, ran his fingers along her windpipe, shortening her breath further.

"My beautiful sub. There she is. Wanting everything her Master will demand of her. Keep your chin up."

The collar was next, and her eyes closed at the sensation of it being buckled and secured, snug against her throat without hampering her breathing. He caught his fingers in the ring attached to it, tugged so her eyes opened.

That tender expression was there as he stroked her cheekbones, around her eyes. He nodded toward the table set up with the candles and the toys. "Your Master was going to break his own rules tonight. I was going to take you home, no matter what I said about waiting. But because I've let you see that, I also need to show you that was my decision. Your Master is in control. Not you. You earned a punishment tonight. So we start with that."

Holding his fingers in the D-ring, he moved around her. She experienced a peculiar leap in her lower belly as his hold made her turn around on her knees, and she had to make a couple awkward steps on them to follow him, relying on the pull on the collar to steady her and help her know where he wanted her to go. Bringing her down on all fours on the mat, he squatted in front of her. As he lifted a length of silver chain from the floor, she saw the other end was attached to what looked like a sturdy cabinet pull, screwed into the floor a few inches out in front of the mat. He attached the chain to the ring in her collar, holding her there.

Her gaze slid to two other pulls at the corners, the mat tucked up under them. Two more were positioned parallel to the mat at the midpoint on either long side of the rectangle. If she could turn around, she expected she'd find a pair at the back corners. While they looked like guides to keep the mat in place, they had another purpose, since each had chains and cuffs waiting at them.

He wrapped the two front cuffs around her wrists and clipped them to the corner pulls. Rising off his heels, he circled behind her, did the same to her ankles. The cuffs at the midway part of the two sides of the mat were wrapped around her thighs. He made adjustments to those chains so her knees had to stay spread shoulder width.

After he had her restrained, he stood up and walked around her, trailing his fingers over her back, her hip.

Her stomach was doing flip-flops, her hands tight in the bonds. When he circled behind her, the tautness of the chain between the collar and floor kept her from looking at him. But when he came back to the front, she could lift her head enough to stare up at him. He was pure virility standing over her like this, his aroused cock impossible to miss under the jeans, his steady but lust-inflamed look leaving no doubt what he planned to do to her.

Whatever he wanted.

He'd silenced her tongue, kept her from moving. That dark part of her that wanted to fight twitched against the chains, and she despaired as she felt the ugliness of it stirring, but he'd taken away her ability to safe word. She had to rely on him to completely care for her. To know what she needed. To protect her.

Insane, right? But she was shaking with desire, fear and need, and couldn't think beyond what he would do to her next.

He picked up the short whip that looked like a rolled piece of cloth. "This is called a dragon tail. I don't usually start with it, but I want you to have a taste of it up front. Your punishment will conclude with this, and I want you dreading and anticipating it."

He threaded it through his fingers, moved to her side. In the corner of her eye, she saw him take hold of the tip end of the rolled cloth in one hand, his other grip sure on the handle. The position reminded her of a tennis backhand, a sport she'd played briefly in school with borrowed rackets and old balls devoid of bounce.

He released the tip in a short, snapping movement.

Holy Christ. She yelped at the sting against her side, as bad as being popped by a wet towel. She tried to jerk back, but he followed that blow with another one on her buttock. She cursed him against the gag, but it came out a petulant mewl.

"Maybe one more to emphasize the point."

She shook her head violently, but he'd already moved to the other side, hit her on the rib cage. "And maybe just one more, because I'm all about balance."

She jerked against her bonds, screeching as he popped her other buttock harder. He laid his hand over the burn, rubbed it briskly. When he dropped to one knee to kiss it, she tried to jerk away, glare over her shoulder.

"There's my brat. Let's play with that some." He shifted and she caught a gasp in her throat as he seized the chain on her collar, jerking her head down so that the only thing between her nose and the floor was his fist, closed around the chain, right against the D-ring of the collar.

As he held her that way, he pressed a kiss to her spine, worked his way along that valley toward her raised hips. She dipped her head, tried to scratch his hand with the semi-stiff corner of the gag. If she hadn't been wearing it, she would have bitten his hand, but since his large fist looked like all hard bone and knuckles, and was the size of a grapefruit, she was sure it would have been as ineffectual as a newborn kitten exercising her tiny teeth.

He *tsk*ed, hooked the neck chain to the steel handle with another clip so she was forced to stay in that position, her ass high in the air, face close to the floor. Getting to his feet, he left her there, returning to the table. She was relieved to see him put down the dragon tail and pick up the paddle. Despite her anxiety over her vulnerable position, she could handle that, actually yearned for impact play.

He began to use that on her ass, firm strokes that made her buttocks wobble, and followed it up with kneading fingers that stayed frustratingly far away from her slick pussy. She lifted up to him, trying to tell him what she wanted.

"That a girl." He cupped her between her legs, his fingers like a hook under her body, curved over her pubic mound, his palm against her labia. His grip there kept her in position as he started to alternate blows around his hold, swatting her bottom with more and more strength. Too much... It started to burn, burn fiercely. Her fingers clenched and she cried out against the gag, tried to lower her hips, tuck them down. He just held her up higher.

When she was sure her ass was on fire and bruised as hell, he put the paddle aside, parted her buttocks and slid his tongue around her rim, his fingers now pushing inside her cunt. *Oh God...* The change in sensation was mind-boggling. As his thumb stroked over her clit, then pushed under it, finding a million nerve endings, she struggled anew, pleading, the sensation overpowering, overwhelming. She was screaming, yet with that gag, it was just a muffled, desperate squealing sound, no louder than a squeaky door.

When she thought she might die from the agonizing pleasure, he eased that pressure and returned to a light brush of her clit and the sensitive flesh around it. He played at her rim with his mouth, the tip of his tongue teasing the crinkles around the opening, then slowly pushing in.

God, it felt so good. A shudder racked her, a climax rising, but he closed his fingers over her swollen clit and twisted it, roughly enough it kept her grounded, though her body pulsed like an alarm.

He rose again, went to the table. With his back to her, he opened the snaps of his shirt, shrugged out of it, revealing the white tank beneath it. He pulled that over his head, the rippling movement of a powerful male animal, and her gaze slid over golden skin, dropping to his ass. The denim snugged over it briefly when he unbuckled the belt, stripped it.

He picked up one of the condoms and turned toward her. Showing he definitely had a cruel streak, her Master moved back behind her so she was denied the sight of him unzipping his jeans, tearing open the foil and rolling the condom over his turgid shaft. She heard a squirting sound, like maybe there'd been extra lubricant in the packet and he was applying it. A moment later, he put the head of his cock where his mouth had been.

She hadn't been entirely prepared for that idea, hadn't made the connection that was where he was going with this, but his hands were on her back, stroking then gripping her hips, holding her fast as he began to ease his substantial cock into her.

"Such a pretty little thing you are. So delicate."

She'd had something pretty enormous in her ass once upon a time, since the Dom at Club Surreal had been over-endowed, but that had been a long time ago and Leland was no lightweight either.

"Easy, darlin'. Just push out. You can take me. This is the way it's going to be tonight. I'm fucking your ass, cunt and mouth a couple times each, just to make sure you get the point. You're mine. You can act up all you want. I'll beat your pretty little ass, fuck you into submission as often as I need to do it. And I'll enjoy every minute of it." He dropped over her then, his forearms braced on either side of her shoulders as he slid all the way home, introducing a burning sensation that had enough pleasure wrapped around the pain she was shuddering, whimpering.

"If you cry, Celeste, I want it to be the right kind of tears. Understand?"

She nodded, her forehead all the way to the floor as he withdrew, pushed back in. He wasn't hard or cruel about it, just relentless and irresistible. Her thighs quivered against the restraints holding her open as he took his good, sweet time fucking her ass. He stayed away from any clitoral massage, so though she was insanely aroused from him shoving into her backside, and then even more from the way he straightened and gripped her hips so he could pound into her more smoothly, she couldn't come.

"Your climax is up to me, Celeste. But you can beg through that gag all you want. Just makes my dick harder. I can fuck you until you're sore as hell. But I'll take care of my baby, make it all better."

He pushed in deep, withdrew slow, then speeded up again. He caught the hair on her crown, jerked her head up so she felt the pull of the collar against the back of her neck as he worked his hips into her, rotated, drilled in deep. She cried out against the gag as he came for the first time, grunting, hips working against her thoroughly, the open zipper of the jeans biting against her sensitive ass.

When he was done, he slowly withdrew, leaving another line of kisses down her spine, all the way to the dimples over her ass. The condom was stripped and tossed in a small waste can under the table, his jeans fastened and zipped. Then he picked up the rose-tipped flogger.

He straddled her, standing over her to bring the length of the flogger beneath her and catch it with his other hand, tightening the straps in one twisted line over the top of her breasts. As he constricted the hold, her breasts tilted up from the pressure, the nerves tingling to emphasize how aching the peaks were, begging for the touch of his mouth, his hands. When he released the whip, he draped it over her neck and slid his hands under her. As he cupped her curves and began to fondle, her hips jerked in a coital rhythm, begging for release, to be fucked, arousal trickling down her thighs. With her legs spread, she was sure she had a pool growing on the floor between them.

Not until she was making utterances of hungry need did he pick up the whip and move back. She looked down beneath her, and saw she was right. The mat had a small puddle beneath her legs, and she could see the glistening tracks along her thighs. He put his hand on her hips.

"You'll like this."

The flogger's rose tips were like drumming rain against her back, buttocks and thighs, curving up under her to tease her breasts, lick at the insides of her thighs. He landed a few blows against her pussy, the stroke of the stiff braids compelling her to undulate her hips like a lap dancer.

"That's it, darlin'. Show me your cunt. Show me you want to be fucked by your Master."

It was all she wanted, everything she'd ever wanted. Time had stopped outside this room. It was about him, whatever he was doing to her. Her helplessness and panic that she couldn't stop any of it was balanced with the reassurance that she couldn't stop any of it.

"Time to get back to your punishment." He picked up that flexible rod that shone in the candlelight. He slid it under her chin first, teasing her collarbone with light flicks. Then he dropped to one knee before her, and took off the second clip of the chain so she was back to having about a foot of chain between her and the handle in the floor. He curled his fist around the chain right against her collar once again, though, so she had to stay in place. Since that let her stare at his chest, the gleaming light mat of hair on it that arrowed toward his groin, that didn't seem bad. Plus his position, resting on his heels with his thighs spread, let her see the curve of his testicles under denim. Then he started using the rod.

He flicked it beneath her, short movements that shouldn't have been anything, but it licked stripes along her breasts, outside, inside, over the nipples. As it started to sting like little paper cuts, he increased his hold, which drew her eyes up to his face. His implacable expression, the heat of lust in his gaze, only grew as she protested against the gag, tried to yank back and was held in place. His unwillingness to stop made her so aroused she couldn't separate physical pain from sexual frustration. She bit down on the phallic gag, lips and tongue working against it, her hips jerking in the air.

He was a gentle bear, but he could also be this, do this to her.

She tried to resist it. She glared at him, cursed him through the gag, fought. He just kept doing what he was doing. He didn't stop until she figured it out and stopped protesting. She held as still as she could, shaking, aroused, absorbing the blows. Her gaze clung to his face, the set of his mouth, the intent focus of his eyes, the steady strength that held her in place for him to do as he wished with her.

At last he set the rod aside. Bending, he kissed her brow, her wet eyes. He moved to her ear, bit and nuzzled. He hadn't released the chain, his knuckles against the collar so she felt them through the vinyl against her throat. Her ass and breasts throbbed with pain. They wanted his soothing touch, those big hands stroking her. She willed him to do that, staring at him with a pleading look she'd never admit to having on her face. But he'd taken away rational thought. Even her desires were under his command, because she knew that she wouldn't have wanted the soothing touch alone. She'd wanted the punishment as part of it. Some things had to go together.

When he finally drew back, she saw he was more than ready to take her again. His cock was an enormous impression against his jeans, no mistaking what it was. All she could think was *Yes, God yes.*

As he ran his hands slowly over her breasts and nipples, massaged, she moaned, closed her eyes.

"Yeah, your Master was cruel to you. He'll also be the one to make it better. It all begins and ends with me, Celeste."

He kept stroking and massaging her, taking the hurt away while leaving the arousal intact, her nipples stabbing into his palms. He teased them with his knuckles, sometimes keeping a hair's width cushion of air between her flesh and his touch so that she was straining for him. Yet when he stopped doing that and simply cradled both curves, his touch did more than soothe the physical abrasions. It reconnected the two of them, made her feel he was with her every step of the way, every strike of the rod or paddle a give and take of energy that bound them more surely together. She couldn't parse that out or define it. It simply was.

She watched with glazed eyes as he rose and went back to the table. She couldn't stop the pitiful noise as he picked up the dragon tail again. No, she just couldn't. No.

He came back to her, dropped to his heels, hooking a finger in her collar to lift her chin. "Ssshh," he murmured as she shook her head. "Okay. I know you don't like this, but I said your punishment would conclude with this. You know you need it. I'm not going to let you get away with tearing yourself down, Celeste. So here's the deal. Take it like the brave girl I know you are. Lift up your ass and keep it lifted, as much as you can. Then, when I'm done, I'm going to fuck you, Celeste, and I'm going to let you come. After that, I'll take care of you like the sweet baby you are. Be good for your Master, and he will be very, very good to you."

There'd be no "byline" spoken this time. He'd understood what she'd been asking at Darla's, her need for him to prevent her from crying wolf. But it had the side benefit of teaching her she could rely on him to understand if she'd truly reached an unbearable point. The way he studied her reactions so closely, the stroke of his fingers on her throat, told her he was waiting her out, evaluating.

She was trusting him to understand her better than she did.

She'd never let anyone have that kind of control over her, but somehow he'd put her in a position where she'd made the choice to have no choice. That dark part of her writhed and twisted in her gut, a rabid animal consuming itself. She should say fuck you, should fight him, damn it. But she didn't want to. All she wanted was this.

A part of her just...let go. Let go of all of it. She was afraid of that sharp tip, afraid of that stinger, but she thought of him inside her, taking her so deep, driving that dark part away.

Meeting his eyes, aware that her own were filled with tears for some inexplicable reason, she slowly, slowly made herself lift her hips.

"Higher."

His voice was quiet.

She complied, shook harder. Closed her eyes, squeezed them tight as she heard him shift, move behind her. Then she jumped as his mouth touched her ass. His hands smoothed over the marks the paddle had left, soothing her skin the way he'd soothed her breasts. In the meantime, his lips worked around the curve of her buttock and then over, closing over her pussy, which was so wet she heard the sucking sound between his mouth working over her and her labia. "That's my sub. Good girl. Brave girl," he said.

She was so close to climax when he drew back, she was seeing black spots in her vision. Then he straightened and she knew what was coming. She imagined her spine as a rigid tree branch to keep her ass up. The dragon tail stung her ass and she jerked, cried out at the pain. With the very next strike, her spine became a willow branch bobbing in the wind, because the subsequent snaps kept her dancing, ass wiggling this way and that as he hit low, high, middle, on the sides, on her thighs. She tried hard to keep her ass up the way he said--don't tuck--but it was so damn difficult.

Every sense should have been razor sharp, cursing him and fighting a pain that was in no way pleasant. Instead she couldn't hold on to a single protest or coherent thought. The pain tore her grip from reality and spun her into a place all about the next blow, her need for him to make it better when it was all over. He had to create this pain to open and heal the deeper wounds. *You know you need it.* Her remarkable faith in that astounding statement, her intuitive sense of what he'd meant, became more important than anything, which told her she'd lost her mind, a temporary insanity where she handed it all to him.

Enough, please. For the love of God. She was begging for mercy against the gag, chewing on that hard rubber, sucking on it, caught in a crazy haze of lust and agony. When the stinging stopped, she had her head to the floor, gasping against the gag. She groaned at the bliss and relief as his mouth came back to her buttocks and thighs, along with the caress of his hands. She was so sensitive, she flinched at his initial touch, but then she pushed into it as much as her bonds allowed. His touch slid over her rib cage, cupping her breasts as he knelt over her.

He released the chains attached to the cuffs on wrists, thighs and ankles, steadied her while he unhooked the chain attached to the collar. He didn't remove the collar or the gag, a reminder that she still belonged to him right now. He was her Master. He gathered her up and lifted her as if she weighed nothing, cradling her in his arms with a tenderness that made her heart hurt. Everything hurt, inside and out.

He carried her out of that room and into his bedroom, laid her on the bed with its earth-tone pillows. She had a brief impression of a dresser, a closet, a couple pictures. He was prepared here as well, for as she watched him in the semi-darkness, he pulled straps from under the mattress and secured the cuffs on her wrists and ankles to them, keeping her spread on the bed. Not uncomfortably straining, though she could only raise her arms a few inches off the mattress and slightly bend her knees but not close them. The mattress was bliss against her sore ass, but not as much as his hands there had been.

He moved to the end of the bed where she could see him and stripped off his jeans and boxers. He was standing naked before her spread, vulnerable body. The man was solid, the golden skin a terrain of layered, rolling and knotted muscle in all the right places. Hard and seasoned, like firewood. His cock jutted thick and stiff out from a trimmed pelt of pubic hair that let her see the heavy weight of his testicles hanging below. Under her gaze, he rolled on another condom and then straightened, his curled fist stroking himself as he simply stood there.

Her stomach quaked as his eyes slid over her with leisurely pleasure. Possession. All his, to do with as he desired. He owned her, every reaction. He'd said he was in charge of everything. She hadn't entirely understood that at the beginning, but she did now in a way that normally would terrify her and raise every defensive shield she had. But her mind was as securely under his command as the rest of her.

Her cunt was slick again, inner muscles contracting as

she remembered his promise. She'd been good for her Master. Hadn't she?

"As much as I love fucking a sub, this is always my favorite moment," he said. "When she realizes she's mine, her eyes all pleading, mouth soft, her pussy wet. And the longer I stand here, looking like I want to take everything she's got and then push her twice the distance beyond that, the more she trembles. Afraid and wanting at the same time. There's some of that inside a Master as well." His voice was low, conversational, but those golden eyes were alive with fire that was licking over every inch of skin he was studying. "Afraid I'll want too much, demand too much. It's like I want to work you so hard I'll destroy you, even as I want to protect you from the whole damn world."

She was shaking, more violently with every word. The noises she was making were similar to when he'd been using the dragon tail. *No more. Have mercy.* She was cracking inside, and the poisons deep inside would take her over, overwhelm her. She'd have no defenses left with him. Which she was pretty sure was his intent.

He stretched out over her, settling his body between her spread legs, his bare flesh against hers. Bracing his elbows by her shoulders, he framed her face in his large hands. He was keeping his weight mostly lifted off of her, his cock brushing her pelvis, teasing her clit with the length pressed between them. He was a big man, so his hips forced her thighs out wider, emphasized that she was spread and held down for him. She stared up at him, spoke against the gag. He couldn't understand the words, but he understood the emotions.

"Ssshh. No, we're leaving the gag on. I'm not giving you anything to protect yourself, especially that sharp tongue. I'm the one protecting you now."

He stroked her cheek, dipped his head to press warm kisses on everything around the gag. Forehead, eyes, cheekbones. "It's all right, Celeste. I've got you."

Her right hand flexed, flexed again. Clenched. Suddenly she needed something, one simple thing that held all the importance of life itself to her. The need for it swept through her like a convulsion. She stared at his hand, then turned her head back toward her own. She hit the mattress with her knuckles like a flopping fish, looked at him again. He followed the motion and shifted his gaze back to her. "Ask me, darlin'. You don't demand anything from your Master."

She swallowed. In another frame of mind, she would have spit at him like a cat, but that mental state was way beyond her grasp. She verbalized *please* in a questing note against the gag, gazing up at him. Then, thinking it through, hard, she swept her gaze down, a gesture of submission, and let her hand relax on the mattress, palm up, fingers curved.

"Nicely done." His approval sent a shot of pleasure through her that should have been ridiculous, but it wasn't. Her eyes closed in blissful relief as he reached out and clasped her hand, his warm fingers closing over hers. It was okay. He was holding her hand. It was uncanny, what it did to her. Miraculous.

"Look at me."

Lifting her lashes, she was absorbed by those intent golden-brown irises as he adjusted his hips and fitted his cock to her opening. She made another inarticulate sound and his gaze flickered, mouth going taut as he began to push inside her. She lifted her hips the amount her bonds allowed, and his knowledge of a woman's body did the rest. She arched her throat and back as he slid home. He stretched her, pressed in deep, and it felt so damn good her legs strained against her bonds, wanting to take more.

"Easy, darlin'. Just let me do it all, carry you where we both need to go."

He ground himself against her, a slow rotation that increased the friction against her clit. Sliding one hand beneath her, he cupped her ass and tilted her up against him further. He released her hand to keep the bulk of his weight off her, but he braced it next to her fingertips, so she could still touch him. He was caring for her as he destroyed her.

"Christ you are a tight fit. Been a while, hasn't it, darlin'? Your vibrator's one of those clit stimulators, I'll bet. Nothing that goes inside."

She was tight, but he was also good-sized. The combination was excruciatingly pleasurable. Then his grip on her ass constricted. "Answer me. Has it been a while?"

Her gaze flicked up to him, the hard mouth, the piercing eyes. She nodded, a quick jerk, and his look of satisfaction, all territorial male, sent a primal surge through her. He pulled partially out, came back in, rotated his hips, ground deep again, pushing up against her clit. He kept doing that, exploring her with cock and rhythm, finding out what made her writhe and gasp, what made her plead for an orgasm.

In the end, all of it did. He was thrusting with intent at that point, and she was crying out against the gag with every stroke. The climax built to a higher and wider point than before. A focused shot of sensation targeting her clit was certainly nice, but this started to rock her whole body, involving every erogenous point, sweeping through muscles, nerves, organs and taking over mind and heart to plunge deeper. Every time he took her this deep, this high, he left no part of her detached, uninvolved or safe from the demand of his body, his cock, and those penetrating eyes.

"Go over for me, Celeste. Tear it all loose for your Master."

Her body shuddered, quaked. A howl of protest came from those subterranean parts of her that were deathly afraid of where he was taking her, but they couldn't hold out against him. The climax grabbed hold, ripped her away from the cliff edge and tossed her into fire, flames dancing over her and through her as she bucked, shrieked her pleasure over and over against the gag. Her tongue slid over and around the phallus, teeth snapping down on it as he took her further, increasing the power of his thrusts. Muscles rippled over his broad shoulders, the veins in his neck pulsing, his eyes fierce and holding hers. His lips stretched back in a snarl as he found his own release, hips rising and falling, slamming against the inside of her thighs. Spread open the way she was, she felt every sensation, could protect herself from none of it, and her screams of pleasure were also screams of deeper, crazier, things. Yearnings and wants as he hammered into her core, breaking down the walls beyond which she'd never let anyone go before.

Help me, Leland. Please...help me.

Chapter Eight

It was a cry from her past, she knew, but it twined with the present. The climax was over, and her breathing was still shallow, fast, fingers curling and uncurling in her bonds. She needed him to let her go. She needed to curl up around that center which was ugly and exposed, shield it with her body.

Instead, he put his mouth against her ear, her neck, nuzzled and kissed his way to the point of her shoulder. He then followed a track across her breastbone to the other shoulder, neck and ear before he lifted his head. As he touched her, she was torn between two states. One that wanted his mouth on her like this, his arms around her. One that was like a wild animal, feeling cornered. He saw both things.

"I'm going to remove the gag, and then I'll remove the cuffs. You're not leaving this bed, Celeste. Not until I'm good and ready to let you go. And you're staying here tonight." He curled his fingers in the ring at the front of the collar and gave it a sharp little jerk, making her chin snap up and wary eyes meet his. "You understand?"

She nodded.

"*Yes, sir* would be the proper response."

She said it against the gag. It could be any two syllables, since it came out as a hum of sound, but it was clear she'd responded as required. It did unexpected things to her, settling down that weird panic, the need to flee. Unfortunately not enough.

He removed and disposed of the condom, then he unbuckled the gag, slid it from her mouth. She sucked on the phallus as he pulled it free, trying to get rid of any unsightly saliva. A smile touched his mouth as he noted her self-consciousness about that. His fingers traced the impression the rectangle had left on her skin, then he turned his attention to the cuffs. All she had to do was give in to the way she was feeling, let him hold her, care for her. That naked, vulnerable soul trembling deep inside her longed for that like nothing else. Why couldn't she give herself over to it, the relief of subspace where the Dom would cuddle the sub and there was nothing but a drifting haze, no worries or thoughts? She'd briefly experienced it, seen it done. But Leland had gone below that layer. She couldn't give herself to that. As soon as he released the fourth cuff, she didn't think about how irrational her reaction was. She wasn't built that way, not when it came to relating to another person. Not this deeply.

She made it barely halfway off the bed before he had his arm around her waist and brought her back against him. She kicked into the air, tried to get away, and found herself put down with a decisiveness that told her she was fighting a male used to subduing suspects. He'd put her on her back though, so she clawed at him. An instant later, her arms were neutralized as he adjusted to a high straddle on her, sitting his fine ass just beneath her breasts, his knees and shins holding her arms at the biceps. Which put his cock up close and personal. She rocked against his hold, but the man was just too heavy and had her pinned too firmly. Her biceps were pressed into the bed, but she had mobility past her elbows. She slapped at his hips, clawed ineffectually at his buttocks and thighs. He just gazed down at her meditatively while he gripped himself over her quivering breasts and began to stroke.

He'd just come, so he wasn't erect yet, but he was an impressive length even in that state. She lifted her head, tried to snap, and couldn't quite get there. "You want me to put the gag back on?" he warned.

She shook her head, though she wasn't talking as if she was still wearing it. She didn't want to talk, and didn't really know why. She preferred this purely physical response. She also couldn't seem to stop looking at his hand, the way he held himself, stroking, gripping, and fondling. She could smell the heavy musk of their combined climaxes. Before she could stop herself, she licked her lips.

"We're only a third of the way there," he remarked. "I've fucked your ass once, your pussy once. Once more of each to go before this night is done. Plus you have to suck me off twice. I expect you could get me hard now, couldn't you, with that dangerous mouth?"

She lifted her gaze to him and curled her lip. A shadow

passed through his gaze, a muscle twitching in his jaw. "Yeah, it's like that right now. You make this real difficult on yourself, darlin'. I've got a ring gag that will take care of those teeth. As embarrassed as you were about a little saliva, you'll be blushing like a girl with her panties around her ankles in front of her daddy when that ring gag's making you drool all over my cock. That what you want?"

She shook her head, and he pursed his full lips. "Even so, I think I'll just take care of getting myself hard right now."

"Let me go." Her voice had a horror movie rasp, and she cleared her throat. "I need to get free. I need to…please, Leland. It hurts. Inside. I hurt inside."

"I've got something to help with that." He leaned over her, pulled the strap at the corner back across the mattress. He knotted it in the ring of her collar and then eased off her, but only to flip her to her stomach, hold her there with a knee in her back as he retrieved a coil of rope from the nightstand drawer. A blink later, he'd turned her onto her hip and wrapped her wrists in the rope, brought her legs up and tied the slack around her thighs, cinching them snug against her wrists so she was curled on her side in a fetal position. She pulled against the bindings, found them fast.

She wasn't free, but the position curled her around that empty, throbbing pain, eased it some.

"Better?" he asked quietly.

She wasn't going to ask how he understood or knew what she'd meant. It didn't seem to matter how he did that; just that he did. She nodded and he rose, moving away from her and into the hallway. She watched the fine flex of his ass, the roll of muscle across the wide back and shoulders before he turned the corner and disappeared. She felt an unreasonable panic about his absence, but he wasn't far. He was in the bathroom, and her Master wanted to be sure she knew it. She heard running water and his voice. He was humming that Toby Keith ballad with a few random notes thrown in, maybe playing with the rhythm as his mind considered various possibilities concerning her. The thought made her swallow and tremble some more.

He returned with two washcloths. When he slid onto

the bed behind her, he laid one against her pussy. The cloth was blissfully hot. Her fingers curled against her thighs as he rubbed her tenderly, splitting her labia to clean the damp crevices. He did the same around her rim, pressing that soothing touch against her there.

The other cloth was for her face. He stretched out on his hip behind her, leaning over her to wipe the area the gag had covered; under her nose, around her eyes, wherever stress and emotion had coaxed forth a visceral human response of tears, mucus, saliva. "This shouldn't embarrass you," he said. "If your Master intends you to lose control of everything, including bodily functions, that's his will."

It was like she was a baby again in his hands, trusting him with all of it. As he took the cloth away, she shut her eyes, hunching into a deeper ball. He passed his hand over her nape, along her spine. "I can't go to the wedding with you," she said.

"Why not?" His tone was reasonable, as if they'd been having this normal conversation all along, instead of a mind-shattering BDSM session.

"I have a wedding to attend that weekend myself."

"Well, if they're different times, we could go to both. Unless you don't want me to go with you to yours. Baton Rouge and New Orleans aren't all that far from each other."

"The one I'm attending is in New Orleans, too."

"All the better. We could drive up together." He cupped her face, made her look up at him, his body against the back of hers. "Don't lie to me, girl."

"I'm not." She tried to jerk her face away and had no luck in that at all. "I really do have a wedding that weekend. It's mid-afternoon. It's outside the city, at this big plantation house."

His brow lifted. "Ben O'Callahan and Marcie Moira's wedding?"

She blinked at him, and his lips curved. "Sounds like fate to me, darlin'."

Leland settled in behind her, his hand resting on her hip, fingers stroking over her buttock as he nuzzled the back of her neck. Her feet pressed against his shins when he brought his legs up enough to cradle her in the curve of his body. Him carrying on a conversation while she was tied helplessly was disconcerting. But he'd somehow known tying her in this curl would be easier, suiting both their purposes.

He rolled away from her to open a drawer, then came back to her. He shifted behind her, but the strap tied to her collar didn't give her enough slack to lift her head and look over her shoulder. When he parted her buttocks and the tip of an applicator pushed into her rectum, the question of what he was doing was answered. She twitched at the lube being squirted inside her, and his fingers replaced the applicator, spreading oil over her rim and then dipping inside with casual familiarity.

"What are you doing?"

"Getting you slick for my cock. Once I'm hard, which shouldn't be too long from now, I'm fucking your ass again. Maybe once I've fucked you enough, you'll behave enough to be released."

"It's not because of that. I'm not doing it because--"

"I know why you're doing it, Celeste." He threaded his arm beneath her head so it was pillowed on his biceps, giving her comfort while he worked his fingers in deeper. Remarkably, a tendril of arousal unfurled from that point, teasing and tickling her clit and deeper inside her pussy as well. Her nipples tingled against her bound arms.

"I should have figured out we were going to the same wedding," he continued. "When I was looking at the articles you wrote for the business social columns, I remembered Jon talking about the snarky reporter who gave them the Knights of the Board Room name. You didn't like them much early on, did you?"

"No. But the later articles..."

"Yeah. Something happened to change your mind about them, didn't it?" He stopped, two fingers inside her. He was stretching her, scissoring, so her mind was fragmenting between the stimulation and the faint burning she was sure he was doing on purpose. "Your earlier articles had that sneer most reporters take toward anyone rich. Then, after that point, the tone was gone. But what's interesting to me is how your writing started to change then, too. You had more confidence, a better voice. That was about the time you moved over to the crime section."

"Have you put in for your detective's badge, Sergeant? Or stalker membership card?"

"As if you haven't looked me up on the police blotters to see what busts I've been on, how long I've been with the Baton Rouge PD, and everything else you could find, down to my scores at the academy."

She sniffed then let out a strangled sound as he did something...interesting. "Oh."

"Yeah. Don't give me attitude, darlin'. I'll make you suffer for it."

"Are you there as a friend of the bride or groom?" she asked, her breath short.

"Groom, though I know them both. Well enough to know he's getting far better than he deserves. He wouldn't disagree. You?"

He set his teeth to her shoulder, nipped a bit more sharply than was comfortable and sent electricity running down her spine. His fingers were still working in her ass, a slow thrust and retreat that had her thighs moving restlessly. Thinking was getting more difficult, not that she'd had a lot of brain cells to scrape together after the last orgasm.

"Uh...Marcie and I did MMA class at the same gym when I was in New Orleans. But um, the way we met... Well, Ben's boss, Matt, helped me get the NOLA crime beat job."

He lifted his head. She felt his gaze sliding along her profile. She was usually much better at obscuring the truth without lying. To say she was off her game was a massive understatement. She was hell and gone from the stadium and off in the weeds somewhere. Regardless, she wondered if he'd ever done interrogation, because that stare could peel every layer back to find the truth. He'd already proven that earlier, and she was still feeling way too exposed.

"Celeste. I know they didn't buy your good graces with a job."

"No."

"That night that was too good to be true. Who was the Dom?"

Damn. Bull's-eye. She couldn't stop herself from

stiffening and he added a third finger, thrust firmly. When she whimpered, her pussy creaming anew, he curved his hand over the collar, tangling his fingers in the tether. "I know what they are, darlin'. Every one of Matt's executive team is a Dom. I've played with them on rare occasions. You aren't betraying their trust if it's one of them."

"Ben. It was Ben. Please…"

"I like hearing you beg. It's getting me worked up again. Gotta make sure I'm just as big as last time, because I want you to feel every thrust. Knowing what I know about Ben, I may be the only one with a dick big enough to compete with that freaking circus act he carries around in his pants."

Startled by the dry humor, she strangled on a laugh against his grip. He kissed her temple. "Tell me how it happened."

"No."

"Yeah. Else I'll go get that dragon tail."

"You wouldn't." But she knew he would. He was teasing her, yet there was an edge to his tone that said he was still very much her Master right now. He was coaxing things out of her she inexplicably did want to say to him, though she knew she shouldn't tell him so much, give him so much. Yet her lips parted, and she started to speak. Finding her throat dry, she cleared her throat, but he stopped her before she could start.

"Wait."

He withdrew his hand, the mattress dipping as he left the bed. Again that mouthwatering view of him going out the bedroom door. She heard him go into the kitchen, open the fridge. As he came back with a cold bottle of water, she saw he had no self-consciousness about his nudity, showing no shame at his erection, which was recovering just as he'd promised and threatened. A twinge between her legs told her she was anticipating it, a senseless reaction given her body was already being wrung out to its last drop of energy. But that wouldn't matter to him. Or rather, it would, because that was the point. Unlike his body, which required a certain state to perform, hers was a receptacle for the desires of his, and he would take her until he used her all six times.

The harrowing thing was how he was approaching it.

Receptacle or not, she was sure he'd be making her come just as often. He wasn't allowing her to detach from any of it. Making her climax over and over was part of claiming every ounce of her will and energy. Though she automatically strained against her bonds at the thought, it was knee-jerk resistance. She hadn't used her safe word since he'd removed the gag, had she? Probably because she already knew he'd discarded that as useless, a message he'd sent with the gag. Her well-being was entirely in his hands.

He freed the collar from the strap, and shifted her into a cradled position in his arms so she could comfortably drink, holding the back of her head as she leaned against him. When she'd managed several healthy swallows, her tongue swiping the moisture across her lips, he laid her back down on her hip, reattached the collar. She could tell him he didn't need to do that, but in truth it gave her a more complete sense of security. She couldn't go anywhere without his say-so. He'd left her no easy way to fight.

"Yeah, I think we can do this now." She made a surprised noise as he probed her rim with his fingers to test how lubricated she was. Another tearing sound as he rolled on a new condom, which she knew would also be pre-lubed, and he pressed his cock against her rim. "I'll get even bigger inside you. Press against me and let me in, Celeste."

She bit her lip as the sphincter muscles released. He sank into her, deep and full. Laying his palm on her stomach, he held them close together as he slid his other arm under her head again and captured her breast once more, tweaking the nipple, rolling it in strong fingers. She laid her head back against him.

"Tell me about that night," he prodded.

"You're making that difficult."

"I know. I like hearing you try to focus when I'm getting you all hot and wet again. Talk, or I stop and go get the dragon tail."

"Asshole."

"Yeah. I can be mean as a snake when you need it, darlin'. Did he put that monster dick inside you?"

The segue was unexpected but thrilling as she detected the obvious edge in his voice, punctuated by a deeper thrust of his hips, a thickening of that shaft inside her. "Yes."

"Yes. What?"

She let out a grunt of reaction as he was more forceful about it this time. "Yes, sir."

"Your ass, your pussy, your mouth?"

"Ass...mouth. Not between my legs."

"You cuss as good as any of my men. But you're shy about saying pussy in the bedroom, darlin', aren't you?"

She flushed a little. "So?"

"So, it's sweet. I like that about you." He started a slow rocking rhythm that had her cunt clenching on empty space, jealous of the fullness in her ass. "So how did it happen? Tell me a story."

The man was evil. *Christ.*

While working business social news in New Orleans, she'd developed an intense dislike for the executive management team of Kensington and Associates. She hadn't really analyzed the why of it too much. She'd given them the mocking name "Knights of the Board Room", because she didn't want to believe Matt and the other four men were what they presented on paper. Five outrageously handsome, irritatingly alpha dominant males who were not only extremely successful in business, but who were some of NOLA's top philanthropists. They'd upgraded one of NOLA's battered women's shelters and provided aid and hands-on volunteer help during Katrina. Those were only two bullet points on a long list of charities who'd benefited from their time and money, most of them organizations dedicated to protecting the most vulnerable members of society.

But it didn't stop there. The five men were reputed to be devastating to a woman's senses, such that business rivals never sent women negotiators to meetings where they wanted to keep the upper hand. Though in truth, very few competitors outmatched Matt and his team regardless of gender. At the time, Celeste had ignored that, though. She'd been offended by everything they were and unwilling to turn the mirror on herself to find out why she took their existence so personally. Always on top of their world, successful, in control, with what she'd viewed as patronizing, overly protective behavior toward women.

Because of a tip from an irate business competitor, she'd suspected Matt and his team were into some "freaky S&M shit," as she'd put it to Valerie, her roommate at that time. She'd decided to pursue a freelance scandal piece on the executive team. The lead she'd been given had brought her to Club Surreal, a place the men frequented.

She'd only been able to afford a three-visit guest membership. On her third visit, she'd been nursing her drink at the bar, feeling pissed off. She hadn't witnessed them doing anything beyond viewing the public play, not enough to get her reluctant editor on board to skewer them as sexual deviants. Then she'd been approached by Ben O'Callahan.

He was the lawyer of the team. He'd challenged her to go behind closed doors in one of the private rooms and try a Dom/sub session with him. See what it really was all about. The carrot he'd held out had been the agreement to tape the session with her face masked and his revealed. She could have the tape and do what she desired with it. She'd have on tape a K&A executive beating a woman, restraining her, all the proof she'd need to run a scandalous article that would have all of NOLA buzzing. It would put her squarely at the top of the heap at the paper, because the story would make front-page news. Maybe national.

As she relayed the story to Leland, she hesitated over that part, but she wouldn't let herself shrink from it. "At that time, I was no better than any of those reporters you love to hate. Just looking for the sensational angle, a way to rip someone else apart to make my career. I'm not proud of who I was then."

"You learned from your mistakes. Got better. That takes character." His fingers rolled her nipple again and she pushed up into his hand, which impaled her ass deeper on him. Her clit was spasming on open air. She was hot and bothered, just as he'd said, needing him to touch her there, but he wasn't in a giving mood.

"What about the tape? Do you ever watch it?"

God, had she ever. Yet as the experience became further distant and nothing in her current life or attempted relationships matched it, watching it hurt and put her in an angry place, so she'd put it away. "Not in a while."

He set his teeth to the sensitive skin under her ear, nipped it so she drew in a gasp. "One day, you'll give me that tape, Celeste. I'll watch it with you sitting at my feet, and you'll show me every reaction you have to it."

She shook her head, but he wasn't in the mood to argue either. Instead he slid his hand down her front, threading his fingers into the small triangle of space her tied-together thighs provided. He dipped into the wetness in her pussy, pushed up to find her clit to circle and tease, worry that swollen bud.

She rocked against him, then moaned in protest as he withdrew from her ass, stripped the condom and tossed it. Leaning over her, he caught her face, made her look up at him. "Truth, Celeste. No one since the last physical? And never without protection?"

Her heart leaped eagerly as she deduced why he'd asked. She gave him the gift she wanted for herself as well. "And I'm protected from pregnancy. Can you..."

"Yeah. No one for me in the past couple years either."

She liked hearing that, and it showed enough that his eyes glinted. "My sub has a possessive side."

So did he, enough that it had things fluttering all up inside her chest. Hearing about another man having intimate knowledge of her body had changed the nature of his touch and his tone. Noticeably more caveman, in a very sexy, thrilling way. But while Ben had gotten inside and shone a mirror on her, making her face some hard truths and emotions, Leland was just inside her, period, every side of himself a mirror that reflected back and forth between them, so she couldn't figure out how to separate herself from what he was doing to her.

He dropped back behind her and she let out a sound of bliss as he guided himself into her pussy, flesh to flesh. His cock made a slow, irrevocable invasion into a very tight space, thanks to the rope holding her legs closed. He wrapped his arms around her again, whispered against her ear. "Did you call him Master?"

"No, not like this. I did, as a joke...on a bet..." Then she lost the explanation, boiling it down to what was important. "No, Master. I didn't. You're the first."

"Good answer. This one's just for me, darlin'. To mark you as mine." He let her feel the power of his body as he took what he wanted, thrusting into her pussy, hands holding her so securely she was little more than a helpless doll in his hands. He'd said this one was just for him, and he meant it, because at that angle, her clit was frustratingly out of reach. Her hands were tied to her thighs in a way she might be able to dip her fingers in between, place them against herself, but she wanted this to be all for him, too. She embraced that sense of being his. Pleasuring him as he denied her, made her wait and want to the point she perversely was ready to tear him apart to get to that peak. But he'd tied her, denying her that as well.

He came with a guttural noise, biting her neck again as he gripped her breast with a deliberately rougher touch, pinching the nipple hard enough to wrest a cry from her lips. She'd have bruises and bite marks tomorrow, and she'd get aroused from seeing them on her skin. Then he proved he wasn't a selfish bastard, not entirely, because he slid his fingers up between her legs, laid them against her clit and started making feather-like movements that had her wiggling and straining.

"That's it, darlin'. Show me how much you want it. Rub yourself against me, squeeze down on my cock."

She came in a bare instant, a shudder of sensation that she was fairly sure he kept less intense from the last time because he wanted her reaching and wanting more.

The night was only half over, after all.

Regardless, that climax left her weak as dishwater, and she suspected he was feeling some of the effects as well, if his satisfied grunt mixed with a groan were any indication. He removed the tether holding the collar, unwound the ropes around her. This time she stayed where he put her. When he withdrew from her cunt and turned her, he let her sprawl over his chest, his arm securely around her back.

"Good girl," he murmured, giving her that tiny thrill. She didn't question why it felt so good to hear those words, the inner child bullshit psychobabble. She was too tired to be intellectual, too easy with the moment to analyze, too sated and mindless to promise herself to do it later. Time began and ended in this room. He stroked her, turning on his hip so he put both arms around her, held her close inside that cavern formed by his body, surrounding her with heat.

"We're going to that wedding together," he said at last. His voice rumbled through his chest like distant thunder, vibrating against her cheek.

"Maybe." She smiled as his arms tightened and he tapped her ass, a warning and a promise.

"I still owe you...twice?" She was shy about saying that, too--giving head, blow job, no real romantic way to put it-- but it unfolded in her mind in graphic detail. Her on her knees, lips wrapped around his cock as he held her hair and thrust in with singular male demand. She wanted his rougher side. Not right now, when she had zero energy, but later. Definitely.

"Not yet, darlin'. You still have a lot of shit boiling up in you. I'm not going to risk getting bitten. You're not going to get out of having to wear a ring gag for that. Do it the hard way first so you'll know what's waiting for you if you misbehave in the future. I've got one with a nice big ring to fit my cock. It'll make your jaw ache. Maybe keep you blissfully silent for a day or two."

She tried to kick at him, wiggle away, but it was halfhearted and he held her secure, chuckling so she didn't know if he was kidding or not, about any of it. He proved he wasn't near as depleted as she'd expected, because he rolled her to her back, pressed her down into the mattress as he kissed her with leisurely thoroughness, moving his hips so he stroked his cock against her clit and pussy in slow circles, giving her simple pleasure in their aftermath and a hint of future plans. As his tongue swept into her mouth, his lips moving on hers with a firm demand that made everything whirl away, even her immediate resistance, her arms slid around him. She held on as if she'd slide off the curved side of the world if he wasn't holding her.

She lifted her legs, twined them around his hips, rubbed her heels over his muscular ass and upper thighs. As he drew out the kiss, her fingers curved, short nails biting into his shoulders, and then she let out a breathy sigh as he broke the kiss to curl his hands in her hair, turn her cheek to the pillow as he nuzzled her throat, nipped and kissed, suckled that sensitive area.

"Can't get enough of you," he muttered.

The feeling was mutual. She wanted to touch and taste, and he hadn't let her do much of either. Not that she was complaining about the things he did to her, but it was like smelling cake fresh out of the oven without ever being given the chance to taste it.

She ran her fingers up his arms, learning the shape of his biceps, the slope of forearm, inhaling his scent up close and personal, turning her head to rub her cheek against his arm. He moved down to her breasts, began to explore them with his mouth, closing over a nipple to suckle. She hummed with pleasure. Her hand moved to his neck, his head, fingers sliding over his short-cropped hair, learning the texture and feel of him. He had a sexual confidence that showed he knew how to arouse a woman, over and over, take her to peak, satisfy her. But he also had the hunger of a demanding Dom, and she responded to it, lifting her whole body to his touch, his desires.

Her fears and worries were so far away, in another world entirely. He must have sensed it as well, because as his cock started to revive once more, he lifted his head, gazed down at her with lust and calculation.

"Fuck it, I'll live dangerously," he decided. He shifted off of her, but he didn't put her on the floor on her knees as expected. Instead, he rolled to his back, his head toward the foot of the bed, and put his hand on her hip, shifting her over and onto him. The first time she went down on him he intended to have his mouth between her legs as well. She tried to help, but it was mainly his strength that moved them both into the right position, her stretched out on top of him, him guiding her knees past his shoulders until his mouth grazed her cunt, his arms banding hard around her hips and ass.

"Suck me, darlin'," he ordered. And then he started eating her pussy as if he had all the time and energy in the world to bring her to the brink of insanity again.

Her tissues were so sensitive, but the feel of his mouth there had her working herself against him, lifting and lowering her hips so he was stroking her with his tongue in a rhythm that made it difficult to focus. But as much pleasure as he could bring her there, she wasn't wasting her first opportunity to serve her Master in such a basic way.

It gave her pause, how quickly her subconscious embraced the idea of him as her Master. She curled her hands around the base of his cock, and slid her lips over the broad head, tasting herself on his flesh as well as his semen. Semen he'd shot inside her, that was drying on her inner thighs, that he was teasing with his tongue when he wasn't thrusting it inside her or playing it over her clit. That iron hold he had on her hips was quickly making the sensations intense and overwhelming. She had to work all the harder to take her time, take him in, slide him into the cavern of her mouth, as far as she could take him. What she couldn't take she gripped to stroke and pump him into her mouth, thrilled at the hardening, the twitch of that massive organ that said her efforts were making him bigger. Her other fingers stretched out, caressed his testicles.

She groaned as another lightning bolt of sensation shot between her legs, thanks to his ministrations. She took him deeper, worked over him more intensely as well, fingers slick with her saliva and with the pre-come she tasted from the tip when she worried her tongue in that opening. His hips lifted, thrusting deep, and she fought her gag reflex, not wanting him to be any less forceful. When she accidentally scored him with her teeth, she jumped as he gave her a stinging slap on her wiggling ass. Then she let out another needy sound as he dipped his thumb into her cunt, working it around until it was slick, and then gripped her ass anew, shoving that thumb into her rectum.

"Ahh...." Now she simply attacked him the way her desire dictated, lips sliding up and down his fully erect length, the shaft glistening from her agile tongue. She gripped his balls again, holding, stroking and rolling them in her palm, her thumb sliding beneath to tease the perineum. He was like a powerful rodeo bull, she thought, the way he bucked up into her mouth, the way his muscular body rolled and rippled beneath hers.

He was going to make her come, but she wanted to give him pleasure first. "Master..." she gasped. "Please...I want you to come first. Please..."

It was essential, important. His voice was a growl, vibrating against her wet flesh. "You want to serve your Master before your own pleasure?"

"Yes. Please."

"I'll think about it." She bit back an animal cry as he worked that thumb inside of her ass. Now he was keeping his mouth off her pussy, though she could feel his measured breath. It didn't help her self-control at all to visualize his position, his face inches away from her wet pussy as he watched it get slicker for him.

"Please..." She had her mouth on him, over him, but he understood the garbled plea well enough.

"All right. Serve your Master."

She obeyed, resuming the ascending and descending motion as she sucked him in, dragged her mouth along his length, licked and teased, stroked his testicles. She clasped her hand around him, gliding along velvet steel. She rode his movements as he thrust his hips upward, taking himself deeper, faster as she moved to accommodate him. He held on to her hips, kept his thumb slowly moving inside her, a sensual torment, especially when he occasionally passed an idle finger over her labia, just an easy rub that kept spirals of sensation coiling in her lower belly. His breath was getting rougher. Now he started to spank her again, random, hard blows, as if he were driving her onward. Then he was past such coordination and gripped her hips in bruising hands, held her fast as his cock began to pulse toward climax.

"Fuck, yeah. Suck me harder, darlin'. I want your jaw aching."

She obeyed with fierce pleasure, and was rewarded for it. She savored the first jet into the back of her throat, his rough undulations into her mouth, the hiss and curse as he released, pumping his seed into her mouth. She worked her ass off to swallow him down, loving the way he shoved into her mouth without care now, all demanding male animal.

At last, he reached down, put his hand flat on her back, a mute command to cease. She drew off of him slowly, cleaning him with her tongue to draw out the experience, and then she laid her head on his thigh, staying there because he kept holding her. When he turned his mouth back to her pussy, it took no more than a couple slow circling strokes with his tongue to send another orgasm ripping through her. He held her fast as she writhed and squealed, his mouth working her, sucking her juices. During the climax she put her mouth over him again, just wanting to hold him there as she came. She stayed that way in the aftermath, panting against him as he softened. She drew off of him reluctantly, hand still curled around his base, knuckles resting in the damp nest of his testicles. She put the tip of his cock to her lips, teasing the slit with her tongue, working around the corona. She owed him once more, and she wanted to let him know she was ready at any time. She wanted to do it.

Another replete male groan came from between her legs, making her smile. Despite her protest, he turned them once more. This time he dropped a pillow on the floor and then eased her down to it on her knees. He sat up on the bed, keeping her between his splayed thighs, guiding her so her head lay on his inner thigh. His firm pressure on it kept it there and the way he slid his fingers beneath the buckled back of the collar trapped her mind in a slow spin.

"Keep your eyes on the floor, sub. You just sit there while your Master recovers. You're trying to kill him."

"You set the number at six," she reminded him, smiling as she focused on his bare foot. Reaching out, she slid her fingers over his toes, traced the bones to his ankle. "You don't have to prove anything to me, you know. Most men overestimate their sexual stamina."

Though privately she had no doubt he'd summon an erection for that sixth time. Nerves between her legs twitched in anticipation of it.

He chuckled, tugged her hair. "You little bitch. That was a gauntlet if ever I heard one."

"I think your masculine pride will remain intact. My blog will say: 'Regardless of a shortfall of erections, Sergeant Leland Keller did rock *my* world with half a dozen orgasms. So all in all, the night wasn't a complete letdown.'"

"Let me go get that ring gag." He started to stand up, and she wrapped her arms around his leg.

"No, no, no. I'll print a retraction."

"Yeah, on page twenty behind the obituaries and car ads." But he sat back down.

She laid her head back on his thigh. Drawing a breath, she let it out slow. Wow. She was starting to tire. She'd probably need another massage to get out of bed tomorrow. His bed.

It was already past midnight, and he'd told her she was staying here tonight. Though it gave her some uneasiness, she didn't have the willpower to cater to her insecurities. He was stroking her hair. Tender, easy.

"That night with Ben," she said slowly. "He gave me a lot of pain the way you did tonight. Why does that help?"

"Because when I treat you gentle, it opens up scary things inside you. Things you're afraid to want. You need to be angry, need the pain. But the pain brings you back to this point, where you can be held and I can be gentle with you. Gives you those things you're afraid to want. You're like a tide, darlin'. Keep your eyes down."

She'd been about to lift her head and expected she'd telegraphed it through tension in her neck. She'd forgotten. She kept her eyes on his foot.

"You asked about the wrong kind of bratting earlier," he continued. "When you demand pain and punishment with your rage, you're really wanting the opposite, but you need to reach it through the pain and rage." He curled a lock of her hair around his fingers. "That first time, after your punishment, you shot right through subspace, bounced down into subdrop and went right back to bratting. That's hard on you emotionally and physically. It broke my heart not to give you the aftercare you really needed then."

He had an uncanny way of pulling thoughts out of her mind, giving them clarity. She bit her lip. "I couldn't."

"I know. And that's okay, darlin'. It's all okay. I'm here."

"What do *you* want, Leland? Truthfully." Tightening her arms around his leg, she pressed her forehead a little harder against his thigh and lied. "It won't hurt me if I'm not it. I just want to know who you are. What you want."

He leaned over, his lips to the top of her head as he wound his arms around her. She curled her hands over his forearm, burrowed her face into his chest and shoulder as he spoke against her hair.

"I want a very special kind of submissive. She might use her claws to tear me apart, but each time she's done with that, she'll know she can be the kitten she really is with me. She knows I'll be her port, the place she can trust to keep every fear, pain and ugly feeling safe, keep her safe. It doesn't matter how often she scratches and bites. She'll know when I look at her, I see the kitten with all the rest, her vulnerable heart. I'll always treat that kitten gentle, even when everything else she is needs the rougher stuff."

She was glad she had hold of his leg, because her world just dropped away beneath her. She closed her eyes to stave off the vertigo. "Leland..."

"Be quiet now. Just hold on to me."

Joey W. Hill

Chapter Nine

He'd kept her on her knees on the floor, talking of this and that. Sliding his finger into the D-ring on the collar, he'd idly played with it, giving her little tugs, reminding her of what it meant. Eventually, he told her to go get them both a beer. Made her walk naked to the fridge and back, the chill in the front room peaking her nipples. When she returned, he took the beer from her, set it on the night table and then pulled her down over his lap to run his hands over her ass, see how the marks he'd put on her were doing. He refreshed them with a few more healthy slaps of his broad palm, commanding her to keep her knees spread, her toes straining for purchase on the floor. He had her yelping when he put the ice-cold beer against her sore ass and between her legs, ordering her to shut her legs tight over the glass bottle until she was begging him to take it away because the cold had become painful.

Chuckling--the sadist--he put her on her knees again, in front of his once again erect cock, and had her suck him off that one last time. When it was over, she was amazed to find herself vibrating with need, despite being exhausted, physically and mentally. But Leland told her it was bedtime and she didn't disagree. Scooping her up, he took her to the bathroom door, politely giving her the chance to answer nature's call. It oddly touched her when she emerged and found him still there. He carried her back to the bed, despite the short distance between the two points.

He put her down, tucked her in and slid in behind her, curling around her. Reaching over her hip, he slid his fingers down between her legs and began to stroke, slow and leisurely, but with obvious intent. Her body hummed, even as she tightened her legs, thinking she couldn't possibly make that climb one more time.

"Denying your Master, darlin'?"

His other hand settled around her throat and tipped her head back onto his shoulder, an inexorable hold that raked fingers of desire down her weak body. Her thighs loosened, no thought needed. He made a noise of approval and brought her to that climax in a way that reminded her of a slow, rich spiral of caramel winding its way around her. She clung to his arm, keening out her pleasure as he worked her through it.

When it was over, he loosened that hold on her throat, kissed her temple. "There you go, sweet baby. Go to sleep now."

I'll take care of you like the sweet baby you are...

She'd never relaxed in a man's arms after sex like this. Never been carried, cuddled to sleep. Cuddling was not part of Celly Lewis's MO.

She fell into dreams with his hands curved possessively over her throat and pussy, still stroking. Her dreams were peaceful and blank, like a clear blue sky with the sun beaming on her skin.

When she woke at dawn, she was sure those dreams were the direct result of having him up against her back, still coiled around her. She wished she could carry the peaceful feeling into wakefulness, but as she pressed her face into his biceps under her cheek, inhaled him, she knew it was time to leave. That familiar weirdness in her belly was stirring, warning her she'd been shoved way too far out of her comfort zone. She needed to regain some control.

When she pushed up with some vague notion of retrieving her clothes from the other room, his arm went around her waist, an iron band holding her fast, and he put his mouth to her neck.

"I have to go to work," she said. "Do things. Back to real life."

He grunted. "Do you make coffee?"

She smiled, despite her uneasiness. "I've been known to push a button on a Keurig, yes."

"How about we share a cup before you go?"

It was a reasonable request. She could act reasonably, not be foolish. She slid from the bed, silent acquiescence, though she noticed his arm loosened reluctantly. Since it was chilly and she didn't know if he'd left the curtains open in the living room, she picked up a T-shirt he'd left over a chair and slipped it on before she headed for the kitchen.

He already had the coffee ready to go. Just a button

push, after all. She poked her head in his refrigerator and discovered some boiled eggs. Since her stomach was growling, she snagged one and a bottle of water while the coffee was brewing. Going into the room they'd occupied most of last night, her gaze lighted on the aftermath. The chains and cuffs in disarray on the floor, the paddle, rod and single tail now not so neatly arranged on the table. The candles were stubs in pools of wax, but their scent still permeated the room.

Looking at the mat on the floor, she could see herself, chained on all fours, him moving around her, using the dragon tail, the paddle. Holding the chain right up against her collared throat as he stung her nipples with the rod. A shiver ran over her skin, recalling the orgasms he'd wrung from her, her screams vibrating against the gag. It was on the table as well, waiting to be cleaned.

She shifted from foot to foot. He probably had special things he used to clean his tools. It wasn't her job. But it felt weird, leaving a mess. Quelling the ridiculous notion that somehow, as his sub, it was her job to clean up, she snatched her clothes and hurried from the room, closing the door behind her. That scent clung to her, though, as did the images from last night.

Going into the bathroom, she concentrated on making herself presentable not only for the man in the bedroom, but for when she left the house, which would be soon. Very soon. He had some mouthwash she used in lieu of a toothbrush, and she combed damp fingers through her hair after washing her face. She needed a shower, but she'd get one at home. She wasn't using a guy's shower and toiletries after one night together. No matter how incredible that night had been.

She found the coffee ready to go. Taking a deep breath, telling herself to act casual and normal, she headed back to the bedroom. She had her clothes over one arm and a coffee cup in each hand. He was sitting up and had pulled on a pair of dark-blue flannel pajama bottoms that rode low on his hips. She expected she was wearing the T-shirt he'd been planning to pull on, but having the chance to see his brown, bare chest and shoulders and the ripped abdomen, made her glad she'd snagged it. It conjured another vivid image from last night. Him shirtless, only in his jeans, which were tight over the crotch because his aroused cock was taking up all the room. When he'd squatted in front of her, held the chain, she'd been staring right at that part of him, the way the inseam cut in to shape his balls for her greedy gaze.

That was all about the sex. A much safer thing to dwell upon than all the rest. Safe sex. She snorted at herself and handed him his coffee, shaking her head at his quizzical look. But she couldn't keep her mind in such safer realms. Instead, standing this close to him, she imagined moving closer, between his spread knees. She wished she was comfortable enough to hand him the coffee, sink down between his knees and do like she'd done last night, lean against his knee, her cheek against his leg and arms twined around it. He'd drink his coffee, stroke her hair, and her mind could be as still as he'd made it last night, after doing all those amazing things to her.

She didn't do it, though. She backed up to the dresser, laid her clothes there and then leaned on it, taking a sip of the coffee. Looked out the bedroom window since he'd cracked the blinds. It wasn't far past dawn, but the gold tone of the sky said there would be sunshine today. Good. That was good.

He clearly wasn't a big morning talker, which was either the cause or effect of him working later shifts, but his lips against her neck when she'd woken, the strength of his arm around her, had made her feel welcome in his bed, not a morning-after regret. But morning-afters were likely more problematic for her anyway. She wasn't used to hanging around.

"Where did you get the scar on your stomach?" she asked, nodding to the shiny, small indentation in his skin there.

He glanced down. "Ricochet. Damn drunk idiot waving a gun around and it went off. Bullet hit the pavement. Gravel and asphalt punched through the uniform."

"Is that the only time you've been shot at?"

"As a cop, yeah, pretty much. Had a few blunt objects swung at me during takedowns or in domestic disturbances. Have to especially watch the women in those situations. They aren't shy about using hammer, skillet or toilet brush."

"Assault with toilet brush?"

"You laugh, but those bristles are prickly. I don't think it had been cleaned since it was bought. Lucky the skin didn't break or I probably would have died from infection."

"The dangers of the job," she said with a lightness she didn't feel. "You said as a cop. How about not as a cop?"

He grimaced. "Damn reporter. Better at picking out the details than a cop."

"Well, that's not much of a compliment. Wave a donut in front of most of you and you lose your train of thought entirely."

She scampered around the dresser to the door as he made a quick lunge at her from the bed. He settled back, chuckling. "Come back in here and give me that attitude, darlin'."

"I think I'll stay here," she said prudently, taking an exaggerated step into the hallway and winning a grin. The chuckle made her feel better. "So what about not as a cop?"

He lifted a shoulder. "I served overseas, saw some action in the Middle East. Wasn't ever hit. Some buddies I was with weren't so lucky."

"I'm sorry."

"Yeah. Me too." He sipped the coffee, gave her an unreadable look. "Most people don't understand how quickly a situation can turn bad or violent. Or just how violent it can get. They expect life to have a certain rhythm, routine, and they assume that the rhythm protects them. They don't realize how fast it can hit a sour note. Like a reporter who gets too comfortable rubbing shoulders with gang members and calls one of them out on his own turf."

She stiffened, stepped back through the doorway. "Mike is a rat. And I didn't get in Dogboy's face. I'm not stupid, Leland. I know how to do my job. I didn't push him to the point he felt like he had to prove himself."

"And you learned that how?"

She didn't flinch at the ominous tone. "By trial and error. Luck, good and bad. I've had to take a few hits in the face to figure out where the lines are. But that's the deal. Just like your rookies, I had to take those blows to learn the ropes and do the job."

His jaw tensed. "A rookie has a backup, body armor, weapons. A radio. You're out there with nothing but your wits."

"I think wits are the one weapon most people tend to underestimate." She scowled at his look. "Don't go all Neanderthal on me like you did the other day. If you do, I'll tell you the same thing I did then."

He lifted a brow, gave her a sweeping appraisal. "I wouldn't do that, darlin'. If you have all that judgment you claim to have, you'll know this is my turf. You think I won't put you over my knee and beat some manners into you?"

She bristled. "We're not doing that right now. It's not Master/sub. That's just...bedroom stuff. Today is today."

"And what was last night?"

Alarms went off as he rose. With the loose fit of the pajama bottoms, it was obvious he was still experiencing that impressive turgid state males had upon waking. Or maybe the argument was working him up, which should in no way inspire the leap low in her stomach that said she was responding to such a primal reaction. When he moved toward her, her gaze was filled with the impressive play of firm skin over hard muscle at his abdomen and hips. The bottoms were low enough to show his hip bones. If she was behind him, she'd be able to trail her fingers over the taut upper slopes of his ass.

So fine. He was overwhelming to her, sexually and emotionally, a combination that had her pulse pounding, but he was attacking the most important thing to her. That gave her the fortitude to plant herself, not back away an inch. He wasn't going to intimidate her.

"It was amazing," she said coolly. "But today is today. We're not Master/sub right now," she repeated.

"Hmm. Could have fooled me." His gaze went pointedly to her throat. "Did you realize you were still wearing it, darlin'?"

The collar. Her hand went to it. Fuck, she hadn't. Well, she had, but she hadn't. It had felt like a part of her when she got up, a part she didn't want to remove. Panic shot through her, but before she could back away, he curled his fingers in the ring and brought her up onto her toes in a smooth jerk that flip-flopped her stomach.

"You matter," he said flatly. "And everything that happened last night tells me you're mine."

"I need to get dressed," she said tightly. "Please let go of me." The pull of the collar against the back of her neck, his hold on her, had a tremor running through her legs. She closed her hands into fists against his bare stomach, straight-armed him.

She was sure he read the body language. But he waited just long enough to make it clear it was his decision to let her go. She might claim things weren't Master and sub right now, but that energy was still humming strong in the room.

When he released his hold on the collar, she muttered something about getting dressed again and escaped to the bathroom. Once there, she closed the door, leaned against it. She didn't lock it. No point to that, given how flimsy it was, but beyond that she knew the punch sound of the lock would be a direct insult. It might push him over a line her body and mind were too eager to test. She needed to get out of here.

Despite that, she stripped off the T-shirt with as much reluctance as he'd demonstrated when he let her leave his bed. She took time to inhale his scent, rub the fabric against her cheek before setting it aside. When she donned her clothes, they felt strange, as if being naked and under his command had been far closer to her natural state.

She put her hand on the collar. He'd startled her by pointing it out, so it should have been the first thing to go when she went into the bathroom, but she hadn't taken it off even now. She made herself tear her gaze away from the mirror, quelled the desire to run her fingers over the wide strap. She wanted to hook her fingers in the ring as he had, so she could imagine he was tugging on it again. Instead, she finally unbuckled it, coiled it over her knuckles and left the bathroom, returning to the bedroom doorway. He was sitting on the edge of the bed, sipping his coffee.

Putting the collar on his dresser, she turned and faced him. "You know, I'm damn good at my job," she said. "Nothing pisses me off worse than to be treated like an idiot child by a cop who thinks women belong on their knees and obeying his every whim."

His gaze sparked. This time, he didn't move at all, but she still instinctively moved a step back into the hallway. His jaw tightened again, but he remained where he was as he took another swallow of the coffee. "Does it make you feel better to boil what happened last night down to that?"

No. It made her feel like shit. But no one was going to give her crap about her job. It was the only thing she was good at. No one was going to take that away from her.

As she put her earrings and choker in her purse, she was aware of his gaze on her, his silence. "I belong to myself," she said. "Not to you."

His eyes flicked over to the collar, back to her bare neck. "Those two things don't have to be in conflict," he said mildly. "I know you're damn good at your job, Celeste. That's why I worry."

"Got it." She didn't want him to talk anymore. He'd say something like 'you matter' again, knowing how such words could scramble things in her mind. So much of last night had been accomplished without words. Words only ruined things. She wouldn't let them ruin this.

She straightened, met his gaze with dignity. "I noticed the bus stop is just a few houses up. You don't have to drive me. I don't want you to drive me," she corrected herself. "I need some space to think about last night."

He gave her his steady look, holding a silence that drew out until it took every ounce of willpower not to fill it with inane words. Like an apology for being such a bitch. It didn't do any good to apologize for something that was unchangeable.

"All right," he said at last. He rose, setting aside the coffee. She turned and walked to the doorway, knowing he'd follow because he'd have to deactivate the security to let her out. When she reached that door, she wished she could keep staying just a step ahead of him, ahead of what he was making her feel.

She felt him behind her. He reached over her shoulder, unhooked the chain and flipped the dead bolt, but before he deactivated the alarm, he turned her toward him, tipped her chin and caught her mouth with his. Easy and brief, though with a lingering feel that made her press her lips together to hold in the tingling response. He kept his face close. "You watch your ass out there."

There was kindness and concern in his voice, but the look in his eyes added a few extra words, too. *Else you'll answer to me, darlin'*.

"You too." She kept her voice steady, reined back her spinning emotions. A whole lot more was simmering between them, waiting to see what direction they'd take it. Right now, the only direction she needed was the exit.

He deactivated the alarm and let her out. As she strode to the bus stop, she didn't look back, but it didn't matter. She felt his eyes on her. When she arrived at the bus sign, she turned, sure that she was being fanciful. Or paranoid. He'd retrieved his coffee and come out onto the porch, sliding a hip onto his porch rail while he sipped from the mug. He'd stay there until the bus came, to make sure she was safe. Why that tore things up inside her heart, she didn't know. Any more than she could comprehend why she could take the most amazing night she'd ever experienced and drag it back down into the muck of her dysfunctional emotions. He'd probably decide he was better off without the crazy reporter bitch. That was fine. Maybe it was best to leave it that way.

As the bus approached a few minutes later and she turned her back to him to face it, she put her hand to her throat, laid her palm over where the collar had been.

Where it still felt like it was.

§

Even without seeing the victim being brought out of the alley in a body bag, she would have known it was a homicide. A homicide always had a larger police presence. More uniforms were needed to corral and keep any witnesses separate, maintain the police barricade, and then there would be the arrival of the detectives and crime scene techs.

The death would be drug-related, since the spot was a popular one for dealing. It looked like the police had snagged three witnesses for questioning, and that many was a miracle. Unfortunately, they looked like homeless people or hapless junkies who hadn't melted away fast enough when the shooting happened. The detectives wouldn't get much from them, but it had to be done.

One of the witnesses she recognized. Dirty Harry, a homeless guy who lived in a nearby alley. Having spoken with him in the past, she knew the nickname wasn't a comment on his cleanliness. He had a rasp a lot like the Clint Eastwood character and did passable imitations of him if he was in a good mood. She made a note to visit Harry later when they cut him loose.

For now, she followed her usual routine. She approached the barrier, razzed a couple of familiar faces enough to get a smile, but she didn't get much from pressing them. So she picked out a strategic spot where the wind direction and location gave her snippets of conversation and a good view of the goings-on. Unfolding her stadium chair, she took up her position to watch and listen.

Cops had to be detached to a certain extent to do the job, yet she thought the way they related to each other at a crime scene helped them deal with the underlying frustration or affront of the crime. Sure, their demeanor was different when it was "dope dealers killing dope dealers." But even when the victim was a criminal, she knew they weren't as callous about it as people often assumed. Those who thought the police didn't care weren't paying attention. Standing over a body was standing over a waste. Their job was to serve and protect, and a body meant they'd failed.

When Leland pulled up, she didn't want to be so thrilled to see him. All these months they'd managed not to cross paths, and now she was tripping over him everywhere. The gods must be screwing with her. She told herself she hadn't wanted him to show up on her radar at all today. She needed to pull herself back together after that out-of-body experience he'd given her last night. Out-of-body experiences weren't a good thing to overdo, like indulging in dessert every day. She had to figure out where this could go with them, though she knew the best thing was to make it a one-time shot.

Even if she did that, though, she'd keep seeing him like this. And unless she backed out of Ben and Marcie's wedding, they'd be seeing one another there as well. Damn it. It was too much to hope the city would be hit by some kind of natural catastrophe, like a hurricane or meteor shower. Just affecting Baton Rouge, keeping all members of the BRPD on duty. She didn't want Marcie's wedding ruined. A lot of planning went into those things, after all.

As he emerged from his unit, a big man who made the vehicle dip and lift as he stepped out of it, her gaze slid over the line of his shoulder and hip, the way his uniform fit. Had he taken a shower this morning after she left? She was sure he had. She could picture him in the small shower, the water sluicing over all those muscles and golden skin, his hands following the soap's track to cup his balls, rub soap along his cock. Would he have thought of her? Of how he'd had her bound and helpless, calling him Master? Would he have worked his hand up and down himself as he imagined doing it again, as soon as humanly possible?

She'd certainly had some similar thoughts in her own shower, though she'd kept her hands away from herself. She'd told herself she was testing her control, not obeying that lasting instinct that felt like her climaxes belonged to him. Then his gaze met hers across the police barrier, and she knew that for the pathetic lie it was. She remembered how she'd swept her gaze downward last night, and had a sudden, unwise compulsion to do it as a gibe, exaggerate it. She suppressed the urge. She needed to cut back on her stupid impulses, since her version of flirting with Leland was akin to tossing rocks at a pit bull on a frayed rope.

She'd only be doing the submissive gaze taunt to cover her weird compulsion to do it for real, anyway. So she kept her expression as inscrutable as his. He gave her a nod, which she returned.

He was probably measuring how far she was from the crime tape, to determine if it was far enough for his tastes. Since she wanted to watch him too much, the way he walked and moved, or tune into that deep voice as he spoke to the officers on scene, she busied herself with other tasks. She checked her email and then scrolled through the notes she'd made from her interview with Dogboy's foster mother.

Mavis Roberts had wild bushy hair, a sharp voice and hands quick to slap out at any of the seven rambunctious children currently under her care. She'd verified he'd attended the same high school as Loretta. School records showed they'd been in the same Spanish class, when he chose to show up.

"No ma'am, we couldn't keep no pets with that one in the house. He hated dogs and they hated him. So his brothers and sisters called him Dogboy to tease him. Took the name and owned it, though." The woman's brow had creased. "He did that about the time the only dog we had left got hit by a car. I thought he did it because he liked that one. It was a male. The others were female. Dogboy, he likes girls, but he doesn't know how to be patient with them. Boy doesn't know how to be patient or kind with nobody. Gonna end up dead, but it won't be my fault. Did the best I could by him. Sometimes they just start out rotten. Know what I mean?"

Though her hands were quick to fly out, Celeste noticed none of the kids seemed all that afraid of her. They were also well fed and clean, and all of them were girls. When she asked Mavis about that, she shrugged.

"Girls are just easier, honey. Got tired of dealing with boy shit."

She needed to try to find some of Loretta's friends, determine if Dogboy had ever come on to her. She'd bet money he had, and Loretta had shut him down, recognizing him for the trouble he was. Celeste had already sent her interview with the foster mother to Detective Marquez. He'd need to follow up and conduct the same interviews, but if Dogboy had killed Loretta Stiles, that was going to be his undoing. A murdered prostitute might regrettably pass under the radar, but a middle-class teenage girl's death enraged a community and galvanized a deeper investigation.

Leland had disappeared down the alley. Though she was ostensibly paying attention to everything else about the scene, her gaze kept returning to that opening, anticipating his return. When he'd left his car, it might have been her imagination, but she thought the wind had brought her a trace of that peppermint scent he carried on his skin.

Olfactory memory was almost as dangerous as hormones in driving a woman's decisions. She thought of the strength of his hand closing over hers, his whisper in her ear, and she closed her eyes, sensation washing through her. He'd been all hers last night, and then she'd spooked this morning.

But all of it hadn't been cold feet, damn it. He was trying to tell her how to do her job. Typical cop. They saw everything in black-and-white, civilian versus police. She covered stories that required taking risks, but he took risks by putting on that uniform every day.

She thought of how he'd come down on her about getting in Dogboy's face. Okay, yeah, now that she thought Dogboy had a thing for killing women, she'd be steering clear of him, at least the face-to-face encounters. No woman, no matter how confident she was or how public the meeting place, would be safe attracting the attention of that kind of person. She wasn't a moron, no matter what Sergeant Leland Keller thought.

But she knew it wasn't that. She'd spent the past few years around cops, so if she stepped away from her personal hang-ups about people fucking with her about her job, she understood he'd have pretty black-and-white lines about keeping her safe. Mike or Billy might react the same way. Mike had come into the cul-de-sac just to check on her, hadn't he? It was the intimate nature of what was happening between her and Leland that had lifted her hackles. He'd said she was good at her job, after all. *That's why I worry.*

Sighing, she looked up to find he was emerging from the alley. As he stopped to talk to the officer on that side of the barrier, he was facing her. Though he appeared focused on the officer whose back was to her, she crossed her eyes, stuck out her tongue. Warm swirlies kicked up in her stomach as a hint of a smile appeared on his face. The little hop stirred up the effects of last night, sent other desires pulsing through her. Who was she kidding? No matter what she'd resolved earlier, she wasn't going to cut the cord between them yet. The glint in his eyes, suggested he wasn't planning on cutting her loose yet, either.

The thump-thump of a car stereo with too much pumped up bass disrupted her pleasant imaginings. It was coming out of a black sedan with one tan-colored door, a battered back panel and expensive rims. It wasn't the first car that had cruised past, slowing down to see what was happening in that taped-off area. There was far less rubbernecking, though, since most of the normal traffic would be people coming to score drugs. The police had blocked off the right lane so any traffic had to swerve out, which slowed the vehicles further and gave the barrier cops a good look at the driver. If they thought the occupant was a regular patron, they might stop and question the driver.

That was the case with this car. Officer Manny Brown, who'd been in District 1 about three years, a slow-talking Texan with a young face but sharp dark eyes, stepped forward, raising his arm to slow the driver down, bring the car to a stop.

The driver punched the gas.

Leland had said a reporter was like a cop when it came to noticing details, but one thing they had that Celeste didn't was an impressive level of vigilance. The second the car accelerated, Leland, Manny, and the other two officers on the barrier drew weapons. Suddenly they were all bellowing orders at the car to stop, Leland's baritone roaring over all of them. The back windows came down and one of two figures shadowed there thrust a weapon out toward the barrier side.

"Down!" It was a thundering command from all the cops. Gunfire cracked through the air. Celeste saw the flare of the discharge, Leland standing in the line of fire. *No.*

She'd sprung to her feet and started forward, despite the stupidity of such a knee-jerk reaction. Later, she'd remember she'd screamed his name, but in the next second, she was scrambling for cover as gunfire erupted out the other back window. Bullets struck her stadium chair and knocked it backward like a fly hit by a flyswatter. As she stumbled away, another bullet ricocheted off the light post, a sharp ping, then the concrete, sending up a spray of dust and gravel.

As she ran for her life, cracks in the curtains of the buildings across from her became smooth lines again as the occupants of the apartments retreated from the vulnerable position. The door of the nail salon slammed as the store owner took cover. She was holding her tablet up to cover the side of her face. The car couldn't stop or the police would catch up, so as she heard glass shatter in the storefront behind her and heard the nail salon employees screech in alarm, she knew the gunman was being carried away from her. She spun around when she was pretty sure she was in the clear and saw the car rocketing toward the end of the street.

Her gaze shot to Leland. He was all right. He was helping Manny back to his feet as the other two cops sprinted toward their units, one shouting into his radio.

She pivoted and ran down the alley behind her. This was why it was critical for Billy and all the others to know the streets inside and out. The car was most likely to turn left so they could shoot down the parallel street. It was the quickest route to a warren of neighborhoods with rabbit holes for a fleeing vehicle. If she could run fast enough, she could see them as they passed by, get a better look at their faces. Rage accompanied the adrenaline now. Bastards. Thinking they could shoot at the police, at Leland. The police hadn't returned fire, no time for it. Plus, a moving target was too great a risk to the civilians behind the windows. She'd been sitting on that same sidewalk herself.

She'd been on scene at a police shooting a couple years back. She'd known the dead officer. Tom had been twenty-nine years old, with a young son and a five-year marriage. He'd been gunned down on the street. By a stroke of unlucky fate, she'd arrived right before police backup had. 911 had already been called, officer down, but she'd been the one to see the life die out of his eyes while she held his hand impotently. She hadn't been aware of the police arriving, of hands moving her out of the way. Eventually she'd found herself sitting in her car in an empty parking lot, no idea how she'd gotten there, with smears of his blood on her shirt.

Now she visualized Leland in the same position as Tom, that strong handclasp going limp around hers. Her speed doubled. Son of a bitch wasn't going to get away with shooting at her man without her seeing his face.

She was glad for every punishing workout as she skidded out of the alley on the other side, right by Jai's place. Triumph surged through her as she saw the black sedan come screaming down the street. The tinted windows in the front were raised, so no chance of identifying the driver, but she saw one of the two in the backseat. Shock froze her as Dogboy's dead eyes pinned her, his lips peeling back. Fast as she could blink, he thrust his gun back out the window.

He could send a dozen bullets across her body faster than she could move. But it was harder to hit a moving target than a sitting one. Pure survival instinct had her dropping to the ground. As she went down, something grabbed her around the waist, swung her back into the alley, hard enough she hit the concrete with a bone-jarring thud. She was covered as the whine of bullets shot over her, then the weight on her back lifted.

She shoved herself up in time to see Leland spinning and lunging out of the alley, weapon drawn. He fired one shot before lifting the muzzle, the fury in his face indicating the car was making its getaway.

"Dogboy," she gasped.

He didn't hear her, so she said it louder, repeated it again and again before she realized she sounded like an answering machine stuck on a loop. Shock, probably. Yeah, she'd been in some sticky situations before, but that was the first time someone had tried to kill her. Christ. Dogboy. Teenage psychopath. The asshole had shot at her. Multiple shots.

Despite her legs feeling like noodles, she was on her feet and out of the alley, breaking into a half run to go after the car. Leland caught her around the waist. "Hey. Celeste, they're gone."

"Son of a bitch," she snarled, fighting his hold. "Thinks he can take a fucking shot at me and make me scared of him. Bastard will wish he'd never been born."

"Easy, *easy*." He gave her a hard shake, snapping the red haze out of her eye. "Stop clawing at me. Settle down."

She knew she was acting irrationally, fought it back, but she pushed against his hold. "I'm all right. Let me go. Let go."

"Okay, but you stay right there." He kept a hand on her shoulder, fingers curled in her shirt while he spoke into his radio. "Black Chrysler sedan, bullet hole in the back trunk, Louisiana license plate Delta-Hotel-Lima, 5756."

"Dogboy," she said again. "It was Dogboy doing the shooting in the back. Earl Edward James is his real name." She took a breath, suddenly remembering standing at Leland's door this morning. "Guess neither of us watched our asses, did we? Good thing we were watching each other's."

It was a weak joke, and he glanced at her, concern etched on his face. There was a ringing in her head, a keening sound like a frightened woman. That wasn't her. She'd shoot herself before she'd make such a noise. As she focused, she realized it wasn't her. The unidentified sound widened her focus so she could take in more of her surroundings. As soon as she did, she wrenched herself from Leland's hold and was off like a shot, but not to chase down a car that was long gone.

One of Jai's windows was gone except for jagged glass teeth, and there was a trio of bullets in an arc along the thick glass door. She jerked it open and saw a woman on her knees by the cash register. She wore a yellow tunic and brown leggings. The tunic was stained red. A dozen tomatoes were around her, but they were unbroken. They weren't why her tunic was stained and her hands were red and wet. She lifted them to Celeste, eyes frantic. "Help us. Help…"

Leland pushed past her, already back on the radio. "We need an ambulance at the Mini-Mart at 447 Weller Avenue for…" His voice hitched as he reached the end of the counter. "Multiple GSWs to the chest. One male, mid-forties… Ma'am are you hurt? Are you hurt? No? I need you to move back then, let me help him. Step back for me."

Celeste, her heart in her throat, moved forward. Leland briefly met her gaze as she eased the woman away. Jai was crumpled behind the counter, a thick puddle of blood soaking his shirt. His head lolled toward her, his eyes glazed, but she thought she saw a hint of the half smile he always gave her. Muscle memory. Shock as well. *I'm not really shot if I can smile and say hello like I always do, right?*

The woman was crying louder now. Despite wanting to

stay right at Leland's side, Celeste moved the woman further away, in front of a display of Hostess cakes. Jai had teased her about those.

"Two for a dollar. Makes your butt bigger, Celeste. A man likes at least two good handfuls. You see any skinny porn stars? How about the classics? Marilyn Monroe, Jane Russell, Sophia Loren. Those are women, the ones men fantasize about it. Not these pencil thin super models."

The Mini-Mart had a small supply of overpriced folding stadium chairs, cheaper versions of her own. Thank God Jai had one set up so his customers could see how they worked. She sat the woman down in it and checked her over, made absolutely sure the blood wasn't hers. It wasn't. It was all Jai's. Celeste's hands shook as she turned the woman's palms over. Pulling some paper towels off the shelf, she ripped them open and helped her clean off the blood. It gave them both something to do.

Celeste wondered if she was the lady who brought the tomatoes, or if she'd just knocked them off the counter. She'd assumed she would be an older woman, but this woman was about thirty, pale under her hazelnut skin. She had a figure Jai would like. Wide backside and generous breasts. Right now she smelled like blood and a fragrant hair spray, mixed with cigarettes. They might have been flirting before the shooting. If so, it would have been harmless fun, like how Jai teased Celeste, because Jai was faithful to his wife. His wife and two daughters. The one who was studying to be a doctor and the other dedicated to partying, to giving her father sleepless nights.

Celeste swallowed on a hard lump.

"Monsters," the woman sobbed. She had a heavy Jamaican accent. "They are monsters. Jai did nothing to them."

Celeste held her, uttered something pointlessly soothing, but her gaze clung to Leland. He was doing what his training allowed to slow the blood flow, keep Jai responsive. His hands were covered in blood, too. When his gaze slid back to her, checking on them, she saw in his face what she already feared.

Jai's head turned, his hand fumbling to rest on Leland's arm. The store owner coughed, muttered something. Leland bent to hear him. As he did, his full lips twisted in an attempt at a smile. Jai's hand closed in a fist, beat a weak tattoo against his arm. Leland took his hand while holding pressure on the gunshot wound in his chest. So she saw when Jai's fingers loosened and that stillness set in. It was over.

§

Marigold was the woman who brought Jai those non-USDA approved tomatoes. Her gaze couldn't seem to leave them, the way they gleamed on the floor. When someone accidentally stepped on one, Marigold winced as if she'd been punched. There was about ten feet between her and Celeste, and they were under the supervision of one officer, Jack Bronski. She knew his job was not only to see to their comfort while they waited, but to minimize conversation between them. Witness statements tended to be more accurate if they hadn't discussed the scene with other witnesses.

Jack explained that to Marigold, but she looked as if she heard none of it. She was fixated on the tomatoes, mumbling to herself. Celeste asked Jack if they could collect them in a basket, give them back to the woman. Bless him, Bronski checked with the detective on scene and the crime techs and received the go-ahead. She suspected the officer who'd stepped on one had made the case for removing them from the floor before a bigger mess happened. When Celeste automatically rose to help, Jack put a firm but kind hand to her shoulder, keeping her in place on another stadium chair they'd opened up for her. He had one of the crime techs hand him a grocery bag from behind the counter, then squatted to collect the tomatoes. Marigold stifled a sob as Celeste stared at his long fingers closing over the shiny red spheres. For some reason, she felt a similar desire to cry over the simple, normal act. Gathering up tomatoes, putting them in a bag. Bronski brought them to Marigold, who held them like she was cradling a baby.

They were at the back of the store. Normally they might

have been parked outside until the detectives decided where they wanted to take their statements, but perhaps the death being caused by a drive-by had driven the decision to keep any material witnesses in the store. Most reporters would donate a kidney to be allowed to sit this close to a crime scene, but given that Jai had paid for her privilege with his life, Celeste couldn't derive any satisfaction from it. It was automatic for her to log comments and information as she heard and saw them, but the largest part of her mind was oddly fuzzy and disjointed. Besides which, her tablet was shattered on the concrete in the alley outside the store, and she had no idea where her paper notebook was.

Detective Toby Allen eventually came over and pulled her aside to get her statement. It was a relief to shift into her reporter mode and recall as much detail as possible. Yet when she was done, she couldn't remember a word she'd said, like a driver who couldn't remember parts of a long trip, lost to highway hypnosis. Detective Allen's gaze was approving, though, and he touched her shoulder, telling her she'd helped. He told her she was free to go, because they knew how to get hold of her. Nodding numbly, she moved toward the door.

"You okay?"

She found herself staring into the wall of Leland's body, standing in front of her. Celeste's gaze shifted to Leland's hands. He'd cleaned his off as well, but there was some on his shirt. He'd used something to dry the excess blood on his trousers where he'd knelt next to Jai, though she could still see the stains.

Her attention lifted to his face, the flat hardness of it. Yet when he said, "You okay?" she could tell her answer meant something to him.

She choked on a near sob, startling herself, but firmed her chin, never mind that her eyes were glassy with tears. "I'm good. You do what you have to do. Are *you* okay?"

"Yeah. No. He told me..." He shook his head. "Tell you later."

"Sarge?" Bronski had shifted forward, his eyes narrowing. "Are you..."

Celeste followed his gaze, and saw it too. Before Leland

could stop her, she yanked his shirt from his belt with enough force to make Leland wince. The tear in the fabric had been concealed by the bloodstain, and she'd assumed it was all Jai's blood. "You've been shot."

"Grazed," he corrected her, guiding her fingers along the wound so she could feel it was indeed shallow, no puncture. The blood had already clotted and dried over it. The firm touch of his hand had its usual steadying effect on her, though this time it also cracked open something deeper, and she couldn't pull away. As if he knew she needed it, he held on to her hand, let it stay resting on his waist over that graze. "Nothing to worry about, darlin'," he murmured, for her ears only. He touched her face, made her look at him, meet his gaze. "Okay?"

"Sarge, you know we have to--"

"Bronski, you finish that sentence, a report has to be filed. Every time my aunt sees 'officer-involved shooting' on the incident reports and finds out an officer was hit, she calls the captain and makes him tell her if it was me. He can withstand the press, the Mayor-President, the damn Metro Council, but we went to high school together and she can pull a lie out of him like giblets from a turkey's ass, same as me. He'll spill."

Bronski blinked. "It's just a graze," Leland said calmly. "But it will ruin her whole month and she'll be calling me every time I get off shift to make sure I'm home safe. If you put me through that kind of aggravation, I will dedicate my life to making yours utter hell. Are we clear? Besides which, it could be a scrape from the concrete when we went down. Or she did it." He looked at Celeste. "She tried to claw me to ribbons so she could chase the damn car like a rabid pit bull. We could charge her with assault on an officer, but I don't want to do that after the kind of day she's had. Wouldn't you agree?"

Celeste's mouth closed like a trap, her gaze narrowing to slits. Despite the seriousness of the situation, Bronski had to suppress a chuckle, covering it with a cough. "Yes, Sarge."

"Good." Leland looked at her. "You're not okay to drive. Bronski will take you home--"

Celeste latched both hands on him. "No," she said.

She wasn't sure what she was refusing. She knew she needed to go home and take a shower, put some antibiotic ointment on her leg. But he'd almost been shot, and Jai had died. Died in Leland's arms.

She could tell that hurt. Hurt deeply. They really didn't know each other that well yet, so she wasn't sure what he'd need in this kind of situation, but the image of him standing squarely in the sights of that assault weapon was pummeling her like a migraine.

"Don't make me leave," she said, low. "I want to be where I can see you. It was too close, Leland. Way...too close."

I just found you. Thank God she didn't say that aloud.

His jaw eased. "Yeah. Same goes, darlin'."

She stepped closer. Despite the speculative looks she was sure he'd get from the cops on scene, he didn't move away when she rested a hand on his chest. "What did Jai say to you?"

§

If she wanted to crack him open right here, she'd chosen the right thing to ask, but when Leland met her gaze, it was as if it was just the two of them. When an officer had to shoot someone, tunnel vision could set in immediately after. They were trained to immediately sweep their front, back and sides to keep that from happening, so no one could sneak up on them. She came right up in front of him, and she still took him by surprise. He closed his hand over hers, too rough because she winced, but he couldn't make himself release her, not immediately. But he did ease his grip.

"He looked at you, and said what he said that night. 'Pretty girl. Girls are good. They make you happy.' Then he looked at me and said, 'You tell my girls they made me happy.'" Leland cleared his throat. "I told him that he'd tell them that himself, but he said, 'A man knows. When he's not afraid, he knows.'"

"If I hadn't chased them, I wouldn't have given them an excuse--"

"Don't," he said shortly. "This is all on them. Thanks to you we have the plate and an ID on one of the shooters."

Her gaze dropped to his hand, gripping hers. Neither of them were letting go, and she could feel his eyes locked on her face. He raised his voice. "Bronski?"

"Yeah, Sarge?"

"I'm going to take Miss Lewis home. Can you escort our other witness to her home, make sure she has someone there with her before you leave? She said she has a sister in the same apartment building."

"Sure thing, Sarge."

When Leland escorted Celeste out of the store and onto the sidewalk, moving her toward his car, Celeste had a brief glimpse of the alley. Her shattered tablet had been thrown violently to the cracked sidewalk when Leland had shoved her down beneath him, and then one or both of them had stepped on it when they'd scrambled out of the alley. Thank God she'd backed it up this morning.

A couple crime techs were pulling bullets out of the side of the store. She saw at least four or five holes, and though her perspective could be skewed, when she pictured herself there, she knew they would have punched through her chest. Dogboy might be a psycho, but he had good aim.

He hadn't gotten her, though. Every muscle hurt like she had the flu, and she had a bad scrape on her leg, her slacks torn where Leland had tackled her and taken her to the pavement. But if he hadn't, she'd be headed the same direction as Jai was now. In a black bag to the morgue.

She was shaking again. Leland pulled a coat out of his car and wrapped it around her, guiding her hands into the roomy sleeves and bundling her into it like a cocoon.

"I'm fine," she said distantly, though she couldn't tear her eyes from that wall or pull away from him. "I'm good. I'm all right."

Chapter Ten

She was better than all right. She'd been fucking heroic. He shouldn't be surprised that she'd responded to getting shot at the way most cops did. She'd been full-blown pissed and ready to go after the asshole with her bare hands. Leland kept a watchful eye on her as he navigated through traffic.

He'd had to deal with the Shooting Review Team and IA on-site since he'd fired his weapon, but he'd tried to keep an eye on her as much as possible during that time as well. Hell, after what had happened, he really didn't want her out of his sight for the next decade. While she was waiting, Bronski had escorted her to the bathroom Jai had in the back. When she returned, she'd cleaned herself up some, more to steady herself than for vanity's sake, he was sure. She was still pale, but her gaze was steady and sharp. Yet when they'd walked out to the car she'd lost that focus again, her gaze going to the alley. He'd put a firm hand on her lower back, ushered her into the car.

He'd been glad they'd taken Jai away when she was in the bathroom. Watching a person you knew get zipped into a body bag was a wrenching feeling he wanted to spare her. The coroner would notify the family, but Leland would find out when the funeral was so he could pay his condolences. Celeste would probably want to go as well.

He didn't expect Jai's family would know either of them as anything more than one story among the many that Jai brought home to them. Yet hearing from people who thought well of the victim usually helped the family. Jai had been one of the good influences in a tough community, which meant today that community was a notch bleaker. It filled him with anger, made him wish his bullet had shattered the back window and blown out the back of Dogboy's head. Which wasn't a good thought to be having, he knew that, but it didn't make it less true. Or any more useful than his wish that they'd made that happen before the car turned the corner and headed down Jai's street.

He reached out, put his hand over hers on the seat.

She'd remained silent, an unusual state for her. Any other time, he would have teased her about that. But neither of them was in a teasing mood.

Her head tilted away from the window. In his peripheral vision he saw her looking down at their clasped hands. She moved her other hand to cover his. Then she lifted it with both hands, pressed her face into his palm. The gesture created an eye in the storm inside him, a still, potent place as she kissed his callused skin, her lashes feathering against his fingers. He felt the precise slope of her nose beneath them.

He'd just watched the life slide out of a man, as impossible to stop as a child who'd pushed off that no-going-back point on a tall waterslide. The child left nothing behind to hold except the last image of a laughing face. Whereas a man's body did what it did as it succumbed to death, the blood no longer pumping out, the eyes getting that vacant look.

In the organized chaos that had happened after the drive-by, the shouting of orders, the status check to ensure no one had holes in them, he'd been pulling Manny to his feet. It had been pure chance, the fortunate angle of his body, which had allowed Leland to catch the quick movement across the street, Celeste disappearing down the alley. If he'd had his head down an extra second, he wouldn't have known where to look for her. If he hadn't pushed himself during every workout, telling himself the bad guys didn't give any breaks for him being forty instead of twenty, or if he'd been born any shorter, with legs any less long, he might not have caught up to her. He'd shouted at her as he'd run down that alley, but she'd been flying on adrenaline, unable to hear him. The time between when he caught her about the waist and threw her down beneath him and when those bullets had pulverized the wall above them had been less than an indrawn breath. The impression of slim bones, quivering muscle and silken skin, the smell of her hair, was even briefer before he'd shoved himself up to get a shot off at the vehicle, but they'd imprinted themselves upon him like a brand.

He pulled into the driveway of her small rental house. It wasn't in the best area of Baton Rouge by a long shot, but it was a friendly neighborhood, mostly working-class young families with kids, if the scattering of tiny bikes and toys left in a few yards were any indication. He used his opposite hand to turn off the vehicle, because she wouldn't let go when he began to pull away. The press of her lips against the heel of his hand became more purposed. Her lips parted and he felt the moistness of her breath, the touch of her tongue on his life line before her lips closed there again. Her eyes had closed, but he could feel the tension thrumming through her as she dipped her head, nuzzled him. Moving to his wrist, she put her teeth there, bit, then rubbed her face there as well.

Sometimes if the late night sports didn't have anything of interest, he'd switch to a documentary. Her behavior now reminded him of one he'd seen about lions. A pride whiling away the afternoon in tall golden grass, one of the lionesses cozied up to the male just like this. Showing her affection, marking him as her mate with the stroking of her face against him.

Reaction surged through him. Fury, need, and something too primal to voice. Her gaze lifted and met his, and he saw a mirror of his own feelings in those vivid hazel eyes.

"Stay there," he said. He extricated his hand and exited the car, grabbing a fresh shirt out of the trunk before he circled around and opened her door. Her eyes were wide, her face still too pale. He took her hand, brought her out of the car. When they reached her porch, she gazed up at him, as if waiting for him to open her door. She wasn't fully registering that they were at her place. She was still in a state of detachment, but what was humming off her skin wasn't detached enough. It was as if she was in a different dimension with him right now, everything sharp and vibrant. He couldn't stop thinking about her scent, the way she'd trembled beneath him. The glory of her rage at a guy carrying an assault rifle, as if her rage alone could incinerate him. His need was a fire in his blood that could match hers.

"Keys, darlin'."

She blinked, focused enough to fish them out. He unlocked the door, swept his gaze over the interior. He was pretty certain of the answer, but asked to be sure. "Do you live alone?"

"Yes."

"Good." He secured the door behind them, unbuttoned the bloodstained shirt and stripped it off his shoulders in a blink, leaving him in the dark-blue T-shirt beneath. She was staring at him. Clamping one hand on her upper arm and banding the other around her waist, he lifted and pinned her against the wall with his full weight, slamming his mouth onto hers.

If he'd had any doubts about the signals she'd been giving off, they were gone in that first second. Her legs and arms locked around him and a harsh moan ripped from her throat, her body shuddering.

It wasn't about foreplay or seduction. Hell, he wasn't sure it was even about sex. He kissed her hard and deep, tongue taking over her mouth, teeth scraping her. She clung to his shoulders, rocked against him. Too many clothes. He put her down, yanked open her slacks as she was toeing off the shoes. When they tried to shove the slacks and underwear down and off, they damn near bumped heads. He caught her by the throat, pinned her against the wall, gave her a hard look to make her stay there as he dropped to one knee and pulled the pants off either leg. Her fingers whispered over his back, his shirt collar, caught there and clung. He spread his fingers out against her thighs, the contrast of alabaster skin against his tan-brown skin, and made her cry out as he put his mouth between her legs. He forced them open wider with the grip of his hands and the insistence of his invasion, tongue-fucking her and finding her already slick, ready for him. He sucked on her clit and she damn near came from that, arching up against his mouth and almost walking up the wall with the writhing of her body.

Setting aside his belt with his weapon, he rose, opening his trousers. As he gripped his turgid cock, he coiled an arm around her waist and gave her the hitch to put her up against the wall again. Her hands slid up his chest, locked around his neck. Another rough, needy sound broke from her throat as he pinned her once again, this time by thrusting his cock as deep into her cunt as he could manage.

She let out a gasp, her eyes widening at his size, filling and stretching her. Yeah, it was one of the weird ironies of life that fear could make a man's cock shrivel up and hide, but surviving a brush with death turned it into a pile driver.

He needed to take it easy, but the bite of her nails, the parting of her lips, said otherwise. He kept ramming into her, a steady tattoo of impact against the wall as their two bodies strained to get close and even closer. She hiked herself up further, arms wrapped fully around his shoulders, her back rounded so he felt the vulnerable ridge of her spine under her shirt as she laid her face against the side of his, breath rasping in his ear. For his part, he had one hand gripping her ass so hard he'd leave bruises, the other remaining banded around her waist as he kept bringing her down on him.

"Don't mean...to hurt you..." he said, the apology the best he could do.

She shook her head and gripped him tighter inside and out, cunt muscles squeezing down on him. "I want it to hurt. Please..."

He shifted his hand from her ass up to cradle the back of her head, first to protect it from him hammering her against the wall and next to dig his fingers into her hair, pull her head back and set his teeth to her throat. She emitted a feminine growl, a spirited surrender. He felt her body start to gather itself, knew she was trying to keep herself off the edge, waiting for him. He was more than ready.

"Go over now," he demanded. "Let me hear you."

She did both, a beautiful symphony from her arched throat, her pussy convulsing on him and pushing him over the same edge. He came harder and longer than he expected, but he couldn't stop. Not with her. Not until every drop was spilled inside her.

When they finally coasted in for a bumpy landing, he was aware of the bite of her nails through his shirt, how tightly he was holding her head and waist. He hadn't removed his shirt or hers, yet they were still melded together from groin to chest, and he wasn't sure her arms could be removed from around him without a crowbar. He didn't mind. He didn't want to let go of her either. He braced his forehead against the wall next to hers and inhaled her hair. He didn't think he'd ever get tired of doing that. She streaked the chestnut brown with some kind of blondish highlights and the scent of the thick strands was fragrant and elusive. Delicate but memorable and enduring, like the woman herself.

She was still breathing erratically, but she brushed her lips against his ear. "What do you have to say, Sergeant?"

"Girls are pretty. Girls are good."

She snuffled against him, part chuckle, part sob. He cradled her face, holding them temple to cheek as they drew a different kind of strength from one another. "Damn it," she said. "Life is just too hard sometimes. Poor Jai. His family. That stupid, awful, fucked-up kid. Damn it, damn it, damn it."

"Yeah." He was so steeped in her, his phone rang twice before he identified the muffled sound from his belt. "Hell, I didn't log out. Let me get that."

"It would have taken longer to log out than to do what we just did," she said dryly. "You do get coffee or smoke breaks, right?"

"Smart-ass." He gave her a pinch, but eased her down, made sure she was steady before he fastened his pants, zipped up and fished out the phone. "Keller."

He scooped up her slacks and panties and offered them to her. Trying to be a gentleman to make up for the beast he'd been, though his beauty didn't seem dissatisfied. Celeste gathered them to her with a faint smile, then hooked her thumb in the general vicinity of what he assumed was her bedroom and plucked at her shirt, stained from Marigold's bloody hands clutching at her. He nodded and she disappeared that way.

"Keller, you there? I said, it's Detective Allen."

"Yeah, Toby, sorry. What's up?"

"Are you still with Miss Lewis?"

"We just got to her house." Leland donned the fresh shirt and tucked it in, then picked up his belt, buckled it back in place as he held the phone under his ear.

"Good. Just wanted to give you a heads up. We've still got some work to do, but the bullet track on your side of the street at the drive-by was high. At first we figured whoever was shooting just had lousy aim. But what didn't make sense to me was them shooting out of both windows of the car. The opposite side of the street is mixed use, a few stores with apartments over them. No cops were over there, no one from the Reigning Kings or MoneyBoyz was hanging out. No reason to shoot in that direction at all. Then we noticed the shots on that side only hit where Miss Lewis was sitting. They dogged her escape path like a coonhound."

Leland's gut went cold. "If I hadn't seen that," Allen continued, "I would have assumed shooting at the two of you at the convenience store was incidental, but looking at what I've got so far, I think the initial shots at our crime scene were to pin us down. The shots at her--"

"She was their target. Son of a bitch. One of the shooters, she was in his face recently about the killing of that prostitute on Compton Court. Had her suspicions he was the doer."

"It's looking like he didn't just do DeeDee. I work with Marquez, who's running the Stiles case as well. She apparently made a connection to the same guy for that. He's done some follow-up, and Earl Edward James has gone from a person of interest to our main suspect as of this afternoon. Maybe he didn't realize she'd already shared that information with us."

"I don't think that matters to him." Since his talk with Mike, Leland had pulled up Dogboy's rap sheet and talked to a few others on his shift who had dealt with the teenager. "My guys say he's probably a loose cannon with a looser screw. If he killed both of the women, he's no Ted Bundy. Just a dumb, fucked-up kid who's gotten himself hooked on killing and can't stop himself. The question is, will the MoneyBoyz help him out with Celeste?"

"Hard to say. You know none of these groups are all that organized yet."

Thank God, Leland thought. They caused enough trouble as loose affiliations. "But he might have a few friends willing to help him out. Like today."

"Yeah. Until I find out more, she needs to be somewhere else for a few days. Out of town, preferably, and she shouldn't be showing up at any of her regular haunts. Like her home. I've already sent a couple uniforms your way to flank the place."

Leland glanced out the window to see them pulling up. They'd had enough units today, so Mike and Billy were driving separate cars, Billy looking like he'd been given the keys to his first Camaro. Stepping out on the porch, Leland acknowledged them with a wave so they knew all was good inside. "They're here. Thanks, Toby."

"You got it. Talk to her about getting out of town. Word is the two of you are dating."

"The word does travel fast."

"Nobody does gossip like cops," Toby said dryly. "We all know she broke her unbreakable rule about dating cops for you. It's probably asking a lot, but dig deep and summon up some charm. See if you can't get her ass out of town. Lot of the guys are fond of it."

"Tell them to keep their focus on her journalistic integrity and off her ass." He injected humor into his voice, but it was forced, too many serious variables running through his mind.

"Yeah, like that will happen. Gotta go. Tell her to call if she remembers anything else."

"Will do." When he clicked off, Leland knew the reminder wouldn't be necessary. Her trained mind was probably already running back over the details, trying to remember every scrap of useful information.

"Celeste?"

"Here." She emerged from the back, wearing jeans and a clean, long sleeved shirt covered with a swirling gold-green version of Van Gogh's *The Starry Night*. It picked up the colors in her eyes. She'd brushed her hair, the strands falling over her brow. The three studs in one ear winked brown and green. "Okay, I feel more like myself. Not really, but armor is everything, right? Protects all the squishy stuff inside. God." She shook her head. "I sound like an idiot."

"No, you don't." He came to her, took her hands, which were nervously fluttering. He wasn't sure if the day's events were understandably keeping her at loose ends, or if she was unsettled by what they'd just done, or some of both. In truth, the intensity of it had surprised him as well. He hoped her lack of balance would help him now, though.

"You need to pack a bag for several days."

She looked up at him. As she did, she saw the additional units parked out front. Her brow furrowed. "Why are they here?" She put a hand up to her mouth to stifle a giggle. "Thank God they didn't arrive ten minutes ago. That could have been awkward."

She was experiencing the fluctuating emotions, both appropriate and inappropriate, that accompanied this kind of ordeal, but he couldn't help but smile at her. It helped lessen the weight on his chest as well.

"Dogboy was after you, Celeste."

She blinked, refocused on him. "What?"

"You were the target. They were firing at us just to keep us pinned down."

He could have broken that news a little less harshly, but she'd want the truth, unembellished. Part of him also wanted to scare her, make it easier to protect her. Knowing her, that wasn't going work for more than a heartbeat, but the cop in him was all about keeping her safe, no matter how much of a bastard he had to be about it.

She listened to what Allen had told him. "I agree. He's about as clever and subtle as a punch in the face. So he'll be picked up, go to prison and that will be that."

"Yeah, once he's picked up. He lives with a couple guys in a shithole about a mile from our crime scene. We might get lucky and he'll go back there, but I think it more likely he'll hole up in another shithole and keep moving around. It's probably going to take a couple days for us to use our eyes on the street to figure out where he's gone, and that's if he doesn't try to skip town."

"True," she said. It was both alarming and impressive that she didn't react with fear, but her next words told him the reporter had taken over. "I'm not sure he will, though. He starts with a high-risk victim like Loretta Stiles, then kills a prostitute? And marks both crime scenes with the dog signature? I don't think he's interested in covering his tracks. More like challenging the world to gun him down, daring you to stop him."

"Suicide by cop," he confirmed. "So go pack a bag. Do you have someone you can stay with out of town for a few days?"

His first extremely strong impulse was to have her stay at his house, but being near her stomping ground was too much of a temptation. She could get bored when he was on shift and decide to go talk to just one source, or something foolish like that.

She shrugged. "There are always things I can do in New Orleans, but I really don't think it's necessary. Dogboy was looking for me at a crime scene he'd know I cover, not at my home. I don't advertise where I live."

"All he'd have to do is follow you home. Or have one of the MoneyBoyz do it." He put his hands on her shoulders again. "If he has their support in this, you're not looking at one person gunning for you. It could be the entire gang."

That elicited a flicker of concern from her, but her brow creased. "I'm not seeing it. An unstable personality like his is going to be a liability. They're not going to take out a target whose murder would expose their trade and suppliers to extra scrutiny. Jai's death"--she hitched over the word but pressed on--"is already going to turn up the heat."

"But you've written articles that take swipes at the Baton Rouge drug business. They might see settling Dogboy's issue as a benefit for them, long term."

"Swipes only," she said frankly. "I was following some leads, but I hadn't even dinged them yet. So right now, I'm not worth the effort."

The idea of her following leads to the heart of the city's illegal drug trade was enough to give him nightmares, but he set that aside for now, with effort. "Maybe not. But violent criminals aren't always as reasonable and clear thinking as you'd expect." He tightened his grip on her. "Celeste, I'm about a breath away from being a hard-ass about this, and I know that means you'll get your hackles up and we'll fight." He touched her face. "I'm not in the mood for a fight. How about you?"

She held his gaze, then shook her head, took a deep breath. "No. So...the wedding's Saturday anyway. Right?"

"Yeah."

"Well, I'll pack a bag and go check into a hotel in New Orleans for a few days." She shifted her gaze to the right of his shoulder. "Maybe you could join me at the hotel and we could spend a weekend there, go to the wedding together."

"So if it's your idea, us going to the wedding together is okay?"

"Of course." She tossed her hair out of her eyes.

"Trying to hold on to control," he noted. "You know that's not going to work that often with me, right?"

He touched her chin with a curved finger, slid it down beneath and along her throat, making her eyes get that wary yet needy look that made him wish today had gone differently. That they both weren't too wired up to slow it down, make those Dom/sub vibes come to full, pulsating life between them.

"And you think you being all macho and domineering will work with me?" she retorted.

"In a way, yeah." He leaned down, feeling the pulse in her throat jump as he came closer. "Especially if I tell you I'm going to tan your hide for chasing after that car."

"But you wouldn't have the plate number if I hadn't. You said..."

"Two different things, darlin'. I'm proud of you for being brave and doing such a fine job, just like I'll get a kick out of busting your ass for risking it."

She processed that, visibly struggling with whether he'd just paid her a compliment or insulted her. He almost had to bite back a grin at her expression. Yeah, she wanted that punishment now, but she was going to be spitting and clawing all the way, just to get back at him at the same time.

"Go pack a bag," he said. "Now."

She sniffed and pivoted, but he caught her arm, pulling her back to kiss her sneering mouth until it slackened and the claws she put into his forearm eased into a sensual bite. When he lifted his head, she was staring at him. As he stood still, she put her hand on his face, outlining his cheekbone, the corner of his mouth. Wariness had turned into that vague panic mixed with irritation he was beginning to recognize as her bratting cue. Or, given they had no time for that kind of interaction right now, the prelude to an actual fight. But he was betting she was where he was on it. It wasn't a day for fighting.

"It's all right," he said quietly. "We'll work it out, Celeste. It is what it is. Don't question it today."

She bent her head, which put her temple against his jaw. When his arms closed around her, she let out a little sigh. Her willingness to accept his comfort gave him an injection of strength he didn't expect. She whispered something against his shirt he couldn't decipher, so when she pushed away, he caught her fingers before she could head for her bedroom.

"What was that?"

"Nothing. I called you a jerk."

"No you didn't." He only had three of her fingers in his grasp, and those only at the last knuckle, but he saw her discomfiture when she couldn't get him to let go. "Tell me, Celeste."

Her gaze lifted at that, because he'd deliberately employed the tone he would have used with her in session. She pursed her lips, started to shift her gaze.

"No. Look at me when you answer me."

That increased her discomfort. When he felt a tremor go through her, saw the sudden misery in her eyes, he relented. It wasn't a time for pushing, so he set aside his Dom nature and let her go, though he gave her an even look that said they'd pick it up another time. Her hand slipped from his and she moved across her small living room toward the hallway, but when she reached it, she paused. Looking over her shoulder, she met his gaze. Her lips quivered, uncertain petals, her eyes too large for her slim face.

"'Yes, sir.' That's what I said."

Then she vanished like smoke.

To settle his own reaction to that, Leland went back out on the porch. He nodded to Mike, leaning on his car, talking to Billy, and both men gave him a brief acknowledgment in return. Leland took out his phone, dialed. The guy he was calling always answered his personal cell, an indication that the very small selection of people who had that number were those he'd consider a priority call. Not surprising, since Matt Kensington, the CEO of Kensington and Associates, was pretty particular about who he let into his inner circle.

"Leland." The Yale-educated Texas drawl on the other end was filled with warmth. "Always a pleasure to hear from you. If you're calling to tell me you can make it up here Friday night, Peter's got a Kentucky bourbon with your name on it. You're welcome to join our gathering to keep Ben from bolting."

"I've met his fiancée. If he even thinks of bolting, shoot him between the eyes because he's too stupid to live."

"I wouldn't dare deprive her of that pleasure. But she'll let us hold him down for her to do it."

"Marcie's a Southern belle through and through."

Matt chuckled. "What can I do for you?"

That was another thing he liked about Matt. The man knew Leland wasn't much on chitchat and wouldn't be calling without purpose.

"You know Celeste Lewis."

"Very well and with great fondness. I subscribe to her blog and follow her articles in the papers when she freelances. She's a hell of a reporter."

"Yeah, she is." And he meant it. "She's run into some trouble up here."

Briefly, Leland explained the situation. Normally the details of an ongoing case weren't discussed with a civilian without clearance, but he considered Matt and his four-man executive team trusted confidants.

"What can we do to help you protect her?" Matt's tone had changed in a blink, now sharp and serious. "What do you need?"

"A safe place for her to go for a few days. I don't know if he's going to have gang support on this or not. They're small time, but there's always the chance they might have their own sources for hacking email accounts and tracking credit card use. I'd like her to stay somewhere where they won't expect her to be and where she doesn't have to have a paper trail."

"Marcie's back at Lucas and Cassandra's this week. Something about the tradition of the groom not seeing the bride before the event, though I think there's more to it than that, because Ben's been broody as hell. Nothing the wedding won't fix. Celeste could stay with them."

Leland felt a twinge of conscience. "She said she and

Marcie were friends, but I'm not sure how well." He for damn sure was aware of how well she knew Ben. It was absurd to have any territorial growls over a one-night session she had with another Dom, but he knew that was exactly what had prompted him to strip the condom the other night and take her without it, marking her in a way as primal as the Neanderthal she'd accused him of being. He'd told Celeste she'd show him that video eventually, but it would be as tough for him to sit through it as it would be uncomfortable for her, for far different reasons.

Yeah, okay, he was a caveman. Whatever.

"When Celeste lived here, they used to spar at the gym together weekly," Matt said. "They exchange birthday gifts and usually grab lunch when Celeste comes here for a story. So I'd say pretty tight. Celeste came up for one of the wedding showers a few weeks ago." He paused. "What's the likelihood this bastard would track her down and try to get at her in that kind of environment? That will tell me how to reinforce things there."

"I wouldn't ask if I thought it was anything more than a lightning strike possibility. This guy is starting to unravel fast, and my guess is his associates will give him up pretty quick rather than risk him jeopardizing their day-to-day."

"All right. Unraveled can be unpredictable. I'll assign Max there for night duty. I'm sure he'll ask his friend Dale to take shifts with him so one of them is on the property or with her at all times."

Leland felt a surge of emotion at Matt's generosity. Max, the head limo driver at K&A, was a former Navy SEAL, and his buddy Dale was a retired SEAL.

"Janet will make me pay for that. Are she and Max married yet?"

"Still considering it, but it's a moot point for them. They know they're it for each other."

"Yeah. It can be like that, I guess."

"I guess." The amusement in Matt's voice as he parroted him had Leland hunching his shoulders. "Okay. I'll bring her up in the next few hours. Should I call Marcie?"

"No, I'll handle that. She and Cassandra are out until late tonight doing some things, but Lucas will be there. You just focus on Celeste."

"Thanks, Matt. I know this is bad timing. I'm sure you're all up to your eyeballs in wedding planning."

"The women are up to their eyeballs. They just want us out of the way. Janet is the head of that ship, so she'll probably be fine having Max assigned elsewhere for a few days. I had to type up a memo by myself this morning because she was resolving some worse-than-famine-or-flood crisis involving wine glasses."

"Memo typing. Can't imagine anything more traumatic than that."

"Janet put far less effort into hiding her sarcasm when she said almost the same thing." Matt's amusement registered through the phone. "I appreciate your restraint. Oh, and Lucas said to tell 'The Duke' he'd have a hitching post set up to park your white horse at the wedding."

Leland chuckled, tension easing. "Asshole. Listen, Matt, I know Celeste is going to resist the idea, so if it's at all possible for Marcie to give her a quick call and ask her to come, I think it would go over better."

"That's what I was thinking. She'll see through it, as will Marcie, but Marcie likely can use an additional hand."

"I wouldn't ask, except--"

"You're sure it's necessary." Matt sobered again. "Don't give it a second thought, Leland. Marcie would be the first to tell you that keeping a friend safe trumps everything else. Especially if that person is more than a friend."

Leland pursed his lips. "Yeah."

"So how long have you two been seeing one another?"

"You asking for me or for your wife?"

"My wife, of course."

"Good. I thought I was going to have to pull your man card."

"You know if I crack the seal on that bourbon, it'll be long gone before you get here. Answer the question."

"Long enough." If there was anyone who could understand that statement, the man on the other end would. Like everyone else who knew Leland, Matt was aware he hadn't been dating much these past couple years, so if he was seeing someone now, she mattered. It wasn't casual. Matt was a Dom through and through himself, which meant he'd deduce the nature of their relationship, or at least the way it seemed to be headed. As that *Yes, sir* went through Leland's mind again, he increased his grip on the porch rail. Did she know that every step she made toward opening up to him like that just made him want to bind her to him all the more?

"Fair enough," Matt said smoothly. "We'll be having a more intimate get-together that night after the reception, at Ben's Garden District place. You and she are welcome to join us if you feel comfortable. It will just be the core group plus a very small handful of trusted friends. Ben's converted the whole floor into a private dungeon. You'd have some excellent options to explore together."

"Appreciate that." The idea definitely sparked some interest, now that he was feeling a little less uptight about her whereabouts for the next few days. But he wouldn't get ahead of himself. She still had to agree to stay with Marcie, let alone agree to anything else. "We'll keep it in mind. Thanks, Matt."

"Not a problem. See you in a few days. Marcie will call her within the hour."

Leland clicked off, putting the phone at his belt as he stepped back inside. He heard Celeste moving around in her bedroom, so now that he had some time, he took a closer look at his surroundings. The night he'd picked Celeste up, she'd practically met him on the curb, but he could see why she'd been reluctant to let him into her house.

She didn't have a home. She had an office and storage facility. Clippings were spread out on the kitchen table, some fanned out together, some grouped in stacks. The back wall of her kitchen nook was all corkboard, covered with clippings, pictures and sticky notes.

He swept his glance around the room. The couch had a bed pillow and a rumpled blanket on it, a fitted sheet over the cushions telling him that was where she preferred to sleep. No pictures on the walls. Just bare and white, not that the starkness was too noticeable with the magazines, books, notebooks and files stacked up on chairs and scattered over the top of the entertainment center and coffee table. Her TV was a painfully small flat screen, sitting on top of some books in the middle of the much larger opening provided by the entertainment center. From the furniture's scarred appearance, he expected she'd picked it up from a secondhand store.

Except for some pretty little figurines on her kitchen window ledge, he didn't see any indication she was into decorating or personalizing her space. However, she was conscious of cleanliness. No dirty dishes in the sink, and the one countertop in the kitchen she wasn't using for her work was clean. The place smelled good, like her, that vanilla flower fragrance, mixed with the smell of books and paper. The wood floor was vacuumed. She didn't mind clutter, but she didn't like dirt. Other than her bedroom, it looked like the house had one other room beyond the hallway bathroom. That room was probably a guestroom she'd turned into additional office space.

He was curious about her bedroom and backyard, to know if anything more personal could be found there. She'd had a couple potted flowers on the front porch, lush groupings of purple-and-gold pansies, easy to find in a city devoted to its LSU Tigers. He could hear drawers opening and closing, the occasional mutter as she talked to herself about whether this or that might be the right thing to take. He only caught snippets of that, but he registered the tone of her voice. Still unsettled by the situation, but doing okay. He'd rein himself back, stay out here, give her space.

Stepping closer to the corkboard wall, he saw that her surroundings might be cluttered, but her mind was extremely well-ordered. He quickly found the relevant pieces she'd used to put together Dogboy's involvement in the murders of the hookers and Loretta Stiles. Who would have thought to connect animal control reports on dead dogs to two murders? And she'd asked the right questions, been in the right places to find out about Dogboy, his involvement in the store owner beating.

Figuring out crimes was the detectives' bailiwick, but looking at the details she'd put together, Leland understood why the captain had a good opinion of her. Her generous heart was evident here as well. She'd pinned up a school picture of Loretta Stiles, a pretty fifteen-year-old with a shy smile and intelligent eyes who would never get any older.

Leland remembered her face had been severely beaten, her body stabbed both by knife and rape. He put his hand on the picture. When his gaze shifted to another picture in the same section, he fished out his reading glasses and leaned in to get a better look.

The snapshot had been taken outside. The woman, obviously a prostitute, had struck a sassy pose and smiled at the camera, a tight-lipped gesture likely to hide bad teeth. She had sharp cheekbones and a delicate wrist, revealed under her sleeve because she'd lifted her hand to hold the side of her head as she threw it back, a jaunty starlet pose with her hip cocked. He saw a drug habit in the set of her face, the look in her eyes, but there was also laughter in her expression. As if it had tickled her to be asked for a picture.

"When I get to know my sources well enough, I take a photo of them," Celeste said, coming to stand beside him. She folded a garment bag over a chair and propped a small rolling suitcase next to it. "DeeDee obliged."

Just as he'd done with Loretta Stiles, she stepped closer to put her hand on DeeDee's picture. "She was smoking a cigarette, offered me a drag. I hadn't smoked since I was a teenager, so I said no. She acted all outraged. 'Bitch, you think I gonna give you a disease? You too good to put your lips where mine have been? Shit, can't blame you on that. You'd run screaming if you had to put your lips where mine have been.'"

Celeste did a credible imitation of a street hustler, such that Leland's lips twitched, though he didn't smile, because her eyes didn't smile. They stayed focused on DeeDee. "So I reach for the cigarette, fine. She jerks it out of reach and smacks at my hand. 'Bitch, you crazy? You don't smoke the cigarette of a skanky ho. Your pretty lips will rot and fall off.' Then she laughed at me and strolled away. 'I gotta work. You go do what you do. We both make the world a better place, right?'"

Celeste's gaze slid from there to a clipping from the newspaper. Just a couple paragraphs, no headline to it, though she'd penned the date in the corner. She put her hand on it, two fingertips covering the scrap of paper. "When someone is killed," she said, "the killer becomes the important one. The one who gets the press as we all speculate why he did it, how he did it, how much suffering did he inflict. Rather than how much suffering she endured. It bugs me. There are so many that don't seem to matter, but everyone matters. There are all sorts of voices in dark corners of the world, where they feel like if they screamed at the top of their lungs, no one would ever hear them."

He reached out to touch her, but she moved away. Without her hand on the article, he saw it was a clipping from the newspaper's crime report summary about DeeDee's death. No name given. He shifted his gaze back to Celeste, who had pivoted, her gaze sweeping the room as she grimaced.

"It's like Mel Gibson's place in *Conspiracy Theory*. I was going to clean it up, and then I figured I'd be better off just renting someone's house for the day and telling you that's where I live. Especially after I saw your place. What guy is that neat? Makes me feel like a freak."

"Celeste." He stepped up to her again, closed his hand on her wrist to hold her in place. She turned her green-gold gaze to him.

"I wish you'd killed him today," she said. "I don't care if that's right or wrong. I know he probably had a fucked-up childhood, but a lot of us do. Doesn't give him the right, you know?"

"No, it doesn't. If I had killed him, I wouldn't be sorry in the least. Because then you wouldn't be in danger now."

She shook her head. "I'm not dismissing your concern, but I really can't imagine he's going to go out of his way to track me down. He went the easiest route to find me today."

"Maybe, but I'd rather not take any chances. I called--"

Her phone started to ring and Leland stifled a curse. He should have told Matt to give him at least thirty minutes. He hadn't wanted Marcie's call to be the first Celeste was hearing of his plan for her. But when she glanced at the view screen and her expression clouded, he knew that wasn't the expression she'd have if she was receiving a call from a friend.

"Hey, Trice. What's going on?"

§

"Not a lot." But her sister didn't really call unless she needed something, so Celeste made a noncommittal sound and waited for her to continue. Fortunately, Patrice didn't make her usual effort toward pointless small talk, a pretense that she'd called for social reasons. Good. Celeste just wasn't in the mood today.

"Can you do me a big favor, Celly? I know it's a pain in the ass. I have a small box of stuff at Mom's. I know I should have picked it up last time I was in town, but you know how she is. I was just wanting to get the hell out of there and forgot it. Well, she called to say she needs to dump some stuff because she might be selling the trailer, et cetera, et cetera, but basically she's moving another new guy in with her. I'm afraid if I ask her to hold it for me until the next time I'm in town, she'll just toss it. There are a couple things in it I'd really like to have."

"Who's the guy?"

"Don't know and didn't ask. She sounded in a hurry when she called me anyhow."

As usual. Celeste closed her eyes, rubbed her temple.

"I'm really, really sorry to ask. I know you hate going out there." Her sister sounded suitably chagrined. Celeste didn't blame Patrice for calling only when she needed something. There was no reason to pretend they were poster children for World's Greatest Family. As the oldest child, Celeste had made sure her two brothers and her sister finished high school, got out of that trailer park, but there hadn't been room for a lot of touching *Little House on the Prairie* scenes during that struggle.

"No, it's okay. It might take me a few days to get to it." At Leland's quizzical gaze, she put her hand over the phone. "My sister needs me to pick up a box at my mom's."

"We can get it on the way if you want."

It was bad enough Leland was seeing her living space. Letting him see where she'd grown up and having him meet her mother? Not happening.

So she shook her head, ignored the disappointment in Trice's voice. "I promise I'll do it soon, Trice. Hopefully before the end of the week. Don't worry. I'll call Mom and tell her to hold on to it until then."

"Oh, okay." Relief took over from disappointment. "You're the only one she halfway pays attention to anyway. It should be fine, then. Uh, I have to get back to work. Hope everything's good there?"

Translation: Please just say fine so we don't have to stay on the phone with one another. "Yep. All's good here. I'll text you when I ship the box."

"Celeste, we have time," Leland said when she clicked off. "Unless she's hell and gone in the opposite direction."

Her mother lived just outside Baton Rouge, right on the route toward New Orleans. She was tempted to tell him she lived in Texas or California or Alaska, but what would happen when he found out differently? Thinking about her relationship with him lasting that long was unsettling enough. She wouldn't inject a lie into the mix.

"Not today," she said shortly. "I just can't deal with my mom today."

"Even if you have a cop at your back?" His brow creased. "Is that the problem? Why I'm escorting you to New Orleans might upset her?"

"No, not really." She could show up on her mother's doorstep with a Secret Service protection detail, have open boils on her face and be wearing a clown costume, and her mother would never think to ask her anything about herself. Then she bit her lip, because she could have seized that opening as the best reason not to go by. She needed to work on her ability to lie to him. Yeah, because that was the secret to a successful relationship, right?

Leland stepped closer to her again. If he took her hand, it gave her that feeling of safety, of warmth. When he gripped her wrist as he did now, his fingers caressing her pulse and palm, that feeling was enhanced by a weakening in her knees, a funny feeling in her belly, especially when he combined it with the chin tip, holding her face. "Celeste, what's the problem? Mama will have a stroke and die if she sees you're involved with a black guy?"

"If I thought that would happen, I'd take you there in a heartbeat." Oh Christ, she hadn't meant that. She shook her head at his look. "Sorry. When we were growing up, the white girls in the trailer park would do that sometimes. Bring black boys home to upset their parents. It's sort of like that, but not what you think."

"Are you ashamed of being with me?" He asked the question neutrally and her brows shot up to her hairline.

"Seriously? No. Double no." She sighed. "The worst she'll do on that score is pull me off to the side and say something like 'Is this the best you think you can do?', as if you're less, because you're black. Typical white trash reaction, but I don't want her to treat you like that. I don't subject anyone I care about to my mother." She tried for a smile. "Don't let that go to your head. I would include casual acquaintances on that list."

He considered that. "You have enough to worry about, and I don't want you stressing about that box. Let's go by and get it. You'll introduce me to her, and she'll do what she's going to do. I'm going to respect her as long as she respects you, because she's your mother."

"I'd really rather not go there."

"Will that be any different when you get back? It's already been a shitty day, what with getting shot at and what happened to Jai. Why not just get all the shitty stuff done in one fell swoop?" He dropped his grip to her hand, laced fingers. "And you get to do it with someone watching your back."

She couldn't give in to him on this one. It was beyond a bad idea, especially after everything else today. But she didn't want to talk to her mother about keeping the box for a few days, either. If she went by and picked it up, it would be over.

"You like watching my back just because it gives you an excuse to look at my ass," she said, putting him off, trying to rally a defense that would end the conversation before she agreed to something cosmically stupid.

"Don't need an excuse. I plan to do a lot more looking at it. Among other things." He touched her face. "Let's go stop by your mom's and head for New Orleans. And as tempting as the hotel idea sounds, I have a better idea for you. Marcie is staying at Lucas and Cassandra's this week. They have a big place. I want you to stay there until the wedding. I'll drop you by there tonight and come back tomorrow night after my shift."

"Are you insane? The last thing Marcie needs this week is--"

Her phone started to ring again and she glanced down, saw the screen. This time her eyes flashed. "I don't need to be handled."

"I didn't say you did. But I figured you'd feel better about it if you heard it from her lips."

Celeste put the phone up to her ear. "Marcie, what an astounding surprise," she said, caustically enough he had to school himself not to wince. "Let me guess. You got a call from one sexist asshole, who talked to another sexist asshole, and they came to the brilliant conclusion that your wedding plans needed to be disrupted to give me a place to stay that I don't really need."

He narrowed his gaze at her, temper flaring, but then he saw her mouth tighten. "Yes, but that's beside the point. A hotel would serve the same purpose, and I wouldn't have to worry about disrupting... Max and Dale? Yes, I'm sure I'll be safe, but... You know I'm happy to help you with that, but you're just making up stuff for me to do. If I came, I'd hide in a guestroom and you wouldn't even know I'm there." Her eyes sparked as she realized she'd walked neatly into that. He could almost hear Marcie saying in her practical way. "See? It's all settled then."

"Fine. I'm going to talk this over with Leland, though. I'll call you when I get to New Orleans."

She shoved the phone in her jeans pocket and whirled on him. "Really? You drag my friends into this, risk them? Make them think I can't handle my own life? You and I have already been down this road. Yes, there may be things about me that respond to...things about you, but this," she swept her hand around the room, "this is me. This is who I am and what I do. If you can't handle that, then you need to step the hell back and let me get on with my life."

"You really think I'd take you to them if I thought there was a significant risk?" He bumped toes with her. It made her have to tilt her head to look at him, which obviously irritated her more. Since she'd already found out that slapping her hands on his chest and shoving would be as effective as moving a brick wall, she stalked around him, put the kitchen table between them before she pivoted to face him again. He curled his large hands on the chair on his side and glared at her. "No one associated with Dogboy or the MoneyBoyz would expect you to be there. Max and Dale on the property is an added measure of security. You shouldn't use your credit card or do anything that sets up a paper trail for the next few days. Staying with a friend can help with that."

"But you didn't ask me how I felt about that. You just set it up like I didn't have a brain in my head."

"I set it up because my first priority is keeping you safe," he snapped. "I can't drag you there by your hair, woman. It's your choice to go or not to go, but if you don't go, I will take personal days and fucking sleep on your doorstep. I will hound your every step until we find this guy. Because I'm not going to let something happen to you just because you think this is some fucking political statement about you being a woman. A bullet kills a big, strong man as easy as a sharp-tongued woman. Just ask Jai. And this particular bastard doesn't just want to shoot you." He stabbed his finger at her corkboard. "He strangles them, stabs them, rapes them. You really think I'm going to let you getting pissy stand in the way of doing whatever the hell I need to do to protect you from that?"

He didn't raise his voice often, but she had him snarling. She'd taken a mirror stance during his diatribe, white-knuckling the chair on the other side. Her eyes were still angry, but he saw other things there, too. It had been a fucking stressful, crappy day, and now he was shouting at her.

"Damn it, Celeste," he said, his voice softening, but she shook her head. Gazed down at her hands, the table, all those clippings she'd yet to pin onto her board.

"I'll pack up a few of these notes to take with me. Other than that, I'm ready to go."

She leaned over to pick up an empty tote off the arm of a chair. His height gave him the reach to place his hand over hers.

"No. It's okay," she said, drawing away. "Let's just go."

Chapter Eleven

They stopped at Leland's house for him to change into his street clothes and to pick up his truck. Celeste didn't want to come inside. Rather than argue with her about it, he settled her on his porch swing which was screened behind lattice. She suspected he was keeping an eye on her through the blinds of his front window. She told herself he was smothering her but she couldn't stay worked up about it too much. She gazed at the mum plantings around the lawn jockey painted like a police officer. The lattice turned everything into small, manageable squares. Across the street, an elderly lady was sitting on her porch reading a paper, an ancient-looking, brindle-colored dog lying on her feet. She wondered if the woman was Gilly.

Leland stepped back out on the porch, dressed in blue jeans and a dark-green button-down, tucked in and belted. Dressing was so easy for men. A shirt shrugged over those broad shoulders, jeans pulled up over the fine ass, and he was good to go.

"Fast as Superman," she muttered, and he slid a glance her way. He had a plastic container in one hand and a couple bottles of water tucked under his arm. He lifted the container.

"I have cookies. Better be nice to me."

Charm was not going to work on her. Or cookies. But she took his offered hand and let him guide her back down the steps. "Is that Gilly?"

As he glanced across the street and saw the woman, she gave him a casual wave and a warm smile. Her speculative look at Celeste was far less friendly.

"Yeah, that's Gilly. Don't let the sweet little old lady act fool you. She's sharp as a switchblade."

"I got that from her look. I think she sees me as competition for her granddaughters."

Leland opened the passenger door, helped her up into the seat. Celeste made herself let go of his hand though she wanted to keep holding it. She was pissed at him, she reminded herself.

"Yeah." Leland rolled his eyes. "I'm in for the 'What, colored girls aren't good enough for you?' speech. She'll probably spit in the next batch of tea she makes me."

He closed the door and circled around. When he slid into his seat, he asked her for her mother's address. He'd probably expected her to fight him again about stopping there, and she'd thought about it, but she found she didn't have the energy. She gave him the address. She didn't know if he recognized the area as a run-down trailer park, but his expression didn't change when she gave him the directions. He backed out, swerving around his parked police unit, waved to Gilly again, and they were on their way.

For the next ten minutes, they didn't talk much. He asked her a few things about how giving the statement had gone, how Detective Allen had treated her. Another silence reigned. She thought of a hundred ways to renew her attack about him contacting Marcie, but she saw Jai bleeding in his arms again, and found herself struggling with a different set of emotions. A couple more miles, and she spoke.

"I'm not used to someone caring about me like you do."

He glanced in the side mirror, changed lanes to pass a beat-up pickup. "I'm sorry I sprung it on you like that. You're right, I probably should have told you first."

"Before you went ahead and did it anyway." She gave him a glimmer of a smile and received one back. It warmed her more than she should have allowed it to do, but when he laid his hand on the console, palm up, she put hers in it, felt that little easing inside when his fingers closed over hers. "This is going to suck," she said bluntly. "There are story leads I can follow up in New Orleans, but I'm assuming you want me to stay incommunicado with everyone for the next few days so I don't send up any alarms."

"It would be wise. I'm sure the MoneyBoyz have some contacts in NOLA. I wouldn't make any calls from your phone, either. We'll pick up a burner phone you can use."

She knew it would be suicide for her to go out and pursue face-to-face interviews until it was resolved. But it still rankled to be prevented from doing her job.

"It's too easy for them to put eyes in my neighborhood,"

he continued. "Else I would have had you stay at my place. My bed or my couch," he added, giving her a look. "Your choice."

She wasn't ready to tell him there was nowhere she'd ever felt as safe as when she was curled inside the curve of his body, in his bed. "You can stay in the car at my mom's, if you want. It should only take a second."

"I'll come in and meet her, at least say hello. So it can chap her ass that you're dating such a good-looking stud as myself."

She managed a better smile this time. "You know, I'm a bitch all the time. It doesn't really wear off, so the effort you put into buttering me up is kind of wasted."

"It's my time to waste," he pointed out. Lifting her hand to his mouth, he kissed her fingers, squeezed as she considered the unexpected feelings such a courtly gesture sent through her. "And the bitch part may be skin-deep, but when I get down to your heart, I don't see a trace of her there, Celeste. I think that's why you need me to push you so hard as a sub. Because that heart is who you really are, and you need to pass a stress test to feel comfortable letting that show."

She didn't know what to say to that, so she let another, more comfortable silence prevail for another few miles before speaking again. "So I guess you'll want me to meet your family at some point. Like your aunt, or brothers and sisters?"

"That'd be nice. My aunt and my sister live together in Raleigh. They might give me some of the 'What, you couldn't find a nice black girl?' attitude, just like Gilly will, but I expect they'll really like you once they get to know you."

"Most people like me more when they don't."

He grinned. "Not me. The more I know, the more I think I want to keep you."

"You make me sound like a stray cat."

"I'm fond of your claws."

"So you don't date black women?"

"Didn't say that. I just don't choose my relationships based on the same criteria I'd use to match my drapes to my couch. And I don't date, remember?" He kissed her hand and kept it, their fingers a loose tangled knot on his thigh, the worn denim against the side of her hand.

He had a good memory for directions. Before she had to cue him, he'd already flipped on his right signal to make the turn off the highway into a rural neighborhood. She watched the houses go by, small but neat homes with elderly long-term residents or working families who had ambitions for more. As they drew closer to their next turn, those houses gave way to less maintained structures, with algae-stained siding and buckled roofs, the occasional black trash bag duct-taped over a broken window. Rusty cars and old appliances sat in yards that never saw a mower, and suspicious-eyed inhabitants sitting on their porches didn't smile as they went by. She lost count of the No Trespassing signs on mailboxes.

Mrs. Davidson still had chickens, she noted, the hens scratching and busy in her bare front yard. Leland made the turn at that corner. The bumpy road had been that way as long as she could remember, potholes from the rain making the truck rock, the weeds choking the roadsides. It was all fields on either side for about a mile, fields that had once been farmland. When they reached the place where the trailers were, the "Haven Trailer Park" sign that marked their location was faded and peeling, almost unreadable.

She clenched her hands in her lap. "Leland, maybe we should just keep going. I really can pick this up later."

"Hey." He touched her leg, met her gaze. "It's okay, darlin'. I'm here. It'll be all right."

They pulled up to the trailer. About eight years ago, her mother had bought a new one, a double-wide. She'd had to replace the one that had become so rusted there were holes under the thin carpet. The new one was five years old when she bought it and her mother treated it no better, so it was already just as crappy-looking as the previous. There were two doors, one at either end of the front of the trailer. A cracked set of concrete steps led up to one, but at the other end, a small porch with a ramp had been built recently. The golden pine gleamed. An awning off the side rail protected a gleaming grill.

So the new guy had some money, but not enough to move her mother off to a fancy house, her mother's lifelong ambition. The ramp made Celeste frown. She knew her mom hadn't had an accident, let alone one serious enough to require a structural addition to the trailer. If she had, she would have immediately called Celeste to care for and help her.

Her mother opened the door then, confirming it. Ginny Lewis had always kept herself in good shape. She knew her figure was her best asset, whether for her many waitressing jobs or hooking a man with money. Her generous breasts and rounded hips were showcased in a snug T-shirt and jeans, her thick brown hair carefully dyed to conceal the gray pulled back in a ponytail. Though she had the calculating mind and narrow vision of a mean-spirited whore, she didn't make herself up like one. She'd spent plenty of time at department store makeup counters, taking advantage of the free makeovers when she had a lucrative fish on the line.

She'd had a brief period of glory in high school as a cheerleader, before she got pregnant with Celeste. She'd seduced the high school principal and tried to pin a molestation charge on him when he refused to leave his wife. He was fired, and ended up working for an auto parts store. Since the wife forgave him and they left Baton Rouge, Ginny spent a few years living off of the dubious good will of acquaintances and temporary boyfriends, which was when Celeste had lived in the inner city apartments she'd mentioned to Leland.

When Ginny got pregnant again, her mother let her move back in with her at the trailer park. Celeste's grandmother was a tight-lipped woman who always looked beaten down but never raised her voice. She died when Celeste was still a child and the trailer became her mother's. Celeste's three siblings had three different fathers, all of whom paid Ginny to go away and then disappeared themselves. One of the earliest pearls of wisdom Ginny shared was that men felt guilty when a woman's belly swelled with child. "A smart woman can get something out of them for that. Before your piece of shit daddy skipped town, he paid me fifteen hundred dollars. In cash. If I'd gotten rid of you at the clinic, I wouldn't have gotten that."

Celeste knew the value of a healthy white baby on the black market would have been far more, but while Ginny had less than no morals, she didn't have the guts to break the law. At least not in that way. Thankfully, she'd finally concluded that getting pregnant was no longer worth the aggravation to her.

When she saw Celeste wasn't alone, Ginny's practiced smile upped up in wattage. If Celeste landed a good catch, she might benefit, after all. Celeste felt vaguely nauseous, a feeling that grew when Leland stopped the truck and stepped out of it. Her mother took in his appearance, the color of his skin, and her smile became far less warm. He offered her a cordial nod, coming around the front of the vehicle to open Celeste's door.

"This is a mistake," she said.

Putting his hands to her waist, Leland slid her off the seat with easy strength so her feet didn't touch the running board. They were screened by the tinted window as he leaned down, pressed his lips to her temple. "No matter how bad this goes, Jai and his family had a much worse day. When we get to New Orleans, I'll take you out for a nice dinner and buy you a dessert that'll make everything better."

How could any woman avoid falling in love with this man? No wonder she'd let him insinuate himself into her life so deeply in a handful of days, when no one else had ever gotten halfway this close. Leland was right, of course. She was the one freaking out, not him. Time to pull it together.

"You should have called, Celly." Her mother's voice had a touch of shrillness. Nerves. That was odd.

If she'd called, and her mother didn't want anything from her, she would have told Celeste she was busy and not to come by. Celeste pasted on a faint smile, the best she could muster, and stepped away from the shelter of the door. "I'm just here to pick up Trice's box, Mama. We're on our way to New Orleans. This is Leland Keller."

"Ma'am." Leland put his hand on the small of Celeste's back, a subtle but potent gesture of support as they moved toward the porch. "Pleasure to meet you."

Celeste's mother nodded, marking his size. She didn't

offer the same greeting back. Then Celeste heard a voice inside.

"Is that our little Celly?"

She stiffened, everything locking up. Her attention snapped to her mother's face, and she saw a combination of emotions. Triumph, jealousy, worry. The first two increased the nausea in her stomach. God, she was so glad she hadn't eaten since breakfast, even if the emotions that swamped her now made her light-headed. She forced herself to stay rigid, lift her chin, as her mother stepped aside on the porch to allow the man behind her to come out onto it.

He was in a small transport wheelchair, which explained the ramp. He was older looking and thinner, the tousled hair streaked with gray. He was still handsome though, the type of man most women would consider a harmless charmer.

She savagely told herself she was not going to squeak or rasp. "Don."

"See, I told you she'd remember me, Gin. Even with this." He smacked the arm of the chair. Celeste flinched. Though she thought she'd managed to internalize it, Leland's fingers stroked that vulnerable dip in her spine, a reminder. He was here. He had her back. "Damn car accident, if you can believe it," Don said. "Remember that sweet GTO I had? Tore it up and totaled it. Can't feel nothing from the waist down, which sucks, but other guys have it worse, don't they? Didn't want to stay in California anymore after that, even after winning that big insurance settlement. So I remembered how good your mama and you all were to me, and thought I'd stop in. Just to say hi, that was the plan, nothing more than taking her out for a drink for old times' sake. But wouldn't you know it, we just seemed to pick up where we left off, like I'd never been away?"

She'd just bet. All he'd had to do was say those magic three words, "big insurance settlement." Her mother slid an arm around his thin shoulders, throwing him a dazzling look as her hard eyes went to Celeste.

"Don says this here is all just temporary. We're going to move into a nice house in a few weeks. He's just shifting some money around for the down payment. There's a little yard in back. I had to wait so long for my dream, what with all the sacrifices I had to make for you kids, but now all that giving is finally coming around. And I have Don to thank for it. He always did take such good care of me."

"Yeah. Do you have the box, Mom?"

Her mother straightened, her expression becoming more brittle at Celeste's brusque response. "Why don't you come on in here and help me get it. Don and..."

"Leland," Leland supplied.

"...can talk." Her mother threw Leland a dismissive look and gestured to Celeste to come inside. Don made way for her, rolling forward.

To use the stairs, she had to move away from Leland's supportive hand. She did it, reminding herself a woman who leaned on a strong man forgot how to stand on her own two feet when that hand went away. She wondered what Leland was thinking. When she glanced at him, his shrewd gaze was shifting from her mother to Don. Though his expression was impassive, she saw the cop in his eyes. He knew he was looking at trash, through and through.

She'd called her mother white trash herself, but it wasn't the trailer or the poor surroundings that made her that way. There'd been other families here, white, black and Hispanic, all in the same economic circumstances, but some of those families had been different. The kids had mothers who tousled their hair or hugged them. Or fussed at them in the right way.

"Clarence, this is your home, not no barn. You wipe them feet or I'll tan your hide..."

Mrs. Jarrett's voice was as clear in her head as if she was still standing in the door of the trailer twenty feet away, rather than speaking across twenty years. Instead of flinching when his mother came onto the porch, expecting a slap or a verbal cut-down about how stupid or ugly he was, Clarence had dutifully wiped his feet, then did it in a more exaggerated way, shaking his hips and doing an improv funky chicken while his mother rolled her eyes. "Boy, you nothin' but a fool. Get in this house and get your dinner." But she'd cupped his neck, given him a smacking kiss and shoved him gently in the house. She loved him. Even a child without that knew what it looked like. Maybe especially one without it.

"Celeste?"

She'd come to a stop at the top of the ramp. Don was less than three feet away, was saying something she didn't hear, that shit-eating look on his face. His eyes were warm but wary, waiting to see what she was going to do. She gave him the barest of nods and stepped into the trailer.

Stale cigarettes and things that needed cleaning. Cold. Those were the things she remembered, the things she inhaled and felt now. Her stomach roiled and she had to fight her gag reflex. Her mother pointed to the small area she used as a pantry. A medium-sized box was pushed back against the wall on the dirty linoleum. Celeste moved to get it, but her mother put a hand on her arm.

"Don came into a shitload of insurance money because of the accident," she whispered, her eyes gleaming. "Nearly half a million dollars. And he came back here to find me. That's no coincidence, Celly. Him being paralyzed doesn't bother me none. Fact, it's a blessing to be with a man who won't care about that. Less work for me."

Celeste tried to move away, but her mother held on. She'd had a manicure. Little sparkles on her nails, painted slick and pink. "Don't mess this up for me, Celly."

A tremor went through Celeste, so hard and sudden it jerked her from her mother's grasp. She pushed through the haze that had formed over her eyes, bent and picked up the box. It was light, and through the folded flaps she caught a glimpse of a doll, a couple notebooks, an old T-shirt. Whatever few memories Trice had wanted to keep from her childhood were in her hands.

Her mother had gone silent. She was probably trying to figure out what was going through Celeste's mind, how to work things. How to get her to react. "Can't believe you went for dark meat, Celly. You can do better."

God, it sucked to be right sometimes. She thought of Clarence and Mrs. Jarrett. Mrs. Jarrett hadn't had the time of day for Ginny, but she'd been kind to Celeste. When Ginny was away as she often was between boyfriends, Mrs. Jarrett had come over and taught Celeste how to sew so she could mend one of Patrice's torn shirts. She remembered the woman had given her hair a brisk stroke when she'd done the stitches right. "You're a smart girl, Celly," the woman had said. "Smart enough to survive all this."

She hadn't been old enough to really understand what the woman meant, but she did now. She turned. "You say another word about Leland, and I *will* ruin this for you. And you sure as hell know I can do it. Got it? He's a cop. A sergeant."

Whatever she saw in Celeste's face made her mother's eyes widen. Maybe it was resolve. Maybe it was murder. She just needed out of this trailer. Now.

She heard Leland and Don talking. Don's voice was muted to her, whereas Leland's baritone was the lifeline she followed into the open air again. She gulped it in, but the dank smell of stale cigarettes was on the deck as well. She had a brief impression of Leland offering to take the box as she came down the ramp, but she didn't really register it. Don said something again, but she didn't hear that. Putting the box down beside Leland's truck, she kept walking. Fast, faster. She managed not to break into a run until she turned the corner around an old, white trailer. She didn't know the occupant anymore, but the road to the pond was still behind it.

She took it, running until the cramping in her stomach stopped her. Doubling over, she heaved into the tall grass on the side of the road. Her breakfast hadn't been completely gone, but it was now. Her legs trembled. She'd never had to throw up standing, and she found it was hard to balance. She was going to stain her jeans with mud, a dull thought that crossed her mind as her knees gave out. But she didn't, because Leland's arm was around her waist, holding her, steadying her. His other hand touched her hair, gathered back those longer strands that might get caught in her mouth.

"Sshh. It's okay. Just let it out. Get it done and you'll feel better."

She dry heaved a few more times, the smell of cigarettes and her mother's body spray still in her nose. She wanted to strip off her clothes, burn all of them, but like most of her clothes, they were designer wear she'd picked up at consignment shops. Maintaining a professional image for half the cost, because every dollar counted. She didn't have the money to toss her clothes because of an emotional breakdown. But it was all an image. *When you are shit, you have to make up an image different from who you are, and keep at it until the past starts not to matter...*

She straightened, sucking in deep breaths. He stayed behind her, letting her lean against him without making her face him. Laying her head back on his chest and shoulder, she found he was as comfortable as leaning against a broad, smooth tree. His angles and curves were right where they needed to be to support her.

"I'm really glad you're this big."

"It's useful sometimes." She glanced down at a nudge on her hand and saw he was offering her a pack of cinnamon Trident. She took a stick, unwrapped it and put it in her mouth. The cinnamon helped. His smell helped. After she chewed the gum, she turned and buried her nose in his shirt. It wasn't enough. She unbuttoned a couple buttons with quick, jerky movements to get to his skin, inhale there. He stroked her back, her nape, giving her all the time she needed. He didn't ask, didn't say anything beyond murmurs of reassurance.

When she could draw a steady breath again, she stepped back, wiped at her wet eyes. If he'd asked her questions, she probably would have clammed up, but his compassionate silence reached into her and drew out the poison.

"My mom always had a string of boyfriends," she said. "Most of them we only saw in passing, because she preferred to go to their places, so they weren't reminded that she had four kids. But Don came to live with us for a while when I was eleven. When my mom was at work and he got horny, he taught me to play a game. Suck on the lollipop and win a prize. Every time I did it for him, he'd make me cookies. Or buy me a toy at the dollar store. Never forced me to do it, but when I told my mom about it, because it made me uncomfortable, she said, 'A girl's never too young to learn how to give good head, honey.' And then she said, 'Don't mess this up for me, Celly.'"

"Christ."

She swallowed. She should stop. She really should, but she couldn't. She'd never told anyone. Never had a friend she'd let get that close.

"She made me promise I wouldn't mess it up for her, or for us, because Don was helping her pay the bills. Pay 'our' bills, she said.

"Nobody ever tied me up, hurt me. It was just what it was. It wasn't even sex. Just blow jobs. Coercion, of a sort. I guess I didn't really think about what I thought about it. About how I stopped having friends that year, stuck more to myself. Then one day, I'm on my knees doing for him, and my six-year-old sister Patrice comes in, though I'd told her to play outside until I called. She asks what we're doing and Don says, 'Playing a game. Pretty soon, you'll be old enough to play too. But maybe I can let you play just this once...'

"I don't remember my mind telling me to do it. I had an iron heating because my mom told me I had to iron her shirts for work. She was working at this cocktail lounge that required dress shirts and black miniskirts. I turned around, picked up the iron and jammed it against his stomach. Honestly, I was aiming for his dick, but I was pumped up on adrenaline and rage, all nerves. I grabbed Trice's hand and we ran. We hid with a friend for two days until they told us he'd picked up and left...guess he was afraid we'd be found by the cops and his secret would be out. My mom didn't speak to me for about three months. She took every opportunity to tell me what a dumb little bitch I was. Would just come in, dump her dirty laundry on me and then be off again."

She shook her head. "It's crazy, but I didn't really think about him anymore, about any of that. Maybe because then Mom met Vince. He was so nice. He took us to the zoo, places like that. He was...like a father. He wanted to spend time with us. His wife had the kids in his divorce and she'd moved to California, so he didn't get to see them. He had a job here he couldn't leave and still make the child support payments, though he was always sending off résumés to California. I helped him type them up."

She took a breath. "He didn't live with us, but we had him for about five months. Then he lost his job because the company had layoffs. My mom dumped him. She said, 'You don't saddle yourself with a man who has no money, Celly. He has to pay for what you give him.'"

She stared out at the pond in the distance, wondered if there was still an old raft in the high weeds. She and other kids would take it out into the middle of the pond to fish and while away warm afternoons, slapping at mosquitoes and jumping into the murky water when the bugs got too aggressive. "Losing him was harder than dealing with Don, if that makes sense. Things being hard and difficult, that I knew. Losing someone who was kind, who made me think about what it was to be loved the way a kid should be loved, and having to go back to the other, that was worse. I thought about killing myself once or twice, but instead I got angry. Really angry."

It really was time to stop. This was like a complete childhood info dump, but she had to finish it, to make him understand about everything that kept boiling up in her. He needed to know why it would never work between them.

"I told myself I was done with it. I went wild for a bit, drinking, getting in trouble, but then one day I looked in the mirror and saw my mom looking back at me. Nothing really significant had happened that day. It was just one of those moments, and I pulled my shit back together again."

She straightened, her chin set as she stared out at the pond as if it would disappear if she looked away. "I used the anger. I wanted to spite her. Made sure my brothers and sister got through high school, got on their way. They're all over the country, no shock there. The farther they can be from here, the better, right? As for me, I'd already figured out life is the same no matter how far you run. You have to make yourself a better life, and that's not geography, that's what's inside yourself. I did community college and got the hell out. I made one friend in high school that stuck, Valerie. She and I lived together in NOLA for a few years before she got married and moved away and I came to Baton Rouge. I've lived my life the way I want to live it since I left that trailer. Yet the anger never goes away."

"Because you've used the anger as your weapon, darlin'," Leland said quietly. "It helped you survive. When someone takes that anger away from you, you have to be sure he's offering something just as strong."

"No. I wish it was that simple, but it's not." She looked at him. He'd moved to stand next to her, and her shoulder was against his arm, but he didn't touch her, as if he knew she needed to stand on her own two feet to say all this.

He was right. Quality wasn't a skin color or a class status. It was in the heart, and his was as big as the ocean. Big as the world was cruel.

The bitch part may be skin-deep, but when I get down to your heart, I don't see a trace of her there, Celeste.

Sadness filled her. "You're a really good man, Leland. The best kind of man. Any woman in her right mind would look at you and see someone who will stand by her, no matter what. But there's nothing you can do that will make me believe I can depend on you. That I can let go of the anger to accept what you're offering in its place. I don't know how to be with someone, love someone the way they deserve to be loved. Every time I fight you, every time we go through all this shit I have inside me, I know you don't deserve any of that. And it tears me apart inside, because I honestly don't know how to be anything different. I'm just better off alone. I'm sorry, but I am. I'm so sorry."

Her voice broke. His expression changed and she knew he was going to try to touch her, hold her. So she bolted again, but this time he didn't let her get past him. He caught her arm, held her as she rounded on him. When she tried to shove away, he turned her, put her back against him, wrapped both arms around her, her chest and waist, held her fast. She struggled, begged him to let her go, but he didn't. Just held her. When she started to claw at his arm, started to struggle in earnest because she didn't want to be trapped, didn't want to be held or stopped, he changed his hold, crossing her arms over her chest and holding her wrists at the base of her throat with his strong hands as she kicked out, lost her footing. He held her off the ground until she settled again, somewhat.

"Stop. Let me go."

"No. You're going to settle down now, because I've got you. I'm not going to let you run off, I'm not going to let you be alone with this. You're used to being able to push people away. I can't be pushed anywhere, darlin'." His fingers eased enough to stroke her crashing pulse, his thumb rubbing over her collarbones. "We're going to have that nice dinner and dessert I promised you. Then I'm going to take you to Lucas and Cassandra's place. I'll carry your bag to your room. Once we're there, I'm going to put you down on the bed and blister your ass with my belt because you need it. After that, I'm going to bury myself to the balls inside you, make you climax. Then I'm going to hold you until your tears run out and you sleep."

Her body was shaking harder with every word. He shifted her wrists to one big hand so he could spread the other out on her sternum, fingers sliding into the neckline of her Van Gogh T-shirt to stroke the upper curves of her breasts, tease the edge of lace on her bra cups. She knew he wasn't trying to arouse her. He was reminding her he was her Master. He wasn't going to let her run. Her stomach hurt a little less at the thought, even as counting on that frightened her.

"After you do all that, you'll leave me." She made it an accusation.

"No, I won't leave you. I'm going to curl up around you just like I did the other night, sleep with you and make sure you're all settled down. I'll get up early to go back to work, see what I can do to help catch this asshole who's after you. Then I'll be back Friday night. The marks I leave on your ass should be fading by then and you'll need a new set."

"I don't want to go back to the truck. Not there."

"I know. You don't have to. You can wait right here. I'll come back and get you. But I better find you here when I get back, or I'll spank your ass wherever I happen to catch up with you, no matter how many people are looking."

She must be hysterical, because her lips quivered in a near smile, despite his stern tone and her certainty he meant every word. "I think you might get written up for that, Sergeant Keller."

"Most of the guys I work with know you. They've probably wanted to paddle your ass more than once, though if they've had that urge, they'd better keep it to themselves." He sighed, kissed her temple, made a soothing noise when she let out a short sob.

"It's all right, darlin'. It's okay."

"I meant what I said. You shouldn't be with me. I shouldn't be with you. This isn't going to work."

"That decision's up to me."

"I have no say in it?"

"Nope. Not until I say. Understand?" He slid a hand under her jaw, and her breath caught as he pulled her face up, his grip firm. "I want to hear the words you said to me at your place. Don't you give me that weak-ass whisper this time."

She stared into his eyes. She wanted to look away, but he wouldn't let her. The words were like bullets burning in her chest, a pain she couldn't release, a pain that competed with the anger and--at least this once--overrode it.

"Yes, sir." It was still a whisper, but the tear that rolled out of her eye though she tried to stop it, seemed to make up for the lack of volume. He kissed the tear away, caressed her face. "Stay here."

"Can I..." She shifted her gaze away, because she was so unsure of herself like this. "I really need to walk, Leland. The road from here to the turnoff is about a mile. I'd like to walk that way, just clear my head. Just to feel like...I need to pull myself together. It's safe, just fields on either side. You saw it."

It was a trek she knew well, since as kids they'd walked that route to catch the school bus. He studied her, then nodded. "I'll go get the truck."

§

Based on the pace she set as she moved away from him on that bumpy road, Leland calculated he had at least fifteen minutes before she reached the turnoff. As he went to get the truck, he used the time to take a few breaths himself. A lot of things were boiling inside him she didn't need to deal with.

He thought of his parents. He'd seen them fight, sure, but they'd also laughed together, cried together. They'd worked side by side to protect and care for their kids to the very best of their ability. It had taught him that whether parents lived in a big house or a small shack, the ones who loved their kids had the same hopes for and worries about them.

Looking at the trailer as it came back into view, he wondered that Celeste ever came back here at all, for any reason. Celeste's mother was on the porch, handing Don a beer and twisting the top off her own. When she noticed him, he could almost see her calculating whether or not Celeste's reaction had adversely impacted her plans with her latest cash cow.

She was a whore, plain and simple. He knew plenty of prostitutes. He didn't bear them ill will. He had pity for the ones who were strung-out junkies you couldn't trust. He'd developed a rapport with a few others who carried on with him when he did his drive-bys and checked on them to make sure they were okay. Not every cop felt as he did about it, but he had decided long ago they should legalize and regulate it. If that happened, then those he saw selling their bodies--women of all ages, and mostly young men barely out of boyhood--might be able to get the same basic protections that everyone from factory to office workers had. There'd still be problems, but they'd sure as hell be far safer than they were now.

Beyond that, those who chose to offer their bodies for money as a professional transaction would gain more respect, whereas someone like Celeste's mom would stand out as the piece of shit she was. Celeste might tease him about a cop seeing things in black-and-white, but he saw no reason to muddy water that was clear enough to him.

Don should have gone back inside. In Leland's current frame of mind, Don being where he could see him was an unwise move. *Never forced me... Don't mess this up for me...*

Leland stared at the trailer, thought about how poor he himself had grown up. He thought of his mother. She'd never made his dad feel as if there were any man in the world she wanted more than him, no matter how rich, educated or handsome. She hadn't seen his father as a means to an end, a personal trophy. They were partners, who'd promised to be there for each other throughout their lives, for better or worse.

Was there any wonder he wanted the same thing for himself so much? And how did he convince Celeste of that, or rather, help her understand it? The only example she'd had in her life was this. He'd suspected the reasons for why she acted like she did, but it didn't give him any pleasure to have it confirmed. Her history had taught her she was never more than a step away from being alone, that any pleasure or bond with another was temporary. His girl didn't want to face loss again. A simple problem to understand, not so simple to solve. But he knew refusing to let her go when they were at the pond had been the right tactic. He'd keep hanging onto her every time she felt like she had to bolt, until she figured out he was like a damn millstone around her neck.

"We'll be going now," he told Ginny. He kept his voice cool, even. Professional. She shifted uncomfortably, picking up on the tenor he used toward anyone thinking about making trouble in his general vicinity. That tone usually took care of it, if that person had any sense at all. He tried to detach himself from who they were to Celeste, to think of them as just another couple of troublemakers he encountered on his watch. Else he might burn the fucking place down with them in it, like trash in a metal barrel.

He put the box in the car without saying anything. He felt Ginny watching him, considering options. He wasn't surprised when she wasn't smart enough to keep her mouth shut.

Ginny put on a bright face, glancing toward Don. "You tell Celeste she's welcome to come see her mama anytime."

Leland met her gaze. "I think you and I both know that's not true. But if I have anything to say about it, she won't be coming here again." His gaze shifted to Don, to the wheelchair that had deadened everything from the waist down. "The Lord does work in some pretty damn amazing ways, doesn't He?"

Ginny's features froze, showing panic then anger. She knew exactly what he was talking about. If it was possible, he found her more despicable than Don himself.

"Well, that's fine," she said abruptly, the mask falling away to show an aging woman who was pure ugly on the inside. "Just because Don has money, she shouldn't think she can come sniffing around here."

"Funny how often a thief always thinks someone is

stealing from them."

When Ginny flushed beet red, gaze darting back to Don, Leland let out a short, harsh laugh.

"Honey, you don't need to pretend. He knows exactly why you've taken him back, and he's grateful because you're the only option he has now. He knew you were the fish that would bite. Best to keep it open and aboveboard. You're cut from the same cloth."

Shut up, he told himself. Just shut up and go. But he couldn't. "It will be up to Celeste if she ever wants to see you again, but you try to reach out to her, hurt her in any way, I'll be the brick wall in your way. Count on it."

His attention returned to Don, and the face he showed him now was all cop. "Whether your dick is dead or not, if you're anywhere near a girl under the age of consent for any reason, you're going to get nailed. Because I know that woman enough to know she's going to keep tabs on you. She wants nothing more than to forget you, but she'll put that aside to protect another little girl. That's the kind of person she is. I don't have to tell you how long a crip child molester will last in prison. Might as well hand those guys candy and call it Christmas."

As Leland reached for the driver's side door, he had the empty satisfaction of seeing Don whiten.

"Don never done anything to that girl she didn't want," Ginny said belligerently. "That's the honest truth. Celeste was a wild child. Always went her own way."

Given the emotions that surged up hot and hard in him, he wasn't surprised to see her whiten under his hard stare. "Good-bye, ma'am. Remember what I said. You step out of line, and you'll lose what little you got left here."

As he closed the door, he saw Ginny's face twist in a snarl, heard her shout a few typical things at him as he was backing away. He bared his teeth at her. "Yeah, that's original," he murmured. "Being called a nigger by a white trash whore. My feelings are hurt."

He caught up with Celeste pretty quickly. She was walking slower now, arms crossed, head down. As he bumped up behind her, his gaze covered the delicate line of her shoulders under the pretty shirt, the faint imprint of her bra strap, the way the jeans clung to her hips.

Sometimes a man looked at his woman and felt lust stir from how she was put together. Other times, the exact same things could cause a stirring higher up, making it hard for him to find words for his feelings. He hadn't been bullshitting Don. Despite how desperately she'd want to distance herself from this, he already knew she'd force herself to keep checking up on them while Don was here-- which would be until he and Ginny blew all his money. Celeste wouldn't let Don ruin the life of any other child if she thought she could stop it.

She thought so little of herself, and yet he could see so much. It was going to take time to change her opinion of herself, help her see what he saw, but he could at least help her with one thing. He had friends in the sheriff's department. He'd contact them, let them know about Don. They'd increase their patrols here, probably conduct a child safety session with the parents and kids in the park to remind the kids of the way adults were supposed to behave and teach the parents the warning signs. They could maintain enough of a presence that Don would know he was being watched. The sheriff's department could research his time in California, see if there'd been any complaints out there.

If Leland could put all that into motion, it would minimize what Celeste would have to do. It wouldn't add to the weight of what she already had to handle when dealing with her mother.

He pulled ahead of her, stopped the truck on the shoulder, got out and went around to open her door. She'd left her light jacket in the truck. From how her arms were crossed over her, he could tell she was cold. The air was humid, not cool, but there were other things that could make a woman cold. When she reached him, he put the coat around her shoulders. At first she stared at his chest, but then she looked up at him. She was tense as a board again under his hands, so he didn't draw her in for an embrace. He'd made his point earlier on that, but obviously her walk had stirred some of it back up. That was okay. It was a little over an hour to Lucas's place outside New Orleans. They'd work on getting her to a better place, not just geographically.

He lifted her into the truck the way he'd brought her out, pulled the seatbelt over her and fastened it. When he got back into the truck, he turned the heat on low and angled it toward her feet. She'd been shivering under his hands. He picked up one of her hands, cupped it between both of his, blew on her ice-cold fingers. She was watching him, still tense. She probably expected him to talk. To ask questions and expect something of her. Was it so unusual to her that someone would simply take care of her, watch over her needs more than she would do for herself?

She'd said she wasn't used to someone caring about her, so he guessed he had the answer to that question. Whereas caring for her was the only expectation and desire he had at the moment.

"Did you torch the place?" she asked.

"No, but I was sorely tempted. Did you want me to?"

She shook her head. As they began to trundle toward the turnoff, she looked out the window, tugged her hand out of his and tucked it inside the coat. "No," she said. "I dealt with the rage a long time ago. Now it just seems so pointless. Like being mad at the grass for being green."

Yet she had so much anger in her. He'd felt that volcano tempest within her plenty of times. He expected what she was saying was that expelling the rage didn't make her feel better, that it just filled her right back up again.

He remembered what she'd said. *It was just the way it was.* And that made his girl think she was broken past repair, unable to handle a relationship with him.

"You want anything to eat, darlin'? You didn't have any lunch."

She shook her head.

"Okay. I'll probably hit a drive-through." Once they reached the highway, it wasn't too long before he saw a fast-food place. He picked himself up a couple burgers and a large fry, and made sure the open bag was turned in her direction. He turned on a country station, hummed along as they covered the miles in companionable silence. Eventually the bag rustled, and he saw her take a couple fries out of it, chew and swallow. Take a few more. Then she borrowed some of his drink to sip. When he broke off half of the second burger he'd bought, she took it. As she bent her head over it, that gave him the opening he wanted to lay a hand on the back of her seat, then move it from there to stroke her hair. When she was finished with the sandwich, she ate one of Gilly's cookies and he took a couple for himself. Then she turned on her hip toward him, laying her cheek against the seat. She kept her eyes closed as he stroked her face, dropped his hand to her lap. Her hands curled around it, fingers tangling.

"When we're in session, and you're doing the Master thing, I'm a sub, it's not real. But it feels real enough. It helps. With everything."

"It is real, Celeste. I'm not playing a game and neither are you."

He lifted one of her hands to his mouth, kissed it. Her fingers tightened on his, held on, so he let her keep his hand, leaving it inside the loose knot of both of hers as he drove one-handed.

"I don't want to fall in love with you," she said.

He glanced at her, startled. From the distant expression on her face, her closed eyes, it was possible she hadn't realized she'd said it aloud. The words hit him hard in the chest, but not as a rejection. When it came to her emotions, she tended to state things backward, so he translated it easily enough.

I'm falling in love with you, but I don't want to.

Chapter Twelve

She maintained her silence after that, but his favorite country station helped him finally rouse her. When they played some old-school Hank Williams, Jr., he sang along with a twang that had her rolling her eyes and begging for elevator music. From there he eased them into casual conversation. Nothing heavy; the passing scenery, his work, her work. While he didn't ask her anything that would pull her back into the nightmare they'd just left, he kept it open enough, if she did want to talk about it. She didn't. She asked him questions about himself instead, which left him wryly amused, since once again it showed their respective professions were more about seeking information than giving it. She looked thoughtful when he pointed that out.

"I always wonder if it's chicken or egg," she said. "Are people who become cops and reporters drawn to those jobs because it gives us an excuse to be the one holding the control?"

He considered it. "Maybe. But for a cop, over time it becomes less about your nature and more about the nature of the job, until they become one and the same. What we do, there's a lot of shit to it that we don't want to take home with us. Because it can take over everything and drive your family away."

"But if you don't figure out an outlet for it, it could poison everything anyway."

"Yeah. It's a bitch to figure out the balance. It's like when we take a life in the line of duty. We have to go on paid leave for the usual investigation, but counselors are made available to us. While it isn't required here, there are departments that make talking to a counselor mandatory. I won't say it on the record, but that might be for the best. A cop doesn't have to say he or she needs to talk to someone; they have to do it, so they save face but have a way to get it out of their system."

"You don't do that in the military."

"If a soldier had to go to counseling after every firefight, it would cause a severe shortage of man power. But the mind-set is different. In the military, you're trained to kill, so you know up front it's a very real part of how the objective has to be met, so you're more prepared for it. Cops' ultimate job is to protect and serve." He grimaced. "Though both cops and soldiers have to deal with the shit the media spits out about us being racist thugs and soulless killers. No offense."

"None taken. If the time comes that I can't make money doing it the way I'm doing it now, I'll do something else. I won't go back to working for a paper or TV station. That kind of crap is why I'm not part of that machine anymore. And I don't want to be."

"You're exceptional, darlin'. On a whole lot of levels."

"Well, damn," she said with a sigh. "Now that you've said nice things, I might have to scrap that smear piece I'm writing about a police sergeant who threatened me with bodily harm at a crime scene."

"Be sure and include all the details on that. I'd like to hear your reaction on his follow-through."

Her cheeks pinkened and he grinned at her. Continued to do so as she fished around in the fast-food bag and retrieved the other half of the sandwich to finish it.

The rest of the trip was equally amicable, until they drew closer to New Orleans. Then he saw her tension returning. If the line of her shoulders, like an overdrawn clothes-line, didn't give it away, the direction of the conversation certainly did.

"You know, maybe it would be better if I stayed at a hotel."

"You'll be safer with Lucas and Cassandra."

"I don't want to endanger anyone."

"You won't. Just do the things we discussed. Don't use your cell, limit your work stuff to what you can do via that burner phone or anonymously online. You have the cash you pulled out of the ATM in Baton Rouge before we left. Use that if you need it. Nothing that lays down a paper trail. We might be giving the MoneyBoyz credit for way more resources than they have, but better safe than sorry."

He'd intended to take her out for that dinner he'd promised, but his gut told him to go a different way. Since she'd polished off the second burger and fries, dinner could wait a while anyway. So instead of going into the city, he took the turn to follow the outskirts, heading for Lucas and Cassandra's house.

She thought the best way to deal with it was all by herself. He respected her feelings, but he thought he had a better idea of how to handle those festering emotions than being alone a hotel room, where those emotions would likely galvanize her into doing something unwise to avoid feeling them.

When he turned into their quarter mile long driveway, Celeste didn't say anything. The plantation-style house Lucas and Cassandra had bought just outside New Orleans had the square footage and acreage to accommodate the couple and near half-dozen siblings Cassandra had raised on her own, until Lucas came into her life to help share the load. Three were still living at home, Nate, Talia and Cherry at various points of middle school and high school, but Jessica was in college and Marcie had been living with Ben since their engagement.

Leland had first met Matt and the other K&A men at one of his visits to Club Surreal, the classy and discreet Baton Rouge BDSM club whose membership he couldn't afford. He'd purchased a three-month temporary card to check it out, regardless. While he hadn't played there, he'd ended up sharing a drink with Matt and meeting the other men. The relationship had grown from there. All five men were Doms, and that orientation infused and guided their lives, far beyond a preference exercised in a club environment.

They were each married--or engaged, in Ben's case--to a submissive who complemented that degree of commitment, though the couples exercised it in different ways.

Leland understood that. While the desire to exercise his Dominant side was something that admittedly manifested itself in ways large and small in his relationships, he wasn't as much of a sadist as Ben, or primarily a psychological Dom like Matt was. He fell somewhere along the spectrum between them, but that spectrum put him well within the men's circle. Some people just clicked, and he'd felt the click with the five men, enough to enjoy time with them socially since. He went to the Super Bowl party that Matt hosted every year and to cookouts at Peter and Dana's. On Labor Day, Cassandra and Lucas had a big picnic, and then there was the Christmas party that Jon and Rachel had. He had a standing invitation to join them all at Matt's for Thanksgiving every year, and he'd also worked side by side with the men in their volunteer efforts during Katrina. He was glad Celeste had a friendship with Marcie, because he knew without a doubt she'd be safe here, emotionally and physically.

If she got out of the truck.

Stiff body language and the hard glint in her eyes told him she was back to having problems being handled. In about three seconds, he'd bet she was going to return to the hotel idea, except instead of a wheedling suggestion, she was going to put her foot down and make it a demand. Yeah, that wasn't happening.

He got out, came around to her door. When he opened it, she didn't look at him, just kept staring at the house.

"Take me to a hotel. I'm not staying here."

"Two seconds longer than I thought it would take."

Her gaze snapped to him, and he saw the fire there. "Don't mock me."

"Don't test me." He gave her an even look.

She shifted her gaze back to the house, crossed her arms over her chest. "I mean it, Leland. I just...I can't be here. Not after everything else today."

"Which is exactly why this is where you need to be. You need to trust me, darlin'."

Reaching in, he closed his hand on her shoulder, ran his thumb down the side of her neck, over her thudding pulse. When he came to rest on that sensitive juncture of her shoulder, he saw her get still, anticipating him. Using that pressure point had a decided effect on her, but he chose to use his voice alone this time, an implacable tone. "Come inside, Celeste."

She pressed her lips together, but when he put his hands on her waist, she let him slide her out of the truck.

"I don't want to talk to anyone right now. We really need--"

"You're not going to talk to anyone. Not right now. I

want you to stay quiet unless I tell you to talk."

He heard the door open at the top of the steps, but didn't turn right away so he could meet her startled gaze with an expression that told her he meant it. He'd surprised her enough to render her speechless. At least for a couple more seconds. More than that would be a miracle, so he'd best take advantage of the small window of opportunity he had. Taking her garment bag and overnight tote from behind the seat, he shouldered them, then grasped her elbow and guided her up the steps.

Lucas was at the door. His casual outfit of faded jeans and a well-worn T-shirt with the LAMBRA logo, the Louisiana/Mississippi Bike Riding Association, emphasized a lean and athletic form. His hair, a blond mix like tarnished gold, indicated how much time he spent outside cultivating his passion for amateur cycling. Nate, Cassandra's youngest sibling, now shared his interest in it, and they'd done the last marathon together. The CFO of Kensington and Associates had a sharp mind for numbers and a steady calm in the midst of any tempest. He also had the insight to know when one was brewing on his steps. He glanced at Leland with shrewd silver gray eyes, his brow lifting.

"I need to take Celeste to her room. She's glad to be here, but we need to deal with something first."

Leland wasn't the type of Dom who took it to this level in a public way, not usually, but the good thing about having friends who were Doms down to the bone was they understood the weighted meaning in a simple statement. After a brief flash of surprise, Lucas merely nodded.

"We made up a bedroom for her on the second floor, at the end of the hall. I'll be in my home office if you need me."

Celeste looked like she wasn't sure if she was going to spit, hiss or say something just to spite Leland, but when he tightened his fingers on her elbow, putting pressure on the sensitive nerve point there, he felt that telltale tremor that distracted her. It sharpened his own appetite to lance the boil inside her.

Lucas gestured them inside and closed the door. He gave Celeste a look of warm welcome, then he left them there, moving back through the large living room off the main foyer and disappearing around a corner. Celeste looked nonplussed at his abrupt departure. As Leland ushered her up the curved staircase with its wrought iron balustrades and polished wood hand railing, he felt her resistance and uncertainty. She was dragging her feet toward that room, wondering what she would face there, but he also sensed a different kind of anticipation humming through her blood.

It was as she herself had told him. She fought it, because she had to fight it. Not because she didn't want the feeling he could give her. He just had to have the balls and a bit of Dom meanness to see it through, because in truth, after seeing what she'd dealt with as a child, he wanted nothing more than to comfort and stroke her. Which wasn't what she needed. Not at first.

Though the house had many preserved historical features, Lucas and Cassandra didn't skimp on modern amenities. The guestroom had a king-sized bed, a flat screen and small fridge probably stocked with an assortment of beverages. A bowl of chocolates and fruit was on the dresser. The wide brace of windows offered a view of the pond and a scattering of weeping willows and mature live oaks. When he closed the bedroom door behind them, Celeste ignored all that, moving to the center of the room, arms crossed over her chest as if she was in a much smaller space. "He's going to think I'm rude."

"No, he's not. He understands what's going on."

"Well that's one of us." She tossed her hair out of her eyes. "I don't want to stay here."

"Hmm. You know what's going on, Celeste. It's why you've started to tremble."

He began to unbutton his shirt, matter-of-fact and efficient. She latched onto the movement, as well as noting his position in front of the closed door. *Yeah, I wouldn't try it, darlin'.* Now that the door was closed, fortunately his own volatile side was rising, overriding that nurturing compulsion. It was one of those perverse things. Seeing a threat to his sub made him want to stress to her, in no uncertain terms, that she was his. Not just to reassure her, but to enforce the lesson that she could rely on him. Especially when he was dealing with a sub who had a hard time believing she could rely on anyone.

"What are you doing?" she said unnecessarily.

"I want you to kneel, Celeste."

"I want a hotel room and a bath. We can do this better there. Everyone would be happier. Especially me."

He shrugged out of the shirt, and then removed the cotton tank he had on beneath it, pulling it loose from his jeans. He saw her eyes latch onto his bare chest as he tossed the clothes over a chair. "Take off your coat, Celeste."

When she kept standing, he could tell she wasn't openly defying him. She was just at a loss, her busy mind scrambling to keep up. So he moved behind her, slid the coat off, put it over the same chair as his shirts. He put his hands on her tense shoulders.

"If you don't take me to a hotel, I'll call a cab as soon as you leave and go to one."

"When I leave, which won't be until morning, you're barely going to be able to walk, let alone call a cab." He put his body up against hers, a reminder of his strength. "On your knees, darlin'."

She resisted, but he hooked her ankle and took her down anyway. He shifted his grip so it was a controlled descent, careful as lowering a baby into its cradle, despite her struggling.

Once he had her down, he used his weight and strength to hold her there. She pushed against him, but in this position, he had all the leverage, and she wasn't fighting him as much as herself. He understood that, but held her like that until he was sure she understood. He was the force that would take her down the road she needed to go. The struggle lasted thirty seconds, maybe a minute, then she stilled, her head lowering, breath short.

"Stay where I put you now. Understand?"

"No cuffs or ropes?" He'd eliminated the physical component of her resistance, so now she went to her stronger line of defense, her sharp tongue.

"Don't need them." He tipped her chin, met her eyes. "You'll stay where I put you. Tell me you understand, Celeste."

"Okay," she said sullenly.

"Okay?" His tone sharpened and he felt her pulse jump under his grip. The hazel eyes held a flash of resentment, more confusion, and a longing that was stronger than all of it.

"Yes, sir. I understand."

"Good girl." His hand gentled then. "My very, very good girl. Such a good girl."

§

The words brought a lump to her throat. The way his eyes became kind and his voice lowered, soothing, devastated her. She closed her eyes. "Ben said I needed pain to let go. But you...you do things like that and it's like I'm falling out of a tree and can't hold on to the branch anymore."

"You do need pain. But you need this as much, and sometimes more. It's all about timing, Celeste. A Master knows what his sub needs, and teaches her to trust him to get there, even if she doesn't know what she needs."

"I didn't want you to know any of that about my family, see any of it. Hell, I don't want to know it. I try to pretend it doesn't exist. I imagine I grew up in a happy family, with a picket fence and a dog. That I hung out with my friends at the mall and used my allowance to buy designer jeans."

He squatted in front of her. "Lift your arms, darlin'."

When she obeyed, he pulled the T-shirt over her head, set it aside. He caressed her skin, knuckles sliding over her breasts, quivering in the hold of lace cups. Unhooking her jeans, he brought her to her feet, steadying her with one hand. "Take them off."

She managed to unzip her ankle boots, step out of them with his assistance, then she removed the jeans.

He drew her over to the bed and sat down on the edge of it, bringing her to stand between his spread knees. He perused her body, clad only in bra and panties, for another weighted moment. When he brought her closer, she rested her hands on his shoulders as he unclasped the bra in the back and pulled it down her arms. She made an uncertain noise, but he shook his head, keeping her silent as he moved her back again.

Putting his hands on her hips, he slid his thumbs along the elastic of her panties and took the garment off of her, a whisper of silk along her legs. He had her step out of them, then he rose.

"Stay," he reminded her. She watched him put the other garments on top of their shirts, then he stepped behind her to the dresser. She looked over her shoulder to see him open the top drawer. "Eyes on the wall over the bed, Celeste. You don't look at what I'm doing."

She obeyed, though she didn't want to do so. The glass front of the picture over the bed, a landscape with soothing greens and blues, let her see his reflection, but she couldn't tell what he removed from the dresser.

He returned, standing behind her. If he'd taken anything from the drawer, he'd tucked it in a pocket or laid it in a guest chair, because he placed empty hands on the crown of her head. Smoothing his hands over her hair, he traced the shell of her ears and stroked the sides of her throat. Once, twice, again, as she swayed under the caresses, her shoulder blades brushing his chest. Sliding one hand down her sternum, between her breasts, he brought her back against him fully. Shoulders against his chest, ass against his groin, an intimate temptation and reassurance at once. The ache returned, growing stronger in her stomach and spreading out beneath her rib cage, traveling upward as he fanned out his fingers, stroked her abdomen, cupped her breast, played with the nipple. Bending, he pressed his mouth to her shoulder.

"Leland..."

"Not my name right now, darlin'. Not to you. Call me what I am."

She swallowed. She couldn't. She twitched as blue gauze dropped in her field of vision. A scarf, wide enough to fall to her navel as he held it level with her chest. He passed the fabric over her breasts, over the peaks as they tingled from the stimulation. She arched into it with a sigh, pressing her backside against the hardness under his jeans. She needed it rougher, faster, not this slow seduction that unfurled all these unbearable feelings in the pit of her stomach, that made her legs weak and her mind spin out of control.

Yet she didn't say anything, couldn't figure out what to do to make him go faster, not with him teasing her. Slowly, he gathered it up into his hands, turning the wide, translucent cloth into a folded strip in his hands, the tails falling down on either side of her. It was long, the ends tickling her thighs, her knees. When he brought it up to cover her eyes, she drew back, resisting, but he was behind her, so she couldn't stop his intent. He tied the scarf firmly behind her head and brought the ends forward, putting the fabric in her mouth and tying a knot there, too, before he wrapped the tails around her head again, once over the bridge of her nose, then down a second time over her mouth before he tied it off at her nape. It was similar to what he'd done with the rope, reminding her of that deeply emotional Ichinawa session between them. Despite the freedom of her hands and feet, her face wrapped in gauzy cloth was a powerful restraining effect he emphasized when he curled his fingers in the knot beneath her occipital bone and used his other hand to put her back on her knees again.

Help me, Master. She couldn't say it aloud, but it was there in her mind. She couldn't stop it, any more than her reaction now. She tried to push back up to her feet, to get away. He just put her down on the ground, her body folded over her knees, his weight keeping her in that curled ball as he began to lay kisses on her spine. His gentleness was killing her.

"Stop," she said through the gag. She bit down on the knot as he ignored her. Sweeping, lingering kisses on her back, the rise of her buttocks, her nape. He turned her head, kissed her mouth around the gag, through the thin cloth, as she wept and cursed him. When he eased his fingers inside her, began to thrust, rotate and play with her clit, there was no urgency to it.

"Please..." *Just fuck me. Use me.* The knot wasn't large enough to muffle her words entirely, so she might have said it out loud. His response, which came long, eternal moments later, made her think she had. Or that he was inside her mind in a way that was terrifying.

"You're my sub, darlin'. I cherish you. Worship you,

even as I own you. Fight all you like; it's not me you're fighting. It's yourself. I won't let anyone take away the pleasure you need and deserve. Even if it's you doing the taking, the denying."

"No." She wasn't disagreeing with the ownership thing, the thing she *should* be protesting. It was the worshipping and cherishing that were going to kill her. Ben was right. She needed pain. Needed it like air. She tried to jerk away from him, force the issue, and all he did was hold her fast. The climax he was inspiring was going to destroy her, but in this position he held all the power.

"You're going to go over for me. You're going to say 'Yes, Master.'"

She shook her head. He put his mouth against her ear. She was curled up on her knees on the ground, his large body arched over her, so he could surround her with his voice, his demand and heat.

"Your tears are making the scarf wet, Celeste. It's breaking my heart, darlin'. I'm going to keep doing this to you, make you cry even more, until all the tears are gone. Until you know it's okay again. That I've got you, safe and sound, beautiful and whole. All mine."

He eased another finger in, stretching her, and she gasped at the bolt of pleasure. He worried his finger over her clit. "So swollen, and what's this? Your pussy, wet as morning dew. We'll spread some of that over your clit, make it easier for me to stroke and play with it. After you come, I'm going to suck all the juices off it with my mouth, because I love the way a woman squirms and shudders when everything is still so sensitive. If I order you to be still through that, you'll try so hard. Because you act like a brat, darlin', but what you want to be is my good girl. You're just afraid. And you don't have to be afraid with me. Break, darlin'. I've got you."

She started to come on that note, and the strength of it brought her hips off her heels, pushed her forehead deeper into the carpet. She was glad for the gag as she tried to muffle her response. A cry became a scream as he removed his fingers, shifted around to straddle her head, his thighs against her shoulders, and replaced his fingers with his mouth. Curved over her, he licked her rim and cunt, sucking on her clit as she came so hard, she had to rely on the cage of his body to hold her up.

"No..." The aftershocks came together, like fast ripples of sound. She kept rocking against him, her fingers clawing the carpet. She wanted him inside her. She was so empty. She needed to be filled up. She begged him to fuck her through the gag, a muffled plea he ignored.

Instead he teased and cleaned her with his mouth, little licks and a sweet, long sucking on her clit and labia that had her whimpering, squirming against his face, just as he'd said. He put her down on her side after that, her body still curled up beneath his. He had his knees planted on either side of her head, and she wrapped her hand around his calf, digging her fingers into the denim of his jeans as he kissed the line of her hip, nipped her buttock, massaged her rim and slid his fingers down between her folded legs again, working into the wet petals of flesh to stroke.

He didn't stop until she was making tiny little moans, her body twitching. Bringing her back onto her elbows and knees, he made sure she was steady before he stepped away from her. It was only a second, a scraping sound suggesting he'd picked something up off the dresser. He passed something cool and hard with uneven ridges against her buttocks.

"It's an antique hairbrush," he said. "The back is metal, the surface shaped like a garden of flowers." He stroked something else over her like a line of felt fingers. "This is a pussy willow branch. Not a real one. It's designed to look like it's part of the flower arrangement on the dresser, but it's a switch. Cass and Lucas have made sure their guestroom has a few improv tools for a visiting Dom, without it being obvious to their more vanilla guests. Makes them pretty damn good hosts, in my opinion. You'll be sure and thank them for their hospitality, won't you?"

She was trying to wrap her mind around what he was about to do with those two items, and then he hit her with the switch. The contrast between the fuzzy buds and the sting of the whiplike stem had her jumping. "I asked you a question, Celeste."

"Yes. Yes, sir." The damp knot of fabric muffled her

words, but the responses he was demanding were simple, easy to understand.

"Good."

This wasn't her. She didn't obey so easily, didn't capitulate to calling a man Master or sir as if she'd been a sub all her life. But before she could think about pushing up on her knees, renewing her resistance, he'd put the thick tread of his shoe on the back of her neck, his heel braced on the ground next to it. "Stay," he reminded her.

She couldn't see anything except blue through the scarf. It, as well as what he was doing to her, kept her in a hazy world as he struck her. It wasn't as painful as the dragon tail. It merely got her twitching and off-balance before he brought the brush into it. The metal studs were painful, yet she lifted up for more of it. She embraced the agony, needing the punishment for everything...for nothing...for herself. For him to call her a good girl when it was all over.

She was letting out tiny muffled yelps with each strike, especially as he ramped it up, alternating it so she wasn't sure if she was going to get the stinging slash of the switch or the hard thump and painful pressure of the back of the brush. Then he ran the bristles over her throbbing skin, between her legs, and she jerked at the uncomfortable prickle over her labia.

"Please..."

"Please what?" He paused. Hooking his fingers in the scarf at her nape, he brought her up on her knees, settling her on her heels. When he moved in front of her, she saw his shape through the blue layers. "Tell me, Celeste."

"Please, Master."

"Hmm. What do you want, darlin'?"

She couldn't give voice to it. 'Please, Master' covered all of it. It was a plea for anything he could or would do to her, whatever would make her lose control, stop wanting to fight. Otherwise, the tides inside her shifted too suddenly. Like now. She struck out at him with closed fists, hitting his upper thigh, his hip. He caught her wrists. She tried to jerk back but he simply clasped both wrists in one impossibly strong hand and removed the scarf with the other.

"Un-unh. Settle down." As he pulled the scarf away, she blinked. He was on one knee in front of her, his mouth set and serious eyes seeing everything. He threaded his fingers through her bangs, stroked them back from her eyes and then he rose to his feet, shifting his grip so he had one wrist in either hand. He pulled her arms around his upper thighs so her hands were molded against his muscular buttocks, a pleasing place to pin her palms. Her fingers curled against the pockets.

"Put your mouth on me, Celeste. Occupy those lips of yours with something other than getting you in trouble."

He hadn't removed his jeans, so she was frustrated by the barrier, but she gave it full effort, opening her mouth and pressing against the fly, licking the denim, stroking her tongue up the length of the hard shaft beneath. She breathed heat through the jeans, used her teeth on the stiff fabric to increase the pressure. He kept his firm clamp on her wrists, and weirdly, though she was gripping his buttocks as much as the fabric allowed and trying to give him oral sex through it, she kept pulling against him, trying to get away even as she mouthed and tongued his cock and held on to his ass as if she never wanted to let go. Her own bottom hurt from the strikes of the brush and her come was trickling down her thigh. Or maybe that was more arousal, because it didn't seem that she'd had an ebb period from that last climax. She needed more now.

"More," she muttered against him. She bit down on the thick denim of his fly harder, trying to inflict pain, an instant before she remembered he'd said he couldn't yet trust her not to use her teeth. She couldn't control the surges of anger that hit her at odd points like this one. The truth of it defeated her, filled her with despair, but he wasn't letting her go there. Instead, he shifted her in one smooth movement, putting her on her back as he straddled her face. He pinned her arms with his knees as he'd done before. With that cue, her lips parted, a savage eagerness rising in her breast. She watched him open his jeans, stretch that beautiful cock out, thick, hard and long. Her lips were already parting as he pushed the smooth broad head into her mouth. As he made her take his full length, even when she choked, he kept his eyes on her face. The golden-brown eyes were brilliant and ruthless now, convincing her he was her Master, whether she said it or not.

"You bite me, and I'll beat you within an inch of your life," he promised. He gripped her hair, used the pull on her scalp to thrust in and out. Her gaze clung to him, the plea in her eyes. Her pussy was aching, empty.

"Get me nice and slick and I'll see where else I can put this."

Thank God. Nothing like giving a girl a goal to distract her from the unwise compulsion to do exactly what he'd warned her not to do--use her teeth. She sucked his length, ran her tongue over him, got him as wet as she was between her legs.

She made a noise of protest as he removed himself from her lips, but his eyes flashed, telling her he'd have his way. He moved down her body, hiked her thighs up over his elbows, holding her up high, hips off the floor. He nudged her anus with his cock, telling her he might fuck her there, but in the end he pressed his thick length against her cunt, holding her gaze as he pushed deep into her snug channel, as she rested in his arms, helpless as a doll. Fucking her temporarily ended the fight, all control ceded to him as he took full possession. The man could destroy every ounce of resistance she had with his pacing, that leisurely rhythm that built her to an excruciating level of sensation. Their position gave him all the control over rhythm and force. Though she did tighten her thighs and stomach muscles and try to increase the rate of thrust, she was unsuccessful.

"Who's in charge, Celeste?"

"You are."

"Who?"

She met his gaze, was swallowed up in it. Inside those honey-gold depths she could trust; she could be brave. "Master." *You're my Master.*

He began to come, his seed marking her inside, his strength holding her as he carried them both to a place where she didn't have to think about anything else. Not right now.

"Come for me, Celeste. Come now."

How could she resist anything he commanded?

§

When it was over, he didn't leave her, just as he'd promised he wouldn't. He bid her stay where she was, went into the guest bathroom and ran the water. When he returned with a washcloth, she'd sat up and was trying to get on the bed despite legs weak as noodles. He sighed, helped her get there, then promptly put her over his lap and gave her a spanking that, on top of the switch and brush, hurt like fire. She struggled and cursed him, but when he was done and laid her down on her stomach on the comforter, the fight went out of her. Especially when he used the warm cloth to clean her, and tucked her under the comforter before she could get cold.

He took the items back to the bathroom, and was in there long enough to suggest he was cleaning himself. She drew circles on the comforter, tried not to think of anything. Upon his return, he pulled back the covers, bent and brushed his lips over her sore ass. Cupping his hands under her thighs, he started eating her pussy. In no time, she was clawing the covers, on the cusp of climax once more. The man was a freaking machine, and he was going to kill her.

Confirming it, he stretched out on the bed, turned her over and made her straddle his body. Hands clamped on her hips, he lifted her up and set her on his cock, shoving up into her hard enough she gasped. He held her there, spread cunt firm against his pelvis, as he picked up the scarf he'd left on the pillow and looped it behind her neck. Twisting it over his fingers, he rested his closed hand against her sternum and brought her down so she was leaning over him, their eyes a few inches apart.

"You hold me tight inside, Celeste, and lift off of me slow. When you get to the head, you rotate your hips once, and push all the way down to the hilt again, just as slow. At my pace. You listen to my voice and follow direction. Starting now. Squeeze it and push up onto your knees."

It required taut stomach and thigh muscles, and

excellent control. She was already so close to coming from his mouth, she found her control faltered within three rounds, but he kept her doing it, kept her to his pace.

"Do you want me to let you come, Celeste?" His eyes were on fire, his mouth set in a fierce line, and from the ripple of muscle all along his body, she knew he was just as close as she was.

"Yes, Master. Please."

"All right. I'm going to hold you just like this, Celeste. You work your hips on your Master until he comes. I want to see you working hard, your face all flushed. You rub those beautiful breasts against my chest some more. When you make me come, you can come."

Christ. Who'd have ever thought she'd be with a male partner who'd have better control over his climax than she did? She wanted to hate him for it, and wanted to give him everything in the world to keep doing what he was doing. She couldn't hold out. She started to shudder within seconds, and her panicked look shot to his face.

"Ask, Celeste."

"May I?"

"Yes. Fucking yes. Come."

They came almost at the same time, him only a hat drop behind her. He kept his fingers hooked hard into the twisted folds of the scarf, pulling her down so her face was against the side of his as her hips pistoned on him, as he gripped her ass with his other big hand and worked her on him until the full measure of the climax was so pleasurable she could have blacked out. She muffled her shrieks against his thundering pulse, and was afraid she'd maybe deafened him, but he didn't seem out of sorts about it.

He guided her limp body into a curl against the side of his, keeping the length of the scarf wrapped around his hand like a tether. The tails of the blue fabric were in a folded line across his chest, his hip bone. She played with it, looped it around his cock and earned a chuckle.

"You leave that on me, and I'll stick to it when I dry, darlin'. You'd take too much pleasure in pulling my skin off."

Freeing it from his cock and her throat, he rewrapped it around her wrist, knotting it there. She left that hand resting on his chest as she listened to his beating heart. She traced the graze mark in his side, now a thin scab, caused by the same objects that had pierced Jai's chest, killed him. "I don't want you to go."

"I know." His arm tightened around her. "Believe me, darlin', I don't want to leave you, either. By the time I get back tomorrow night, you'll have decided you shouldn't have done any of this, and be pushing me away again."

"Yeah. I'm sorry." Didn't change it, though.

He gave her a squeeze. "I didn't ask for your apology, Celeste. Seems like it works out pretty well for both of us, working through that. I've got no complaints." He shifted, glancing out through the sheer curtains, where night had fallen and the moon was rising. "I still owe you that dinner, but I have a feeling you need sleep more."

"I should get up and at least say hello to Cass and Marcie."

"No. Not tonight. It'll keep. I think Cass and Marcie are still out dealing with wedding stuff, and Lucas understands where we're at tonight. None of them will be surprised if they don't see you until the morning. Though I'll go root you up some food if you're hungry."

Celeste struggled with the dictates of courtesy, but in truth, she was relieved to concede the point. She wasn't up to social chat tonight and she wasn't hungry. Remembering he'd leave in the morning brought on a whole other set of discomfiting emotions that filled up her stomach.

"I'll miss you." She would, terribly, and that worried her worse.

"I'll miss you. We'll touch base tomorrow, don't worry. You answer that phone when I call, even if you've talked yourself into a snit. Don't make me call Lucas to make sure you're okay. When I come back, I can bring things a lot worse than that brush."

That gave her another shiver. He chuckled again, a bear's growl. "Yeah, you'll test me to the limit, won't you? Shut up for now and let's sleep."

"I didn't say anything," she protested.

"Darlin' you say more with your silence and your body than most women say with their mouths. Then you have that sharp-assed tongue on top of it. Lucky I'm a patient man."

She sulked a little over that, but worried the scarf around her wrist, plucking at it. He'd kept the other end twisted around his own hand. "You're not going to take this off?"

"No. Not while we're sleeping. I'm making sure my sub stays right where I put her. Go to sleep. Turn it off for a while. It's all right." He kissed her forehead, held her close.

She closed her eyes, hoped he was right. She wanted the feeling in her gut that said things were going to get worse to be wrong. But the more he proved his worth, the more she'd push him away. She knew it. Or did she?

There was a first time for everything. She carried the hope into her dreams.

Too soon, she woke to him sliding out of the bed. A bleary look at the clock showed it was a couple hours before dawn. She knew he wanted to have time to get in before his shift, see what was happening with the case and how he could help. She knew that because he explained it to her in a murmur as he bent over her to capture her mouth in a kiss. She was still groggy, but not so much that she didn't slide an arm around his neck, press her bare body against his clothed one and do her best to convince him to stay. He put his hip on the bed and pressed her back into the pillows as he took over the kiss, making it demanding and hot, his arm banded around her back, crushing her to his chest. He slid his other hand beneath the covers, between her legs, making a sound of approval as her thighs loosened and parted for him. He had her rubbing up against his fingers and the heel of his hand in no time. When the climax rolled through her, quiet and intense, she made tiny little feminine cries against his mouth. He massaged her through it, kept kissing her mouth, her cheek, her ear and throat.

When he drew back, he was looking at her with fierce and focused eyes that roved over her face, over her breasts that he'd exposed by pulling the covers down to her waist. He bent and closed his mouth over one nipple, suckled it to a rigid peak, then moved to do the same to the other as she curled her hand in his short hair, the back of his neck, holding him to her.

"Please don't leave." When he was gone, she'd start re-erecting her walls, wonder what the hell had caused her to surrender so unconditionally to him, to give up with what seemed like barely a fight. She didn't want that to happen.

"Christ, you don't make anything easy." He framed her face, ran his thumb over her lips. "I need you to make me a promise, Celeste. It's important."

At the serious look in his eyes, she closed her hand over his to hold it between her breasts, her slim fingers sliding over his large ones. "I'm listening."

He studied her. "It's one thing to act out with me. It's part of what you and I are exploring together, and I told you I have no problems with that. You're not going to drive me away by being a brat. Understand?"

Not sure where he was going, she nodded, because she could tell he wasn't going to continue until she acknowledged it. "But you pursuing a story lead here or getting a cup of coffee with your credit card just to prove I can't tell you what to do?" He touched her chin with his free hand, a tender reproof. "I'm asking you not to do that. If you follow the directions I gave you, you'll be safe here. Don't take risks with your life just to piss me off."

"I'm not an idiot, Leland. At least not about that." She traced the silhouette of his face with her fingertips. Every part of her hungered for him, wanted him to stay in the bed with her. So she did her best to paste on an indifferent look, give him a haughty sniff. "And it's not all about you, you know. I would have used the credit card or pursued the story lead because it pissed me off that a piece of shit like Dogboy was keeping me from living my life."

His lips curved, eyes warming. "Just imagine how good you'll feel when you hear he's caught and going away for a long time."

She sobered at that. "I'm not sure that will make me feel good, a teenager so messed up he's ruined his life before it barely started, but I'll be glad he can't hurt anyone else." Her fingers dropped to his shirt collar, curled around the fabric. "You be safe, too. Okay?"

She'd spent so much time around cops, but it had never hit as hard as it did now, the kind of job he did. A lot of police work could be tedious, but it could change on a dime. And he worked the most dangerous district in Baton Rouge. Yesterday he'd been right in the thick of things. For her.

"I don't know how long you'll put up with me," she said, staring at his chest, "But I'm going to say it once more, just in case. Thank you for being there. For keeping me safe yesterday. And today."

He considered her. Sitting down on the edge of the bed, he dug in his pocket, stretching out one long leg to get his fingers into it. When he straightened, he clasped her wrist, wound something like a rubber band over it. Reaching over, he switched on the bed lamp so she could see it.

It was a girl's hairband, the kind they wore around a ponytail. The band was blue with silver threading, the pair of marbleized balls that formed the clasp twisted over one another. On her thin wrist, the hold was snug but not constricting. He verified it himself by running his fingers under it, then he tugged lightly on one of the balls. When he let it go, it knocked against her wristbones, enough to be uncomfortable. She looked up at him, surprised. Leaning in, he kissed her mouth firmly, shooting her that eye-to-eye laser look of his.

"Every time you start to put yourself down, Celeste, you pop that against your wrist. That's an order from your Master. You keep count of it, because when I see you again, I'm going to ask how many times you had to do it."

She set her mouth in a thin line. He read her reaction, closing his hand over her wrist. When her biceps constricted to pull back, he merely increased his grip. "No," he said.

She stilled at the look in his eye. "Why are you carrying a little girl's hair thing around with you?" she asked, letting the reporter take precedence. It was easier than facing the other feelings.

"I picked that up on a domestic violence call. Mom tossed her little girl against the wall because she got in her way when she was high. Put her in a coma, and she died. There were other kids in the home, two boys, and the only good thing that came out of that was we were able to get them out of there. Placed with a grandmother who'd been doing her best to get custody of all the kids. The system sucks, because it took killing one of them to make it happen."

He looked down at the hairband, twisted the balls, caressed her wrist around them. "I think about that little girl a lot, about what she would have dealt with as she grew up. How she would have found a sense of self-worth with a mother like that." He looked up at her, holding her with his steady gaze. She wanted to look away, but she couldn't. The things that made her uncomfortable in his expression were the same things that made her need to keep looking, holding that connection.

"I've found people are far stronger than they know. Adversity tests and shapes character. Some tests we pass, some we don't. You're a strong woman, Celeste. Terrifyingly strong." He tightened his hand around her wrist, over the band. As he did, he leaned in again, brushed his lips over her cheek, put them to her ear in that way he had, where everything became about his scent, his heat, the whisper of his voice echoing inside her. "Let this remind you that you have someone in your corner. Someone who knows how strong you are, who wants to be with you. Who doesn't 'put up with you.' I can't wait to see you again, and I'll be counting the minutes before I'm touching you again, talking to you, listening to what you have to say about damn near anything."

He kissed her and rose, headed for the door. Her eyes landed on the nightstand. "Wait."

She left the warmth of the bed, coming to him naked and bearing the container of cookies. His eyes slid over her, and then reached her face, a smile on his own that made her heart stutter. She put the container in his hand and, on second thought, took out two oatmeal cookies for herself and let him have the rest. "Because I ate most of your lunch and didn't let you get any dinner," she said.

"I had better things to eat last night," he said, and then captured her lips in a hotter kiss as her cheeks warmed. He cupped her bottom, gave it a rough squeeze. "Get back in bed woman, before you freeze."

But he cupped the back of her skull, holding her one extra second before he pulled back and left her, sliding out the room and closing the door behind him. He left so swiftly, she realized he was having a hard time tearing himself away from her, too. And that wasn't a bad way to start the day.

She'd wondered what was waiting at the bottom of that downhill slide. Since last night, she'd discovered the answer.

His arms. Him. Ready to catch her.

Chapter Thirteen

"Get up, lazy bitch. Daylight's wasting."

Celeste came out of her doze to hear the cheerful, sultry voice, a mix of Lauren Bacall and Marilyn Monroe. A scant second later, she yelped and rolled out of the way, nearly tipping off the side of the bed as the owner of the voice jumped onto the mattress with both feet and tried to come down on her in a wrestling pin. Celeste would have vacated the bed entirely and taken a defensive stance, but she hadn't left the cocoon of covers since Leland had departed, not wanting to disrupt the scent of him on her skin or the bedding. She'd dozed back off with her head on his pillow, nose against it.

"Hey, perv, I'm naked here," she protested, blocking Marcie's jabs as best she could while hanging onto the sheet for modesty. "Is this how you treat a guest?"

"You're not a guest. You're practically family, and it's okay to abuse them." Marcie settled back onto her heels in the tangle of bedding. "I've already been to the gym and kicked the asses of three guys twice my size. You should have been there. You could have helped." Her brown eyes surveyed Celeste's face, her bare shoulders. "But I see you had your own sparring session. Wish I could have helped with that."

The wicked spark in her gaze had Celeste smiling. "Back off, skank. You got your own man."

Marcie chuckled, then seized a pillow and began to beat Celeste about the head and shoulders with it. "Hey, hey," Celeste yelped again, diving for the other pillow and fending off the blows as she grimly clutched her cover. "What the hell?"

"Oh. My. God. Leland freaking Keller? You couldn't have mentioned you were dating a hot cop via email, text, phone call, carrier pigeon? Dana and Rachel nearly shit bricks."

"Rachel eats too much healthy stuff to shit bricks. More like neatly packaged pellets that smell like rosemary and cilantro and fertilize organic gardens." Fully awake now, Celeste managed to locate her clothes. Leland had left them folded neatly over the top of the occasional chair. Her garment bag was hanging in the open closet, her rolling tote on the floor beneath it. "And we're not dating," she added. "He doesn't date."

Marcie sat back on her heels again. She had her blonde hair pulled up in a ponytail and still wore her workout clothes, black leggings and a Danskin tank that showed off her fit body. She worked corporate investigations and excelled at it, but she'd been talking about applying to the Municipal Police Academy in New Orleans. Having just experienced how precarious a police officer's life could be, and knowing how protective Ben O'Callahan was of all the women in his adopted K&A family, let alone his fiancée, Celeste wondered how Marcie and he would work that one out.

"Can you give me a minute to get dressed?"

"I've seen you naked before. We've taken showers at the gym, so I know all about your impressive rack and skinny ass."

Except her skinny ass was sore and she was certain it bore noticeable marks, which made her self-conscious.

Marcie was marrying a hard-core sadist Dom. To Celeste's mild mortification, it only took her a moment to put it together.

"Oh." Her expression went from teasing to practical. "I have a great ointment from Rachel that helps you heal fast and keeps the skin sensitive. I'm kind of surprised, though. Leland isn't usually that heavy-handed. Not that I know that firsthand," she hastened to say, as Celeste narrowed her eyes. "Just info I've pulled out of Ben. I've never seen Leland play publicly. He doesn't go to the clubs that often. Maybe because he's a cop and has to be more careful about being recognized, but Ben thinks it's more because it's not his thing. He likes to be more one-on-one, all about him and his sub."

"Marcie." Celeste ran a hand through her hair. It bothered her, hearing it discussed like a singles tennis match, rather than something more personal. Which was stupid, since they had hardly been seeing one another long enough for her to be jealous. "Let me get dressed and then

I'll come down. Okay?"

"Sure. Okay." But first Marcie came around the bed, and sat on the edge of it. Before Celeste could anticipate her friend, she slid her arms around her, hugged her close. "I'm so sorry about yesterday, Celeste. But I'm glad you're okay. Really glad. Sorry. I should have come in a little more low-key. Wedding stuff has me in hyperdrive."

Her strong arms were more welcome than Celeste had expected. She smelled like happiness and love, eau de bride-to-be. Celeste sighed, hugged her back. "You shouldn't worry about me at all. This is your week. That's why I didn't want to intrude."

"You're no intrusion at all. Are you kidding? I'm happy to have you here." When Marcie drew back, all Celeste saw in the young woman's lovely face was sincerity. "If you remember, months ago I told you I wanted you to be here for as much of it as you could. You just forgot because you're always in hyper-workaholic mode. So though I'm not glad of the reason, I'm glad you're able to be here early. You can hang out at the house, do whatever you want today, but we do have a champagne brunch this morning out on the gazebo, my version of the bachelorette party."

"What? You didn't want to get drunk off your ass and do the pelvic grind with a bunch of hot strippers?"

Marcie chuckled. "I'm such a lightweight, I'd wake up in some biker lair with a tattoo of a pink poodle on my ass. Dana would make sure of it. No way. Besides, that 'last night of freedom' thing doesn't make any sense to me. When Ben asked me to marry him, that's when I felt like the whole world opened up to me. Everything that mattered."

"Ugh. Eww. Gross." Celeste pretended to stick her fingers down her throat and Marcie shoved at her, grinning.

"See, if you were still writing the business social column, you'd have a great quote. Very touching."

"Thank God I'm doing gang warfare and violence. The most affectionate thing I hear on the job is 'Bitch, get out of my face before I fuck you up.'" She shifted and winced, and Marcie's fingers stroked her arm.

"C'mon, let me see. I want you to be comfortable today, and Leland wants us to take care of you."

"I'm sure inspecting my naked butt wasn't what he meant."

"When it comes to a protective Dom, you'd be surprised what that means."

Celeste shook her head. "Seriously, I appreciate it, but leave it be. I'm not like you guys, you know. In that inner circle where you can run around naked together and play in front of each other. I'm a bit shier about things."

"Okay. But look for aspirin in the bathroom cabinet, and I recommend a hot shower. There's a body scrub in there that is awesome. You'll feel like a new person. Come join us whenever you're ready. Brunch is at ten, and the food is going to be to die for. That's why I did the extra workout today. I have a dress that's going to make Ben's tongue roll out of his head, but it fits like a second skin."

"Moron."

"Yeah, I know. The plan is to have him rip it off of me before oxygen deprivation results in long-term brain damage." Marcie smiled, but Celeste noticed a tension to the gesture that raised her curiosity. Marcie didn't pause for breath, though. "It's crazy. I decided to do this week apart thing before the wedding, but he got his revenge. Told me I couldn't do *anything* to take the edge off. You know you're hurting for it when you switch the phone off vibrate because that weak-assed hum might shove you into full-blown orgasm."

"TMI, girlfriend. Way too much."

"Not. You know you're eating it up. I agreed to it only because he agreed to the same."

Celeste raised her brows. "You're depriving a sexual sadist of an outlet for a week, when he practically has sex with you six times a day to stay on an even keel. There's a good plan. You're going to be the one who'll need medical care."

"I'm looking forward to it." Marcie winked, slid off the bed. "See you in a bit. Really, though, take your time. Cassandra had the whole thing catered, so we don't have to do a thing."

Reaching out, she ran her fingers lightly over Celeste's jaw. "You have a whisker burn. Might want to conceal that, unless you want to brag some. Oh, and don't be giving me that stink eye when I say things about Leland. You got to sample my man. I think fair is fair."

"Don't make me hurt you. That was years ago, long before Ben knew about your diabolical plans for him."

Marcie grinned again. "You're possessive. It's a good sign."

Before Celeste could get uncomfortable or defensive about that, Marcie moved toward the door. Once there, though, she stopped, looked over her shoulder.

"I'm not all that surprised to see you and Leland together. He's one of the good ones, and I don't know anyone who deserves that kind of man more than you."

On that entirely unexpected statement, one that hit Celeste right under her rib cage, Marcie slipped out, leaving Celeste looking down at the hairband still fastened around her wrist, her Master's reminder of his presence. *And that you have someone in your corner... I'll be counting the minutes before I'm touching you again.*

That made two of them...

§

She thought about not going, just opening up her computer and writing up some of her latest notes, plotting out other storylines, but in the end, she couldn't do that to Marcie. Plus, she didn't really want to be alone with her thoughts. Maybe she wanted to be around women who might understand, in a variety of ways, the conflicting feelings she was having.

The screened gazebo in the beautifully landscaped backyard had been set up for the breakfast, a round table with white linen and six place settings accented by a center arrangement of sunflowers nestled in a frame of white roses. As she approached it, she found the women drinking champagne outside the gazebo, chatting together on lounge chairs or standing. As she hung back, her gaze moved over all of them. The reporter in her automatically reviewed the basics about each of the women, though a deeper, personal part embraced the warm energy of their company. She could feel it reaching out to draw her closer, even before they noticed her.

That didn't surprise her. The Kensington and Associates executive team were indescribable, both in their bonds with each other and with the women in their lives. Each of them had found the submissive of his heart and made her his, and every one of those women was an accomplished, strong individual in her own right.

Dana Winston, Peter's wife, was an Army veteran who'd lost her sight, hearing and almost her life in Iraq. Reconstructive and plastic surgery, as well as a cochlear implant, had taken away most of the outer scars and improved her hearing, and now she was a minister at a local church that served a poor inner-city population. Peter, K&A's operations manager, overseeing both their domestic and overseas physical plants, had been a captain with the National Guard and had served tours overseas himself. That experience, as well as his nature as a Dom, had helped pull Dana out of the despair and PTSD. Her submissive nature had responded to his command and unrelenting love, a yin and yang that gave both of them life again.

Rachel Forte was a physical therapist and yoga instructor who'd crossed paths with Jon through Dana's therapy. Jon was the most spiritual of the K&A men, a male with genius-level engineering and invention skills. Rachel was thirteen years his senior, yet Jon had a steady core that left little doubt of his skills as a Master, especially when a woman met his gaze and saw it simmering there, ready to take control of her pleasure and her needs. Only now all of that skill was dedicated to Rachel. When Celeste had first met Rachel, she'd been shy, unsure of herself. Though Celeste didn't know her full story, she'd suspected some type of extreme psychological abuse. There was almost no trace of it now. When Rachel fully embraced her submissive side with the right Master, she'd bloomed anew.

Celeste's brow creased as she thought about that. There'd been a time in her life she would have sneered at the idea of submission being an avenue to confidence and personal strength. Even up to a few days ago, she'd had only an academic acceptance of it, but she thought about the way she and Leland played off of one another, the way he'd simply put aside her assertion that he didn't deserve someone as messed up as she was. He'd treated that like a bullshit defense tactic, and somehow transformed her into a quivering, passionate creature who called him Master and was eager to please, filled with pleasure at his desire for her.

"Celeste, we're so glad you could join us."

She emerged from her thoughts to find Cassandra Adler had noticed her and left her conversation with Savannah to come and draw her into the group.

Lucas's wife was a top negotiator with Pickard Consulting, a division of Pickard Industries. Supposedly she and Lucas had crossed paths during a negotiation with K&A where Cassandra had done what most women couldn't. Holding her own against the full charm and force of will of the executive team, she'd brokered a pretty even deal for the Pickard client she'd been representing. About twenty-four hours after that, she'd been engaged to Lucas. Celeste had always suspected there was more to the story, but until her friendship developed with Marcie, she hadn't found out what it was.

Celeste was getting ready to move to Baton Rouge, branching out on her blog, doing freelance work between Baton Rouge and NOLA, when Marcie graduated college and began her pursuit of Ben O'Callahan. It was a passion she'd nursed ever since she was sixteen years old and Lucas had married her sister, bringing Marcie and her family into the K&A fold. She and Celeste had met at the MMA gym where Celeste was already a member. Celeste had been quick to tell Marcie who she was. She had a high regard for the K&A men at that point, a direct contrast to how their relationship had started, and she didn't have any intention of being construed as trying to dig up stories by assuming a friendship with one of "the family."

That awkwardness was a blip on the screen and then gone, because she and Marcie had clicked as friends in a way Celeste hadn't experienced in quite some time. Though she'd never let Marcie close enough to know half of what Leland had figured out about her in the first night, and she dodged any topic about her family, Celeste still felt a close bond to the young woman. Marcie was shrewd enough to get the hint and leave Celeste's past untouched. However, the young woman's tact and compassion about anything related to family suggested she'd long ago deduced Celeste was pretty alone in the world.

Yet Celeste had never felt pity from Marcie, and her moving to Baton Rouge hadn't dimmed the friendship. She and Marcie drove back and forth between Baton Rouge and NOLA regularly to visit one another, as well as texted and emailed. So, eventually, Celeste had learned the missing piece about Cassandra and Lucas's love story. They'd met months before that business meeting, a hot, passionate encounter in the Berkshires that involved a motorcycle and Lucas's very clever mouth. Marcie couldn't be budged to say more than that, respecting her sister's privacy, but that brief incident had been enough to leave a big impression on both Lucas and Cassandra. Celeste thought of her and Leland's first meeting in a convenience store, and understood how that could happen, in a way she wouldn't have only a week ago.

For her side of things, as Celeste and Marcie became closer friends and Marcie began to open up to her about her deep submission to Ben, Celeste had faced her own disclosure dilemma. Eventually, she'd taken her courage in both hands and let Marcie know about the night at Club Surreal. In a very high level overview way, one that made cliff notes look like Tolstoy's *War and Peace*. And with great emphasis on how *very* long ago it had happened.

At first Marcie had seemed a little taken aback. When she said slowly, "Ben never told me", Celeste figured their friendship was over.

"He couldn't," Celeste hurried to say. "I mean, Matt promised they'd never say a word about it."

"*...you may be assured that what's on that tape is something that won't be discussed outside this circle. Not now, not ever. We don't impugn a woman's reputation...*"

"Oh." Marcie's expression had cleared, and Celeste had been nonplussed to see relief. Marcie closed her hand over hers. "That's their code. They'd never break that. Their über-chivalry is one of the things that can drive you crazy and yet make you love and trust every one of them beyond anything you ever expect. So...okay. I may have to take a couple face shots next time we spar, but other than that...we're good."

And that had been that.

Cassandra slipped an arm through hers, bringing her back to the present again. The woman with hair like white gold had facial features that reflected the family resemblance between her and Marcie, though Cassandra was a few years older, had blue eyes instead of Marcie's doe-brown color, and was more serious. Understandable for the oldest child who'd had to raise her siblings with an absent father and a mentally ill mother. Since that was a scenario that Celeste understood down to her bones, she'd always felt a special connection to Cassandra, seeing things in her eyes she expected the woman saw in hers as well.

"Normally I wouldn't try to put a guest to work," Cass said, giving her a squeeze, "but I do have a favor to ask."

"I'd be thrilled to help with anything you need," Celeste said, and meant it.

"Good." Cassandra lowered her voice, glancing over at Marcie, currently engaged in conversation with Dana. "Marcie could use a friend today. It's different, having a friend to talk with, instead of a sister. She's worried Ben is getting cold feet."

Seeing Cassandra was serious, Celeste blinked. "Is she insane? He's obsessed with her."

"He is, but Ben...he sometimes has difficulty when it comes to things like this. A couple times this week, Marcie has almost talked herself out of the 'week of separation before the wedding' thing, but I think it was a good idea. Breathing room, so she knows that trust and love don't need constant vigilance."

Celeste pursed her lips. "Well, whether or not Ben deserves her is a moot point. She can't live without him and he can't live without her, so he's just going to have to get his shit together and figure it out. He tries to bail, I'll run him down like a dog and beat him with a tire iron."

Cassandra smiled, gave her another squeeze. "You'll have to beat me to it."

Celeste thought of Ben that night at Club Surreal. There'd been a moment where she'd caught a look in his eyes, one she was pretty sure he didn't let anyone see that often. "He won't bail. He might be worried he doesn't deserve her, but he wouldn't hurt her like that. Not for anything. He loves her just as crazy much as she loves him."

"Yes, he does. It's scary and wonderful to watch. Oh, the caterer is waving at me." She handed Celeste the champagne bottle. "I could have hired waitstaff, but our discussions tend to be the private kind. If you don't mind making sure we all stay refilled, I'll be right back."

"Sure."

Just like Marcie's welcome, Cassandra's warmth toward her didn't suggest a knee-jerk hostess response. She was treating Celeste like a welcome friend. But then, ever since she'd met the K&A men and then their chosen brides, she'd never noted anything false about them. They simply made a person feel good, special.

A person they deemed worthy, she corrected herself, though she didn't mean that in the wrong way. She'd seen Matt Kensington's cool reaction to a reporter or business competitor that stepped out of line with him. He could cut someone off at the knees with merely a look. Most people didn't cross him. Except the woman wearing Christian Louboutin heels and an Ann Taylor classic style short dress in a sea-green color, who was currently handling a champagne flute in her elegant, long-nailed fingers. Her flaxen hair was loose in waves around her deceptively delicate features.

Savannah Tennyson Kensington, Matt's wife. Out of all the K&A wives, Savannah was the one who could always stand toe-to-toe with the formidable Matthew Lord Kensington, even while loving him with everything she was. More remarkable to Celeste--at the beginning, at least--Savannah was a submissive who softened at his merest touch or a look out of his piercing brown eyes. She and Matt had been blessed with a baby girl in the past year, and Celeste hoped to get a chance to see Angelica with her parents. She might not be doing business social news anymore, but those were the things she'd liked the best about that job. Seeing a real love match, and the happiness that came with the birth of a child. She couldn't capture the depth of those events in a way that fit the fluffy tone of the business social news, but she could feel them herself.

Celeste had once been no more educated than anyone else about BDSM, thinking a submissive woman was a subjugated one, weak-willed and a discredit to her gender. Or a victim of psychological or physical abuse. She'd injected those misconceptions with her own poison, resisting the craving for submission deep within herself. Which was why that night at Club Surreal had frightened her to the core, the way she'd been overcome by the heady need to surrender control to the right male. Leland was reopening that chapter and adding to it, offering her the chance to read a whole book about what lay within her. A journey it seemed he was more than willing to take with her.

But it would end, because every book ended.

Dana's glass was nearly empty, so she moved across the gazebo, putting herself squarely inside the circle of women gathering there. "There she is." Marcie smiled at her, taking her hand. "Stop moving, Dana. She's going to fill your glass."

Dana put her hand on Celeste's wrist as a guide for herself as Celeste topped off the glass. The woman with skin the color of caramel had short-cropped hair and wore dark glasses. She said she preferred that, since her unfocused eyes tended to be a distraction to someone looking at her. She wore dark slacks and a silk blouse that clung to her petite frame. A chain of jasper beads with a set of dog tags as the pendant was around her slim throat. Sliding her arm around Celeste's neck, Dana gave her a warm hug. "Heard you stirred up some trouble in Baton Rouge. Good for you."

Celeste chuckled. "Not so good for me. I'm getting behind on my deadlines as we speak."

"Eh." Dana waved a dismissive hand. "There will always be work. I'm thinking you had damn good timing, doing it a couple days before Marcie's wedding so you could come hang out here and be part of the fun and chaos. About time for Freak Girl to be married off."

"*I* wasn't the one dragging my feet," Marcie reminded her. "This was all supposed to happen in the spring, and I let myself be talked into waiting a few more months, 'to be sure you're sure,' he said. Even now, he's probably thinking of all the reasons this isn't a good choice for *me*."

"That's why Peter is shadowing him this week. So he can punch Ben's hard Irish head through a concrete block whenever he needs it."

Though Marcie smiled at Dana's declaration, Celeste saw the shadows in her brown eyes, the worry that Cass had mentioned. Dana had heard them in her tone, because she slipped an arm around Marcie's waist. "The boy's just a little fucked in the head when it comes to things like this. Once he sees you coming down the aisle in that spectacular dress, it'll all be over for him. He knows in his heart you're meant to be together."

"I get it. It all makes sense to me logically," Marcie said impatiently. "But having someone constantly telling you in ways large and small that he's not good enough for you, and you're better off without him, starts to wear on the nerves, you know? Especially when you have those moments that aren't about talking at all. I just look in his eyes, and I see that we're all wrapped up in each other, that there's no one else either of us wants. So why can't he focus on that instead?"

"Maybe because when you feel like nothing, you can't believe someone who's everything could possibly see the real you."

Celeste hadn't intended to say anything, but the words were out before she could stop them. Feeling the other women's attention turn to her, she frowned into her champagne and took a swallow to cover it. "I mean, it's just a possibility," she said lamely.

"A very good one." Rachel was on Marcie's other side now, her arm overlapping Dana's. She wore dark slacks as well, with a gorgeous flowing tunic in a swirl of earth tones. She gave Celeste a friendly nod, though her eyes were pensive. "Ben is afraid of not being everything you need him to be. He's been down some very dark roads in his life. But you have nothing to worry about. He's impossibly addicted to you. As Dana says, once he's standing at the altar waiting for you, nothing else will matter. To either of you."

"You know, you should just call him. Or go see him," Celeste said. "Neutral place, like a coffee shop. What's bugging you is how you left things before you stomped over here."

"I didn't stomp, I drove." Marcie shot her a look. "And I didn't tell you we fought over it."

"Yeah, you just did. Someone doesn't fret this much over something like that unless they left things hanging with the other person in question."

Cassandra joined them then, with Savannah at her side. "You didn't tell me you two fought over it."

Marcie shot Celeste a "gee thanks" look. Celeste shrugged that off. "So what did you tell him before you 'drove' over here nearly a week ago?"

"Fine." Marcie brushed her thick hair back over one shoulder. "I told him I'd had enough of the dumb-ass hints and foot-dragging, and I didn't want to see him until the wedding. I told him if he was going to bail, he'd have to do it at the altar, in front of all our family and friends." Marcie took a swig of the champagne, lifted her chin. "Bastard." Then the chin started to quiver and her eyes filled with tears.

"Oh Christ. I wasn't trying to make you cry." Celeste was set to dash forward to hug her, but Cassandra waved a hand, stepping forward to blot her sister's eyes with a ready handkerchief before her makeup was ruined.

"Don't worry. She's been like this all week. Like an emotional Ping Pong ball. Though now I know a little bit more why." The two sisters exchanged a look, Cass's older sister/motherly side showing. Marcie shook her head.

"It was between me and him. And would have stayed that way if it wasn't for nosy Lois Lane over there."

"Hey, the public had a right to know," Celeste gently teased her. However, feeling chagrined, she put down her champagne and slid closer to her friend.

"I was already glad to have Celeste here. Now I'm doubly so." Cassandra sent Celeste a reassuring look. "But Marcie, no tears, damn it. You'll get us all going. C'mon. The caterers are ready to serve and the food is so awesome, you'll forget all about him."

"Yeah. And I'll be back at the gym until the wedding."

"Not my fault you picked a 'fuck-me-right-in-front-of-the-minister' dress to wear for the wedding," Cassandra said mercilessly, making the women chuckle. At their hostess's gesture, they all moved into the screened gazebo, taking seats at the table. The napkins were placed in the center of the elegantly ridged white dishes, the silver napkin rings embellished with a fresh black-eyed Susan twined with a white rose, to match the sunflowers and white roses in the center arrangement.

"It is a very hot, very beautiful dress," Dana agreed, taking a seat next to Rachel. Celeste sat on the other side of Rachel, Marcie to her left, with Cass and Savannah completing the circle.

"I personally felt her up from head to toe when she had it on," Dana continued. "So I can say with great certainty that Ben will lose his freaking mind when he sees her in it. And there will be no fucking in front of the minister," she added.

"So says the minister herself, who just talked about feeling up the bride." A smile flirted around Savannah's mouth as she nodded a greeting to Celeste.

The caterer's waitstaff arrived to serve the breakfast, but Celeste noted they melted away after that. Only one female staff member, clad in black slacks and white shirt, remained, but she stood at a discreet distance outside the gazebo. She was close enough to be summoned, but she was well out of earshot, guaranteeing them the privacy Cassandra had noted would be needed. Considering the tone of the conversation, Celeste wasn't disagreeing. She also thought Marcie was right about needing a workout after the meal. The table was loaded with temptations, such as small quiches, croissants stuffed with goat cheese, berry tarts and chocolate truffles.

"There's a proper time and place for everything," Dana said. "Plenty of time for fucking after the wedding and the reception. You can let it all loose at the private after-party, in Ben's loft."

"Matt invited Leland to come," Marcie said.

Five sets of bright, curious eyes turned toward Celeste. "Bride can do no wrong," Marcie reminded her, giving Celeste a wide grin as she threw her to the wolves.

"On her wedding day," Celeste said darkly. "This is not your wedding day. A black eye wouldn't go so well with that hot dress."

"If three guys couldn't get through my defenses this morning, you have no chance."

"Yeah, yeah. Big talk."

"So, someone at the table has caught the attention of the world's most ineligible bachelor," Dana noted. "It's a miracle. How long have you been seeing one another?"

"Less than a week. But it's not like that. We're not really seeing one another. It's just...it's not dating." *Shut up*, Celeste told herself. *Stop talking*. Nervous people tended to fill up silence with information they shouldn't reveal. She used it as a tactic herself in interview. She picked up a platter of cheese straws and offered it to Marcie. "Here. Get fat. Tell me about the wedding. Music, self-written vows, what?"

Marcie waved that away, took one cheese straw and nibbled. "He brings you up here himself for your protection. Stays the night with you. Sounds to me like you're seeing one another."

"Stop poking at her, Marcie," Cassandra said. "You know what it is."

"Of course I do. I'm just hoping I can get her to give up details. Leland has so rarely played publicly, it's hard to know what kind of Dom he is. Well, I mean what type of things he prefers. You can see what kind of Dom he is in the eyes."

Yes, she could. Celeste waffled over it. She shouldn't want to talk about it. After all, talking about it as if he and she were together, as if she belonged to him...she wasn't there, was she? Okay, yeah she'd as much as said so in the heat of passion, but that was the heat of passion. To say it out loud now, for real...

Her gaze fell on the hairband, subtly visible under the long sleeve of her lavender knit shirt. Who was she kidding? "He's gentle. And stubborn. Sometimes ruthless, in a way that's hard to...resist."

Marcie's hand covered hers. "They can be like that. It's scary and wonderful at the same time. Like a roller coaster. Sometimes you don't know if the supports are going to give out at the most thrilling part."

Celeste's eyes lifted, met Marcie's. Earlier, she'd spoken

about Ben's motives without thinking, exposing too much of her own bitter emotions about the past. However, seeing the worry behind Marcie's eyes, and remembering what Cassandra had said, Celeste knew she could help. She could talk about herself in a way that wasn't about herself. She'd built her career galvanized by how much she wanted to leave her past behind, after all, which meant her past had helped her achieve that success.

"It's not that Ben doesn't love you, Marcie," she said slowly. "The problem is probably how much he does. You open up his heart in a way he never thought was possible. And he doesn't know how to trust that, because it's not something he ever expected to have. It's hard for darkness to believe it won't swallow light, because he's probably seen it happen so many times. He found a safe spot for himself, above all of it, where he had everything at arm's length, but you're right up inside him. You've made him feel clean, a part of the light, too. And that's a gift so big…he keeps looking for it to be a mistake, like a package delivered to the wrong house."

She was wrong. She couldn't talk about it without making it too personal, because she had a hard ache in her throat. She'd stopped talking, but Marcie's gaze was fixed on her, and she felt the attention of the other women again. "I'm sorry," she said. "That was so wrong. I'm sorry, I don't know why I said all that. This is your day."

"Yes, it is," Marcie said, her hand over Celeste's. "Which is why it's good for me to hear that. That night you spent with Ben, you saw it in him, didn't you? And Leland sees it in you."

Only in this company could Celeste imagine talking with a bride about the night her husband-to-be met another woman at a BDSM club and broke her open like an egg. Before ass-fucking her into climactic oblivion.

"I've only known Leland a few days. It's too much, too soon. I'm just babbling. You need to ignore me."

"For some people, it only takes a few days," Savannah said. "For some of us, it's a single moment."

"I met him in a convenience store," Celeste blurted out. "How do you find forever love in a convenience store?"

"Conveniently," Marcie quipped.

As the women chuckled, Dana shook her head. "We all know Leland. If that man was ever going to find forever love, that's where he'd find it. So did it happen by the nachos and cheap coffee?"

"Yes," Celeste said, and couldn't help smiling at the laughter that exploded around the table. Marcie squeezed her hand, hard, and let her go to snag another cheese straw and a berry tart.

"I recognize the men by their smell," Dana confided, mischief flirting around her bow-shaped mouth. "Like Ben. I can smell pasty white Irish boy a mile away. Leland's scent tells me I have a big, fine sexy black man headed my way, and the crappy coffee smell tells me exactly which one."

"And lemon," Celeste added. "Old wood, like from a historic house. Sometimes peppermint. He keeps a jar of peppermints on his coffee table." She flushed a little under their amused regard, but it was kind. They'd all been there. Every woman here had fallen hard for their chosen Dom.

"Jon smells like sandalwood," Rachel added. "My favorite time of day is when he gets home from work, and I put my nose against his throat, right there at the base, and inhale all of that. Especially when it's warm outside, so the smell just blends with his scent."

"Show of hands. Who hasn't snagged one of their shirts to wear to bed when they're away on a business trip? Except maybe Rachel, because Jon's got the lean sexy thing going on and she's got big tits," Marcie teased.

"I can wear one of his T-shirts," Rachel said with dignity. "They stretch."

"So, um...why hasn't Leland gone out with anyone in so long? Do you know?" The banter was making Celeste feel more comfortable, giving both the woman and the reporter in her permission to find out more about him. She expected she wouldn't find a better source, since this group seemed pretty familiar with the man's personal side.

"That's just Leland." Dana shrugged. "He decided he wasn't in the mood for casual anymore. He wanted it to matter, so he said he'd pursue a relationship with a woman when he felt the right spark from her. He's a 'still waters run deep' kind of guy."

"A reason he and Max get along well," Savannah put in. "Janet says they can have whole conversations sitting out on the porch together, trading nothing but the occasional grunt."

"Oh, I don't believe that. Max is such a chatterbox, I can hardly get him to shut up when he drives me to church," Dana teased. "Speaking of which, I hear that fine man is on the premises."

"He's here," Cassandra said, glancing toward Celeste. "He said he'd stay out of our way. He's just keeping an eye on things. Dale will come relieve him in the evening."

"I'm sorry for that," Celeste said, feeling a guilty pang. "I told Leland I should have stayed at a hotel."

"They're here for you," Savannah said with firm purpose, reinforced by the other expressions around the table. "We fully support that, every one of us. Matt would have done the same thing if you stayed at a hotel. You did something incredibly brave, Celeste."

"It didn't seem brave at the time. I was just so pissed that they were shooting at Leland, and then Jai…" She broke off at that. "It was such a waste. He was a good man. No matter what happens with the two of us, I think he'd like knowing Leland and I met at his place."

"I agree with all that, but what I meant was your determination to find out who killed those women, even when it brought you squarely into the sights of the man who killed them." Savannah kept those blue eyes on her, unwavering. "Your past may shape your future, your character, but it's your actions that determine your worthiness in this life, Celeste. I think Leland is very fortunate to have finally found a woman who can match his own integrity and inner strength."

Great. Now she was going to tear up as well. She shot Marcie a glance. "You need to call him, dumb-ass," she declared, fighting back her emotions.

"Leland? That is *so* nice of you. Quid pro quo and all that. A lot of brides have a last-minute fling, right? Is it true what they say about black men…ow." Marcie yelped and slapped at her as Celeste pinched her arm, hard. "Quit it."

"Call Ben, bitch. Tell him you'll meet him at Café Beignet. I'll take you. I want to do some shopping. Haven't bought you a damn wedding gift yet."

"I do have a gift registry, you know."

"Yeah, yeah, stuff I can't afford. I want to find you something cute and tacky you'll have to haul out every time I visit and tell me how much you love it."

"I'll just say I accidentally knocked it off a shelf and broke it during violent sex."

"Do you and Ben have any other kind? And thanks for the tip. I'll make sure whatever I buy is sturdy plastic."

"You don't have a car," Marcie hedged.

"Max will take you," Cassandra said brightly, shooting Celeste a pleased, conspiratorial look. "That way you don't have to worry about parking and driving."

"Here." Celeste produced Marcie's phone from under the table. She'd slid it off the edge when Marcie was talking to her sister. By glancing down, she'd quickly found the speed dial button for Ben's number. "It's ringing."

"You bitch," Marcie said, but she snatched the phone just as Celeste heard Ben answer. Marcie left the table, moving away for privacy. Savannah nodded.

"Nicely played, Celeste."

Cassandra agreed. "If I'd done it, I would have been the interfering big sister."

"Well, it's eating at her. And I'm just the irritating friend from Baton Rouge who visits her every few weeks. She can be mad at me."

"They're both terribly stubborn," Rachel said, fondness in her expression. "It won't ever be a tranquil marriage, but it will be a passionate and loving one. They're meant for one another."

Celeste had always scoffed at what seemed like a pat phrase, but as the women continued to chat, Celeste watched Marcie's body language out of the corner of her eye. She'd started with the phone to her ear, her other arm across her body, a defensive posture. As they talked, she began to wander and her hand fell to her side. Pressing the toe of her shoe against invisible divots in the grass, she curled a lock of hair behind her ear, her lips pressed together. She responded to something he said, and her gaze softened, as did the set of her mouth, lips curving. Celeste turned her attention back to the table then, her heart aching and every part of her missing Leland. She fingered the burner phone in her pocket, wishing it had come with a texting plan. But she could just call him, couldn't she? He was probably working. He said he'd call, after all. She'd just wait for that. No need to seem desperate.

§

Max was the head limo driver for K&A. Celeste knew that he and Janet, Matt's executive assistant, had become an item recently, but Marcie filled in some intriguing details while Max brought the car around. Janet was a Domme and Max...well, Max wasn't a sub in any way, shape or form. Celeste had to bite back the intense desire to interrogate him about how that worked.

Max pulled up and got out to open the door for them. Though a former Navy SEAL, his mannerisms and the superior fitness of his mouthwatering body suggested he considered himself still on active duty. The black jeans hugged strong thighs and a tight ass, the K&A logo polo shirt stretching over his wide chest and muscular biceps. His firm mouth didn't smile, but his storm colored eyes did. "Doing all right, Miss Lewis?"

A nice way to confirm that he was assigned to oversee her protection without being overt about it. Celeste nodded. "Thanks. For this. And to your friend Dale as well."

"It's our pleasure," he said.

Leland shouldn't have set this up without her say-so, but Celeste couldn't argue his choice of location or the type of people he'd put around her. When Max closed the door and returned to the driver's seat, she *really* wondered how a Navy SEAL acting as a sub worked. Having that powerful body, firm mouth and the simmering fire in those gray eyes at a woman's command...

"Don't worry," Marcie whispered, seeing Celeste's expression. "Janet comes to our monthly girl dinner parties. I'll make sure you get invited sometime soon. I bet we can get her to talk."

"You'd have a better chance of getting an al-Qaeda suicide bomber to spill," Max offered from the front.

"Donkey ears," Marcie said, sticking her tongue out at him in the rearview mirror.

"Don't make me pull this car over, young lady."

"Promises, promises." She batted her eyes at him and Max sighed.

"Incorrigible. All of you. It's bad enough I have to put up with Dana."

"He loves us," Marcie informed Celeste. "Wouldn't know what to do without us."

"Stretch out on a beach in Bimini, drink fruity drinks and read the latest *Guns & Ammo* magazine. I think Janet's due for six months of vacation time, at least."

"Yeah, and if you think Matt's going to approve that, think again. According to Savannah, he can barely survive a week without her, let alone six months."

"Matt can adapt."

Marcie gave him a look of mock horror. "I'm going to tell him you said that."

He chuckled and then focused on traffic as Marcie and Celeste chatted about the wedding and less-intense subjects for the drive into New Orleans. Celeste bit back another sigh as they passed areas where she'd be only a hop and a skip away from some story follow-ups. It was only for a few days, she reminded herself. Surely they'd find Dogboy quickly or verify he wasn't that much of a threat to her. Even if he had gone out of his way to take a shot at her yesterday, maybe the MoneyBoyz would set him straight and he'd give it up.

Yeah, because a psychopath killing women could turn off that urge like a faucet.

"I know you're going stir-crazy," Marcie said, touching her arm. "Don't worry. You'll be back to work in no time. Just think of it as a short vacation."

"I'm a workaholic. We abhor vacations."

"Turn it into a feature piece. 'Waterboarding or Vacation: Pros and Cons.'" Marcie smirked at her while the limo pulled up in front of Café Beignet. As she started to get out, Celeste held up her burner phone. "I'm going to go check out the Blue Dog gallery and the antique place across the street from it," she said. "Just call the burner number when you're ready to hook back up."

"I'll go with you. This will just take a second," Marcie said, surprising her. "Wait here."

When Marcie closed the door behind her and moved toward the front of Café Beignet, Celeste saw Ben was already waiting for her. It had been quite a few months since Celeste had seen him last, but she noted immediately the changes their relationship had wrought. Despite the conflict they were having, there was an easiness to his features, a warmth around his mouth and in his green eyes that had been missing during his and Celeste's evening. Some of the weights of his past had been lifted.

Celeste had dug into the backgrounds of the K&A men enough to know some things about Ben she was sure most outside his circle didn't, things that had prompted her insights to Marcie. Even at the height of her bitter and misguided state toward them, nothing would have compelled Celeste to expose his private struggle as an abandoned orphan. Or those empty blocks of time when it was obvious he'd chosen the streets over whatever the foster care system had offered. But here he was, top legal counsel for K&A, standing on the corner in tailored Hugo Boss. And all his attention was riveted on the woman who emerged from the car and came toward him as if the two of them were magnets.

Marcie had changed as well. She'd always been lovely and accomplished, but there was a grace and maturity to her movements, a deeper level of confidence that said she'd found the person she wanted to love and cherish forever. Despite Marcie's tears this morning, Celeste could tell her friend was sure he felt the same way, no matter his dark spaces. She went right to him, slid her arms around his neck and brought her mouth to his in a no-holds-barred kiss he took over in a heartbeat, his strong fingers in her hair, his other hand gripping her skirt at her hip in a possessive hold. The passion he injected in the embrace, the depth of the kiss, had Celeste blinking and Max suddenly looking at the dials of the temperature control with great interest.

New Orleans being what it was, a few catcalls and encouragement came from Café Beignet patrons and shopping pedestrians, but the couple seemed oblivious.

Both of Ben's hands were at her hips now, holding fast, and when Marcie pulled back, Celeste felt a shiver low in her belly at the look in his green eyes. She'd seen that look before, and knew exactly what he wanted to do to Marcie. He was a Dom who could masterfully administer extreme levels of pain, tangling them inexplicably with nigh-unbearable pleasure. He broke a woman's mind into tiny pieces, gathered them up and closed them in a fist, applying more pressure, somehow making her beg for more.

He'd been a one-time-only experience for Celeste, something she didn't need to repeat. Leland had proved his point. His unique blend of gentle force and relentless seduction as a Master had broken things loose inside her that even Ben's talents couldn't, probably because, despite the intensity of her session with Ben, there had been no intention that night to create a relationship. To start something for the long haul.

Acknowledging the thought gave her the usual spurt of panic, but she noticed it wasn't quite as strong. Not since yesterday, when Leland had come face-to-face with the core of her issues. Not only had he not run, he'd done everything right. She'd been upset, she'd fought him, she'd gone back to that sense of self-loathing, and he'd pulled her back from that edge, several times, until all that was left was being in his arms, exhausted...and content.

Celeste decided to leave the thought right there before she could twist it into something negative, and focused on the tableau in front of her.

Marcie was a different animal from Celeste. Her hunger for the extremes Ben had to offer was obvious in the strain of her body against his. Celeste had seen Marcie spar with men at the gym regularly. The blonde might take hits to the body and sometimes the face, but she'd just spit out the blood and come right back at them. She knew how to embrace pain. More than that, she'd obviously known how to reach through it to find Ben's heart, twine them together and take them on a rushing ride to physical and emotional bliss together.

That ache was back. Celeste dialed Leland's number before she could doubt herself. She almost hung up, but he picked up on the second ring.

"Celeste? You all right, darlin'?"

His voice sent a rush of pleasure through her so strong, she closed her eyes, told herself to pull it together. "Yeah. I just...um, anything new on the case? That you can share with me, I mean."

He paused. "That's not why you called."

"Let's pretend it is."

"Let's not. Did you wake up missing your Master?" His voice had lowered and she suspected he was moving away from someone so their conversation could become more private.

She glanced toward Max, who was checking some sort of log he had on his phone. Whether he was doing it to give her the illusion of privacy or not, she appreciated it. "Yes. I did."

"Good. I've had some pretty graphic thoughts about what I plan to do to you next time I see you. Things I think we'll both like."

"How soon do you think that will be? This is New Orleans. Lots of temptations here. I'm watching the bride-to-be have a heavy public make-out session with her over-the-top hot fiancé right now."

"Over the top, hmm?"

"I only report the truth."

"I'll keep that in mind. I'll be there sooner than later, so you behave." She heard the smile in his voice before he sobered. "Dogboy's gone to ground, but the detectives think it's just a matter of time. We put out an APB and released his picture to all the news outlets. We're patrolling his favorite hangouts and haunts in the applicable districts. They're also rounding up and talking to his friends and neighbors, anyone we can get our hands on."

"Good. I'm going back to work on Monday, no matter what. Otherwise, I'll claim you're guilty of a First Amendment violation."

"I suspect there isn't a force alive that can inhibit your freedom of speech. Except a gag. Got a couple in mind for you."

"I think it's illegal for an officer of the law to be doing phone sex. Or at least inappropriate."

"You started it. You okay, darlin'?"

"Yes. Yeah. Just come back soon, okay. I...I'd like to see you."

She ended the call before the frogs jumping into her chest could overcome her. Marcie had broken the embrace with Ben and was backpedaling. A totally besotted grin was on her face as he held her hand, refusing to let it go. She said something and stopped. He cocked his head, a light smile on his lips, replied. Whatever he said came with a look that should have ignited everything flammable in a fifty-foot radius around them, but he let her go and slid his hands into his pockets. As she moved back to the limo, Ben glanced toward the front seat. Celeste saw him and Max exchange a nod of acknowledgment before Marcie jumped back into the vehicle. "Okay, how about the French Market after we check out Blue Dog? I can show you what I want and you can buy it."

Her skin was flushed, her lips swollen with that kiss, and she was practically vibrating. Celeste shook her head. "So what did he say? 'I'm done with you, ho, and have a nice life'?"

Marcie flicked her neck with long nails. "No. He said he'd meet me at the altar and if I valued my gorgeous ass, I'd better be on time. I told him I'd be there as long as I didn't have anything else more pressing. Hair-washing, a manicure, that kind of thing."

Celeste shook her head, then squawked as Marcie threw her arms around her, squeezed hard. "I'm getting married," she announced in giddy delight.

"Ow. You've been working out way too much. Let me go, Butch." But she caught Max's amused glance in the mirror and couldn't help smiling back at him.

Marcie settled back, tucked a lock of her blonde hair behind her ear and glanced out the window to see Ben still standing there. He was watching her window as if he could see her, despite the black tinting. For her part, Marcie put her hand on the glass as if she could touch him, then cleared her throat. "Let's go shopping."

Chapter Fourteen

Celeste lay in the king-sized bed that felt too big without Leland in it and played with the hairband, slipping it on and off her fingers, threading it through her knuckles, and then wrapping it back around her wrist again. She was lying on her side, looking through the sheer panels out into the back yard. The storage pod was a large block-shaped silhouette, the chairs, tables and other assorted items necessary for the ceremony and reception inside it. They'd be set up in the morning. Today a small army had strung white lights in the trees and set up the altar platform. The arbor of greenery over it threw shadows like lace against the lawn, thanks to the lit trees. Marcie had wanted the tree lights to stay on through the night. "So I can look at them from my window and dream about tomorrow," she'd said. Celeste couldn't bring herself to tease the girl for her unabashed schmaltziness, since her own heart had tilted at the simple purity of her happiness.

Tomorrow they'd fill in those spaces on the arbor with fresh flowers and more greenery. It would be a beautiful wedding. The weather was predicted to be a gorgeous fall day, sunny with temperatures in the low seventies, a light breeze and moderate humidity. The latter was of major concern for the bride, who had thick, natural curly locks. Cassandra had reassured her little sister. "Vivian's getting here mid-morning to do your hair. She'll shellac it with Gorilla Glue if needed."

Celeste had helped the sisters wherever needed, making some calls and helping with wedding favors, wrapping gifts for the groomsmen and bridesmaids. When they hadn't needed her, she'd slipped off to her room or the gazebo and caught up on some projects, fleshing out two articles she'd started, one on budget conflicts between state agencies and the governor's office, and the other on the local impact of New Orleans adding parishes to their metro area. Between her own notes and checking online resources, she had enough to work on those stories without making calls or pursuing avenues that would reveal where she was. It still chafed, however.

Even if she had been kidding Leland--and she wasn't sure she had been--she'd only play it his way through this weekend. If Dogboy was still at large on Monday, she was going back home. She had a gun and she knew how to use it, as well as her pepper spray. She'd carry both. He wasn't keeping her from her life.

Up until recently, her life was her work. But today had reminded her she did have a couple important friendships, and whether she shied from the idea or not, she was smack in the middle of a budding relationship. She twisted the balls of the hairband to tighten its grip. It made her think of Leland's hand there, but there was no comparison between the thin friction of the covered elastic and the energy in his grasp. He'd called back in the afternoon to tell her they'd had a double homicide in his district. Unfortunately, that made it impossible for him to get there that night to join the K&A men for their private get-together with Ben, or to be with her, but he'd promised to be there Saturday, bright and early.

She was disappointed enough that her neediness irritated her, so she'd told him fine, it didn't matter. She also told him she had to help Marcie with something and couldn't talk, so she'd hung up before he had a chance to say anything else. Or she could get snottier about him not coming back when she was hoping he would. She understood his job, understood the demands of it. It didn't make her feel less bitchy about it.

When she hung up on him, Marcie had given her an odd look. She'd been stretched out on a couch, Cassandra painting her toenails. Celeste just shrugged and went back to looking at the newsfeeds. A couple weeks ago, she hadn't had a man in her life and she'd been just fine. Better than fine. She was torn between rushes of feeling that went all the way to her toes, thinking about him, and a violent rejection of them.

Proving that she was suffering a major case of romance bipolarism, now she was lying in bed, cursing herself for being that short with him. If they'd had a longer conversation, she could have been going over that in her mind, rather than debating whether or not she should call him back. She thought of what Marcie had said, her frustration with having to deal with Ben's doubt, his pulling back because he thought he wasn't good enough for her. That had hit uncomfortably close to home, and made her blurt out those stupid things that were obvious self-reflection. Fortunately, none of the women had made her feel uncomfortable about it. Dana had taken it a step further. When the champagne brunch had ended, she'd slid an arm around Celeste, ran her hand down her arm, a comfort.

"It'll be all right, you know," the minister said. "When it's meant to be, these things tend to work out. No matter how hard you fight them. Trust me. Marcie's the only exception in this room. Every woman here had reasons to push away the men we married. Not little reality show dramas, either. Big, important reasons we each thought were totally insurmountable, but they proved us different."

"Why was Marcie different?"

"The shoe was on the other foot for her. She had to convince Ben the reasons didn't matter. That the way they felt for one another could break down every wall, heal every wound, and make him believe in a future together."

Celeste had gazed at the other four women drifting up the path toward the house. Cassandra said something to Savannah, and Matt's wife embraced her. Whatever they were discussing made Rachel chuckle. Marcie wrapped her arms around Rachel, putting her head on her shoulder while Rachel put both arms around her, kissing her forehead and stroking her head, the two of them rocking back and forth together as the four women continued to talk. "It's hard when you're still on the other side of the fence," Celeste said.

"Yes, it is. They could each tell you their story, and it would help some, but you're caught in your story now, and have to work your way through it before you can really hear theirs. Maybe when you've reached that other side, you'll join us one night and we'll all tell our stories, share them. Off the record." Dana nudged her teasingly.

"Sure, spoil all my fun. Marcie talks about those monthly dinners like they're vital therapy."

"Exactly. But better than therapy, because we have

wine and chocolate."

Coming back to the present, Celeste curled up under her covers. She'd been surprised to hear the murmur of Lucas's voice a couple hours ago. Apparently the men's get together with Ben wasn't an all-night bachelor party. His feelings about that must match his bride's, a good sign. If she had to guess, she expected it had been no more than a quiet congratulatory drink between male friends who were close as family. A bonded pack of brothers who understood one another in ways only matched by the relationships they had with the women in their lives.

Leland's smell was gone and she wanted it back. She wanted him back. She'd told Leland she didn't apologize for how she was, how she pushed away more often than she pulled someone close to her. There was no point to it. But she wanted to say she was sorry to him. Sliding her hand up to her throat, she curved her fingers there, thought of the collar he'd put on her. When it was there, so much had stilled, had gotten clearer. Or rather, she hadn't needed to think about her murky psyche.

The phone started to vibrate. Since he and the members of this household were the only ones who had it, she knew it had to be him. She drew it off the nightstand, closed her fingers around it. *Answer it. Answer it.* It was late, he would assume she was asleep.

Fuck it, stop it, you stupid, destructive bitch. She started to put the phone back on the nightstand, and then she hit the connect button.

"I'm asleep," she informed him.

"That's a shame. I was looking forward to having phone sex. That shrewish, nasty tone gets me going."

"I didn't know a Dom could be a masochist. Listen, I know I was pissy earlier today--"

"We talked about you apologizing, Celeste. You only owe me an apology when I tell you that you do."

"How do you know I was going to apologize? Maybe I was going to say 'Yeah, I was pissy. Deal with it.'"

He chuckled, the warmth of the sound unfurling inside her. "Are you in bed?"

"No. I'm at the desk, working."

"No, you're not. Are you in bed, Celeste?"

He could sharpen that baritone like distant thunder sliding along a knife. It focused her on his intent, giving the liquid arousal flowing through her an electric feeling. She thought of him with a knife in his hand, trailing the edge over her skin, so lightly, her slightest movement capable of producing a nick, but he trusted her to stay still when he commanded her to do so...

"Yeah, I am. I told you I was asleep."

"So you did. What were you thinking, right before I called?"

Her hand constricted on the phone. "I was...I put my hand on my throat, thought of the collar there."

"You miss it."

"I miss your hand there more." She curled into a smaller ball. "I'm so bad at this, Leland."

"Actually, you're outstanding at this. Some subs, they play games to test their Dom, or because their minds are all over the map, not sure how to handle surrender. You're brutally honest, darlin'. You lay a trail down in pretty colored lights for me to follow."

She wasn't sure what he meant by that, but he didn't give her a chance to press him to explain. "Put your hand back on your throat. Squeeze it, imagine your hand is my hand."

She did, and this time her breath shortened. "Leland..."

"Put the phone on speaker," he ordered. "Lay it on the pillow. You're not going to talk. I am."

"Okay." She did as he bid. "It's there."

"Cup your breasts with both hands. I love your breasts, darlin'. I've got big hands and you fill them up nice. Your nipples press into my palms, and I just want to suck on them all night long, bite on them, play with them until you're so wet I can lick all that honey off your thighs, rub my face in it, in your cunt. You'd spread your legs for me because I told you to do it, wouldn't you?"

"Yes." She wanted to do it now, so she slid on her back, still cupping her breasts, and let her thighs fall open. "I don't resent your job. I don't ever want you to think that. I just want you to be here." She sounded plaintive, and hated that. But his response drove that negative feeling away.

"If we hadn't had that double homicide, I'd be settling

between your legs now, easing my cock inside all that wet heat. You're a tight fit, Celeste. I like watching you take my cock, the way you have to concentrate, move your hips to make it fit. Makes me even bigger, makes you have to work harder for it."

She almost whimpered her frustration. "Where are you?"

"You know where I am. I'm inside you, Celeste. That's what's got you so spooked. And you're inside me. I couldn't stop thinking about you today. Tell me what you thought about."

"I thought about Marcie...and Ben. About how he pushed her away, too, and she stuck with it. I understood why he feels how he does. Because I feel that way, too."

"You think if you're not nice to me, I'll go away?"

"Yes."

"That's just not true, Celeste. You know the only thing that would make me go away?"

"I don't want to know. I'll do it, just because I'm me."

"No, you won't. The only thing that would make me go away is knowing you really, truly didn't want to be with me. And that isn't something your mouth tells me. It's something I feel. The more your mouth says go away, the closer you really want me. I feel it. You want me so close you can't even breathe. You'd give up breathing to have me that close."

She closed her eyes. "So why aren't you here so I can stop breathing?"

"Believe me, darlin', there's no place I'd rather be. Did you enjoy being with the girls?"

"They say they've never seen you play publicly. And they wanted to know if it's true about black men."

"That had to have come from Marcie." His voice held fondness. "That girl is trouble up one side and down the other. Are your hands still where I told you they should be?"

They'd started to slip away, but she put them back there as his voice returned to that thrilling note of command. It was probably good she wasn't one of the few female officers in his district. She'd embarrass herself on a regular basis, the way everything in her yearned toward that tone. "Yes."

"Good. If I tell you to do something, you keep doing it until I tell you otherwise. It keeps your mind occupied, keeps your body ready for me, for whatever I want to do to it."

She'd fantasized about phone sex, but hadn't thought it would really be her thing if the opportunity presented itself. She'd been wrong.

"Tell me what you've imagined me doing to you," he said.

"Why do you assume I've been spending any time thinking about that at all? I've been busy."

"Hmm. Well I don't want to interrupt that, so I guess I'll get back to what I'm doing."

"Jerk. Ass." She sighed as her fingers convulsed on her breasts. Her aching nipples could almost feel him there, the powerful suction of his mouth, the stroke of his tongue. Her hips bore down into the mattress, lifted. She was so empty. She didn't want to be empty. "I thought about you being here the other night. The way you just...took over. It's so quiet in here, so dark. I feel like I could do anything with you...for you. You took away my sight, with the scarf. All I felt were your hands, your breath. That was all that mattered."

"Yes. You're learning, darlin'. That's why I don't play publicly that often. It's between you and me. Matt invited me to the after-party at Ben's loft. He has a lot of equipment there. It'll be an intimate group, probably less than fifteen people. Would you like to go and watch, Celeste? Go as my sub? Tell me how your nipples feel."

"You know how they feel. It's you feeling them, at least in my mind."

"Hmm. So I'd say they're nice, firm points. And your breasts are warm from my hands."

"Yes. And yes. I would like to go...as your sub."

"As mine."

"Yes." She closed her eyes tighter. "I don't know about doing anything more than watching. I'm not sure if I'm like that."

"Well, as I said, I'm not much of a public player myself. We'll see how it goes. This is a pretty private group. They tend to be more reserved themselves. I expect they'll enjoy the equipment, but probably as couples, not sharing. Matt and Savannah tend to watch more when they're in a group as well, so you wouldn't feel self-conscious. Not that you'd need to worry about that, even if we were the only ones watching. I need to go, darlin'."

"Oh." She pushed away the disappointment. What had she expected, that he would stay on the phone with her until dawn? He needed sleep so he could get up early, come to her. "Well, I...when will you be here tomorrow? Or today." She glanced at the clock, saw it was after one.

"In about ten minutes. I have to get off the phone because I'm pulling up the drive and I need to let Dale know I'm not someone he needs to break into twenty pieces and then shoot."

Her toes curled in delight at the idea of seeing him so soon, but she tried to sound nonchalant. "Wouldn't he save himself a lot of effort just shooting you?"

"SEALs like a workout. See you in a minute, darlin'." His voice got husky. "When I get up there, I expect to see you naked and playing with those gorgeous breasts, your legs spread, showing me how wet your pussy is, because I'm going to fuck you first thing. No foreplay tonight. I need to be inside you."

He clicked off, leaving her in mid-shudder. She was warm all over, so it was easy to push away the covers. Not as easy to do as he bid, because she felt self-conscious drawing off the sleep shirt, but then she thought of how he'd look as he came through the door, the brown eyes piercing. The light from the decorated trees illuminated the room so he'd be able to see her, the pink of her flesh, the neediness of her eyes, the fullness of her parted lips, their moistness as she hungered for his mouth to be on hers.

It was less than ten minutes, which was good, because she might have chickened out on the pose. He didn't knock, the door opening then closing behind him, ensuring their privacy. The house was silent, though, everyone sleeping at this point, gathering energy for the busy day ahead.

Leland had already had a busy day, and a bad one. She could see it around his eyes, in the set of his mouth. Her Master was exhausted, mentally and physically. Cops didn't bring it home. He'd said that himself, that they didn't want what they saw to touch their family, and they didn't want being home with their family to be about that for themselves as well.

Yet there were things that could bleed over, because there was no setting them aside. She'd expected him to have the fierce light of lust in his eyes, to feel that edgy passion. He had that, could give her that, but she saw something else.

He'd said he needed to be inside her. He needed her, period.

The gaze he slid up her body was pure, desperate hunger. She'd pleased him by doing as he'd ordered, opening her legs, cupping her breasts, offering herself to him, but as he leaned against the door, staring at her as if she was the best thing he'd ever seen, she wanted to do more. She slid her hands down her body, trailed her fingers between her legs, stroked herself. Dipped her fingers inside her slick labia. His eyes darkened, and his barely leashed desire made her breath shorten.

Withdrawing her fingers, she lifted herself off the bed, tucking her legs under her so she could come to the end of the bed, slide off of it. He watched her, still and waiting, as she came to him. He was wearing street clothes, and his scent said he'd showered, trying to get rid of what still lay behind his eyes.

She'd hung up on him, been testy. The problem with being a dysfunctional bitch was the chronic selfishness that went along with it. She hadn't asked about the homicides, hadn't watched the day's news, because it would have just irritated her further, not being able to be right there, digging up all she could on it, preparing notes for her blog.

If she let those negative feelings rise, they would take this over, make her hate herself anew. But for once, she set that aside, because suddenly what was more important to her was being there for him.

She put her hand on his face. "I'm sorry."

She loved him. It was there on the tip of her tongue, absurd, too soon. It couldn't be true. But she wanted to love him, and it had been so long since she'd wanted to love anyone, it was almost the same.

"I'm all yours," she whispered, meeting his eyes. "Whatever you need, Master."

Moving her fingers to his mouth, she painted her taste on his lips. She drew in a breath as he closed his hand on her wrist and licked her skin, taking all of it off. When he released her, she began to slip the buttons of his shirt. She leaned in, pressing kisses to his flesh, between the defined pectorals, along his sternum, her lips whispering across his chest to his nipple, then higher, brushing her nose against his shoulder inside the open shirt. As she went to her toes to reach it, she curved her fingers into his shirt and dropped her other hand to his belt. He cupped the back of her head as she nuzzled him, kissed his collarbone. Then she went back to undressing him.

Pushing the shirt off his massive shoulders, she followed its track with her fingertips, then she began to loosen his belt. His hands went to her hips, his intent gaze on her. Just watching her. It made her fumble a little bit, but as he bent and kissed her bare shoulder, she tilted her head against his. Held it there, cheekbone to his temple.

His hands slid down, cupped her bottom, stroking and kneading. Then he lifted her. She wrapped her legs around his hips, arms winding around his shoulders as he carried her to the bed. Laying her down, he stretched out over her, but he didn't thrust into her right away as he'd said. Instead he slid down so her pussy was against the hard ridges of his abdomen. He cupped her breasts, fondling them with pure pleasure in his gaze. Lowering his head, he began to suck.

"Oh..." She gasped, lifted her hips. His weight kept her pressed to the bed, but as she struggled, it increased the friction of her clit against his sectioned stomach muscles. "Leland... Master." She let it out on a breath. Every worry and fear was beyond her grasp, at least in this moment. "Master." She gripped his shoulders, held on to him.

The climax rose fast, and she warned him as much as she was able, with a desperate gasp, a strangled cry. Rising up, he sealed his mouth over hers, cupping her skull again to hold her in place as she screamed her pleasure into his mouth. Her hips worked against him as her clit spasmed, as the climax gushed, making his abdomen slick with her juices. He lifted his head, stared at her as she came down with tiny moans, her mouth still slack and eyes dazed.

"Open my jeans, Celeste," he demanded. "Grip my cock with those pretty fingers."

She slipped the button of the jeans, pushed the zipper down over the erection. Reaching into the boxers, she closed her hands around him, exulting at the shudder that ran through his powerful frame. He pulled away from her, leaving her with an almost unbearable sense of loss, but it was only for a blink. He stripped off shoes and clothes, came back to her as naked as she was, and she let out a groan of sheer gratitude as he put a knee onto the bed between her legs, gripped his cock and angled it into her. She was already lifting her hips to take him, but he slid an arm around her waist, raising her further and thrusting into her at the same time, a forceful possession that had her crying out again, aftershocks from her climax rocking through her at his size and demand.

"Take your Master deep." Catching her jaw with a firm hand, he wouldn't let her look away. "This is why you won't make me go away. I see it in your face. I see everything you really are right now. The rest is bullshit. None of it matters."

She was helpless to deny it, could only strain to give him more and more as he delved deep, took more than she'd ever known she had to give. When he released her jaw, she wrapped her arms hard around his shoulders, buried her face in his neck, and cried out a second climax when he released, thrusting hard into her, fucking her with the singular, animal purpose he'd promised. She relished the jet of his seed, the excess spilling out around the joining point between them.

It had taken only minutes, yet the intensity of it had stretched out like the boundless universe.

He bent, nudged her cheek toward the pillow so he could put his mouth against her neck, bite. She let out a little quivering sigh, dug her nails into his flesh, lifted her hips to take him deeper, squeeze down on him.

"God." He let out a gusty sigh against her flesh, gave her his full weight for a single, blissful moment before he propped himself up, looked down at her. "You're the most beautiful thing I've seen all day," he said, his sculpted features and golden eyes gleaming in the dim light. "I couldn't wait to be with you."

She'd never been the type of girl who received compliments like that. She wasn't even sure it was a compliment as much as a fervent statement of fact, which was more unexpected. She spread her hands out over his chest, fanning her fingers over that expanse of firm, tempting muscle.

"I'd like to lie on top of you," she said. "If that's okay."

His lips twitched. "Probably a good idea. In another second I'm going to collapse and you'll be squashed."

With a satisfied grunt, he shifted. Though he had to slide from inside her, he curled an arm around her so they were still close together as he moved to his back. He adjusted his thighs so she could lie between them, her cheek pillowed on his chest. His cock was against her stomach, her knee bent and against the inside of his thigh, her buttock braced against the opposite one. She felt cradled in his strength, his hand stroking her back, but she wanted to touch as well. She caressed his side, fingers stroking along his rib cage, his hip. She moved her mouth against his chest, small kisses here and there, random, drifting. She wanted to put him back inside her and thought he'd let her do that when he recovered enough. She thought he would need her more than once that way tonight, and she was more than willing to accommodate him, no matter how deep the circles under her eyes tomorrow.

"What happened?" she asked at last. She didn't want him to rehash it if he didn't desire to do so, but her intuition told her he at least needed to say it out loud, think it through.

He drew a circle on her back, slow, thoughtful. "Things are ramping up between the MoneyBoyz and the Reigning Kings. Retaliation for killing one of their members. Good news is it means that Dogboy isn't going to have much luck getting the guys to help with you. They have too much else going on. I don't think the drive-by was part of their deal. He probably called in a favor from a couple buddies."

She thought of Dogboy's friend, Bobby. "That makes

sense. So did he leave town?"

"It's looking like it. The detectives have intel that he took off to Houston, to lay low with some contacts he has there. They're coordinating with the Houston PD to see what they can turn up."

"Mmm." She didn't say anything else. Just kept laying kisses on his chest, stroking his firm skin. The tree lights outside made the golden-brown color of his flesh smooth and burnished. He was beautiful to her in every way. As he stroked her hair, she followed her own desires and what she thought she could do for him at the same time. She began to move downward, teasing the washboard abs with her tongue, dropping her hands to his hips, stroking the curve of his taut buttocks, his upper thighs. Satisfying pleasure shot through her when his cock twitched, stirring against her body. When she adjusted so she was fully between his legs, her mouth over his cock, she put her lips on the broad head, tasting and smelling herself on him. She teased the corona with her tongue, the slit. His cock twitched further, coming to a semi-erect state. She was in no hurry.

As she glanced upward and caught her Master's gaze, watching her please him, things in her lower belly jumped at his intent regard. Keeping her eyes on his, she opened her mouth wider, took him in, sliding down his length, savoring, tasting, sucking. She traced his contours with her tongue, released him to slide down and lick his testicles, play her mouth along his base, then swirled, sucked and nipped all the way to the top. Pushing up to her knees, she gripped him and found the angle she wanted to slide straight down, take him all the way to her throat and work her way back up again. She didn't care how long it took to bring him to orgasm again. It was all about giving him pleasure. When she saw his thighs tighten, felt him push into her mouth, heard the muttered oath, she reveled in all of his responses.

It wasn't penance for her behavior, which would have made her feel more uncertain of herself. This was service, and for once she embraced the full meaning of it, a giving of herself with no worries about conditions or shortcomings.

"Look at me."

Lifting her lashes, she trembled at the fire in his gaze, his reaction to her obedience, to the way she looked, meeting his eyes while her mouth was stretched over his cock and down his length as far as she could go without choking. He was a lot to take, and she was more than happy to put in the effort. She slid up his length, leaving him glistening with the moisture of her mouth, then went down again, clasping the base in one sure hand, her thumb stroking the pulsing veins. She sucked on the ridges of his head, went back down again. Now he put his hand on her head, dug his fingers into her scalp and started to push her down on him, directing her, letting her feel the strength of his desire.

She was surprised when he stopped her, sliding his hands under her arms and bringing her up his body, but her Master told her what he wanted.

"Ride me, Celeste. I want to watch you."

She straddled him. His ardent gaze coursed all over her; face, breasts, abdomen, the pale lengths of her thighs spread over his hips. She curled her fingers around him and rose up on her knees, positioning the head of his cock between her legs. Putting his hands on her hips, he controlled the descent, lowering her on him inch by inch, his gleaming gaze fastened on her face as her lips parted and eyes clung to him. Once he had her seated, he let her go, gave her that look again. She didn't need him to speak to command her. Every look, the brief press of his fingers, told her what he wanted, how she could please him.

She started to move, rotating her hips on him, rising and falling, her head tipping back at the pleasure of it, at the way his hips started rocking up to meet hers again, at the way his expression became more concentrated. He cupped her breasts, constricting his grip and using it to bring her down on him harder, telling her what he wanted. He wanted to be ridden.

She braced herself on his upper abdomen, squeezing him inside, sliding up and back down faster, so her breasts bounced and drew his gaze and hands again. Then she slowed down, rotating her hips in sensual seduction, arching back and bracing her hands on his knees so he could lower his gaze and see his cock sliding in and out of her cunt. She was catching fire, her flesh glowing, her pussy tight on him and starting to vibrate with another climax rising between them.

He caught her arms then, bringing her down to him, his grip unbreakable on her biceps, holding her fast as he pushed into her, withdrew, pushed in again. The friction on her clit resulted in an immediate reaction, and she saw by the light in his eyes he fully intended to push her over the brink of helpless pleasure once again.

"Master..."

"Come for me, Celeste. Like this. I want you coming when I climax." His voice was hoarse, his body like iron beneath her, from straining thighs to tense shoulders, the muscles bunched in his arms.

He held her still as he pushed in and out, in and out. Her lips parted, drew back, her wild, frantic eyes finding his. The climax grabbed her the same way he could close his hand over her throat and make everything in her center toward one point, one goal, only one thing in the whole world important. It was incredibly powerful with him thrusting into her, his face so close. She was pleading as she came, wailing as her pussy convulsed on him. She brought him along with her to that same peak. His grip moved from firm to bruising, and she knew she'd relish the imprint of his fingers on her flesh.

He groaned out his own release, kept thrusting, harder, deeper, until she knew her arms weren't the only thing that would be sore today. She was glad. She helped, moving her hips as much as she was able, working his cock until she had every drop, until he let her go. It was only to shift his grip, though, for he brought her down on his chest, wrapping both arms around her and rocking them both. He kissed her forehead, her nose, then her lips, holding that one a heartbeat or two before he drew back enough to meet her eyes.

"You'd make a hell of a cop's wife, darlin'."

Her heart stuttered, a flare of panic and delight. "I hope that wasn't a proposal. One marriage is enough this weekend."

"Yeah, but you should have seen the terror in your face. It was worth it."

She narrowed her gaze, and he caught her hand before she could give him a halfhearted slap. "No assaulting an officer. I'm too tired to cuff you. Given how much I'd enjoy that, that's saying something."

He slid her off him, but didn't let her go far, keeping her cuddled up to his side. She wanted to leave his warmth like she wanted to take an ice bath, but nature was calling. With amusement, she saw he was already falling into a half doze.

"What are you grinning about?" he mumbled. "It makes me nervous."

"Even superheroes need a nap after sex."

"It's because you women are vampires."

She kissed the corner of his mouth. "I'll be right back. Bathroom."

"Yeah. Go for me while you're in there, because I'm not getting up until daylight."

She shook her head at him, picked up his shirt and slipped it on without buttoning it. As she passed the writing desk, she snagged the tablet Lucas had loaned her to check things online and held it against her body, hiding it as she took it into the bathroom with her and closed the door.

It didn't take her long to pull up the story. If she'd turned on the news, she would have heard about it immediately. The death of a child was always a ratings kick, and two were a bonus. The media outlets were milking it for all it was worth. Her mouth thinned in sympathy as she read through the few facts available so far. A seven-year-old and a ten-year-old, brothers Tony and Ron Roberts. They'd been killed in the crossfire at an apartment complex. From the location, she deduced it was another drug dispute.

Loretta Stiles had been fifteen, and that was bad enough. Handling a pre-adolescent child was so much different from a fully grown adult or even a teenager. She'd been on-site for a child killing before. When they wheeled the body out to the coroner's van, the adult-sized bag they'd had to use looked like it barely held anything, just air and shadows.

Jai's death and now that of two children were going to turn the heat up against anyone involved. Leland was right. The MoneyBoyz wouldn't be wasting time on one member's vendetta against a reporter, especially with Dogboy hiding out in Houston. By the time he returned, they'd keep him busy with other priorities, but she was betting they'd apprehend him before then.

She wanted to get back to Baton Rouge right away, start putting together a story that covered multiple angles on this. But she reined back that urge. She was here for Marcie's wedding. While Marcie was work-driven enough to understand, she was Celeste's friend. And what about Leland? He was here for his friends too. As a police sergeant and combat veteran, maybe he'd realized a smart person made time for friends and family, no matter the demands of the job. A day like today reinforced how vital it was to celebrate the good things, to help deal with the far-beyond-bad ones.

She used that thought to douse her own impatience. While she usually put a quick update on her blog for the preventive safety aspects of a crime--something like 'a robbery has happened in the so-and-so area, and here's how the suspect did it'--the in-depth details of a crime didn't come through right away. And everyone in the apartment complex knew the boys' deaths were tragically incidental, that the motive of the crime was drug-related. From her knowledge of how the coroner and detectives worked, there'd be more vital and accurate information to harvest on Monday. She'd get back on it then.

So she'd focus on the wedding today...and the after-party tonight. A shiver went through her. She'd told Leland she'd go with him. As his sub. She should definitely go get some sleep.

Yeah, good luck with that. Now that she'd thought of what might happen at the after-party, the possibilities had her mind churning a hundred miles a minute.

When she emerged, Leland's even breath told her he'd succumbed to sleep. She stopped by the bed, gazed down at him. The sheet was draped low on his hips as he turned on his side, arm stretched out and palm on her side of the bed, as if he wanted to know when she returned to him. That hard twist of guilt came again as she thought about how short she'd been on the phone with him when he'd been dealing with the murder of two children. But he'd pushed that aside, had found solace in her arms. *You'd make a hell of a cop's wife, darlin'.*

Since she was obviously having a crazy person moment, she let the idea fill her mind. A cop's wife. What would it be like to be married? To be his, not just in words, but in fact? She didn't want to wake him, but the desire to touch was too overwhelming. She bent, pressed a kiss to his shoulder, brushed her cheek against the back of it.

He mumbled something incoherent, acknowledging her, though his eyes remained closed, his breathing undisturbed. He really was exhausted, and he trusted her enough to sleep while she stood over him, as if even in slumber he knew it was her. She chided herself for the overly romantic thought. For as little as she really knew of the man, he might sleep through hurricanes.

She didn't know details like that, but she understood deeper things about him that called to her. He'd had an inside look at her soul as well, and he hadn't bolted yet. *For some of us, it's a single moment...* Savannah's words went through her mind.

None of this was making her any sleepier. Maybe Leland was right. Women might be vampires when it came to sex. She was wired. If she laid down next to him, she'd keep him awake with tossing and turning.

Drifting to the window, she looked at all the props intended to turn the spacious back lawn into a picturesque wedding venue in a few hours. It was then she noticed something different about the storage pod. Someone was sitting on top of it. Someone whose mind was likely gnawing on some of the same things hers was.

Sliding on her underwear and pajama bottoms, she buttoned Leland's shirt over her breasts and added a pullover over it to ward off the night chill. Then she pulled a pad and pen out of her tote and left a note on the side table.

I'm safe. I went to see Ben on the lawn.

§

She was used to seeing him in his expensive suits, but

tonight he was in faded jeans and T-shirt, sneakers with no socks. It made him look younger than his thirty-something age. Ben O'Callahan had a jump-me-now body and a face blessed by the gods, with piercing emerald-green eyes and dark hair falling rakishly over his high brow. She knew firsthand how strong he was, how ruthless a Dom, but his casual attire and the way he sat on the top of the pod, knees drawn up and arms clasped loosely around them as he tipped his face to the sky, made him seem approachable.

"Is this a private party?"

"Not at all. A good-looking woman is always welcome."

He didn't lower his gaze from the firmament, telling her he'd known she was approaching. He wasn't the only one. The voice that came from behind her was low and relaxed, making sure she wasn't startled by it.

"Let your fiancée hear that, and you'll be limping to the altar tomorrow. Lot of activity out here tonight. Think I need to impose a curfew."

She pivoted to face the man she knew had to be Dale Rousseau. Like Max, he looked every inch a SEAL, albeit a retired one. She was facing a man who'd put in twenty years of dangerous missions in places far from this one. She guessed him to be around fifty, his brown hair peppered with gray, the lines of his face and hardness of the fit body giving him a rugged appeal that would make him a head-turner for the next several decades at least. He wore a wedding ring, so some woman had the good fortune of having him in her bed on a regular basis. She hoped they'd both be at the wedding so she could meet her. If Dale was a close enough friend to be doing guard duty, she assumed he'd received an invitation. Which reminded her of her responsibility.

"Thank you," she said, offering a hand. "I really appreciate you watching out for me."

Dale closed it in his, a light-handed grasp, typical for a strong man. She'd noted Leland had the same tendency, though there were times when he wasn't light-handed at all. Thinking of his grip bruising her biceps, at the pleasurable soreness of her sex now, she knew she loved his gentle side but craved his rougher side. She could still taste him on her lips.

"It's my pleasure," Dale said courteously. "That scumbag tries to reach you here, we'll end any concerns you have about him. Plenty of marsh to dispose of a body."

She had no doubt he meant it, and was greatly reassured as a result. "Mind giving me a boost up there?"

The lines around his eyes crinkled and he obligingly bent and cupped his hands together. Ben now had his long legs dangling over the side, so as she stepped into the stirrup Dale had made, he reached down to clasp her hand. The two men boosted her up and into a sitting position on the top of the pod. "Thanks," she said.

Dale nodded to her, glanced at Ben. "I'll finish my perimeter check now."

"He's going back to his nap," Ben told her. "We woke him up. Old people can get cranky."

Dale shot him an amused look. "Don't push me, son. There's more than one reason you could be limping up that aisle tomorrow."

He moved away into the shadows. Leaning back, Celeste braced her hands on the pod's metal surface and gazed up into the sky, wondering what Ben saw when he looked up there. "I think I'd listen to him. He looks like he could kick butt and take names without breaking a sweat."

"And then some. But he and Max have that whole military discipline thing happening. I have to yank their chain. It's what I do."

"Hmm." She noticed that his position on the pod, the direction he was facing, gave him a direct view of Marcie's dark bedroom window. "Were you waiting for the opportunity to scale the wall, do a Romeo and Juliet thing?"

Ben shook his head, slipped a cigarette out of a pack next to him. The flare of his brass lighter showed a face that was pensive but not unhappy. He was just...waiting.

"You couldn't sleep."

A short nod confirmed it. He drew on the cigarette and blew the smoke over his shoulder, away from her.

She'd never experienced Ben this way. In the times she'd seen him since their night, he was typically charming, a man with an infectious sense of humor who made conversation easily with men or women. But his lack of conversation didn't make her feel intrusive. On the contrary, it made her feel as if he was comfortable enough with her that he didn't have to be charming, funny or engaging.

That night at Club Surreal had been more about Celeste, getting to the root of her surrender, of why loss of control was so difficult for her, but Marcie had been right. Celeste had seen something in Ben's eyes. What's more, he knew she'd seen it. His silence now told her so, a bond between them.

"You were the one who came to me that night, because you knew how I felt, in a way the others couldn't," she said. "You knew what it was to feel unwanted, like nothing, and want nothing more than to be...wanted. But it's more than that. When you're finally wanted, then you have to deal with that feeling, that weird, dumb-ass shit that tells you to push it away and run from it, though that's the last thing that makes sense. You can't explain it to anyone, not even really to yourself. Or worse, to the people you love."

Ben drew on the cigarette again, his eyes on Marcie's window. "I see you have a date for the wedding," he said in answer.

"Yeah. I see you have a date for life."

He slanted her an amused look. "So you think I'll go through with it."

"I know you will. Because you'll break her heart if you don't. As worried as you are about what kind of husband you'll be, you know you have to step over the starting line. You're way past the point of no return. The waiting's the worst part." She gave him an appraising look from head to toe. "So you're doing the Zen thing tonight. Accepting your fate. Really feeling it, and realizing it doesn't suck at all. Not in the least."

His lips did curve then, and she shook her head. "Fucking impossible."

"What?" A silken black brow lifted.

"No man should be as sexy as you are. Tomorrow I bet you'll wear some kind of perfectly cut tux, and every woman will be having fantasies about you."

"Not every woman. Marcie will probably be thinking about Leland. She's always had the hots for him."

"Well, that 'ho' can just keep her greedy little paws to

herself, or you two can limp up the aisle together." Celeste bared her teeth.

"So it's like that."

"I don't know." She emulated his pose, staring up at the back of the house. The guest bedroom window was at the far end. "I never thought I'd feel that way. I met him barely over a week ago. He took me to a country bar and sang to me."

"That bastard. He doesn't play fair."

She poked him in the side with her elbow, but kept her gaze on the house. What she wanted to ask, she didn't think she could if she was looking at him.

"You remember the safe word you wanted me to use that night? The word you knew I needed to say, but it hurt too much."

"I remember." His voice was warm and reassuring now, a friend concerned about her care. As he crushed out his cigarette and braced an arm behind her, she found herself leaning against the inside of it, a comfortable companionship. She drew her knees up, locked her fingers around them the way he had his own earlier.

"When I look at Leland, I keep thinking of that ridiculous phrase, 'Who's your daddy?'" She gave a half chuckle. "If you tell him that, I will kill you."

"I'm getting a lot of threats tonight. And I'm just sitting here, not bothering anyone."

"I know. It makes all of us nervous. It's so not you." Then she looked up at his amused face and pursed her lips. "No. I take that back. You look...okay. Like you're totally you tonight. Nothing added, nothing put on. It's a good look for you."

Reaching down, he tugged on the hem of Leland's shirt, a good foot of the tails extending out from under her pullover to layer over her pajama bottoms. "This is a good look for you."

"Oh, yeah. I plan to wear this to the wedding. Marcie will be so pissed that I outshone her."

He smiled, but she saw the measured calculation in his eyes as he gazed at her. She tried to conceal the little shiver it gave her low in her belly, because it was undoubtedly his Dom look. "You're not quite reconciled to it yet," he decided.

"Being who you really are with him. But you're closer to it than you've ever gotten, aren't you?"

"Yeah," she said simply. "Any advice so I don't hurt him, or do something really stupid?"

Ben tilted his head, lifted a shoulder. "Just more of the same. Be who you are, Celeste. If he can't handle that, he's not the right one anyway. People like us, we spend a lot of time covering who we are, because we think that's something no one will want. But the person who gets past all that not only shows us different, they'll help you let some of that go, so you can finally accept you're worth loving. And that, in turn, helps you live up to it. It's funny, but when someone accepts you for everything you are, the good and the bad, you stop worrying so much about the bad and focus on strengthening the good. Matt and the other guys helped me with that first, and gave me enough of it I could accept the rest of it with Marcie."

She met his gaze with a searching one of her own. "Does it help you believe it? Really believe it, the way they do?"

"Not all the time, but I'm closer than I've ever gotten to it. Else I couldn't say it aloud like that. Therapy. It makes me say all sorts of shit, like a psychobabble form of Tourette's." He gave her a wry look.

She put her head on his shoulder and then, on impulse, hugged him, pleased when he put his arm around her and did the same, dropping a kiss on top of her head.

Ben's male strength and masculine scent made her realize, tired or not, she wanted to be back beside Leland, holding on to him as he slept, feeling his arms around her. "I'm going to go back to my man, before someone looks out here and thinks the groom is having a make-out session with a sexy woman in flannel PJ's and sweatshirt."

"It's all right. My bride is sitting in her window seat, so we have a chaperone."

Celeste turned and looked. She couldn't see through the sheers over Marcie's window, but Ben apparently had better eyes than she did. Or maybe Marcie had had her light on earlier and he deduced she was still there. One thing Celeste had no trouble seeing was the quiet, fierce love in Ben's eyes as he kept them fastened on that window.

"I think she's fallen asleep, though," he said. "Curled up on the cushions."

He turned his attention back to Celeste with a different expression, a different tone. The one that could make a woman's knees weak, particularly if that woman had a good dose of sub in her makeup. She'd have cursed him for it, but she knew it was as natural and unassuming for him as breathing. "When you go back in," he said, "go to her room and tell her I said it's time to get in the bed and go to sleep. Make sure she does."

"If she thinks you'll come and see to it yourself if she disobeys, she'll throw open the window and do the Macarena on the roof."

He chuckled. "Any other night, I'm sure she would. Not tonight. Will you do as I ask, Celeste?"

"I don't think you asked." She tossed him a spirited look, just to show him he might be an über-Dom, but he wasn't *her* Dom. Yet as she positioned herself to slide off the pod, he stood up and took her hands, lowering her back to the ground safely. Putting her hands on her hips, she looked at him, standing tall and formidable against the night sky. Christ, the man wore the hell out of a pair of jeans. "I'll get her tucked in," she promised. "How about you? Are you going to bed soon, or is this like some kind of knight's vigil?"

His lips twitched at the irony, responding to the spark in her eyes. "If you like. See you tomorrow."

"Good night."

Chapter Fifteen

She'd been right. The Armani tuxedo Ben wore was charcoal black, perfectly tailored to his broad-shouldered, lean-hipped body. He had a matching vest beneath, a gray-and-black striped tie tucked into it against the white dress shirt. His dark hair was brushed to gleaming. And he was just the tip of the tasty man-candy iceberg.

Matt was his best man. The Italian-Texas parentage of the CEO of Kensington and Associates gave him the best of both worlds; he was over six feet, with rugged features, piercing brown eyes and burnished close-cropped hair. But it was the sheer presence of the man that made him unforgettable. Even when she was in the throes of her dislike for him, she couldn't ignore the energy and intelligence that made him alpha pack leader in any situation.

Jon and Peter stood up as Ben's groomsmen along with Marcie's brother Nate, all in the same style of tuxedo. Jon had midnight blue eyes and black hair to his shoulders, his slimmer physique undiminished by the larger build of the other men. He was like looking at Michelangelo's best work. Peter, the former National Guard captain who'd done two tours in the Middle East, lived up to that image. He and Max both had battle-ready musculature, dark blond hair and storm gray eye color, leading to a lot of inside family jokes, since Max was Dana's regular driver.

Lucas was a groomsman as well, but he was currently absent because Marcie had asked him and Cassandra to walk her down the aisle.

The K&A men were devastating to female senses on a normal business day, so if one of them so much as smiled or flexed, female brain cells would lock up and hearts would stop. She hoped someone had thought to have a defibrillator on hand.

For her part, she felt mostly immune, because all her energy was occupied with staring at her date and trying not to be caught doing so. He'd worn a copper-colored suit with a black shirt and a tie striped with those two colors. The gold-and-black Semper Fi ring he wore, a gift from his mother after his honorable discharge, was cool and hard under Celeste's hand. He had their tangled hands on his thigh and she was leaning against his side, a comfortable intimacy between them.

"I can't wait to see her dress," she said. "Cass and Dana said it's a knockout." The hard part was going to be looking at the dress and Ben's reaction to it without giving herself whiplash. Fortunately she saw they had hired someone to film the event. She'd be playing the friend card to get a copy of that, for certain.

"You don't have to wait much longer," he said, brushing his lips across her forehead. "It's almost time to start. You look stunning, by the way."

She doubted that. She'd brought the standard little black dress every woman kept in her wardrobe for such an occasion. Pairing it with stockings and heels, she'd fluffed up her hair and tossed on some silver jewelry, and called it done. Yet when his gaze coursed over her in lingering appraisal, she was aware of the mid-thigh hem and the way the neckline gave him a deep view of cleavage. She felt sexier than she'd expected to feel, hyperaware of his thumb sliding over hers with erotic promise. He put his lips to her ear.

"Tonight, I want to reach under your skirt and peel off those filmy thigh-high stockings. Make you spread your legs so I can stroke your panties and see how wet you are for me."

Would he do something like that at the after-party? She'd said she wasn't sure if she wanted to do anything more than watch, and he'd said virtually the same. But when his promise shot hard, hot desire through her right here in the middle of a hundred people, she wondered if any such inhibitions would become moot. Getting their hands on one another might become far more important than their privacy...or lack thereof.

Fortunately, the music had changed and the female attendants were starting to come down the aisle. To settle herself, she focused on that. Jessica and Talia, Marcie's sisters, came first, followed by Savannah. Matt's wife was arresting in a butter-colored sheath, a floret of white fresh roses and tiny green leaves on the gathered hip of the dress, the low back revealing her smooth shoulder blades. Her flaxen-blonde hair had been pulled up and secured with a matching floral barrette. Because she was a romantic at such events, no hope of denying it, Celeste glanced toward Matt to confirm his reaction. Whether today or fifty years from now, it was obvious no bride would ever compare with his wife.

Rachel was Marcie's matron of honor and followed in a dress of similar colors, though hers had been cut with a V-bodice and different skirt line that complemented her lusher figure. Her gaze found Jon in the lineup, and there was a brilliant light to her face that matched the luster in his blue eyes.

Matt spoke a word to Dana, waiting patiently with her Bible clasped against her robed breast. She nodded, gesturing to the audience. "Please rise."

The string instrumental that began to play was one Celeste identified without looking at the program. It was "As Long as You're There" by Charice. Her heart lifted at the choice Marcie had made for her wedding processional. Though she wanted to look toward the back with the rest, Celeste didn't want to miss that first moment when Ben saw the bride. Fortunately, she didn't have long to wait.

The shift in his green eyes could steal a woman's breath. Vivid expectation became a mix of things. Surprise, deep pleasure, sharp desire, and a wealth of emotions Celeste could fathom but not articulate in any way but with a stab of tears behind her eyes.

Murmurs of appreciation rippled through the crowd. Even before she turned to see, Celeste wasn't surprised by the reaction. Marcie was a stunning woman and, if she'd chosen a dress that complemented her looks at all, she would be astoundingly beautiful. When Celeste turned and inched up on her toes, using the prop of Leland's body to give her more of a view, she corrected that assessment.

Marcie looked absolutely mesmerizing.

The bodice of the corset top was white satin overlaid by lace, the wiring lifting and framing her breasts, but that was where solid fabric stopped. The remainder of the corset was see-through lace to her hips, patterned with intricately beaded appliqués. At her navel, the satin backing resumed, but it started in a point and sloped in a widening triangle of solid satin toward her hip bones, leaving translucent lace over her sides all the way to the tops of her thighs. From there satin and more brocade took over, hugging her lower body and backside in a mermaid style skirt that accented the curves of her hips, the graceful lines of her legs. The short train slid over the carpet of white rose petals laid down by her sister Cherry, her flower girl. Marcie's blonde hair was pulled in a smooth, shining twist on the back of her head, a few tendrils teasing her delicate neck, but nothing else was in the way of what she wore there.

Celeste had seen the collar Ben had given Marcie, because she wore it almost full-time. The stainless steel choker had an etching of three forget-me-nots on it. But she'd made it her only piece of jewelry today. No earrings or bracelets, a deliberate message to her groom.

As they passed, Lucas escorting her on one side, Cassandra on the other, Cassandra looking a little weepy but happy, the audience was treated to the back of the dress. There was no space between the lacings that held Marcie's body in such breathtaking relief. White satin ribbons tied in a bow at her lower back trailed over the tempting swell of her hips in the snug mermaid skirt fit. The back of the corset was the same translucent lace with appliqués, all the way to the dimples above her backside.

It was as if Marcie was a young goddess, emanating a heady mix of erotic and all-dreams-come-true promise for one man, making that promise far deeper than just the physical. The one last touch she'd added to the back underscored it. Celeste's gaze was drawn to the bare line of Marcie's shoulder blades. At her nape, a temporary tattoo had been applied, flowing script edged with a silver pearlescent ink infused with tiny pinpoints of glitter like the appliqués. *Always Yours.*

Like the groomsmen and their wives, Celeste knew the significance of the collar Marcie wore, but the words on her back were a statement. They told Ben the collar was more than a commitment to the roles they played in Dom/sub sessions. It was a promise to be his forever.

Celeste recalled the clasp of the collar Leland had put

around her throat. Though it had been temporary, merely functional for their play that night, she'd accepted it so definitively she'd almost forgotten to remove it the morning after.

Leland's hand tightened low on her hip, and when Celeste looked up at him, she saw all of it, everything she was thinking, everything stirring her up, reflected in her Master's eyes. She laid her hand on his chest, fingers sliding around the tie. When she moistened her lips, she couldn't keep her needs out of her eyes, and the grip of his fingers said he'd received all those messages. Everything she didn't know how to say, she didn't have to do so.

Trying to contain a tremor, she focused on the altar. As impressed as the audience was, Celeste could tell Marcie's husband-to-be was the one most under her spell. But that was a two-way street, for Marcie was just as enchanted. Her attention was locked on Ben as if he was the only one watching her.

She didn't break that lock until she reached the altar. Marcie turned to kiss Cassandra and hold her sister in a close embrace. Whether intended or not, it showed Ben the crescent shape of the words delicately scripted on her flesh. His gaze darkened further and he reached out, passing his fingers briefly over them as if he couldn't keep himself from doing so. Marcie drew back from her sister, dipping her head in charming, feminine acknowledgment of her Master's touch before she turned to Lucas. He kissed her cheek, touched her face. Then he offered her hand to Ben, the men exchanging a long look.

As Dana gestured to the attendees to be seated, Celeste knew she wasn't the only one craning her neck to see that significant instant when Lucas stepped out of the way and Ben closed his hand over Marcie's. Except for that hot kiss at Café Beignet, she expected it was the first time they'd touched in a week. The look they exchanged, the way his fingers closed firmly over hers and he drew her to his side, her hand sliding under his arm to hold on, said they weren't likely to let go of one another anytime soon. He leaned in, pressed his cheek to hers, said something. Marcie smiled, then drew back to say something to Matt. Whatever it was, she swept all the men with a glance when she said it, and laughter rippled through the first few rows as a result.

Celeste glanced up to see Leland grinning. Since he didn't suffer from the female sensibilities that had sucked her into the romance of the moment, he could fill in what she'd missed. Men were useful for such things.

"'Pay up,'" he told Celeste. "That's what she said. Matt and the guys had a bet going that Ben wouldn't show up."

Celeste's mouth dropped open. "How could they--" Then she caught the gleam in Leland's eye.

"The proceeds from the bet are Ben's wedding gift," he said. "They all bet against him because of it."

That backhanded male way of telling him they knew he *would* show up. It was the K&A men's show of faith in Ben. She curled both hands around Leland's arm as he settled his hand on her leg, thumb teasing the seam between her thighs, a gesture that spoke of the sexual intimacy between them, but more than that as well.

The wedding was simple and sweet, Dana administering the traditional vows. Throughout the entire ceremony, the bride and groom's eyes remained on each other, all four hands clasped together. She'd never seen Ben so absorbed, so unaware of anything else in the world. Marcie's brown eyes were so full of him, Celeste couldn't stop a couple of tears from rolling from her own. Leland gave her his handkerchief, put his arm around her, pulled her close and kissed the top of her head as Dana pronounced them man and wife. The kiss began as a lingering press of lips, Ben's hands coming up to cup his new wife's delicate jaw, her hands resting on his sides inside his jacket. In a blink, the heat level accelerated, him folding her into his arms and turning it into a demanding embrace, Marcie melting against him and her lips parting underneath his. Applause and whistles broke out, until Dana swatted Ben on his shoulder with her Bible.

"Consummation is *not* at the altar," she said severely. "Bunch of damn heathens."

The audience burst into laughter. Marcie put her arms around Dana and hugged her. While Dana hugged her back, the minister completed the ceremony in a tone of fond exasperation. "Friends and family, may I introduce to you

Mr. and Mrs. Ben O'Callahan."

Celeste joined Leland as they rose to their feet with the rest, whistling and clapping. She noticed Marcie's eyes were wet as Ben took her hand and they proceeded back down the aisle together. Each of the groomsmen took the arm of his respective wife, and Marcie's brother Nate brought up the rear with Cherry, Talia and Jessica following behind, all of Marcie's siblings wearing happy faces.

"Now to the best part of a K&A wedding," Leland told her as she blew her nose. "Free food and alcohol. Enough of this mushy shit."

"Jerk," she said, and stabbed him in the side with her elbow to reinforce the point. But she noticed she held on to his arm as they followed the rest of the audience toward the reception, and he seemed just as reluctant to let go of her. Mushy shit, indeed.

§

A screened pavilion tent had been set up on the lawn to shelter the food and bar areas, with tables scattered around a dance platform. Ben and Marcie did a waltz to Christina Perri's "A Thousand Years," and followed it up with a Cajun fast step to Mindy McCready's "This Is Me," which drew everyone else out on to the dance floor. The men tried their best to get Leland to sing, but were unsuccessful until the bride intervened.

Marcie stepped up to the microphone and pinned Leland with her doe brown eyes. "No one says no to the bride on her wedding day, Sergeant Keller. It's the law, and I know you respect the law."

Celeste had to chuckle at his pained expression, but then he dutifully did as Marcie demanded. He chose to sing John Michael Montgomery's "Rope the Moon," which brought all the married couples and lovers back out on to the floor with the newly wedded couple. When Leland finished, he gave Ben a direct look. "And you keep her believing those lyrics, else there'll be a posse of us to lynch your ass with that rope."

Matt took the stage then. While Ben had acknowledged

Leland's comment with a quick salute, he and Marcie went back to dancing in a slow sway to their own music, not a breath between their bodies. Marcie pressed her face into his throat, one hand on Ben's chest. She reached back with the other one to tangle fingers with the hand he had spread out low on her hip. His grip shifted to her wrist, holding her that way, arm pulled behind her, pressing her body more firmly into the angles and curves of his own. It was a less-than-subtle gesture of the Dominant/submissive relationship between them, and when he lifted his head to meet her gaze, her lips parted and their fingers tightened together, their bodies obviously responding to those overt nuances.

Matt coughed into the microphone, loud enough to cause feedback, drawing their attention as a chuckle rippled through the crowd.

"Thank you. It's almost as difficult to get him to pay attention in a meeting."

Ben snorted. "Because I'm always ten steps ahead of you guys. You have to catch up to me."

"No, it's because he's sexting Marcie and doesn't have time for work," Lucas called out from where he was sitting with Cassandra, arm behind her chair, his legs stretched out in front of him. "Time to fire his ass, Matt."

"I would do that, but then he and Marcie would have to move back in with you and Cassandra."

"Not with what I'm paying her to keep her out of your clutches," Savannah tossed out.

A grin wreathed Matt's handsome features. "Marcie?" He dropped his voice to a dramatic stage whisper. "Just FYI, we offer better maternity benefits than Tennyson, when you and Ben decide the world is ready for little replicas of you."

Tucking his tongue in his cheek at his wife's dagger look, he drew an envelope out of his suit coat, waving it at the crowd to hush the laughter. "We've already given Ben his wedding gift. Of course, every wise man knows what's hers is hers and what's his is hers, so technically you could say we've already given her a gift too. Nevertheless, we wanted to officially give Marcie something as well."

Pulling out his phone, he glanced at it, then crossed

his arms, tapping his toe as more titters ran through the crowd. "Just a few more seconds."

Celeste became aware of the purring sound of an engine. Looking around, she didn't see anything, but Matt nodded, apparently receiving the cue he needed. "Some time ago, Ben put his car up for auction for the battered women's shelter we support. Richard Lewis bought it and funded the shelter's operating costs for a year." He pointed to the man in question, who raised his glass, amusement in his expression. Ben turned, gave him a quizzical look, and then he and Marcie brought their equally curious glances back to the stage.

"There were many reasons Ben decided to do that. But the most important one was that he is a good man, with a good heart, who deserves the love of the woman he's holding right now. All of us"--he nodded toward the table where Peter, John and Lucas sat--"and the women we're lucky enough to have as our own, fully agree on that. We have no doubts. You understand?"

Ben's expression grew still, and Marcie ran her hand over his shoulder, lifting on her toes to touch her lips to his throat as he held her.

"We love you both," Matt said seriously. "And so you understand that we have no doubts, and to remind yourself of that whenever necessary, we decided this was the best gift for us to get Marcie. But I do emphasize"--he waved the envelope--"this is for her. You can't play with it unless she says it's okay."

Another laugh from the crowd, and then Matt extended the envelope toward her.

Marcie approached the stage, holding Ben's hand so he came with her. She released him only when she needed both hands to open the envelope. As she unfolded the piece of paper inside it, her eyes widened. "Oh my God."

The engine sound became a revving noise. Everyone shifted toward the open side of the tent as a silver sports car emerged from behind the house. With Max at the wheel, the Mercedes-Benz McLaren Roadster carefully bumped over the lawn, coming to a halt at the fringe of outdoor tables arranged outside the tent. A large white bow was tied over the gleaming hood.

Marcie squealed in delight. Ben tossed Matt a narrow look, though a smile flirted around his mouth. "I hope Lewis charged you full price," he said darkly.

Marcie flew through the crowd, holding up her skirt, revealing she'd ditched her shoes some time back, so she was now in bare feet as she ran to the car. Max was getting out of it, unfolding his large frame from the bucket seat. When he dropped the keys into her palm, she embraced him enthusiastically and then whirled toward Ben. "This is almost worth marrying you," she called out over the whistles and cheers.

Despite her teasing, when Marcie stretched out her hand to her husband, there was no doubt that he was the only man she wanted, the one that filled her shining eyes with love. Celeste didn't think any man in the world would have been able to resist her, let alone the man who loved her best of all.

As he caught her fingers in his, Ben drew her close, putting his arm around her waist and pressing the backs of her legs against the car when he bent and kissed her throat. Marcie slid her arms around his shoulders, but as her lips parted, Celeste thought she detected a shudder. She had a feeling Ben had just told her in concise detail what he planned to do to her on the hood of that car.

"If the two of them get any more combustible, they're going to incite an orgy," Leland commented.

Celeste slanted him a glance. "Would that be a problem, Sergeant?"

"Private property and out of my jurisdiction. None of my business." He shot her a smile, sliding his arm behind her, then lower to caress the top of her buttocks, his fingers playing in the seam between them through the thin cloth of her dress. "I'm just counting the minutes until that after-party."

Though she was enjoying the festivities, at the look in his eyes, she had to agree. The worries she had about what might or might not happen there seemed far less important than the desire she had to be even closer to her Master than she was right now. Ben and Marcie's obvious desire for one another was a contagion, and she was already feeling fever symptoms.

§

When the reception concluded, there were several hours to endure before the after-party. She had graphic visions of the things Leland might do to pass the time in the privacy of the guest bedroom, but instead he left her with a hot kiss on the front porch, his possessive hands sliding over her hips as he gazed down at her.

"I have to go check on some things with Matt and the others. I'd recommend a nap. I left you a gift, if you decide you want to wear it tonight."

She raised a brow, but he bent to kiss her again. She met him eagerly, doing her best to convince him he needed to come back to the bedroom with her, her body rubbing against his until he untangled her arms from his neck and gave her a mock-severe look.

"Behave, woman." But he ran a thumb over her lips and his warm look said he wasn't displeased with her. It occurred to her then she hadn't been feeling that push-pull inside her she often had with him. Maybe weddings were like Christmas, bringing out a person's better side. If that was the case, she wanted Leland to reap the full benefit of that. His body against hers, the firm pressure of him against her stomach, the way his hands gripped her, made her desire all the more acute.

She thought of Marcie in that beautiful dress, Ben's eyes hot on every inch of her. The love that had woven itself around all that desire made the day perfect for them in every way. She needed Leland to assuage this ache, a tangle of lust and need as well. She couldn't bear another moment. There was too much pressure building inside her, and she didn't know how it would manifest tonight, in front of other people. She might do things she couldn't take back, things she couldn't control.

Okay, maybe weddings didn't help. Or they brought out the brat in a different form, because she could feel the shift inside her from pleasurable yearning to fierce insistence, whatever else was happening right now be damned.

"Celeste. Darlin'." He caught her nape in a firm grip, snapping her attention up to him. She met golden-brown eyes that held that steady calm, that implacable look. "Settle down."

She jerked away, turned and left him. She needed to breathe. Needed to get a grip. What was the matter with her? She went back into the house, up the stairs and to the guestroom. She'd forgotten what he'd said about a gift until she was there and saw the slim gray velvet box on the bed, tied with a silver bow.

She sank down next to it, rubbing her forehead. She'd been fine until she'd let her thoughts run away with her. Sometimes she thought her quicksilver moods happened because of some dark trigger inside her. If she was too happy or content, it sprang like a trap, dragging her back into the shadows. Today everything was about light, good, love. Suddenly she felt out of place here, and she knew she shouldn't feel that way. She wasn't isolated. She wasn't alone. She just kept making herself feel that way.

Setting her jaw, she put the box in her lap, untied the bow. Removing the lid, she pulled back a thin piece of tissue paper to see what lay on the white satin beneath.

Everything whirling inside her came to a portentous halt.

She sensed him in the doorway. Though she hadn't expected him to follow her, she'd hoped he would. That was what he did to her. He made her hope, and he kept making her hope, because he kept doing things she didn't expect. Like being there when she needed him, knowing what she needed to make a bad feeling better.

"It's beautiful," she said in a small voice.

He came into the room, a big man who made the floorboards vibrate as he walked. If they lived together, she would always know where he was, would always feel his presence vibrate through her physically as well as emotionally.

Dropping to one knee beside her, he unhooked the string of black-and-silver beads around her throat, a piece of costume jewelry that worked with the dress. Then he lifted the necklace out of the box. "Let's see if I have the measurements right."

He put the delicate silver chain around her neck, leaning forward so his forearm rested on her shoulder and his body brushed hers. It fit like a choker, the pendant resting just above the center points of her collarbone. "You have such a slender neck. So fragile." His fingers slid over it. "So beautiful. You're beautiful, Celeste. And mine. Aren't you?"

She nodded, unable to speak. The pendant was a pair of linked silver hearts. Two intricate silver roses were woven through them. Where the stems emerged on either side, they threaded into a handcuff, which connected to the chain that circled her neck.

The necklace contained multiple messages, much like the ones he sent whenever he touched her.

"This is a pretty dress." He dropped his hand down to smooth her skirt that stopped at mid-thigh. His fingers teased the lining beneath the hem. "Come with me."

He lifted her off the bed with a hand under her elbow and brought her to the dresser, so she could see the way the necklace looked on her throat. Standing behind her, he had her clasp the two handles of the long top drawer, which spread her arms out to either side.

"I want you to hold on to those. You don't let go until I tell you. Right?" He shot her an expectant look, and those tumultuous feelings settled at a lower spin inside her chest, like disturbed sediment returning to the bottom of a pond.

"Yes, sir," she whispered.

His expression was so serious. When he was like this, she knew what he expected of her. What she expected of herself. Her breath shortened as he stepped back, unbuckled his belt, stripped it out of his slacks. Doubled it over.

He put his hand on her nape again, massaged it, sending a sensuous wave through her shoulders and back, over her breasts. She closed her eyes, dropping her head to her shoulder, wanting to rub her face against his hand.

"Open your eyes, Celeste. I want you to look at the necklace while I'm doing this, think about what it means."

She complied, though all of her peripheral attention strained for him. She bit her lip as he worked the dress up, held it just above her buttocks with one hand.

"Wearing thong underwear to tempt your Master with your gorgeous ass." He *tsk*ed.

"My bad, good girl."

The first strike of the belt was low, on her upper thighs, the next on the widest part of her ass. The sting of it was sharp, immediate, a relief. She had to resist the urge to close her eyes again, absorb it through all her senses more deeply.

He did it a dozen times, until she was flinching and she could feel the throb of the strikes on her thighs and ass. He slid her skirt back in place, moving behind her to smooth it over her buttocks. When he pressed himself against her, she made a hungry sound at his size, her pussy aching to have him thrust his thick cock inside her. But he was teaching her something, and proved it now by catching her gaze in the mirror and locking it in the unblinking regard of his.

"I'm your Master, Celeste. When you want something, you don't get pushy about it. Got it?"

"Yes, sir." Her voice was trembling. He always made her tremble.

He bent to put his lips on her throat just above the necklace. His collar. "I expect you'll remember that for as long as it takes me to leave this room and reach the bottom of the stairs. But I don't mind reinforcing the lesson. I've thought a lot about tonight. About the different equipment Ben has in his loft. I don't want anyone else touching you, but I think I wouldn't mind them seeing how lucky I am, with my beautiful submissive. What do you think of that? What will you do if I want to peel you out of that dress and take you, right there in front of all of them?"

"I think you've got me so worked up I wouldn't care if you did it in the middle of Bourbon Street." She gave a desperate half laugh, dipped her head because she couldn't look at herself in the mirror just then. "Please. I can't think."

He cupped her face, held it to his shoulder as he pressed against her back. "You need your Master to fuck you right now, make it better?"

She nodded again.

"I will fuck you. Later. Until then, I expect you to behave." He touched the necklace on her throat, the linked hearts. "Will you behave?"

"I'll try," she whispered. A person she didn't know was taking her over, the person she wanted to be with him, no matter how much it scared her when she was in her right mind.

"All right then." He turned her around, kissed her lightly. "I'll see you in a couple hours. I want you to wear this dress tonight. Take that nap I told you to take. No work. And keep your hands and all electronic devices away from what's mine."

"How about non-electronic devices? Pillows? Showerheads? Air?"

She'd waited until he reached the door to be that brave. It had also taken her that much time to get her breath back. He tossed her a glance that was full of fire and amusement both. "You can rub up against any inanimate object you want, darlin', but your climaxes are mine. Remember that truck ride? I can make it much worse. Much."

§

It took a while for her to settle enough to take a nap. Her body was humming like a generator, thinking about his belt striking her thighs and ass, the way he'd looked at her. However, eventually she drifted off into a fitful cat nap. When she woke, it was close to ten. The after-party at Ben's loft was scheduled for eleven, so she slid out of bed. She'd left the stockings, thong panties and bra on, and slipped her dress back over them before stepping into her high heels. He was telling her what to wear, and she was getting a sexual charge out of being commanded, following those commands. No, not just being commanded. Being commanded by a man she'd called Master. Who, in those incredibly intense exchanges between them, she accepted as exactly that without question, worry or fear.

Could it be that simple? Nothing about relationships had ever been simple for her. But Leland had a force of will that made things simple for her. When he took control, experiencing it as simple action-reaction, pure feeling, nothing to doubt in herself, seemed so much easier. And the alarm bells that should be going off at that thought...didn't. Not tonight at least.

Bemused, she descended the steps, following the comfortable chatter of female voices. She glimpsed Savannah and Cassandra in the kitchen, standing on opposite sides of a marble-topped island as they sipped wine. Cassandra had a hip cocked and was making some point with her free hand while Savannah smiled, bringing the glass up to her pink frosted lips. The two of them were wearing short black dresses as well. When she found Dana and Rachel in the adjacent living room, sitting on the couch, she verified the same fashion choice. Though the styles differed to highlight and enhance the unique shape and curves of each woman, the after-party obviously required a certain dress code.

Had their Masters ordered them to wear the dresses the way Leland had? She had a feeling the answer to that question was yes. When Cass and Savannah glanced her way and nodded, they exuded the same expectant, simmering arousal and anticipation coursing through her own blood, quickening through her thighs and keeping her sex damp against the narrow panel of her silky thong.

Stepping into the living room, she saw Dana was braiding Rachel's blonde locks and pinning them up on her head. "There," the black woman said. "You'll have to check the mirror to see if it's lopsided, but that should hold until he decides to tear it loose with those clever long fingers of his."

Rachel glanced over her shoulder at Celeste. "What do you think?"

"Not a bit lopsided. And fetching around the face and neck, as if just waiting for a man with long, clever fingers to take it down."

"It's so delightful to have a writer in our midst," Jon's wife responded with a twinkle in her gold-and-green gaze. Like Celeste, Rachel had hazel eyes, though like most people with hazel irises, the blend of colors were different. Rachel's grey, green and gold mix reminded Celeste of the depths of a forest, whereas her own eyes had a brighter green and brown-gold mix. Like fairy wings, her sister had once told her. A long time ago, when Trice still believed in fairies.

"We were just going to check if you were awake. Max is driving us. The guys went to get the loft ready."

"Where's Marcie?"

"You really think Ben is letting her out of his sight for the rest of the month?" Dana snorted. She had her brown legs folded up on the couch, the skintight latex skirt of her dress so short it revealed the ribbon garters at the top of her sheer stockings. "He was probably consummating in the limo while we were still throwing birdseed at the back bumper. Hope Max had the privacy screen up."

Rachel grinned at that, then nodded to Celeste. "To answer your question, if the two of them come up for air, I expect they'll show up at the loft a little later."

"They are really...something," Celeste responded. Feeling a little foolish, she crossed her arms over herself, but Dana cocked her head and Rachel gave her a look laced with empathy.

"Yeah, you're feeling it too, right?" Dana scoffed. "I'm blind and I could feel the pheromones vibrating off them like a nuclear reaction. Left all of us needing to be fucked hard and now against the nearest vertical or horizontal surface. Yet what do those bastards we married do? They all run off together. Insensitive jerks."

As Celeste blinked, Rachel spoke up. "Her Army personality sometimes seizes control," she said helpfully.

It only took Celeste a moment to rally. She'd grown up in a trailer park, after all. "I think said bastards did it on purpose," she rejoined. "To make us more agreeable to whatever perverted thing they want to do."

"That is exactly their plan," Cassandra concurred, coming in to join them, Savannah with her. "And of course we'll go along with it. Celeste, what a beautiful necklace."

"Thank you." She put her hand over it, turning rosy at the protective gesture. Savannah's blue eyes and mouth softened.

"Congratulations."

"Well, I...it's just a necklace." Though she just flushed deeper.

Dana rose from the couch. "May I?" she asked, turning in the direction of Celeste's voice and reaching out with questing fingers.

"Yes."

Dana explored the design, adding in light strokes of Celeste's collarbone. She wasn't wearing the dark glasses right now, so Celeste could see her pale green irises from her mixed-race parentage. "Can you describe it?"

"Um...yes." As she described the detail of the interlocking hearts, Savannah bent closer to take a look.

"Nice, detailed work. Artisan quality." As she spoke, she stroked her own necklace, a choker of polished rose quartz and pure silver.

It was an absentminded but telling caress. Celeste had no doubt it was Matt's collar for his wife and cherished submissive. As her gaze traveled around the room, she could pick out that symbol of ownership on each woman without any difficulty. It emanated a significance another submissive, even one new to all this, couldn't miss.

Dana's was a wide strap that fit her long elegant neck like a second skin. A waterfall of decorative chains fell from it. The D-ring in front had a Saint Christopher's medal as a pendant. Rachel's was a choker of sterling silver wire bound with gold bands. A small sapphire pendant against her sternum was wrapped in the slender silver wire. Cassandra wore nothing on her throat, but instead had a pair of beaten silver wrists cuffs with engraved Japanese characters, matched by thinner bands around her ankles.

Each of those accessories indicated the woman was a submissive who willingly belonged to a Master. And she was part of that exclusive group tonight. The delicate chain on her neck had a symbolic weight that she felt tingling through her nerves. It flustered her, made her uncertain, until she remembered Leland's gaze on her. It was too soon, she knew it was, but maybe just for tonight it would work. She could accept what her heart wanted and not question it.

"You're not wearing your wedding rings," she noted, then bit her tongue. "Sorry. I wasn't trying to be rude."

"You shouldn't feel uncomfortable about asking us anything," Cassandra said. "It isn't about being a reporter tonight, is it? It's personal."

Celeste nodded. She should feel defensive at being so

out of her element, but the thing was, she wasn't out of her element. It was like when she followed a lead on a story. At the beginning, she didn't have all the information. It was asking the right questions, following the right leads, seeking a deeper understanding of what was happening, that resulted in the fully fleshed-out story she wanted. Only this time the heart of the story she was trying to uncover was her own.

"We typically don't wear our wedding rings when we're going to be in scene with our Masters like this, more formally or in a group setting." Cassandra glanced at the other women, then back at Celeste. "A husband and wife are partners, helpmates, a different type of relationship in many ways. Master and submissive requires a power shift. Removing the wedding rings is a ritual that helps us transition to that mind-set."

"Do they remove theirs?"

"No. Because we're the ones handing over power and control. Their wedding rings reinforce the fact we belong to them. Kind of hard to explain."

"No, I get it." She did. She understood so much of this without having to think it through, it was a little scary. It was when she did think it through that she messed it up.

Cassandra nodded. "I figured you did."

Dana spoke up then, dispelling the serious exchange before Celeste could get uncomfortable. "So is Janet going to come and put Max through his paces? I would give good money to hear that, and have Rachel describe it in detail."

Celeste blinked. "I know Janet's a Domme, but Max... Marcie said he's not a sub, not that way. In public...like we're going to be tonight? I mean, I know it's not truly public, but..."

"Oh hell no. He's definitely not a sub, honey." Dana chuckled. She took the glass of wine Cassandra poured her and returned to the couch with Rachel, stretching her bare legs over Rachel's lap. On the left one, Celeste saw a network of faint scars from the explosion that had taken her sight. From how extensive she'd heard the original wounds were, Celeste thought the plastic surgeons had done an admirable job. "But he serves her just the same. SEALs are all about service. It works for them. Which is why I'm only teasing. I don't think she'd ever make Max play publicly, especially not in front of Matt and the guys. I'm not sure who would be more mortified by that."

"It wouldn't be Janet," Savannah pointed out. "She likes showing Matt and the others how she can bring a man to his knees."

Celeste had glimpsed Matt's efficient admin several times during the reception, obviously overseeing a wealth of details involved with the event. The woman who had the build and grace of a ballet dancer and the demeanor of a strict schoolteacher was terrifying, though Celeste was always hoping for an opening to learn more about her. A reporter couldn't resist investigating a fascinating subject, even if the purpose wasn't to write a published story about her. "So they won't be there tonight?"

"Max is going to drop us off and then head back home. Janet worked her ass off today. I expect what she most wants is a foot massage before she falls asleep."

"I'm good with going to sleep, though I want some really hot sex first," Rachel declared.

Dana pinched her. "I told you, I can't do you tonight. I have to take care of Peter. You're just going to have to settle for Jon."

Cassandra rolled her eyes. "Jon and Peter are likely to separate you two. And I know Janet. Yes, she'll go for the foot massage, but she'll order Max to give her fantastic sex right afterward. Make him do all the work, and then go to sleep in his arms."

"I can think of far worse things," Savannah commented. "Matt gives a wonderful foot massage."

"I expect anything Matt massages is wonderful." Cassandra nudged her. "Lucas gave me a full-body massage once while he had me cuffed to the bed. So many levels of ecstasy, I'm not sure Heaven can compare."

Rachel cocked her head at Celeste as she shifted. "Are you okay?"

"Yeah. It's just...you all are so comfortable with this. It's new to me, the reality of it. No matter how long I've thought about it." The environment seemed to encourage honesty.

"It's unsettling to all of us at first." Cassandra shrugged

so matter-of-factly, it eased any fears Celeste had about coming off as foolish again. "But it's easier to talk about it together like this. And tease one another, because it can be scary as hell." She laughed at Celeste's expression. "Yes, you heard me right. Even now, how intense it can be, it's unreal. And the way they play off of one another... Alone, they're each overwhelming. Together, there's an energy that just takes over your reality. It becomes about anything they demand, and you don't think beyond that."

Celeste remembered how she'd sat at a table with the other K&A men after her intense session with Ben. Though that part had been non-sexual--technically--she knew exactly what Cassandra meant. She'd seen it in their expressions, the confident way they surrounded her, cared for her. Tonight she was going to be in a very sexual environment around all of them. The scary thing was knowing she meant what she said to Leland. She didn't think she would refuse anything he desired to do in front of them. When she thought of him laying her down and thrusting into her in front of them, it felt like a territorial act, a statement of who was his, and her body wasn't in the least appalled by the idea.

But she couldn't deny part of that had to do with who they were. If Leland were taking her to a club tonight, planning to do such a thing in front of strangers, she would have had a big *hell no* sign blinking over her head. But in a way, this journey to Leland had started with the K&A men. Though she wasn't part of this inner circle, she was still connected to it, which made the idea not only feasible but arousing. It might be the same for Leland, because when she imagined him taking her in front of people who weren't these men and women, she wasn't seeing it happening for him either. Not with how one-on-one he truly was when it came to their interactions with one another.

Her hand went back up to her throat, fingered those interlocking hearts, cuffs and roses. Virtually the same thoughts she'd had herself had come from Cassandra's lips, and the others had nodded, the expressions on their faces confirming that they'd each wrestled with the surreal nature of these feelings. Each of them had perhaps wondered how her respective Master could make her surrender so completely, and not just as a one-time fluke, but again and again...

Anything was possible tonight.

"Max just pulled up," Cassandra said. "Ladies? Ready to go?"

"Absolutely." Dana bounced up, pulling Rachel with her. "We'll get him to tell us everything that happened in the back of the limo."

"Good luck with that." Savannah shook her head. "With SEALs, everything is classified."

"I'll threaten to strip down and sit in his lap naked while he's driving," Dana said resolutely. "He'll talk."

"He'll spank you, put you in time-out and turn you over to Peter for punishment," Rachel said.

"So a win-win, then."

§

Ben's loft was in New Orleans' business district. When they reached the warehouse, Max handed them out of the limo and took them to the lift. "Have a good night, ladies. If your dates do anything to upset you, just give me a call. You know I'll come back and get you in a heartbeat."

Dana gave him a hug full of affection. "We figured you were going to come up and show them how it's done, Max."

He shook his head at that, his lips twitching. "Not built that way."

"Yeah, damn it. Our loss is Janet's gain." Dana stepped onto the lift, letting him hold her hand to ensure she didn't catch her heels in the threshold she couldn't see. "Tell her she was freaking fantastic today."

Cassandra nodded emphatically and gave Max a warm hug as well. "Tell her no one could have done a better job. We love her dearly."

"She's family," Savannah added, meeting Max's gaze. "As are you."

His smile grew warmer at that, the look reflecting his own love for the woman in question, as well as his regard for all the K&A women. "I'll tell her."

"Be sure and tell her several times," Dana added

impishly. "Thoroughly."

He chuckled and closed the mesh door before entering the security code that would send them to the third floor. As it ascended and he disappeared from view, Rachel leaned against Dana, squeezed her hand. "He's much more relaxed about teasing all of us," she said. "Have you noticed?"

"He's still somewhat reserved around Matt, but I've noticed it, too," Cassandra agreed.

"Well, Matt is his boss. In his world, that's his commanding officer," Dana pointed out. "There will always be a reserve there. Plus Matt is Matt. He gives off that vibe."

"Yes, he surely does," Cassandra said with an exaggerated sigh like a swooning heroine. "He's a walking vibrator."

Savannah elbowed her, but Celeste could tell this kind of teasing was normal for all of them. Though she had done things socially with the K&A circle, some of it a benefit of her past history with them but mostly as a result of her friendship with Marcie, this was the first time she'd been included in the banter and sexual energy they emitted as submissives, charged up about the impending evening with their Masters. It couldn't help but be contagious. Especially with the ball of heat expanding in her lower belly, imagining being with her own steady-eyed Dom tonight. She cleared her throat.

"I hope Janet isn't too tired when Max gets home. It would be a crime to waste all that."

"Oh, I'm sure she'll rally enough to take a morsel or two of that cake. And if not, he'll be there in the morning."

"Breakfast is the best time to eat cake anyway," Rachel added, gray-green eyes twinkling.

When the lift arrived on the third floor, Jon and Peter were there to unhook the lift door and greet them. As Dana and Rachel gravitated toward their men like magnets, Celeste looked for Leland. She didn't immediately see him, but the impact of what she did see caught her attention like a shifting magnetic force, drawing her gaze from one tantalizing possibility to another, and another...

From tidbits of conversation on the way over, she'd learned that Ben had once used this loft as a living space because of its close proximity to the office. Since he and Marcie had made the permanent transition to his Garden District home, he'd converted the whole floor to accommodate BDSM parties with close friends, as well as his and Marcie's own private adventures here. She found herself looking at a well-equipped adult playground, better even than Club Surreal, if on a smaller scale. Slightly.

The theme of the room was monochromatic, the walls white and splattered with black paint in an edgy, artistic effect. The bar was black marble. Oil renderings of enlarged black-and-white erotic photographs were mounted in silver frames on the walls. The pictures depicted shadows and soft flesh, hints of sensual pleasures.

The equipment placed throughout the spacious area and anchored to the hardwood floor was everything a man with Ben's financial resources could want, for restraint, punishment and pleasuring in myriad creative ways. There were several variations of St. Andrew's crosses, spanking benches and frames for restraint. Thanks to her Internet searches, she recognized a couple types of fucking machines and forced orgasm towers. Padded tables offered multiple ways to restrain a submissive, including one with rounded pegs all along the sides to lace thin rope over her. A horizontal frame stretched with latex she guessed was a cocoon bed, where the sub would be placed inside the cocoon and then all the air sucked out of it to mold the latex to the body like a second skin and hold her down.

Paddles, whips, canes, restraints, gags, vibrators and other stimulating items were mounted on custom-designed racks on the walls in several convenient locations. An elaborate crisscrossing of beams and supports in the back corner was intended for rope suspension, if the adjacent board hung with a number of ropes and a variety of clips were any indication.

Everything was positioned at appropriate distances to allow whatever pair or group using them a discreet cushion of space to craft their scenes and become absorbed in the energy they raised with one another. Looking around, Celeste understood why the men had needed to leave earlier. Some of the things she was seeing had to have been brought in specifically for this event, which would have required rearrangement of the other standing equipment to ensure that buffer of space.

In the back shadows on either end of the room several double beds had been set up on frames. She also saw a king-sized mattress turned into a nest on the floor with the use of numerous pillows and a comforter. Between the equipment and the bed areas, groupings of occasional chairs, couches and a couple recliners were set up, along with scattered throw rugs that looked like they were made of one of those thick coverings that felt so lovely on bare flesh, like Sherpa or micro-mink fleece. If anyone wished to move from the equipment to a more comfortable spot for viewing the other players or to conduct a different type of play that didn't involve the equipment, those needs had been accommodated.

Despite the women's teasing about the uncertainty of Ben and Marcie coming up for air anytime soon, it appeared the newlyweds' arrival was anticipated. More white rose petals like those at the wedding were scattered over the wood floor. The loft had a raised platform which a long time ago had likely been the floor of a foreman's office, raised about two feet to allow him to watch the shop floor. The walls of that office were long gone, but the raised floor was still there and a full perimeter of two shallow steps framed it. On that platform, a canopy bed was made up in white linen. Sheer panels were drawn around it, white roses wound over the metal frame. Four white cuffs attached to steel chains were pulled out from beneath the mattress, coiled against the snow-white bedding in artful display. If Ben wished to restrain Marcie to it as he took his pleasure, those would be easy options.

Celeste was feeling flushed, her knees a little trembly. She had her hand on her stomach, a calming gesture that would have embarrassed her except she had a feeling such a reaction might please one particular person. If she could find him. Where was he? She'd seen Jon and Peter. Lucas had his arm around Cassandra, bending to press a kiss beneath her ear as she gripped the lapel of his jacket, her eyes closed. Her lips curved as he said something to her, and Celeste felt the desire to touch her own throat as his hand spread out over her sternum, fingers caressing her collarbones.

Leland had said it would be an intimate gathering, less than fifteen people. Though she recognized all the faces here as people who'd been at the wedding, she was uncertain about being in this environment with the few she didn't know well. She didn't see Leland or Matt, so she made the educated guess that they might be together, handling something that shouldn't matter anywhere as much to Leland as being the fuck here to reassure her before she freaked the hell out.

Stop it, Celeste. Jesus. It's not like some stranger's going to jump you. She needed some wine to calm her nerves. She headed for the black marble bar. It was spread with food and snacks that matched the quality of the reception offerings. There was also a bartender, though she expected he was here for more reasons than that. He was in his mid to late twenties, a beautiful man dressed in a white dress shirt and black jeans, a thin black tie. His long dark hair was tied back, highlighting sculpted, sensitive features that drew her eyes to his sensual lips and the dark, expressive eyes. He was slim but strong looking.

It was then Celeste noticed that all the men were in black and white. Black slacks or jeans, white dress shirts or white T-shirts covered with black jackets. The monochromatic color scheme made her surroundings feel like a black-and-white movie, every detail precise.

A basket of cards rested on either corner of the bar, with a sign to "Take One." A small vial of bubbles was attached to each card with a black or white ribbon. Ben and Marcie O'Callahan was printed on the vial, with their wedding date. Opening the card, Celeste read, *When the music ends, full play may begin. At that time, please maintain silence or whisper to respect those in session. Bubbles may be used anytime.*

"Sorry, we didn't mean to leave you on your own like that." Rachel threaded her arm through Celeste's, nudged her. "I didn't realize Leland had stepped out with Matt. Jon said they'll be back shortly. Leland said not to hook up with anyone before he returned."

"No promises on that." Celeste let out a breath, though, even while chiding herself for being ridiculous. She didn't have to do anything here she didn't want to do. She had a safe word, but Leland himself might be rethinking what he'd said he might do here. He had his own privacy to protect as well, and the extra people here beyond the K&A men might not be known to him.

"So...um, who are the other people?"

"It's a very exclusive group," Rachel said. "Committed couples and one trio, all of whom are close friends, not only in the 'public' world with us, but also this very private one. Ben wouldn't allow anyone here tonight that he didn't trust without reservation, Celeste."

"Of course not. I didn't mean to give that impression."

"You didn't." Rachel ran her hand soothingly down Celeste's forearm. "Your Master is a cop, and you want to protect him. And you want to protect yourself. Nothing wrong with that at all. But don't worry. In this world, Leland knows his way quite well. You can let go of the reins and trust him to take care of you, rather than the other way around."

Rachel had a calming scent. Beneath the teasing hint of lotion and body oil, there was an inner balance that seemed to increase with close proximity, like now. Celeste was tempted to lean against her, which wasn't like her at all. She wasn't the touchy-feely, hug-all-the-time female type. Yet Rachel read her body language and slipped an arm around her waist, letting the two of them lean together in a posture of relaxed affection.

"Nice change from the world out there, where it's all about juggling the balls and holding the reins, right?" Rachel's gaze swept the room. "Someone might look at this and see a circus, whereas to me, it's the outside world that's the circus. Work, groceries, bills. Expectations, worries, loss. Disappointments, fears. In here, it's like standing in a field beside a pond, listening to the stillness spread outward and inward. Close your eyes."

At Celeste's curious glance, the faint lines around her eyes creased, her lips curving. "Trust me. It's a fun experiment."

Celeste complied, and Rachel changed their positions so she was behind Celeste, one hand on her waist, the other linked with Celeste's. "Take three breaths. Slow. In and out. Think about the lack of color here. Everything black, white and silver. Clean lines. Simple. Yet think about the way the black paint is splattered over the white, a show of passion, a hint of volatility. The silver gleam of the equipment reminds you of the edge of a knife, trailing down your throat, around the curve of your breast, a sensual kiss."

Her eyelids twitched, but Rachel spoke again, her voice like a sparkling spring.

"Keep your eyes closed just a little longer," she urged. "Notice all the scents. Men and women. All the things they've put on their skin, their lips, the touches of fragrance at throat and wrists, the clean smell of their clothes. The rustle of the dresses we're wearing, dresses that will get peeled from our bodies as the night progresses. You'll notice new fragrances then. Perspiration, need and want. Release."

Her grip on Celeste increased as she swayed. "Think about what lies in the shadows, hanging from the walls. Whips, floggers, paddles, restraints, gags. The possibilities are a million tiny tingles that spread from your stomach through every part of your body, making you feel alive, anxious, hungry...happy. You can almost feel him touching you already, hear him murmuring in your ear, telling you what he requires of you. You want him to touch you. He won't yet. But his eyes are on you, watching everything you do, your reaction to all of it. Open your eyes slowly and see."

The white and black colors of the room were sharper, her hearing and sense of smell heightened. Which made the impact of seeing Leland all the more powerful.

Standing a few feet away from them, he was wearing a white T-shirt and black jeans that made the most of his impressive physique, a casual black sports jacket over the T-shirt. His gaze was locked upon her, his golden-brown eyes sliding over her face, down her body, as if he owned every inch of her. At the wedding, she'd worn a sassy beaded jacket over the black dress, but she'd left it off tonight. He lingered over the swell of her breasts revealed by the neckline, the curve of her hip delineated by the cling of the fabric. She'd worn a short slip beneath the thin dress at the wedding as well, but here she'd left it off, so the slit in the back of the skirt made it easy for light to penetrate through the cloth, give him the hint of her thighs all the way up to the juncture between them.

This wasn't the reception where physical desires had to be kept in check. He didn't smile, didn't gesture to her. She was acutely aware of the hold of his collar on her throat as she managed erratic breaths. She was held in place, waiting for him to tell her what he desired from her. She'd always run from that, hadn't she? Never waited around to see what a man wanted from her. Yet she actively sought it from him. She'd started calling him Master before he ever prompted her to do so. If he had prompted her to do it first, she probably would have told him to get over himself and fuck off, shut down the urge and never turned back to it.

She could lie to herself, tell herself it was evidence he'd let her take the lead at key points in their relationship, yet in truth she hadn't felt in the lead once. Nor had she really wanted to step into that role. It was as Rachel had described. She didn't have to be in control. That was her choice, an amazing, empowering choice.

She took a deeper breath at the thought. Now that Leland was here, connecting her to him with that penetrating look and full awareness of her, of who she was, what she was to him, those worries and insecurities felt even farther away.

"I have someone I'd like her to meet, Leland," Rachel said. "Is that all right?"

Leland's gaze shifted to the blonde, and he nodded. "In just a minute."

He crooked a finger at Celeste to draw her closer and reached for a glass of wine that the bartender had placed on the corner of the bar near him. When Celeste reached Leland, he slid his arm around her waist, his palm spreading out over her buttock. The simplest contact had her quivering and his mouth tightened as he saw it. "Take a couple sips," he said, holding the glass to her lips. When she began to lift her hand to it, he shook his head.

She put the hand down. He tilted the glass to give her a sip, then another. His gaze stayed trained on her, making sure he didn't give her too much, too quickly. When he took it away, he leaned down and tasted the wine on her lips, a brief sample of his mouth that, along with the wine, spread a steadying warmth through her.

"Go with Rachel now," he told her.

Rachel laced fingers with her. Leland gave her a mild push and a look that made Celeste want nothing more than to stay right with him. She wasn't sure who this docile creature was whose gaze clung to him and whose feet dragged as she was taken away from him, but she couldn't seem to snap out of the enchantment.

"He'll call you when he's ready for you," Rachel told her in a low voice. "They like us to move around, pretend to make small talk, when we all know the whole point is making the anticipation build until we're crazy with it. It's more fun that way."

Fun was not the strongest priority driving her right now. She noticed Matt, Lucas, Jon and Peter seemed to be doing the same thing Leland was doing. Their wives were greeting friends, chatting, but it was as clear as if there was an electrified tether between each couple that both Masters and subs were thinking about all the things that were going to happen here tonight. It was unsettling, arousing. Ironically, the farther she moved from Leland, the more that feeling was amplified.

When she brushed a lock of her hair off her brow, she had to stop herself from sliding her fingers over her mouth, down her throat, trailing her fingers over her breast. Her gaze slid over a divan and she thought of reclining there, letting her fingers descend further, her attention only on her Master as she touched herself.

"I don't think it will be long before the music is turned off," Rachel said, jerking her out of the fantasy. Though there was humor in the woman's voice, Celeste heard a faint strain that reflected her own.

Celeste cleared her throat. "You said there was a 'trio' here?"

"Yes. It's one of that trio I wanted you to meet. A distraction right now would be good, right?"

Celeste had to chuckle at that, and Rachel's eyes gleamed in response. "Here we go, then. Lyda, may I introduce someone to Gen?"

They'd approached a pair of women who were finishing

a conversation with another couple Celeste didn't know. Celeste hadn't had much direct experience with the female side of the Dominant equation, but the woman called Lyda was obviously on the Dom side of the fence. Way beyond that fence, and all the way up the side of a mountain with it. She had gunmetal silver eyes and an enviable figure outfitted in black latex pants that fit like skin. Her black-and-white pinstriped vest had nothing under it except a pair of firm breasts and more silky pale skin. She had a thin tie looped around her bare throat and tucked into the neckline, nestled into her cleavage. There was a diamond stickpin in the tie. Her long and thick dark-red hair was tied back off her bare shoulders.

Celeste deduced Gen was the woman standing in her arm span. A thirty-something with tawny brown hair and green eyes like fresh juniper, she exuded a quiet, humming sexuality. It wasn't the out-front appeal that Lyda had, but it seemed fanned to life and kept to a steady flame by the Domme's attention. Celeste wondered if she would put off the same vibe after prolonged exposure to Leland. Until these past couple weeks with him, she'd forgotten what being in direct communication with herself as a sexual being had felt like.

Lyda gave Celeste a sweeping glance and nodded, granting permission for Rachel to introduce Celeste to Gen. The music wasn't yet turned off, but Leland's behavior, and now Rachel's, asking the Domme for permission to speak to her sub, told Celeste the protocol was already in place. It made those butterflies in her stomach more active, her desire to turn and look at Leland all the stronger, but she tamped it down and focused on being polite. She could move and breathe without her Master's direction, for heaven's sake. Without Leland's direction. This room and all the weird Dom/sub energy was spinning a spell over her. Like being at bondage Disneyland.

"Celeste, this is Gen. I thought you two might want to meet. Something about your personalities suggested to me you could become good friends."

Celeste's gaze flicked to Rachel, startled, but all she read from Rachel's face was the general instinct of a good people person. "Hello," she said, offering her hand to Gen. It didn't seem appropriate to offer it to Lyda. However, since the woman's regard remained intently upon her, Celeste offered her a nod. "Uh, friend of the bride or groom's?"

Gen smiled. "Sort of neither. Noah and Ben know one another." She gestured to the bartender, telling Celeste who Noah was. "Well, Noah knows all of the knights, but especially Ben. Oops, sorry. I meant Matt and his team."

"It's all right." Rachel gave Celeste a teasing squeeze. "This is the reporter who first called them the Knights of the Board Room."

"As if they needed an additional ego inflation," Lyda observed with dry amusement, but no rancor. "Though I expect you might have meant it in mockery?"

"Initially. Then I got to know them, and I realized..."

"They live up to the hype." Gen chuckled, gave Lyda a light nudge with her elbow. "Don't pay any attention to her, Celeste. Typical Master versus Mistress rivalry."

"So Noah is..." Celeste turned to look toward the bar where the beautiful young man was putting together a drink for Lucas and Peter. Her brow furrowed. She might have stepped in it, no real way to classify what he was to Gen.

"Husband, boyfriend, Dom, sub? It's confusing, isn't it?" Gen's warmth made Celeste feel more at ease. Lyda, while far less approachable, didn't seem unfriendly. She was just listening while stroking Gen's hair, her upper arm, and taking occasional sips of her wine.

"I'm theirs," Gen said simply. "And we both belong to her," she added, nodding to Lyda and coloring a little at her Mistress's lifted brow. "It's complicated."

Celeste thought about how she could introduce herself here. Could she really do it, say she belonged to Leland, that she was Leland's sub? That he was her Master? It was easier to say it to him in the heat of their passion, when it was just the two of them. "Um...I'm..." She reached up to toy with the necklace before she thought of stopping herself. "I came with Leland."

"Really?" Lyda's expression became less imperious and far more approachable. Seeing that she was fond of Leland also helped Celeste relax further. Lyda's gaze shifted to Rachel. "A miracle. The dry spell has broken. Think I'll go talk to him about that and get my wine topped off."

With a nod at Gen, she drifted in that direction. Rachel squeezed Celeste's arm. "I'm going to leave you and Gen to talk and check on the other guests. I'm on hostess duty."

Celeste wasn't sure how to take either Lyda's comment or being left in a one-on-one with a stranger, but she'd handled plenty of difficult interviews, hadn't she? The key was knowing what persona to assume, how to act. Except she didn't want anything about tonight to be about acting.

"You seem familiar to me."

She tuned back in to Gen, who was studying her face. "What do you mean?"

"I don't know. But just now, when you were looking a little uncertain about being left on your own, I caught something in your expression." Gen pursed her lips. "Where did you grow up in Baton Rouge?"

Celeste didn't make a habit of saying where, but apparently her hesitation gave Gen the clue she needed. She reached out, closed her hand on Celeste's arm. "The Haven Trailer Park?" she asked, face brightening further.

"Yes."

Gen's eyes lit up. "Celly. You're Celly, aren't you? Do you remember me? You were pretty young. Younger than me by a couple years."

Celeste studied her face more closely, and then a thought bloomed, her heart speeding up as she caught the anticipation and excitement from Gen. "You lived on the back side of the park. Your mom was gone a lot of nights."

"Like yours." A pleased look crossed Gen's face. "Oh my God. Small world. You remember when we tried to figure out how to make that boxed pizza mix?"

"And the sauce exploded? We were so worried your mom would get home before we got it all cleaned up."

They both laughed, but then Celeste sobered, staring hard at Gen. She could remember the moon shape of Gen's adolescent face, a little bit of baby fat on it, though she'd been all stick arms and legs. Gen hadn't lived in the park long, barely a few months, but despite that, she'd probably been the best friend Celeste had until she'd reached her twenties and met Valerie. Celeste realized she'd bonded with Gen the way she'd bonded with Marcie. Instinctively and instantly, though she and Gen had likely been helped along by their shared circumstances. Regardless, Celeste was impressed by Rachel's intuition.

When Gen slid her arms around Celeste and hugged her with great affection, Celeste found herself hugging Gen with equal warmth. Gen didn't let her go when she slid back, gazing at her face. "Isn't this amazing? I can't tell you how often I've thought of you over the years. That was about the only time my mother ever left Florida when I was growing up. It was such a short time, I probably would have forgotten we'd ever left the state, except I always remembered you. When I got old enough, I thought about driving back to see you, but then I thought, 'God, she's got to be hell and gone from there.' Or rather, 'I hope she's hell and gone from there.'"

"I'm still in Baton Rouge, but I'm also hell and gone from there. If that makes sense."

"It sure does. Sometimes the only journey you make is in your own head, but it can be a tougher trip than jumping on a plane and going halfway across the world."

Gen glanced across the room at Lyda and Noah. Noah was topping off her wine glass. As he did, his Mistress touched his face, a light smile playing around her moist lips. She said something to him, her gaze flicking over him with a direct intensity Celeste recognized, enough that she couldn't immediately tear her gaze away. Noah's dark eyes sparked at the direct command. Straightening, he loosened his tie, removed it and then skinned out of his dress shirt and the tank beneath, revealing a lot of smooth, tan skin and lean muscle.

"I figured she was going to have him do that sooner than later. Thank God." Gen grinned. "The surprise is she waited that long."

Noah put the clothing beneath the bar and braced both hands on it as his Mistress leaned over and kissed his lips, teasing his throat with a flick of her long nails. He closed his hand around her wrist and kissed her hand. When she moved away to engage Matt and Savannah in conversation, Noah didn't bother to keep his eyes off every latex slick curve.

Gen sobered then, her attention coming back to

Celeste. "My mom wasn't around a lot, and she wasn't the best mom ever, but I do remember she would have been mom of the year next to yours. I prayed for you, Celeste, when I understood just how bad it could have ended up for you."

She wasn't usually the sentimental sort, but between what had happened to Jai, letting Leland meet her family and everything that had happened these past couple weeks to crack open a lot of long suppressed feelings, Celeste couldn't quell the ache that captured her throat. It was a simple, lovely thing, knowing a friend had prayed for her well-being.

Realizing she might be drawing them down a path far darker than either wanted to go, Gen squeezed her hands. "Those prayers must have done some good. Look at you. You're beautiful, and you look happy. And that..." Glancing toward Leland, she executed a dramatic eye roll that reminded Celeste of the child Gen had been and left them both smiling, dispelling the shadows. "I just met him a little while ago, but I can tell that is a *very* fine Master there."

"Oh, really?" Lyda had returned. She was no longer carrying the wine glass, so both arms were free. She looped them around Gen's waist and placed a kiss on her throat as her hands slid up, cupped Gen's breasts. Gen winked at Celeste, despite having to catch her lip in her teeth as Lyda's touch roved down, slipped between her legs, began to massage her just beneath the folds of the short black skirt. Instead of a black dress, Gen had worn that and a black fitted shirt, transparent enough to show a black lacy bra beneath the line of pearl buttons. Lyda's other hand deftly flicked them open so she could trail her scarlet nails down Gen's cleavage and play with the front clasp of the undergarment.

Celeste blinked at the blatant exhibitionism, the abrupt and decisive way Lyda had taken control of things, turning this moment into an intimate one between her and her submissive. Celeste couldn't move, yet she was sure Lyda would have sent her scampering if she hadn't wanted an audience. But it wasn't as if the Domme had sought one, either. The humming energy Celeste had felt since she'd stepped off the lift was fueled by her intuitive knowledge--

and by the anticipation of the other submissives here--that the Doms could do as they wished, when they wished. Lyda had just taken that truth from an undercurrent to a full wave that swamped Celeste. She could feel the increased heat in the room. Or maybe that was just in and around herself.

It only took seconds before Gen lost the ability to respond to anyone but her Mistress, and only in panting breaths. Her head was back on Lyda's shoulder as her Mistress stroked her pussy. Gen wasn't wearing any underwear, obvious from the glimpses of flesh Lyda offered as she worked her hand under Gen's skirt. Her scarlet-tipped fingers slid inside and Gen went onto her toes, straining as Lyda fucked her slowly, her knuckles coming out glistening.

Lyda's keen gray gaze rose. "Do you like to watch, Celeste?"

She must, because she couldn't look away. Her own lips were parted, her body swept with sensations that made her sway on her heels. Gen twitched, a cry slipping out of her lips as Lyda did something with her fingers. Lyda shifted her grip to Gen's throat. With one hand there and the other between Gen's legs, it reminded Celeste suddenly of a cello, the way Lyda held her, played her sub's body, her own latex clad legs spread out and braced to balance Gen against her.

"She was already hot and slippery on her way here," Lyda said conversationally, keeping her eyes on Celeste. Gen's heels lifted out of her sexy black pumps. "Mistress..." she gasped.

"Mm-hmm. You're going to come in front of your friend, Gen. Right...now."

Celeste's fingers closed in nervous reaction as Gen obeyed, her body bucking against Lyda's hold. The woman was strong, moving with her sub and yet holding her upright. When Gen's legs buckled, Celeste was ready to move forward, but as smooth as a rippling wind, Noah was there, dropping to one knee and closing his hands on Gen's thighs, helping to hold her upright. Since he wore nothing but the black dress slacks that rode low on his hips, Celeste saw the tattoo between his shoulder blades. It was a blood-colored heart with a Celtic triquetra overlay done in black. Below it was the infinity sign, the sideways figure eight, etched artistically inside a rendering of handcuffs. Below that was script. *Yours, conditionally.* A jagged scar bifurcated the two intriguing words.

He offered Celeste a cordial glance before he bent and placed his lips on Gen's thigh. When he licked the trail of release off that pale column, Celeste glimpsed a tongue stud.

"That's my sweet rabbit." Lyda nuzzled Gen's throat, her cheek. She shifted her hand from between her sub's legs to offer her fingers to Noah. He licked Gen's release off of them, then produced a handkerchief from his slacks pocket to dry his Mistress's fingers. When he released her, Lyda ran a fingertip along the side of his face. "I promised Marcie a whip demonstration at the reception, Noah."

"That probably disturbed some of the guests," he commented, a twinkle in his eyes. "Sorry I missed it."

She tugged his hair. "At the reception, I promised Marcie a whip demonstration. Young fool. Grammar nazi. You'll oblige when they get here?"

"You never have to ask, Mistress." He rose then, putting his arms around Gen to support her on that side. Gen looked a little dazed and, when he captured her mouth in a heated kiss, she uttered a noise of pleasure, making him hold her tighter. Watching the three of them together was too much. Celeste needed Leland, now, no matter what the rules were about mingling until the damn Doms were ready.

Fortunately, the overhead lights began to dim, leaving spotlights on the main pieces of equipment and creating plenty of shadows. The music, a haunting, seductive playlist, drifted to silence. Somebody had uncapped their bubbles, because a small cadre of them floated by.

As conversation started to fade, Noah lifted his head and met Celeste's gaze, a light smile playing on his lips. "I think someone is looking for you," he whispered. Then he bent, lifted Gen in his arms and followed his Mistress toward the equipment.

Chapter Sixteen

Rachel had said the Doms would make their move when they were ready to get down to business, and that seemed to be the case. Celeste noticed other Doms and subs drifting in the same direction as Noah, Gen and Lyda. Those who preferred voyeurism or a different kind of play melted toward the places where chairs and beds waited.

She wanted to watch as well, but she didn't want to do it alone. She knew Leland was still at the bar. She felt his presence like the sun at the center of the galaxy. When she turned to see him leaning there, his eyes were fixed on her in a way she was beginning to understand and answer how they both wanted. As she moved across the room, the sensual atmosphere kept a firm grip on her, so that she moved in the sexy dress the way its designers had intended, her hips swaying, her posture straight. Her high heels gave her a pendulum walk. The gleam of the sheer stockings enhanced her legs. She was keenly aware of how every curve of her body was on display for him.

He didn't move, just devoured her with his eyes, more so with every step she made toward him. His lips stayed firm and unsmiling, his gaze intent. When she reached him, she didn't think. She acted on pure desire and intuition. She sank to her knees at his feet.

His gaze turned to flame. She kept her head up, her eyes meeting his, wanting to see what he wanted, needed.

He set aside his drink. For a time he just studied her, intensifying her arousal. Her heart was a deep drum thud inside her body, echoing throughout every cavity. When at last he reached out and touched her lips, she parted them with an erotic sigh. Ecstasy jolted through her from that simple touch. Watching her, stroking her mouth, he fished ice out of his glass to trace over that same path, then lower, nestling the ice in her cleavage. He left it there, leaving it to melt and work its way down her body under the dress as he ran another piece over the curve of one breast, up her throat. She tipped back her head at the unspoken demand and he put the ice in her mouth, watched her suck on it, melt it on her tongue. The ice melting in her cleavage was fire and cold, making her want to squirm, but she didn't. When it melted enough to drop down into her lap under her skirt, it stayed there a few excruciating seconds before it slid down between her thighs, tumbling against the crotch of her panties, then dropping to the floor between her folded calves.

"Give me your hand."

He lifted her to her feet, turning her to face the room. As he did, he leaned her back against him. She rotated her ass against his erection, steel against the fly of his black jeans.

"Nice. Keep doing that." He slid his hands up and down her arms, played with her fingers, tangling them with his, lifting them over her head, holding her arms there as her body moved in a sensuous dance against his. She rocked down on her heels, slid back up, dragging her buttocks over his thighs, his cock, worked herself against it. She didn't do impromptu lap or pole dances. But when every cell, every drop of her blood, was infused with erotic promise, promises she was making to her Master, she couldn't stop her body from communicating those promises.

He brought her to a halt, his hands tight on her shoulders. That, as well as the increased size of his erection, told her she'd done what she'd intended. But he'd made his lesson clear earlier, and she wasn't being pushy. Just offering herself to him however he wanted. He was as cognizant of the difference as she was affected and shaken by it now.

A few minutes later, she realized there was another reason the K&A men had decided to let play commence in earnest. A whir of gears heralded the lift returning, and Ben and Marcie stepped out of it, Ben opening the door for his new bride.

With session protocol now in place, there was no dramatic entrance or fuss to their arrival, obviously their preference. Celeste suspected Ben had wanted his wife to step into the dreamlike black-and-white world, saturated with the sensual play they both knew and embraced. Now everything was about Doms and subs, surrender and mastery, not about the two of them holding the spotlight.

Each play in process was only about the players themselves, and the audience was like the shadows, part of the ambiance.

Ben wore black slacks and a white dress shirt, and he'd been loosening his black tie when he stepped off the lift. His coat was already folded over his arm, so he put both tie and coat over a rack provided for clothing. Marcie stood where he'd left her, watching the multiple scenarios unfolding before her. Her eyes and mouth were soft with arousal and Celeste suspected there'd been plenty of play between them before they arrived. Unlike all the other women here, Marcie wore white instead of black. It was a short slip of a dress, and she had on a pair of teetering high silver heels with ankle bands that appeared to be slim steel cuffs, padlocked so the shoes couldn't be removed from her feet. Slim silver chains ran up her legs from her ankles and disappeared beneath the hem of the dress.

Ben returned to her. His expression was a complement to hers, fully set with a Master's intensity, more amplified than what Celeste remembered. Marcie was already well into the zone where Ben wanted to take her tonight. From his reciprocal absorption, she expected he was in a comparable Dom space. The intensity of the energy around them said the loft could be empty, for all the awareness they had of others.

Under the hands of her own Master, Celeste's reaction intensified as well.

Ben removed Marcie's dress, hung it on the same rack. She stood on display, waiting for him, though her gaze was devouring everything happening around her. Whereas Celeste knew she herself had strong submissive tendencies, Marcie was that way down to the bone. She could live this way 24/7 and only desire more. While Celeste knew she couldn't say the same, seeing it displayed in such a beautiful way between Master and sub was like being given a glimpse of something extraordinary and perfect in nature, a dynamic rarely seen as it was intended to be.

Marcie was naked beneath the dress except for her piercings. She had small silver hoops at her nipples, her navel and her clit. Tonight they were connected by one delicate silver chain that, just past the clit piercing, attached to silver bands on her thighs, and then down to the cuffs at her ankles, forming a glittering web of chain that kept her movements dependent on the guidance of her Dom.

When Ben turned Marcie toward him, Celeste saw more silver strands of chains ran down her back from her collar. She had wide, closely fitted cuffs on her wrists. Ben pulled her arms behind her and folded them, latching her forearms together with the rings on the cuffs and attaching them to the web of chains along her back to hold them there. Fixing a tether to her collar, he put a hand under her elbow and started to walk her across the room. She had to move in graceful, small steps, such that it was like watching a geisha move. The way Marcie stared at Ben, it was as if he gave her the power to soar. Despite having less than six inches of play between her ankles, Marcie could do no less than soar when her Master held her gaze like that.

For all that she'd experienced it only for a short time, Celeste knew that feeling well. She was holding her breath, watching the two of them. Most in the room were watching them just as intently. No matter their level of play or commitment as Doms and subs, Ben and Marcie were the embodiment of all of it, the ideal of all the different hopes and yearnings being realized here.

Celeste curled her fingers in Leland's hands, folded low over her waist, and she let out a shuddering breath, a sound of joy as he kissed her throat, then kept his jaw to her temple so they could watch together, their bodies so close she felt his heartbeat against her back, the way his chest expanded as he breathed.

Ben took Marcie toward the canopy bed. He carried her up the two steps, setting her back on her feet at the foot of the bed. Bending her forward, he adjusted the chains and bindings so her collar was hooked to the foot of the bed, her chin resting on it as he spread out her ankles. Unhooking the chains from the thigh cuffs, he used that length of chain to hook her legs to the rails, then he did the same to her arms. They were all fragile threads she could break if she resisted at all, but she stayed motionless, except for a quiver that was as potent as a ripple through the firmament. Ben propped his Italian shoe on the bottom railing of the bed as he ran one hand down over her ass and cupped the weight of her breast in the other. Playing with the nipple ring, he tugged on it so she let out a moan. The act was purely proprietary. Proof of full ownership.

Leland caressed Celeste's neck, and she shuddered at feeling that same kind of touch from him. He stroked her neck underneath the thin chain of the necklace, and pushed the straps of her dress off her shoulders so he could explore her skin there unimpeded. This wasn't like being near a climax. It was beyond that. She was trapped in the same kind of delicate web as Marcie. Every part of her was stimulated, her mind a still point in the whirling convection of her body's needs.

"Look at all of them, Celeste. What do you like? What do you want me to do to you?"

She slid her gaze from Ben and Marcie, since he was now examining a very lethal-looking silver paddle with holes in it. She wasn't sure if she could handle watching him use that on Marcie. She knew Marcie was a pain junkie, but knowing and watching it could be different. Instead, her attention fluttered over and alighted on Rachel. Jon had taken his wife to a padded St. Andrew's Cross. She was sliding her hands along the sleek wood, pressing herself against it. Slipping a foot out of a high heel, she drew her toes along the sleek wood grain at the bottom of the X, toying with the cuff attached to the ring embedded there. Jon stood a few feet away, watching her. His ebony hair fell to his shoulders, the black slacks and matching shirt he wore making him an enthralling sight to any woman. His stillness added to the sexual tension weaving between the two. Rachel kept her back to him, as if oblivious to his presence, yet her every motion was an exhortation to come closer, to put her on the cross, to bind her and make her helpless.

Her rounded hips and generous bosom, her body toned from her yoga practice, gave her a Mother Earth type sensuality. As Marcie had mentioned, Jon was the leanest of all the K&A men, but the strength and power that emanated from him made him more than strong enough to Master and shelter the woman who responded to his every shift, the low commands he spoke to her.

Jon was a spiritual man, kind and compassionate. But right now he was also a sharply focused Dom who held every bit of control. Closing the distance between him and his sub, he ran his hand over her ass, tugged her to him with a firm handful of her skirt. Bending his head, he kissed her with hot intent, pinning her against the cross with his body as he shifted his hips to rub his arousal against her mound. Rachel dropped her head back, lips parting. The black dress she wore had a snug zippered top with a low neckline, her breasts spilling out of it when he clasped the tab and opened the zipper's teeth a few inches to reveal her bra. As he trailed his fingers over her curves, Celeste felt heat sizzle along the same track between her own breasts.

"Keep looking," Leland ordered in his quiet rumble. His hand slid down Celeste's front, under her skirt, fingers teasing her thighs. They loosened automatically as his other arm clasped her waist, holding her up when her knees couldn't.

"Please..."

"You want me to touch your cunt. Fuck you with my fingers."

"Yes, sir. Please."

"Not yet. I'm not usually this mean, darlin', but seeing all this, I want you to do more than beg. I want you promising me your soul. I want you giving me everything. When that happens, no matter where we go together after this, every time you fight me--and I know you will, again and again--we'll both remember this night, and know this was when you gave it all to me. No, don't look back at me. You keep looking at all of them. Your lips are all wet and parted, and your pulse is racing. It's making me harder, but I want to go beyond that. I want you so needy to be fucked that I'll tear apart the world to be the one to spread your thighs and thrust into all that wet heat. The only one."

Her fingers were digging into the forearm he had wrapped around her waist, her breath becoming more erratic as his voice deepened, vibrated through her. His grip tightened and she couldn't move. She could only do as he commanded.

Keep looking.

Matt was on one of the short sofas, Savannah curled up next to him. His hand rested on her hip, stroking it as they watched the scenes happening around them. Like Leland, Celeste knew they didn't play publicly, preferring to be voyeurs, so what they did next was pretty blatant for them. Matt said something in her ear, his lips and then his teeth capturing it as he put his hand behind her head. He loosened her hair from its twist, then tangled his hand in the thick strands as they fell to her shoulders. Bringing her head down so her cheek rested on his thigh, he kept his grip on her hair, holding it so her face was turned up toward his. Gazing at her intently, he slid his other hand off her hip and behind her. From her shudder, the sensual movement of her hips, he'd found her under her skirt, was playing and stroking her cunt.

When Savannah's legs twitched in their folded position, Celeste saw Matt had bound her legs from ankle to knee with a nylon black-and-white rope. Savannah's hand dropped, caught the fabric of his slacks over his shin as she reached up with her other hand, twisting her upper body in the throes of pleasure to grasp his shirt front, an anchor in the storm. Matt wasn't in the mood to wait on her orgasm, any more than Lyda had been for Gen. It suggested what kind of night this was going to be, since it was still way early.

Savannah made a keening noise, her body arching. Matt leaned over her, shielding her face as he cradled her jaw, held her in place while he massaged her firmly through all of it. Though the position muffled her cries, Celeste could still hear them, and her own body was rigid as if experiencing that climax with her. Savannah jerked, rocked, cried out. Matt never let up on the rhythmic movement of his hand's manipulations inside her. When his wife finally finished, he tipped up her flushed face and crooned to her while he continued to move his arm in what appeared to be a slow thrust and retreat. Celeste's pussy was contracting on itself as if feeling that coital rhythm far more directly.

Savannah's lips parted, eyes clinging to him. Matt gave her a look that was pure sin and all love, a Master's devotion, as he slowly removed his hand from behind her and then pushed two of those fingers into her waiting mouth. She sucked on them, tasting herself, her hand still gripped in his shirt, her body shifting now so she was on her other hip, fully facing him. He gathered her up in a curl around his body, leaning over her once again as he stroked the narrow line of her back, her hip, the round shape of her buttocks and down to the backs of her thighs, the erogenous area behind her knees.

Since Savannah was in his lap, Celeste couldn't see the physical evidence of Matt's own arousal, but she was sure Savannah was feeling that engorged state directly. She wondered when and how he'd find release and wished they did play publicly.

A breath later, she got her wish. They'd joked about the pheromone-like effect Ben and Marcie's chemistry had released upon the wedding attendees, but that, and the trusted nature of this group, seemed to be inspiring the most conservative public player of the K&A group to break protocol.

After succoring her through her aftermath, Matt brought his wife back to her feet, having her stand between his spread knees. Since her legs were still bound from ankle to knee, he kept both hands on her, steadying her as he prepared her for what he wanted. He slid her panties out from under the skirt and left them at her knees, then adjusted her flirty skirt in the back so it appeared he was tucking it into the slim belt that delineated her trim waist.

Though Celeste didn't have a clear view of it, it was obvious Matt was freeing his cock from the slacks one-handed, because he kept one stabilizing hand on Savannah at all times. A good precaution, because Savannah still looked a little unsteady from the force of her climax. Now both of those strong, capable hands were back on her waist, and Celeste's lips parted the same way Savannah's did as Matt obviously guided his sub back onto his waiting cock, seating her with a little extra thrust that made her gasp. The filmy fabric of her skirt preserved her modesty mostly in the front, but it was still undeniably erotic, watching Savannah's face contort, a mixture of pleasure and probably a good kind of discomfort from his size as he held her firm, made her take him deep.

He spread a palm over her back, bending her forward to give them both the right angle as she clung to his knees, gasping. He adjusted his grip to her hair and hip to hold her where he wanted her as he began to stroke slowly, his gaze never leaving the nape of her neck. He was murmuring to her again. She saw the plea break from Savannah's lips. Matt leaned over her, pushing her hair out of the way to put his mouth against her nape, band both arms over her chest. Savannah gripped his arms, held on, and the two of them rocked to a completion, a second orgasm sweeping the blonde when her Master released inside her, thrusting hard enough the couch was vibrating with the force.

When they came to a halt, breathing deeply together, Savannah lifted one of his hands, pressed her face into it. They were still rocking, only it was slow now, the rhythm of a cradle. Matt slowly drew out of her and adjusted, clothing himself once more before he eased her back into the cradle of his lap, turning her so her feet were up on the sofa as she wound her arms around him.

Celeste had been moving sinuously against Leland's groin in an ever more insistent coital rhythm during Matt and Savannah's lovemaking, and his hands were hard on her hips, so that grind rebounded right into her core, but he still wouldn't let her turn. He cupped her breast, thumb passing over her nipple.

"Please..."

"Keep looking, sub. Remember, I want you beyond begging."

What was beyond begging? A state of arousal so fierce it paralyzed the vocal chords and riveted every single sense on the object of her desire, what she needed more than anything else? Something she'd give her soul to have? Wasn't that how he'd defined it?

She jumped at a sharp *crack*. Gen's arms were bound to a vertical frame that kept them straight out from the sides of her body, and her Mistress had stripped her, except for one garment. Though she hadn't been wearing panties earlier, Gen was now, a pair of ivory panties that rode up and creased in a sweetly vulnerable way over her pale buttocks. Lyda moved around her, fondling a breast, touching her face, letting Gen kiss her fingers. Then she adjusted to the right, nodding to Noah.

Noah stood a few paces behind her. He'd changed out of his black slacks into a pair of black latex pants that clung to his muscular buttocks and lean thighs. They revealed in mouthwatering detail how aroused he was. Still no shirt, so the tattoo rippled across his back as he threw the whip, popped it again just above Gen's shoulder. When she flinched, Celeste saw the bloom of a faint red mark. But her friend didn't seem like she minded. She rolled her head, shifted her feet as if she wanted more. When Lyda ran her fingers over the filmy crotch of the panties, her slight smile, the avaricious glow in her eyes, confirmed Gen was soaked with arousal.

Lyda glanced toward Ben. Following her gaze, Celeste saw the two Doms were coordinating their efforts. He'd put Marcie on all fours on the bed, arms and ankles wrapped in the chained cuffs that had been left there for that purpose. In this position Marcie was facing Noah so she could watch the whip demonstration as promised, though Celeste had a feeling she hadn't anticipated her Dom integrating it into their own session in such a way. Ben hit her with that scary paddle right after Noah landed that blow, so Gen's tiny yelp was matched by Marcie's cry. Noah struck twice then, a crisscross, and Ben did the same, hitting each buttock in a sweeping movement.

Celeste's mouth was dry. When Noah ramped up his strokes, so did Ben, until Marcie was letting out a cry with every impact. As her cries escalated, Ben fit his bride with a rectangular gag like the one Celeste had experienced. This one had a larger phallus, something that stretched Marcie's mouth to capacity over it, but the rectangular patch sealed over her lips the same way. As Celeste remembered, it would suppress the screams, intensifying the sensations.

Once she was watching, Celeste found herself entranced, unable to look away from Marcie's subjugation. It wasn't the extreme pain Ben was dishing out--that part made Celeste flinch--but how Marcie gave everything up to her Master, matching every harsh demand with a pleading look in her tear-filled eyes. It was a plea for mercy, but not from the pain. Her nipples were tight, and Celeste was sure she was so aroused the barest touch would send her catapulting into climax.

She remembered vividly how Ben could take a woman past reason into pure insanity, just to please him. She'd told Leland at the beginning that she needed pain to get past her personal shit, and he'd proven that wasn't the case. She needed a mix of things--his total command, some pain, but it was the tenderness, applied at critical moments, that undermined all her defenses.

She didn't have it in her to want or accept Ben's kind of physical punishment for sexual pleasure. Not on a regular basis. But Marcie was yin to his yang. She looked as if she'd let Ben do anything to her and just ask for more.

No matter how true that was, she was worried about her friend, because it looked like Marcie couldn't possibly handle any more. Celeste broke the rules about not looking at her Master, but she knew it was for the right reasons. She glanced up at Leland for reassurance, her hand gripping his thick wrist at her waist.

"It's all right," he whispered in her ear. "Watch how he strokes her between every blow. How he caresses her hair, her ass, how he trails his fingers down her spine, her upper thighs. He never forgets her, Celeste. He knows just how much she needs to fly. She's not his whipping post. She's the center of his world. The way you are for me."

Celeste swallowed, her stomach jumping with thrilling response beneath his hand. He trailed his lips along her throat again, nipped her shoulder. "Keep watching, darlin'."

Noah was proving his artisanship with the whip, striking wherever Lyda indicated, leaving a mix of red marks that had Gen bucking in her bonds. Lyda came to her, kissed her frantic mouth, gazed at her with an assessing look. Her words carried to Celeste. "All done, rabbit?"

Gen nodded, her forehead hard against Lyda's cheek. The woman brought Gen's head down so it was against her shoulder, and curved her arm over Gen's nape, her hand spreading over the crown of her head to hold her there, and met Noah's gaze. "Five of your prettiest strikes, Noah, and then you get to put your cock inside her. Make the last one count. I want her feeling it for a few days."

The strikes *were* pretty, the whip becoming a sinuous

snake in his hand. Celeste wondered how a submissive had learned to handle a whip with such mastery. Noah must step into the role of a service top quite frequently. The one thing consistent about the BDSM world was how it resisted definitions. She only had to look at every different dynamic here to prove that.

His last throw was a short, hard pop on Gen's ass that bloomed into a precise red circle the size of a penny. Gen let out a short shriek, but Lyda caught it, kissing her mouth.

"Pretty damn impressive." Leland pursed his lips.

"What? Making a woman scream?" Celeste muttered. He caressed her arms, reassuring her once again.

"The whip play. Often when a more forceful stroke is applied, it's a length of the popper that hits, leaving a slash mark. To do it off the tip end, that drawback point when it cracks, is when you get that small circle mark instead. Takes practice and precision. Boy has both. And see? Your friend is being rewarded for taking the pain."

Lyda was running her hand down Gen's back to cup her buttock, soothe the offended skin. The succor was balanced by a pinch that made Gen jump, though Noah knelt behind her and followed that rough treatment with soothing licks of his tongue. He moved to her buttocks, cupping them in both hands and parting the curves to give Gen's rim a tongue fucking that had her crying out for different reasons.

"Look there," Leland said, drawing her attention to yet another scene unfolding. Since Marcie and Cassandra were sisters, Celeste hadn't been sure how this group dynamic would work for them. She saw Lucas's interest had been caught by a hammock frame on the other side of the loft from Ben and Marcie. Celeste wondered if the extra cushion of space wasn't merely because of the sexual component, but maybe because Cassandra also had difficulty watching her sister take those incredible punishments Ben could dish out.

Either way, Lucas was keeping her well distracted. He had Cassandra lashed on the hammock frame and blindfolded. He'd tilted her back on the web so her knees were higher than her head. As a result, he didn't have to bend more than a few inches to thread his hands through the ropes, grip her thighs and put his mouth between her legs. She was making harsh noises of pleasure, and when Lucas lifted his head, she saw how glistening wet Cass's cunt was, her thighs marked as if he'd already brought her to climax this way and intended to keep doing it.

They had company on that side of the loft. Peter had Dana strapped to one of the fucking machines, and was squatting on his heels, studying his petite submissive as she fought her orgasm on hands and knees. Peter's military-short hair just emphasized the corded neck and broad shoulders. His black T-shirt drew Celeste's gaze to the *Don't Tread on Me* tattoo on his biceps. Despite his intimidating appearance and the stern Master's expression, his touch on Dana's nape was as gentle as if he was touching a baby bird.

Celeste hadn't had a chance to meet the other couples before the lights dimmed, but Dana was going down on one of the women, a Hispanic brunette with large breasts, dark, long-lashed eyes and scarlet-painted lips stretched back from her teeth in a captivating expression of arousal. Peter held a pair of clover nipple clamps. Based on Dana's urgency, Celeste guessed he was threatening her with the painful things if she didn't bring the woman to climax before her own overtook her. Yet he had every intention of making her fail. As Celeste watched, he put his hand beneath his wife and began to play with her small nipples as the fucking machine kept doing his work. Celeste had to bite back a strained smile as she detected Dana's creative curse.

These were just the opening acts. They'd probably go on well until the dawn. Every coupling, every surrender, every command, would honor Ben and Marcie's union and what such a union could and should mean.

The air was saturated with sex and need, every desire made manifest. Celeste's nape was damp with perspiration when Leland kissed it and pushed her dress to her waist, cupped her breasts in their lace cups, squeezed and fondled. "Rub your ass against me, sweet darlin'. Tell me how much you need me. How much you want your Master to take all your choices away and fuck you until you can't walk without his help."

She was already rubbing herself against him like a cat in heat, and when he reached into the cups, finding her nipples to give them a rolling pinch, she jerked hard against him, crying out. "Please..." It was the only word she knew with him right now.

"So should I do all of it to you, darlin'? Every single thing? Or is there something in particular you just have to have, right this minute? Ask me nicely, and you might get your wish."

She could barely breathe. She knew what she wanted, but that didn't matter. He would make the decision. She understood that, but she also understood why he wanted her to say it. By saying it, she was acknowledging his right to make that decision, and trusting him enough to follow whatever he decided. Wanting what he wanted as much as what she wanted herself, because it was somehow all the same.

"I want...what my Master said he wanted. To take me here, in front of all of them. To show them...I'm his."

"Yeah, you are. Every beautiful, difficult inch of you." He kissed the top of her head. "I want you out of this dress."

He pushed it off, holding her arm to steady her as she stepped free of it, leaving her in her black low cut bra, lace thong panties, a pair of thigh highs and her heels. He took the dress, folded it over a chair. He also stripped out of his jacket, revealing more of his powerful upper torso clad in the snug white T-shirt. Putting his hands on her shoulders, he leaned down to speak in her ear. "Walk to the bed to the right of Ben and Marcie. The one that's under the spotlight, that everyone can see. I'm going to be behind you, watching the way your hips move, the tilt of your ass in your heels, and thinking about how those pretty tits of yours quiver as you move."

His hands slid beneath them again, teasing the lace edges of the bra, the areola that peeked out of them. Her nipples were taut, pushing into his palms, and he noticed, caressing and fondling her as she let out a thready sigh, rubbed her ass against him again. He nudged her away from him, gave her nearly bare ass a firm pat. "Still showing the marks of my belt, darlin'. Do as your Master tells you."

She felt a pounding up in her throat, a rush of blood that made her light-headed. She tried to take a step, but the world tilted in a funny way. Before she had to grab onto anything, he was there, holding her from behind. "Okay?" he said in her ear. "Can you do this?"

"I'm not sure. I want to. I really want to." She wasn't sure what was going on, but everything was so bright. It was as if she was about to step into a whole different world, as if this act was so definitive, there'd be no going back. Oh Christ, she was doing it again. *Stop thinking.*

When he stripped his belt from his jeans, she wondered, heart skipping a beat, if he was going to bend her over the bar and punish her. Instead he looped it around her throat, drew it taut over the necklace. Pulling the slack back toward him, he wrapped it over his fist and rested it on her shoulder. He put his hand on the small of her back. "I've got you, darlin'. Walk."

It made all the difference in the world, that reinforcement. His contact. She couldn't explain it, but rational thought had no place in this. They walked through the different scenes, past submissives in various stages of what she herself was experiencing. Past the Doms like Matt, Lyda or Peter, all of whom registered her submission with a quick flick of intent eyes, acknowledging she was fully under the care and control of her Master. It made her legs tremble even more. When they skirted past Ben and Marcie, her gaze slid over Marcie's backside, angry red and marked with circles from that paddle.

Ben was now snapping a dragon tail over it. He'd removed the bed cuffs, but had her collar and wrist cuffs attached to those delicate chains, which were clipped to the end of the bed, his new bride on her hands and elbows. Marcie was doing her best not to break those delicate chains, and lift her ass as Ben commanded. But as she squealed at each sting, Celeste faltered under another wave of that light-headedness. She couldn't help but notice how wet Marcie was, the slick flush of her cunt. Ben paused just then to press a thumb into that opening as he bent to slide his tongue along her rim, making her writhe and beg all the more. "Yeah, I'll be putting every inch of my cock in that tight ass soon, brat. What do you think of that?"

"Pleeeassse..." Marcie gasped. "Master."

"Leland." Celeste couldn't find him in the shower of stars closing around her vision.

"Hang in there, darlin'." His arm steadied her.

"I need you inside me. Now. Please."

She didn't want to sound pushy, but she couldn't help sounding urgent. Though he might not prefer Ben's extreme physical methods, Leland could be just as much of a sadist, making her wait, making her lose her grip on reality and fly at his command. She thought that was what she was doing now, because she was sure she was walking on clouds.

Leland didn't take her to the bed under the spotlight after all, but to one in a back corner. Though it could still be seen by the others, it was deeper in the shadows, a space cocooned for the two of them. Leland turned her toward him, loosened the belt, set it aside. Her hands lifted, fluttered, caught his shirt. She shouldn't touch him without permission, but she found herself pressed against him, her lips to his throat, her body rubbing against his. "God, I can't..."

"I know. That's why you have me to set the limits." He turned her around, pushed her down on the bed and braced his knee between her legs, holding her pinned there with a hand on her nape as he ran his palm over her ass, gave her another smart slap. When she tried to push back up, a spike of rebellion, he showed her he was tolerating none of that now. His grip immediately shifted to that muscle between neck and shoulder and clamped down until she was begging for mercy, that she would be good.

"Not likely," he muttered. He released the hold but only to put his hand under her hips, yank her up onto knees. He brought her ass up but kept her cheek to the bed. Then he spanked her more fiercely. After that, he began to use the belt.

"God..." She was biting the bed linens. All that overwhelming arousal, all the stimulation here, she wouldn't have thought punishment was what she needed. She needed to be fucked. Yet here she was, getting even more intensely worked up as he reminded her who she belonged to.

A few times, she tried to fight him, but he put her back

down without any trouble. He was past playing. He didn't stop until he had everything good and throbbing, until she had tears on her face like Marcie, and for some crazy reason she wanted more. Just more of everything, as long as it came from him.

Then, in that insane way only he knew how to do, he turned her world topsy-turvy by changing tactics midstream. He lifted her off the bed, cradling her in his arms. He stood at the end of the bed, just holding her off the ground like that. He swayed back and forth, as if soothing a babe in his arms, her head tucked under his chin while she cried. He brushed his lips over her eyes, her nose, catching her mouth in a hot promise before he bent, laid her down on the bed again.

"Take off your panties," he commanded. "Get on your hands and knees."

She obeyed, her fingers fumbling. This way she was facing the wall, but there were mirrors here. She could see behind her, see the others, see who was looking at her. But suddenly that wasn't all that important. What mattered was her Master, who was opening his jeans. She curled her hands into balls, bit into the covers. *Yes, please.*

"I'm not hearing my sub begging. She must not really want this."

"No, Master, I do. Please."

He fitted the head of his cock against her cunt, so wet, so slippery. "Is all that for me? Or you've just been getting off watching all this?"

"No. Yes. But it wouldn't be the same if you weren't watching with me."

"Hmm." He played with her opening, pressing the broad head against it, but when she tried to push back onto him, force the issue, he withdrew, picked up the belt again. "Haven't learned our lesson, have we, darlin'? Who's in charge?"

"You. You." She didn't think she could take more punishment, but her Master wanted to try her in a different way. He ran the belt beneath her arms, brought her up on her knees, the band just above her nipples as he stood just behind her, his breath on her neck.

"Play with your nipples, Celeste. Feel how sensitive

they are when I hold the belt over them like this."

She obeyed, but she couldn't stop herself from pleading. "Please, Master. I really need you inside me. Please."

Everything she'd ever been afraid of, needed, lost or found, had to do with that. She was afraid she'd lose it if it didn't happen this minute, because such a moment always slipped away.

"I am inside you, Celeste. That's what you need to learn, darlin'. What we'll learn together, however long it takes. I'm already inside you. Inside, outside, all around you. I'm here." He let the belt slide away, crossed his arms over her, curving his large hands over both breasts. As he did, he molded their bodies together, moved them in that sway of motion like he had when he'd done the Ichinawa. She molded herself back into him as she had then, trusting his movements, trusting his hold on her. She let out a long moan as one of those movements pushed him into her, full length, his testicles against the back of her thighs as he brought her forward onto the bed, covered her with his body. "There we are. What do you say?"

"Thank you, Master. Thank you..." She gasped it out as he thrust a little deeper, then slowly started to draw out.

"Don't think I heard you."

"Thank you, Master. *Thank you.*"

"Better. Stay still. Don't move unless I tell you to move." He pushed into her slow, wresting a yearning sound from her as she tried to obey. In the reflection of the mirror in front of her, she saw Rachel's head tipped back over the edge of a spanking bench where Jon had her stretched out and was doing something between her legs that had her flushed and near orgasm. He kept drawing back the phallic-looking device in his hand, teasing her, making her beg as well. Her breasts glistened with something that looked like glitter paste. It was having some kind of erotic effect on her, because the nipples were swollen to twice the expected size. She appeared to be begging for Jon to touch them. When he did, Rachel screamed at the pleasure of it, her body bucking on the bench, her climax held just out of reach.

The look in Jon's midnight blue eyes was pure Master, getting off on her helplessness, her throaty supplications.

That look affected Celeste as well, particularly when Leland spoke to her sternly because her hips started to lift.

"Stay still. Don't make me tell you again."

Which made her want to incur the punishment. But she wanted to please him as well, and for once the latter won. She stayed still, every cell screaming to move as he pushed deep inside her, rotated. God, he felt so incredible. She couldn't possibly stay still, but she did, because he'd ordered her to do so.

"Look at them in the mirror, Celeste. I want you to keep looking at all of them."

She did, but eventually she had to close her eyes, overwhelmed enough to grasp the one thing she felt over and above all of it. Love. The way she'd never expected it to feel. Visceral, all-consuming, angry, tear-swollen, needy, unquestionable, unconditional and overwhelming.

He bent over her, pressing his full weight against her, driving his hips so he moved her forward on the bed and wrested a cry from her throat. "Yeah, you understand now, don't you, darlin'? Gonna use you hard tonight, Celeste. Leave no doubt in your mind. Got it?"

Oh God. "Oh God..." *How had he...* It didn't matter how, but the words alone were enough. The ripple started in her abdomen and started to spread, a tide that was no turning back. "Leland...Master..."

"Come all you want, baby. Won't be the last time you come for your Master. Your night is far from over."

She had no choice. She came, screaming without any thought of who might be around them. Someone else, maybe a couple someones, got tipped over by her orgasm, because she heard several thin cries that matched her own, like doves or swans. Those poignant long notes resonated in the heart and mind, driving the pulsing of her body to greater heights than she imagined possible. He was right. She was going to give him her soul before the night was over.

§

Leland hadn't been kidding her about her night being

far from over. After that incredible orgasm, he'd brought her back up to peak at least twice more. The first time was fast and brutal. He'd bound her on the St. Andrew's Cross that Rachel and Jon were no longer using, blindfolded her with an eye mask that deprived her of any light. Through the use of a high-powered Hitachi Wand, he forced an orgasm on her. Coming so soon on the heels of the other climax, she thought she might have shorted out some brain circuits. She struggled against the overwhelming flood of sensation, but he didn't let up until her body was bucking helplessly again and crying for mercy.

But his follow-up was even more devastating. He kept her on the cross, panting and shuddering, and began to press kisses on her body. A kiss high on her thigh first. Then a significant pause, where the sounds of other sessions, gasps, sighs, cries, sharp slaps, the zap of an electric stick, filled her with anticipation and a swirling anxiety. She jumped as his mouth pressed against her navel next, tongue playing there a leisurely amount of time before he drew back again.

He didn't fix the amount of time or establish any rhythm, so she didn't know where his mouth would explore next, but over an endless amount of time she felt like he gained an intimate knowledge of her flesh through taste alone. He stayed away from her nipples, her cunt, as she once again began to get slick for him, needing his mouth, his cock, his fingers, anything. She was shuddering, jerking from every touch of his lips. When he kissed her neck, his body leaning into hers, she wanted to twist her head around, seek the intimacy of his mouth on hers. She needed that contact, because she was starting to feel brittle, the roller coaster of arousal hollowing her out. She didn't think to ask, too busy struggling with it, but when the first tear rolled down her face, his lips were on her cheekbone.

"What do you need, Celeste? You need to learn to ask, darlin'. Trust me enough to ask."

"I feel empty. You're making me want stuff so much it's scaring me. It hurts. Please."

"What will help?"

"I don't know." She felt a frisson of panic at the

question. She needed him to know those answers. She didn't know them. Keep her tied, untie her? Fuck her, or just cuddle? She couldn't work any of that out.

"Let's try this." He released her ankles and then her hands. Leaning full against her, he sealed his mouth over hers, a warm, wet kiss, his strong arms banding around her, lifting her up against the cross as she twined her own arms and legs around him. The kiss took her under, down below sea level. He murmured against her mouth, a soothing reassurance and a command at once. "Hold on."

He was moving with her, and then they were sinking down on a couch, her cradled in his lap, the blindfold still in place. His hand slid between her legs and her thighs parted without thought, a little gasp on her lips as he explored her engorged clit. He lifted his head, breaking the kiss then.

"Drop your knees all the way open. Wide as they can go."

She did and then caught her bottom lip in her teeth as he kept doing those butterfly strokes against her. Labia, clit, circles, tiny taps. After the overstimulation, she expected to be numb. If he'd applied pressure, rubbed too firmly, it would have been uncomfortable. But Leland Keller knew his way around a woman's cunt. Around her whole body, heart and soul, if she was willing to admit that. He brought her back to life with those bare whispers of contact until she was lifting her hips, reaching for his touch, limited in her motion because she kept her knees open, spread at his command. But the intimate position, her cradled in his lap, her now fully naked body--except for his necklace--pressed against him, fixed that hollow feeling. Though he was wearing jeans and the thin T-shirt, she could feel every muscle and his sheer energy in a way that sheltered and surrounded her.

"Do you want to come again, Celeste?"

She was shaking her head, though she meant yes. She dropped it back onto her shoulders, and he had her, his arm around her back. Two of his fingers slowly pushed into her then, and her lips parted as she swallowed air. Then a third. A fourth.

Her head came back down, and though she couldn't

see with the blindfold still on, she sensed his eyes warm on her face. Intent. "Just relax, darlin'. Totally relax. Trust me. You're tight, but you want more."

He did something and suddenly she was feeling fuller, stretched in a not unpleasant but a little unnerving way. His thumb brushed her clit and it was like electricity, making her jump, though his arm constricted further.

"Drop your head back again."

He kissed his way down her throat, over the slope of her breasts, began to suckle a nipple as she shuddered in his arms. Somewhere along the way she hadn't cared anymore about their surroundings, about the question of what she would or wouldn't do in a more public venue. She wanted to do anything with him, trusting him no matter the circumstances. Though there were people here, the dense energy to the room created a heavy, dreamlike state like that which existed when they were alone. The stimulation that came with having witnesses to their pleasure was there, not as a distraction or a worry, but fueling all desires, a continuous build and reinforcement of the releases that were happening again and again, in myriad ways. The scent in the loft was ripe with body heat, sex, perspiration, the fragrances of aftershave, lotions and other oils released from friction, exertion, pleasurable stress.

Every time she thought about how much of his hand might be up inside her, her instinct was to tense up, but then he'd speak or touch or kiss her in a way that reminded her to trust him. Her head would fall back again, her body limp in his arms.

She heard a male voice near her, one that wasn't Leland's. She made a hazy attempt to figure out what was happening, but the obvious occurred to her. She didn't have to. She could trust him.

His hand slowly withdrew, stroking her as he did. Then he removed his shirt, giving her the pleasure of his bare chest and abdomen against her. It was a further intimacy, a reminder of how close he was to her. A second later she understood it was intentional, based on what he planned for her next. His baritone wrapped around her.

"Noah's Mistress has been so impressed by watching my sub, she sent him over to offer me a gift. He's going to make you come, at my command, while you're secure in my arms."

She felt Noah's long, clever fingers on her thighs, slow strokes, learning her. His palms were warm and callused, the roughness a shivering pleasure.

"Keep your knees wide open like before. You're entirely vulnerable, Celeste, but also entirely protected, because I've got you. Right?"

She nodded. "Yes, Master."

"Good girl."

She bit back a tremulous sigh as Noah's mouth traced a path over her mound, her upper thigh. His lips and tongue teased her moistness, learning her, tracing her. As she arched up, Leland made a reproving noise, using the strength of his arm to keep her still.

It was impossible to stay completely still, because Noah's tongue was tracing her clit, down over her labia. A blink later, vibration accompanied that stimulation, and she remembered the tongue stud. "Oh...*oh*."

A deep, tremulous sigh rocked through her as she shuddered in Leland's arms, moving with the rhythm of Noah's pleasuring of her. He and Leland both probably knew he and that vibration could rock her back into a climax in no time, short and intense, but Noah took his good old-fashioned time, working her clit up to a more engorged state, making her labia more slick, playing all around that area, nipping at her thighs, rubbing his face in her cunt so she knew he'd take Celeste's scent back to his Mistress like a trophy.

She kept saying Leland's name, and he'd answer with quiet sounds, the stroking of his fingers on her face, the kneading of her breast, a tracing of her abdomen. The darkness swirled around her like a cocoon as both men's barest touch took her higher. Earlier in the day, they'd both been certain that she wouldn't want another man to touch her, but this was different. It was as if Noah was simply an extension of Leland's will, a gift he was giving them both to enhance her overwhelming desire to serve her Master.

"Leland...close...really close..."

"It looks like it. Your pussy is a deep-rose color, all wet like after a rain. I want you to come for me, Celeste. Noah's going to take you down that slide for me. Right...now."

She had no idea what the man did with the vibrating barbell, the tip of his tongue and the strength of that muscle, the heated moisture of it, but as soon as the words came out of Leland's mouth, she was hurtling up that ramp as if everything had suddenly hit fast-forward. Her fingers clawed at Leland's arm, lying in a steel band over her abdomen, below her bare breasts. "Oh...God...please..."

She wailed out her climax again, and Leland covered her mouth with his own, swallowing the cries, rocking her all the way to the end. She jerked and thrashed and did everything she could not to close her knees. Noah helped, holding them down with strong hands, intensifying her reaction so when she came back to ground she felt like confetti someone had shredded and tossed into the air.

"There we go. I have you. It's all right." Her Master's whisper was like the wind carrying those pieces, turning them, holding them. She pressed her face into Leland's chest as Noah brushed a kiss on her thigh.

"Would you like me to clean her up with my mouth, sir?"

"No. I'll do that. Thank your Mistress for me, Noah."

"It's my pleasure to serve her pleasure."

If she'd had any energy left, she would have summoned a laugh at the ironic humor in Noah's voice. He had such a smooth, easy timbre, one that slid over a woman's nerves like a man's hand. He gave her another teasing kiss on the opposite thigh, a tiny nip, and then he'd withdrawn, leaving her in Leland's full care again.

"There you are. Easy. Just rest now. You're all done. It's all good."

She mumbled it against his shirt, so she wasn't sure if he'd heard her, but he eased her back and slid the blindfold off. She wasn't sure if she was as brave without the blindfold, but when she saw his expression, completely wrapped in her responses, his golden-brown eyes on her face, the rugged planes of his face suffused with desire for her, the words repeated themselves without any reservation at all.

"I can't be all done if I haven't serviced my Master."

How far had she come, that she would say such a thing

and mean it so fervently? She was shaky, but she managed to push against his hold enough to show that she wanted to sink to the floor between his knees. He held her an additional moment, though.

"You want to take my cock in your mouth here. In front of all these other Masters and Mistress?"

She swallowed. "I want them to know I'm yours." His actions had told them that, but she instinctively knew doing that for him, in front of them, put the stamp on it. Plus, his erection was as hard and straining as it had been right before he'd taken her on the bed, and she wanted to give him release, pleasure.

"Could get messy. I've got a powerful need, darlin'."

Her gaze sparked. "I'm not afraid of getting dirty. Sir."

He flashed her a dangerous grin. Letting her slide to the floor to her knees, he opened his jeans, then stretched his powerful arms out along either side of the back of the couch, adjusting to a casual sprawl. In that sexy pose, he gave her an intent look that told her the man could genuinely fuck her to death and she'd just ask for more. Especially when he used that tone of command on her, as he did now.

"Get busy, sub."

Many of the other couples in the room conducting sessions had concluded them, so she could feel their eyes on her, Masters, Mistress and subs, as she gripped his cock, put her mouth on him and began to slide down, down. That was the point. To show him she wasn't afraid to be seen as his, serving him as a submissive should serve her Master. Completely unafraid, trusting him and the environment, because he'd never put her in a situation that didn't feel right and true. At its core, it was still about just the two of them, even if she were doing this in the middle of a football stadium.

The drive between them could be urgent, but taking a page out of her Master's own book, she took her time now, savoring the taste of him, the way the meaty head of his cock stretched her mouth, the salty taste of the pre-come in the slit. When she worked her way down the shaft, she took as much of him as she could, played her tongue over every pulsing vein, every velvety inch of his organ. His balls convulsed when she slipped her hand under them inside his jeans, cradling their weight in her palm. She rubbed them, slow, kneading strokes as she sucked him, went down, came back up. It was like she was at one of those country bars he liked, straddling a mechanical bull, rocking with sensual intent, nothing in the world more important to her than just giving him the same mind-blowing experience he'd given her.

"Look at me when you're doing that, darlin'. You know I love seeing your eyes on me when your mouth is full of my cock."

Amazing, given the multiple orgasms she'd had, but his husky command sent tingles through her belly. She lifted her lashes, held his gaze as she continued to work him in her mouth, curl her hand over his base, squeeze and fondle. He reached out, cupped the side of her face in rough fingers. That, and the fact his hips were now twitching, beginning to add his own force to her movements, thrusting his cock into her mouth, said she was on the right track.

He bit back a growl as his fingers traced her lips, stretched over him. "Yeah, that's it. Going to fuck that pretty mouth all night long. Next time you mouth off to me, that's what I'll be thinking about. How putting my cock in there works better for both of us. Doesn't it, darlin'?"

He chuckled, gave her hair a sharp tug as she nipped him. "Yeah, there's my brat."

Her eyes glowing, she went back to playing and sucking, squeezing and fondling. His fingers locked over her shoulder, and now he started to push into her in earnest. Mindful of his order, she kept her eyes on him all the way until the end, because it was obvious how much harder it got him, seeing her staring up at him like that, his sub serving him on her knees. She could feel the eyes of others on her still, and wondered how many other subs in this room would be serving their Masters the same way shortly, the seed planted in minds on both sides.

His fingers flexed, his cock pulsed and jerked in her mouth, and he started to come. She finally closed her eyes at that first jet, having to turn all her focus toward hanging on, milking the last bit out of him, giving him full satisfaction. She swallowed, choked, swallowed again, kept pumping her head up and down, some of his seed escaping and sliding over her fingers. She didn't stop, kept going until the grip of his fingers told her he was coming down, that she needed to ease up because his cockhead was getting more sensitive. She was tempted to keep teasing him, but she wasn't sure if she could handle another punishment, pleasurable as Leland could make it. She'd save that for another time.

Slowly, she slid off of him, licking the sides of his still hard shaft, getting every salty drop of him on her tongue. She sucked on his ridged head, nipped and then licked her fingers while he watched her with a glow in his eyes.

"Come here." He tucked himself back in and zipped the jeans but left them unbuttoned, apparently too impatient for what he wanted next to wait for that. He drew her back up onto his lap and sealed his mouth over hers in another kiss that promised an endless cycle of wanting between them, no end in sight. She curled her arms around him, held on, hummed her agreement in his mouth, and then let out a little jerk of reaction as he slid his hand between her thighs, putting his fingers back inside her, a slow invasion, cupping her on the outside with the other fingers. "Hold your breasts in both your hands. Tilt them up toward me."

She did, and gasped as he started suckling, holding her with one arm around her back. "It's never enough," he said, a fervent oath he'd uttered before, but one she'd never tire of hearing. Nor could she do anything but agree, because her body started to go up that incline again. She couldn't refuse his demand, even if she gave him her last breath and last drop of energy.

§

He pretty damn well took both of those. A long time later, Celeste was back in his arms again, cradled in his lap, in a near comatose state. She suspected it was close to dawn or just past that time. He'd wrapped her in a blanket but hadn't wanted her dressed. After stroking and exploring her thoroughly beneath it as part of her aftercare, his hand had come to rest over her pussy, his thumb playing over her labia, the other fingers in a loose curl resting on her clit and mound. A not-so-restful reminder of his promise earlier in the night, that he'd own all of her by the end of it, could touch her however, whenever he wished.

She wasn't in the mood to argue, so she'd just let him have that one. For now. Her lips curved sleepily as he kissed her forehead.

"Bastard," she muttered. "You made me thank you for this. Bet you won't let me live that down."

He chuckled. "You're right about that, darlin'. But whenever it bothers you, I'll make sure you want to thank me again."

She gave a half snort at that, but had no energy to do anything else.

Sessions were all done throughout the room, submissives in various stages of aftercare or fully recovered. Those that had been naked now wore light robes or heavier terry cloth ones if they were chilled. The group was in a loose circle spread out over couches and chairs that had been drawn closer to this end of the room. Marcie and Ben alone remained in a private world on the other side, behind the sheer panels of the canopy bed. They were stretched out under the covers, Marcie naked in Ben's arms, her cheek pillowed on his bare chest. It appeared the wedded couple had given themselves to sleep.

Dana was in Peter's arms on one end of a couch, half-asleep, while Jon and Rachel were in a mirrored pose at the opposite end. Peter had his head back on the headrest, the beer in his free hand propped on the armrest as he studied the ceiling, digesting whatever Jon was saying to him. She couldn't hear the conversation, but there was a light smile on the face of Dana's Master.

On another nearby love seat, Cassandra's head was on Lucas's thigh, her gaze still hazy from their latest intense interaction. Across from them, Savannah was fully asleep, leaning against Matt on a futon. As Celeste watched, Savannah's husband gently extricated a wine glass from her loose fingers and put it down on the ground next to him. Kissing her brow, he helped her lie down so her head was on his thigh. She purred, a contented sound, and he patted her hip.

"It's been a long day," he observed to Lyda. The Mistress sat in a straight chair next to their futon, while Gen and Noah were on the floor together, Gen on her stomach, knees bent and feet in the air over her backside. Noah lay on his back in front of her, reaching up to touch her face, tug her bangs and tease her. Unlike the female subs, Noah was still only in the latex pants, and Celeste had no problem with it, given she had a great view of the nice package delineated by it. Lyda had her feet propped on Gen's ass as she and Matt chatted.

"Why is he not tired?" Celeste said to Gen, catching her attention by pointing to Noah. Every female submissive in the room looked wrung out, and it was offending her feminist sensibilities. In a very lethargic, not-all-that-offended way.

"He sleeps weird," Gen responded as Noah tilted his head to shoot Celeste a grin. "He'll drop like a stone sometimes in the middle of the day, sleep a few hours and then be good for the next thirty-six hours."

When Lyda tapped her wine glass, Noah rolled to his feet and went to get her a refill, checking to see if anyone else wanted one as well.

"He's really good with that whip. A master," Celeste observed, tucking her tongue in her cheek. Though sessions were over, she kept her voice low like everyone else was doing, which felt right for the mood. "Between the tongue stud and whip play, he's pretty irresistible."

His head was back on the headrest of the couch and he looked half-asleep, but she knew Leland was listening. She giggled as he tickled her, gave her a pinch. It was an easy, young noise that startled her.

Gen reached up and poked her side. "You have no idea."

Lyda beckoned Gen to sit up so she could share the wine. When she gave Gen a sip, the Mistress kissed the taste off her submissive's lips, then she brought Noah to his knees at her other side so she could exchange a wine-flavored kiss with him as well. His hand rested on her knee, his other one gliding down Gen's back to rest on her hip, joining the three of them.

You have no idea. That was true on a lot of levels.

Before Celeste had met Leland, she'd never have guessed she'd be here doing something like this, and feeling so...right. She turned in Leland's arms, gazed up into his face. He had his eyes closed. It made her feel somewhat better, to see she might have tired him out as well. During their many sessions this evening, he'd edged her out on the orgasm thing, making her come too many times to count, but she'd counted at least four or five times for him. At least three of those times had been, blissfully, while he was inside her. One time he'd come on her breasts, over her pussy, and then made her rub his seed into her flesh as he watched with avid eyes.

Her Master. Her cop. A good man with a strong sense of right and wrong. He was the first man who'd made her think about falling in love. The one with whom she had fallen in love, whether or not she was willing to say it yet. But for the first time in her life, she thought maybe there might be time for that to happen. That he would be here for the long haul, and so would she.

When she touched his face, his eyes opened to slits before he laid his lips against her pulse. Relaxed, easy, natural. In this environment, it was easy to feel like it was real, that it would stand up to the test of time and the million other things that could challenge them. But outside this loft, could she keep believing it was real?

She turned her attention outward again, and found Gen watching her. The woman was in her Mistress's arms on a couch now. Noah was on the floor at Lyda's feet, stroking his Mistress's calf as he laid his head against the points of Gen's folded knees. Much like Celeste, the moon-faced girl had had rough beginnings. Now Gen smiled, and that tired, content smile said it all.

Yeah. Whether or not it lasted, this was the real deal. This was happiness.

Chapter Seventeen

Stopping at house now. Need to pick up more work stuff.

Text me when you're on your way.

Yes, Dad.

Celeste rolled her eyes, then choked back a laugh when two yellow emoticons popped up, one dressed in black leather and spanking the other yellow smiley face, who was hopping up and down with a look of dismay. She shook her head and sent back a raspberry emoticon, times three.

She told herself it was the one drawback to dating a cop--or a Dom--like Leland. He'd become overbearing in no time if she let him think he could run everything. She'd told him there was no reason to get his boxers in a twist. She was stopping by her house in broad daylight. All the intel they had said Dogboy was off in Houston somewhere, and the MoneyBoyz were focused on their drug trade rivalry with other groups, all while dodging the heat over Jai's death and the murder of Ron and Tony. She was the last thing on anybody's radar.

Still, it wasn't bad to have someone worry about her, care about her. She could get used to it. That after-party had resolved some things, maybe. She didn't think she was going to be the world's most easy going girlfriend any time soon, but maybe there was more room inside her to trust than there'd been before. Ever.

She glanced at the mail she'd picked up from her box and set it down on her kitchen counter. Remembering Leland's admonition, she dutifully locked the door after her, throwing the dead bolt. Good Lord, she was only going to be in here for a few minutes, but she did it because she'd promised. Twice. The second time he'd given her that penetrating stare that made her stomach do a sexual dance. Maybe she'd tell him she hadn't done it just to see if she'd earn a spanking. He'd know she was lying, because she wouldn't have given him her word if she wasn't going to do it, but lying to yank his chain could have pleasurable repercussions as well. Good thing the man had said he was okay with having a brat as a sub.

Shaking her head when she found herself smiling again, she took her overnight bag into her bedroom. She needed to unpack the wedding-related things and repack for a few days at Leland's place. As she returned a couple unused pairs of skimpy panties to her lingerie drawer, she considered some other options, running her fingertips over them. For New Orleans, she hadn't been sure which ones to bring, and since it was possible to fit fifty scraps of sexy underwear in the side pocket of a rolling tote, she hadn't limited herself. But she was thinking of some different choices to take to Leland's. Fuck me casual versus fuck me formal occasion.

With a grin, she gathered up the underwear she had worn, along with other dirty clothes, to dump in the laundry pile in her bathroom. She really should buy a laundry hamper before she let Leland back into the bowels of her home to see the disaster that was her bedroom. Let a man tie her up and bring her to screaming orgasm was one thing; letting him see her dirty undergarments would be beyond embarrassing.

Going into the bathroom, she tossed them on the pile, putting her toiletry bag on the counter. She'd need to add a few things to it as well if she was going to be at Leland's for a couple days. Was this like moving in with him? No. Hell no. She pushed down a spurt of panic. She'd stay a couple days, until he realized all was well, then she'd go back to her place. It was a compromise.

Her fingers stilled on her face powder compact, her heart skipping a beat. She swallowed, kept her eyes down, and closed her hand on her nail file. She started to move out of the bathroom, making herself take her time. She didn't bolt, the way every brain cell was screaming at her to do.

Maybe psychopaths had a second sense for when they'd been made, or perhaps it was the time he'd intended to make his move regardless. Dogboy exploded out of her shower, the metal rings screeching on the shower bar. When he caught her around the waist, she jammed the nail file in his hand, making him snarl, but it was dull and didn't do enough. He stumbled coming out of her tub, but his grip didn't loosen. They fell together against the bathroom counter, the side of her face slamming into the mirror, cracking it. He pulled her back by her hair and smashed her face-first toward it. She shut her eyes, cried out at the painful cuts from the glass, but she lifted her feet off the ground. Since he had her around the waist, she shoved against the counter. It pushed them back against the tub edge, and he fell backward into it. It loosened his grip and she threw elbows, scrambled off of him. He was too quick, though, tackling her again and tumbling them out of the bathroom onto the bedroom floor. He pinned her flailing body facedown and wrenched one of her arms behind her hard enough to make her cry out again.

"Shut up."

She took a breath and screamed at the top of her lungs. He flipped her over and punched her jaw, punched it again, then seized a fallen washcloth and jammed it into her open mouth. She thrashed, but he got it in there, and then hiked her arm up again, this time sending a jolt of pain through her elbow and shoulder that put spots in front of her eyes.

"Stop or I'll break it, bitch."

If he broke her arm, her chances to fight would be severely limited. She went still.

Her MMA instructor had said that once a person learned not to flinch from getting hit, they were a better fighter. They weren't worried about getting hit; instead they focused on how they would hit back. She was grateful for that lesson, as well as all the sparring she and Marcie had done where neither had held back, but this was a whole hell of a lot different.

There was no doubt she was fighting for her life.

Her forehead and cheek were bleeding. She saw the bloodstains on her carpet and tried not to let them fragment her mind into helpless panic.

Dogboy had come prepared. He dragged her over to the bathroom door again by her hair. Keeping her pinned on her stomach with his knees and that arm hold, he reached under her sink and pulled out a roll of duct tape. He used it to hold the washcloth in place, wrapping the tape tight around her head. He bound her wrists and forearms together behind her back in a boxed arm position and then pulled her to her feet, shoving her down on the bed. His hands were on her ass, unzipping her skirt, yanking it down.

No, no, no. She bit back the horror, the denial of what he was going to do to her. *Focus on what's important. Yes, he may rape you, but then he's going to kill you, gut you like he did DeeDee.*

She could come back from rape. She would, damn it. She couldn't come back from the rest. She had to focus on what opportunity he would give her between the horror of Point A and the finale of Point B.

He got her skirt off, her underwear, ripped her blouse down the back, got rid of that and her bra, leaving her naked. She shut her eyes as he fondled whatever he wanted, pinching and probing. She forced her mind to detach, thought of everything she knew about rapists, murderers. Those who wanted to be in control, needed it. She made herself go limp. Trembling and letting the tears roll down her face wasn't hard, because that was a dam that wanted to break anyway. She just couldn't let it completely take it over.

"Yeah, you know you lost, bitch. Not so tough now. Not up in my face, are you?" He gripped her hair, yanked her head up so hard she heard her neck crack painfully. "Answer me."

She shook her head, said something through the washcloth and duct tape that sounded like a plea. It was impossible he was sixteen years old, this six foot tall muscular man who had demons in his eyes. But he was. That was important. She was dealing with a teenager, not a mature man. A wealth of terrifying possibilities were wheeling around behind those dark eyes.

"Haven't had a house like this before, where I can take some time. Loretta, her daddy got home too soon. I should have capped him. Could have waited on Momma to get home, and then had both Momma and little girl. Yeah, should have done it that way. I've got time with you, though. Ain't no one gonna come looking for you anytime soon. So you gonna do for me the way Loretta should have.

She just cried the whole time, but I see in your eyes, you a tougher bitch. More fun to make you cry."

He pulled his gun out from his back waistband, backed up off of her. As he stared at her, a feral grin crossed his face. He sauntered back to her occasional chair and sat down, stretching out his long legs. "You stand up for Dogboy, bitch. Show me what you got."

She wanted to throw up. She wanted to run, to fight, but he had the gun trained on her. She made herself stand up. It took two tries with her arms bound behind her, because her legs were shaking so badly. That had to change. She willed herself to become rigid, to keep her limbs from trembling. She had to center, to calm down, so if the opportunity to fight came, she'd be ready.

His eyes had lit with pleasure at her awkward struggles. "No, don't stand there like a damn mannequin. Pose sexy for me. Maybe you work hard to make me happy, I don't kill you."

She narrowed her eyes at him and made it clear what she said through the gag wasn't complimentary. He chuckled at that, but rose. She forced herself not to back up as he approached, but closed her eyes, averted her face as he punched her again. She avoided having her cheekbone broken, but the impact drove her to her knees. He kicked her in the side several times, until she started begging through the gag.

"Yeah, you a tough cunt, but pain hurts, don't it? I'm going to take that gag off because you going to suck me off before it's all done. The first time you raise your voice up over a whisper, I'm going to shoot you in the gut and fuck you while you're bleeding out slow. That's what I did to DeeDee. She didn't like it none and neither will you. You gonna stay quiet?"

Celeste nodded. Her insides felt like something had ruptured. She hoped to God that wasn't the case.

He cut the duct tape with a wicked-looking knife, chuckling at her widened eyes. He scraped it down her cheek, passing over the glass cuts. A new wound opened, more blood trickling down her cheek and jaw. She bit back another moan at the pain. Some of the blood from her forehead had dripped down into her eyes. He used her washcloth gag to wipe it away, doing it with an obscenely gentle hand. "There you go. Don't want you looking all zombie cunt on me. I can do other things with this knife, bitch. Now get back up. You got sexy stuff? I bet you do. You gonna wear sexy things for me."

He stepped back, the gun trained on her. "I saw you putting sexy stuff in the drawer when I looked through the door crack. You fucking somebody? He ain't gonna want you after I'm done with you." He chuckled again, the darkness in his eyes saying that was as much because of how he was going to use her body as the fact she'd be a corpse. Like she couldn't figure that out herself. But his assumption that she'd do anything for him to spare her life was the advantage she had.

"I...I have sexy stuff." Her jaw was having trouble working properly, throbbing the way it was. But she spoke in a tremulous voice. "Do you want me to...put it on?"

"Not yet. I like seeing your pussy. But show me." He cut the tape around her wrists, freeing them, but then made her whimper as he caught her jaw, shoved the barrel of the gun in her mouth. He hit a couple teeth and a lance of pain went through her as one of them broke from the impact.

"You try anything, this is what you gonna get. You know you're done, don't you? Can't fight me, can you?"

She shook her head, tears streaming, and he nodded, satisfied. "Okay, show me what you got."

She moved to the lingerie drawer. He followed her with the gun, but when she paused, holding on to the dresser and trying to manage the pain of her ribs, her jaw and the nauseating level of terror, he made an impatient noise. "I don't got all day, bitch. Or maybe I do, if no one coming. We can make this last a good, long time."

He backed up to the occasional chair again, did that alpha male, king-on-his-throne sprawl, but his eyes on her were sharp as a raptor's. "Give me a show, darlin'."

She stiffened, an entirely different lance of pain shooting through her heart. She'd rather he call her bitch, cunt, whore. Anything but the endearment she'd come to cherish from Leland's lips.

Focus, damn it. She lifted out a pair of thong panties,

spreading them between both thumbs so he could see them.

"Hold them up to you. Yeah, they're nice and see-through. I could see your cunt through them. Show me more."

She showed him a pair of lacy boy shorts he didn't like as much, then a white delicate pair with lace on the edges. Probably like what Marcie would have been wearing under her dress for Ben. She was going to burn every pair she showed him, every pair his eyes crawled over, even as his attention kept roving up and down her naked body. She could feel every place he'd touched her, inside and out.

"You got anything more? I like this little fashion show. Gonna have you try them all on, maybe fuck you while wearing a couple. Show me more."

She nodded, turned and reached into the drawer for more.

Closing her hand on the grip of her loaded nine millimeter, she brought it out of the drawer and pivoted toward him in one swift motion.

Somewhere in a distant, rational place in her brain, she knew she had less than a blink of advantage. She was going up against a killer who already had his gun pointed at her. Though it was resting on the chair arm, her odds were slim and none. But the only thing that mattered was she wasn't going to bear a moment more of this nightmare.

She fired. Once, twice, three times. And kept doing it until the slide racked back, telling her the gun was empty. The sound in the small room was deafening, leaving her ears ringing, but as the echoes died away, she realized she'd been screaming as she fired. Moving forward while she shot, watching his body jerk. His gun was on the floor, dropped from his limp fingers.

There'd been a bare second of surprise in his eyes, where he'd looked like a bewildered teenager. He'd thought he'd beaten her. It had been so hard to wait, to pick up and show him those first few pairs of panties, to see if the "show" would make him relax his guard. She'd watched the gun lower to the chair arm. Then his finger moved, no longer lovingly stroking the trigger. Giving her the only and best chance of survival.

She felt something trickling down her breast and looked. She had a hole in her right shoulder. She put her fingers up, probed it, swayed on her feet. She was bleeding, but she could breathe, so he hadn't hit a lung. Okay. Okay. She told herself to think through the haze of shock, the overwhelming desire to collapse.

Her phone was still in the kitchen. She moved in that direction, the gun hanging limply in her hand. Her hallway had transformed into one of those fun houses where it seemed like the floor was tilting. She held on to the wall as it kept tilting, trying to topple her. She had to get to the phone. It was important. So important. But she was tired. Maybe she'd just stop here.

She slid down the wall. She was naked. Cold. She should have picked up a robe. Christ, she didn't want anyone to find her naked, but it didn't seem as important as it should have been. As she eased down to the carpet, her aching cheek meeting the rough Berber, she closed her eyes. She'd get it later. Leland. She wished Leland was here. She wanted him to be here. Always.

§

You're dragging your ass. Don't open that laptop, he texted.

He shook his head, a smile on his face as he imagined her response. She'd probably hunker down and work for a couple hours, just to spite him. Maybe he was being paranoid, but until Dogboy was behind bars, Leland wasn't going to let her be any place without him that didn't have a security system. He'd taken a new look at Dogboy's rap sheet, which began at age eleven with the killing of his neighbor's dog with a pocketknife. The crime reminded Leland of the glimpse he'd gotten of the kid's face during the drive-by. He had dead eyes, too far gone to come back.

Fuck it. He turned his vehicle in the direction of her house. She was at the edge of the District 1 jurisdiction. He was going to go scoop her up and take her to his place himself. Then she wouldn't have a car and would have to stay there. Yeah, she'd go for that, he was sure. Probably try to kick his balls in his throat and march right down to the bus stop. But he was going to do it anyway.

He was half way there when the call came in on the radio. *"Shots reported in the vicinity of 26 to 29 Newman Way."* Her street, and her address was 27 Newman.

"Twelve-twenty-five responding." He barked it into the radio, hit the lights, siren and accelerator as everything seized up inside him. He shouldn't have let her go alone. *Christ, please God. Celeste.*

He arrived in a matter of minutes, though it felt like hours. Two other units were pulling up, Mike and Billy. They'd recognized the address as well and gotten on scene first, probably because they liked the cardiac-arrest lunch at the diner about a mile away. Hell, they all knew her. They'd be the first of a damn army of cops rushing to her aid. And they might all be fucking too late.

Shoving that away, he was out of the car and headed up onto her porch, Mike with him and Billy only a beat behind, probably reporting they'd arrived and were going in.

As Mike circled to the back, Leland took out the front door with one kick that busted the door on its cheap hinges and ripped the dead bolt out of the frame. His girl had done what he'd told her, and it hadn't done a damn bit of good. He went high while Billy went low. He saw her keys and phone sitting on the kitchen counter, on top of a pile of mail. Then he saw her in the hallway, lying there unconscious. Naked.

"Fucking Christ." He forced away the cold rage, the fear, and focused on what mattered, clearing the scene. Her living room, piled up with junk, her guestroom which was a second office, just as he'd guessed. Billy checked the closet and Leland came back out of the room as Mike came in through the back door and turned off into her bedroom, the last unchecked room.

"Clear. Got a body here."

He let Billy and Mike handle that issue. Leland was at Celeste's side, holstering his gun and dropping to a knee beside her. Because he could already tell she was alive, he radioed for an ambulance first thing, but when she tilted her head to look up at him, his heart still damn near jumped ten beats. She had a gunshot in her shoulder that looked like a through and through. Her face was a mess, forehead and cheek cut, jaw and eye swelling up. There was purpling over her ribs and abdomen. He'd beaten her, the motherfucking bastard.

No, Leland corrected himself fiercely. Dogboy hadn't *beaten* her. Because Leland didn't have to look to know the bastard's body was lying in that fucking bedroom. She still had the empty gun clasped in her hand. No matter what had happened here, that knowledge would help her deal with the aftermath. Help them both deal with it.

"Good girl," he said, putting his hand on her head as lightly as he could, stroking her hair. "That's my good girl."

Her face eased. Yeah, she liked it when he said that to her. He bent down as she said something, then bent down lower, unable to hear her. "What, darlin'?"

She muttered it again. "What happens when…you try to boss me around. Better remember…that."

It was as if someone wrapped their hand around his heart and squeezed it so hard it was in danger of rupturing. He wanted to hold her, wanted to lift her in his arms, but he didn't know how badly she was injured. Where was the fucking ambulance? That bruising on her stomach and ribs was what really worried him. She was shivering. He started to look around for whatever was closest, so he wouldn't have to leave her side, but Mike was already on the same wavelength.

"Here you go." The veteran cop had brought a fleece throw out from somewhere, maybe her bed or the couch. Leland draped it over her, tucked it in as much as he could without disturbing her. Her shaking was increasing. Shock, nerves, cold, probably all of the above. Mike pointed toward the empty nine millimeter she was holding. "Bastard has a bunch of holes in him, Leland. Far as I could see, she only missed once. Hit the wall behind him. That is one hell of a woman."

"Yeah. She is." He bent down over her, pressed his lips to her head, put his arms around her to give her as much warmth as he could without aggravating her injuries. "I love you, darlin'. Fucking love you. I'm here."

His voice broke. Mike gripped his shoulder, a quick

squeeze, then withdrew. Leland heard the sirens of the ambulance and other cops coming. While he stayed crouched over her, his hands on her, letting her know he was there, Mike donned a glove and carefully extricated the gun from her fingers. Distantly, Leland heard Mike tell Billy to stop traipsing all over the crime scene or the detectives would ream their asses. Billy told Mike how the shower curtain was torn, how it appeared Dogboy had jumped her and then figured he'd subdued her enough to have her pulling things out of her lingerie drawer.

Nobody subdued his girl. Her surrender had to be willing and when it was, there was nothing sweeter than that. But try to boss her around... His lips pulled back in a grim smile. She was right. He'd do well to keep that in mind, but he didn't think she'd be letting him forget it anytime soon.

§

Celeste hated hospitals, but who didn't? Leland was with her the whole way, and that helped. He was going to step out when the detectives needed to question her, but she refused to let him go, her hand clasped on his. The questions, while seemingly endless, actually were fairly brief. She was just so tired and in pain, the departure of adrenaline telling her she had received a fairly severe ass kicking. Fortunately, X-rays found only a couple cracked ribs and no significant damage from the bullet wound. No bones in her face had been broken, confirming she had an exceptionally hard head, but she wasn't going to be going to entering any beauty pageants in the immediate future. They used that stitch tape stuff to close up some of the cuts.

They also kept her overnight for observation and comfortably floating due to the mercifully generous administration of pain meds. Even with those though, Dogboy kept coming into her dreams, making her start out of sleep like a jumpy cat. But Leland was there, every time, sitting in her line of sight in the guest chair. Sometimes he was reading a magazine, sometimes watching the TV, sometimes dozing a little, arms crossed over his broad chest, legs stretched out and ankles crossed. Most of the time his eyes were on her like a guardian angel, and she lost herself in their golden-brown depths, sliding back into slumber again.

Toward dawn she couldn't stand that nervous yank out of a sound sleep anymore. She didn't care that the meds were wearing off and everything throbbed. She slipped out of the bed and toddled over to him. She'd had to wear that ridiculous gown that supposedly wrapped over the back but everyone knew never did. At least they'd allowed her underwear. When she'd been so carefully specific about what kind she wanted brought from her house, not really sure she wanted anything from her underwear drawer at all, he'd understood.

She'd been drifting in and out, so she had no idea who he'd dispatched so that he wouldn't have to leave her side, but when she surfaced, he had a brand-new package of Hanes in her size, a three pack with pretty pink, lavender and light-green colors. It was the first time tears had threatened and, as she fumbled to get the package open, the dam broke entirely.

He sat down on the bed next to her, wrapped his arms around her and held her close, as gentle as he always was, but so strong, so solid. "It's all right," he murmured. "It's okay. You beat him, darlin'. He's gone. And I'm so proud of you."

Another man might have railed about not being there, to assuage pointless guilt. She expected he was pissed about that, because any man of worth would be. But whether it was because he'd seen countless victims, or because it was simply the kind of man he was, he'd set that aside. He'd known what she needed to hear, what was more important. When the tears eased up, he opened the package for her, asked her gravely what color she wanted to wear, and then helped her into the lavender, his hands warm and soothing on her body.

"Did Billy bring these for me? You know he has a thing for me."

His lips had twitched, though his eyes remained serious. "One of the hospital volunteers went to the corner drugstore and bought them for me. Otherwise Mike would have probably beaten Billy to it. They all have a thing for you, darlin'."

Sweet humor, mild reproof, all the things she needed to hear to remind her life was going to keep going, and it was going to be all right. He was here.

So now, as she moved toward him unsteadily in the predawn light, she wasn't surprised he woke. His surprise was replaced immediately by concern as he straightened, reached for her.

"What are you doing?"

"Coming to you." She stopped between his knees, holding on to him, swaying. "I want to sit in your lap. I want you to hold me. I don't care if it's uncomfortable." She expected every joint to protest. But she needed her Master more than she needed physical comfort. Dreams of Dogboy wouldn't dare follow her if she was being held in Sergeant Leland Keller's arms.

The benefit of modern hospital rooms was that the guest chair tended to be a recliner, allowing a caregiver a more comfortable sleep. Though it was still undersized for a man Leland's size, he made it work. He eased her into his lap, taking it slow as he cupped a hand beneath her knees, helped her draw them up, guiding her to lie back into the curve of his other arm as he reclined the chair. She dropped her head on his shoulder with a little sigh, face tucked under his chin. She clasped the fingers he had wrapped over her side and crossed her arms over her chest, forming a comforting ball around his hand as she succumbed to sleep again.

Leland stroked her hair, her neck, the line of her shoulder. Each time she'd started out of her sleep, he'd gone to her, held her hands or touched her face until she fell asleep again. While he didn't want to cause her any discomfort, he had to agree with her that this was much more preferable. He cherished the chance to hold her fully in his arms, have her in his lap.

He'd been humbled and gratified by how she'd looked to him for reassurance throughout everything. She hadn't let him leave while the doctor examined her, so Leland knew Dogboy hadn't raped her, though he'd had his hands on her, in her. When he heard that, the surge of anger he felt had been so strong he'd wanted to shoot the piece of shit nine more times, but he'd reined back the reaction at the doctor's sharp look. Even Celeste's desires might be overridden if the doc thought he was interfering with her care. But Celeste herself had dispelled his anger and the doctor's worries. Giving Leland a knowing look despite her abused face, she'd tightened her fingers on his where they were locked together on the padded examining table.

"He can't be any deader than he already is," she said dryly, despite a crack in her voice.

He resisted the desire to hold her tighter now. He knew she had to be hurting, even with the pain drugs. If he could figure a way to reach the nurse's button without waking her, he might ask for some more for her.

"I want to go home as soon as they clear me this morning," she said sleepily. Her fingers slipped up to his neck, touching him in a light, drifting way.

"Do you want to stay at my place a few days?"

She shook her head. "Would you stay with me at mine?"

His brow creased. "Anything, darlin'. But are you sure you want to be there?"

She tipped her head back to look at him. "It's my house," she said resolutely. "I hate cleaning, but I'm going to clean every inch of it, throw out that chair and everything in my lingerie drawer. I may want to wear cotton undies like these for a while. Not sure I can..."

She stopped, swallowing noisily. Pushing down that useless rage once more--*he's dead, she beat him*--Leland cupped her head, kissed her brow. "You can wear flannel PJs and granny panties for the rest of your life and I'll still only want you." He tipped her chin. "You know you can talk to me about any of it, Celeste, right?"

He waited until he had her uncertain nod before touching that abused jaw as if it were porcelain. Precious porcelain. "That said, if you don't feel comfortable talking it out with me, I think you should talk it out with someone. You remember what I said about when one of us has to kill someone in the line of duty? Dogboy deserved it, but taking a life comes with a bad after-kick, especially if you're a civilian and you have what he did to you piled on top of it.

Though we like to pretend we're tough and can handle anything, it can help to talk it out with someone trained to deal with trauma like that. Will you think about doing that for me?"

"Yeah. Okay. Maybe. But right now, I just need you. All right?"

"You have me through all of it, darlin'. Just rest now."

She pressed her face back into his neck. He felt the tease of her lashes as she closed her eyes. For a while they were silent. He was tired, and was glad the recline setting allowed him to keep holding her without worry that she might tumble. Yet as he dozed, he stayed aware of her every movement, every twitch. As well as the quiet whisper.

He surfaced, listened to make sure she wasn't having a nightmare. She wasn't.

"Master?"

"I'm here." He held her close and she nestled into him, said it again, a reassurance to herself, and maybe to him as well.

"Master." That was all.

§

Eventually the nurse came and he had to put her back in the bed for a vitals check. The hospital was waking up, breakfast on its way, and the nurse said that Celeste would be checked out by lunchtime. He answered a couple texts on his phone while she frowned at the bland fare.

"So are we dating now?" she asked as he tucked his phone back in his pocket.

The question was unexpected, her neutral stare making him wary. But he'd never been anything less than honest with her. "I think we've moved way the hell past dating, darlin'."

Her smile was like a shower of glitter to him. "So it's safe to say you're my boyfriend. And if you're my boyfriend, you'll go get me some Raising Cane's. I want the Caniac. I'm starving."

"Is binge eating a thing for you?"

"Men like women with a bigger butt. Jai said so. I've

also heard from reliable sources that black men are all about the booty."

"Stereotyping and racial profiling." He shook his head mournfully, but made sure she saw his answering grin, because she was watching his reactions closely. Typical for the kind of beating she'd taken, her face looked worse today, and from the way she shifted in the bed, every move she made brought pain. Those were the things that told you that you were alive, yes, but seeing her have to deal with them made him want to break something. Instead, he glanced at his watch.

"A little early for Raising Cane's opening time. Got a backup choice?"

"I want comfort food. Two Bojangles egg-and-cheese biscuits. And orange juice. They have that here, but everything in the hospital tastes like the hospital." She sighed. "I look like shit, don't I? I can tell, just from your face. You look torn between wanting to do the King Kong Empire State Building thing and wanting to hold me like a newborn kitten."

He stood and leaned over her, touching her face lightly. "I'll hold off on the King Kong thing. You kind of stole my thunder on that one, taking out the bad guy before I could get there."

"Well, you were running late, and I had other things to do that day." She gave him a smile that became a little tremulous. He would have put his forehead down against hers, but it had a taped gash. Instead, he laid a soft kiss on it.

"Mmm." She closed her eyes, fingers curling over his forearm. "Like *Raiders of the Lost Ark*. Want to kiss everywhere else it hurts?"

"Don't get pushy, sub," he said gently. But he kissed her face several places, then laid another lingering kiss under her ear, that delicate spot on her neck. He hadn't intended to do so, but once there, he stayed a longer time, struggling against a surge of emotions so strong he found he simply couldn't move. His arms had slid around her, holding again. "It's so fucking good to see you smile. Hear you giving me shit."

She let out a little hiccup of a laugh. "I'm going to

remind you of that," she said against his throat. "God...it feels so awful, remembering it. Like it wasn't real, then it's so real I'm afraid I'll wake up and still be right there. And I'll be too slow. I won't have left a round chambered, like I always do when I put the gun in the drawer. Or he'll be smarter than me. Or..."

She stopped, because she'd started to shake. He slid his hip on the bed, closed her in his arms as carefully as the newborn kitten she'd described, but she shook her head, pushed him back. "No. I'm not going to fall apart like this." She sniffled, rubbed her nose gracelessly and gave him a brave, brassy look. "Breakfast. I'm dying of hunger here."

He wanted to insist, but he knew he was riding his own need for comfort, and didn't want to impose it on her. She was close to breaking again, but it needed to be at her pace. So he went back to placid teasing.

"Dying of hunger, but not enough to eat any of this?" He poked at the tasteless-looking scrambled egg mix.

"Please. I have standards. My meals come from fast-food joints or convenience stores. And only ones run by funny, wonderful Indian men who should still be alive, fuck it all."

She dashed at the sudden tears, but again shrugged him away. He normally wouldn't have let her get away with it twice in a row, but he sensed she really was trying to pull it together, so he caught her hand, kissed it in a courtly way that had her blinking at him, surprised.

"Okay. One Bojangles breakfast coming up. I have my phone. You call me if you need anything. Even if it's just to hear my voice, all right?"

She nodded, and he saw the flash of gratitude for him understanding enough to give her space, and still throw her the lifeline. In her current emotional state, he sure as hell didn't want to leave her, and her uncertain look as he left suggested she felt the same way. But it was a good sign that she was determined to send him off on an errand. She was getting her sass back, God help him.

He paused at the elevator at the end of the hall, taking a second to run a hand over his face, the back of his neck. Christ. Fucking Christ. He loved her so much he was

Goddamned overcome with it suddenly, as if he might need to lean against the wall to steady himself.

Instead, the elevator opened and he found himself face-to-face with two friends.

Celeste's ordeal had been splashed across the newswires, and her identity had slipped out faster than shit through a goose. The texts he'd been answering were from those who knew them both, as well as Mike, some of the guys and Captain Teller. He'd let them know she'd be discharged this morning, so he wasn't expecting any visitors, unless any members of the press were unwise enough to try to figure out where she was. He definitely wasn't expecting to see Ben and Marcie, since they were supposed to be headed to Italy for their honeymoon.

Marcie embraced him immediately, and Ben clasped his hand in a firm, reassuring grip. Marcie had a Bojangles bag clasped in her hand. "I know you texted Matt that they're discharging her this morning," she said, "but we all know how long that can take, and nobody likes hospital food. At least not what they deliver to the rooms. They have pizza and ice cream in the cafeteria, but I figured she'd like this better."

"She will," he said, touched. "She'd just sent me out to get some of that."

"There's enough for you both," Ben said. His shrewd gaze covered Leland head to toe, and rested for an extra moment on his face. "Come on, man. You look ready to drop off your feet."

Mike had brought him a change of clothes from his place last night, but some things a change of clothes and a quick wash-up in the bathroom couldn't fix. Leland wasn't the type to let himself be nurtured, not as a general rule, but as the two guided him back toward the room, the relief that flooded him merely from their presence and their understanding told him how tightly strung he was. Marcie stopped a couple doors shy of Celeste's room, put her hand on Leland's arm.

"Mind if I go in first?"

He shook his head. "She's okay," he said low. "But she looks pretty rough."

A shadow went through Marcie's gaze, the set of her

mouth showing she felt the way Leland felt about that. "I'm glad he's dead," she said. "And I'm really fucking glad she was the one who did him."

With a crisp nod to punctuate it, she moved ahead of the men. Just short of Celeste's doorway, she paused, took a breath, tossed her hair back and stepped into view. Her expression was as nonchalant and teasing as if she were picking Celeste up for a girls' night out.

"So here you are, lazy ass in bed *again*."

Leland gave her credit for the great entrance, though the way her hand tightened on the fast-food bag told him Celeste's pummeled face gave Marcie the same gut punch feeling it kept giving him.

"That's a tough wife you've got there. Remind me never to piss her off."

"You have no idea." Ben's grim smile matched the dangerous flash in his eyes. "I'd agree with her, except I'm sure you'd have preferred to be the one to finish him before he got anywhere near her."

"Yeah." Leland searched for some mundane tidbit of conversation. "What happened? You guys were on your way to Italy."

Ben gave him an incredulous look. "Soon as we heard, we rescheduled our flight. Marcie wasn't going anywhere until we were sure she was okay. Neither was I. She means a great deal to us, Leland. Is she going back to your place after she's discharged?"

Leland ran a hand over his face again. "She wants to go home and clean the house, but I think just getting dressed and checked out will be as much as she can handle today. I'm going to insist on taking her home with me and tell her we'll get a start on that when she's more up to it."

"Good plan. Matt has a cleaning crew headed there now." Ben glanced at his watch. "Should be getting there in the next hour. He confirmed with your Detective Allen that they had all they needed from her house. Best not to ask why or how Matt knows them, but this outfit is Molly Maid meets the CIA. When they're done, there won't be a stray hair or skin cell left from that piece of shit. They'll scrub down every inch of the place. Wash every item of clothing, all the bedding, wipe down every dish and knickknack.

She'll be getting new carpet, too. They work miracle fast. Should be done by tonight, if you can keep her out of there until tomorrow."

Leland stared at him, and Ben lifted a shoulder. "Money can't buy everything, but we damn sure know what it can buy. Do you think that will help?"

Leland put a hand on Ben's shoulder, squeezed so hard that the man couldn't conceal a wince. "Ben, I don't know what to say. Or how to repay--"

"This isn't for you," Ben said, a flash of amusement in his gaze. "We knew Celeste before you did. She was our girl first."

Leland knew when he was being goaded, and also knew Ben was giving him time and a way to clear the lump from his throat. "First isn't what counts," he managed. "Anyone who's ever groped their way through their first sex will tell you that. It's not the starting line that matters."

"You keep telling yourself that. I don't grope my way through anything. For most women, I am the start and the finish line."

"Good thing you're in a hospital. Keep that up, you're going to need medical attention. I'll break one of your legs off at the hip and your wife will break the other."

Ben flashed him a grin. "My wife. That sounds good, doesn't it?" He paused, sobering. "You know, much as we like to be the ones to slay their dragons for them, sometimes it's better, afterward, if they did it themselves."

"Yeah." He knew that as a cop. Probably as a man as well, though Leland didn't think he'd ever stop wishing he'd done anything necessary to keep Celeste from going home yesterday.

Hearing a sob, he stepped to the doorway, fast, Ben on his heels. Celeste was crying, but Marcie sat on the bed with her, her arms wrapped around her and Celeste's face buried in her shoulder. Ben's wife rocked his girl in her arms, crooning to her. "It's okay," she said, glancing over her shoulder. "It's okay."

Trauma victims had wildly vacillating emotions, and finding out Marcie had pushed off her honeymoon just to bring her a chicken biscuit more than qualified as a trigger. Hell, if he would admit to ever crying, which he wouldn't, he'd had a near miss himself when Ben told him what Matt and the other K&A men were doing to help Celeste go back home. He would have helped her scrub every inch, but this way, she wouldn't have to worry about it.

As she said, she hated cleaning.

Joey W. Hill

Chapter Eighteen

Celeste knelt on the fleece throw, feeling its silken softness beneath her calves. The square of sea-blue blanket was stretched out over the cream-colored Berber in her bedroom. It still had new carpet smell, tempered with a soothing lavender-and-vanilla fragrance that had permeated the house since the cleaning crew had come in and done their magic. She hadn't entirely believed Leland when he'd told her how thorough they'd be, but every dish in her kitchen had gleamed in a way far beyond the capabilities of her old dishwasher, and the mismatched fabrics on her secondhand furniture looked as if a decade of wear had been removed from the fibers.

The shower curtain had been replaced, a clear door installed. She'd never again walk into her bathroom and not be able to see the interior of her shower. The perception and sensitivity of the K&A men never ceased to amaze her, but the toothbrush and hairbrush choices were all Marcie. The old ones had been replaced by an X-Men set featuring Rogue. When she and Marcie would spar, they'd revert to childhood, pretending to be a matchup of superheroes. Marcie preferred the Black Widow, à la Scarlett Johansson, whereas Celeste had always identified with Rogue from the X-Men comics. The girl who couldn't touch anyone--or be touched--for fear of draining their life essence.

She'd received a postcard from Marcie in Italy and a promise that they'd get together when she and Ben returned. Celeste had a feeling their friendship was going to be even closer, that she'd be opening herself up to her few enduring relationships more than she had before. It was amazing how embracing love could do that for a person. She might have to choose a new superhero to guide her. Maybe Catwoman. She was billed as a super villain, but to Celeste's way of thinking, she was really just a brat looking for Batman to grow a pair and become her perfect Dom, right?

Speaking of which, Leland had added his own touches to the house. He'd simultaneously made her laugh and cry when she opened her lingerie drawer and found he'd bought several more packages of those cotton bikinis. He'd laid them out inside the drawer in a neat fanned out display, good as a Victoria's Secret counter--with one additional touch. Her Walther nine-millimeter was placed in the center of all the pastel cottons.

It scared her, she couldn't deny it, how quickly her life had changed. She'd thought, in the slim but unlikely chance it ever happened, such a relationship would be a far more gradual process, with way more missteps. One step forward, ten steps back, that kind of thing. But maybe the man made the difference. Leland knew how to be tough and gentle, connecting to who she was and what she needed in ways she hadn't understood herself. Yet through him, she thought she was starting to understand herself better.

He'd suggested they go on a cross-country trip in the spring. He wanted to meet her siblings, and she'd said yes before she stopped to think about it. Maybe that was why love was the one thing that even the most skeptical people called magic. Because time didn't constrain it. It could only deepen it, expand the possibilities.

So now she was kneeling on the throw he'd laid out for her. He wanted her in nothing but a pair of those panties--her choice of color--and the locked heart collar he'd given her. He'd turned on a space heater near the throw to keep a flow of warm air moving over her exposed skin. She was quivering, for a variety of reasons. Tonight was the first time they'd be together...intimately. Sex seemed too trivial a word for it. It had only been several weeks, but it felt way longer, that near-death experience a hurdle that had forced them to wait as her body and mind healed. He wouldn't let her rush it, and she'd known he was right, even as she ached for that connection with a sharp longing that surpassed any discomfort her healing body had given her.

She couldn't articulate what she wanted, how she wanted this to unfold, and the Celeste she used to be would have worried herself into a froth over it, until she was irritable and prickly and ready to start a fight. Now she closed her eyes, let herself sink down on her side, curling in a loose ball against the milk-soft fabric. When he knelt behind her, touched her, she vibrated with need under his hands but remained still, docile, as he passed his hands over her, stroking her arms, her hip, the line of her spine, her cheek. He was naked except for a pair of cotton shorts that brushed her skin as he moved against her.

When he turned her face up and bent over her, she kept her eyes closed, savoring the feel of his lips on hers, the tease of his tongue opening them. He slowly turned the rest of her, hand gliding down over her sternum to her abdomen to slide his fingers between her legs. He stroked her through the cotton panel of the panties and then cupped her bottom in his large hand, his other sliding under her shoulders as he brought her up in a half-curled ball onto his lap. He held her that way with all his amazing strength, cocooned as he put his lips on her forehead, the crown of her head.

"My sweet girl," he murmured. She savored the words, the way he said them, as if he could never tire of her sweetness, never tire of being with her like this. She suspected there would still be times she'd fight him. She'd need that edge he could command to combat her bitchier moments, but tonight it wouldn't be needed. For either of them. She wanted to give him succor as well. He might be a big, bad cop, a tough guy through and through, but love made some things easier to read and understand, especially when she dropped her defenses so she could see his heart fully. He loved her. Which meant this hadn't been a picnic for him, either.

He eased her back to her side, removed her panties. She watched him remove his shorts so he was as naked as she was. Then he wrapped the dark purple rope around her wrist, fixed it there with the simple knot. Beginning the ritual he'd shown her weeks ago, he brought her arm up across her throat, molded her hand against her nape as he guided the rope around the back of her neck. Then down over her sternum, binding her other arm against her body. He figure eight wrapped both thighs and drew them up so she was in a tighter curl. Tucking in the rope, he bent over her, mouth cruising over her buttock, the line of her hip, down between her legs from behind, his stubbled jaw scraping the sensitive seam of her ass as his mouth found that oblong space revealed by her closed thighs. His tongue teased her labia, slipping into wetness as his hand gripped her hip, holding her still when shock waves of sensation rippled up through her.

It felt so good to have him there. She'd scrubbed Dogboy away, she had, but it wasn't real, wasn't finished until her Master replaced that other touch with his own. He was so thorough, telling her he knew, he understood, that he was doing this for both of them. Claiming her and reasserting his claim. She was rocking against his face, fingers flexing against the webbing of rope across her chest, desire rising like a slow tide. She had the normal spurt of panic she couldn't explain as control of her own response started to slide out of her hands, but when she tilted her head back, trying to find him, he straightened, came back to her mouth. He stroked her face, letting her taste herself on his lips while he put his hand where his mouth had been, massaging her as those pre-climax ripples kept building.

"Leland..." She met his gaze, her lips parted.

"I'm here, darlin'. Trust me with all of it. Don't fight me."

She shook her head. "Scared...just a little. Don't know why."

He lifted her back into his arms, the rope falling away. He made her smile as he rolled backward, carrying her with him and changing their position so she was straddling him and he was stretched out beneath her. She curled her fingers into his chest. He had her sitting on his erection, stretched out hard and flat against his belly. She rubbed herself against his substantial length, her breath shortening at his thickness, at the steel beneath velvet.

"Who's in control, Celeste? Who's in charge?"

Ironic question, because the change of position should have made the answer obvious. But it wasn't. What was real and true was going on in the connection between their eyes, all the intense feelings she felt there, as well as in the grip of his hands on her hips. "You."

The lines alongside his eyes crinkled, his firm lips curving. "Can I get that on tape? On the record?"

"No." That made his smile deepen, even as he held her more tightly. Her little movements and twitches became more insistent, desire rising over fear. Her hands slid over his wide chest, that smooth butterscotch skin. Well, smooth except for the occasional scar. She touched the one on his abdomen that he'd said was a ricochet. His hand went to her shoulder, traced the bullet wound turning into a small, shiny scar. His eyes darkened, shifted to meet hers.

"Put me inside you, Celeste."

His grip loosened so she could reach between them, curl her fingers around him. She moistened her lips. "You're so big. You always are, but..."

"I've been thinking about being inside you for the past couple weeks, darlin'. I want to drive it all away. Remind you that you're mine so you don't have any thoughts otherwise."

She guided him to the mouth of her pussy, and her tissues were so moist, so eager, she drew him in with barely a breath, sliding down his length, her face tightening at the stretch. As she adjusted to accommodate his size, her breath grew shallower in that wonderful, thrilling way. She pressed herself down on him as far as she could go, resting on his pelvis and feeling his length fill her so there was no doubt he had her. He took control again, holding her fast as he made small movements inside her, increasing the kaleidoscope of sensations. She curled her hands over his forearms, holding on as he started to move her up, down. Deep inside her, then a slow withdrawal, all the nerve endings tingling as she rose and fell.

"Bring your breasts to my mouth. I want to be sucking on them when you start to come."

Just hearing that was enough to tip her over. Her body convulsed on him, but she obeyed, cupping her breasts in trembling hands and bringing the taut peaks to his mouth. He kept her moving on him, and she shuddered at the new angle, even more excruciating. She could feel the inevitability of the soul-shattering climax like the certainty of sunshine dancing on the Mississippi, but it was all at his pace. He bit one nipple, flicked it with his tongue, drew it back in so hard, so she felt the pull all the way to the womb. Reaching up with one hand, he slid his fingers under the choker, thumb stroking her jugular, and she closed her eyes, all of her vibrating with need.

"Master..."

He reversed their positions so smoothly it took her breath away, pressing her down into the fleece throw. He framed her face with his hands, his eyes fierce, mouth firm. "Mine," he said quietly. "Always, Celeste."

She surrendered everything to him. And as she did, the emotions that filled her overflowed and expanded, covering the room, every inch of the house. The cleaning crew had done their part but it had needed this to make it all hers again for real. Now she believed it, with the same miraculous certainty she believed the man in her arms was hers as well.

"Yours, Master. Please. Always."

He shifted so he could wrap his arms around her. As he began thrusting, their gazes never left one another. She locked her legs over his thighs, his pumping hips. He held her closer as he took them both over that edge, a free fall to bliss.

She hadn't needed pain or elaborate restraints to find this place inside herself. Just a Master who showed her surrender was the way to happiness. To bliss. To letting go of all that didn't matter so she could hold on to what did.

With both hands.

###

Now that Celeste and Leland have found one another, would you like to read the FREE novella about Celeste's night with Ben at Club Surreal, the event that started her on the road toward Leland? (Marcie says it's okay. So does Leland, even though he's a little more grudging about it.) The novella is called "Retribution," and it's available on the JWH Connection fan forum, under the Vignette section. Information about the forum and instructions on how to access it are here – http://storywitch.community.

Soul Rest is a Knights of the Board Room book. If you'd like to know more about Joey W. Hill's work or that series, visit her website or the series page at http://storywitch.com *or* http://storywitch.com/series-kbr. *Free excerpts for all the books are available there. Each book of the series can standalone, because each book is about a different "Knight," so see who piques your interest!*

Joey W. Hill

The Knights of the Board Room...

Five powerful corporate executives, five bonded males. Together they help each man find the woman of his dreams, even when it takes the sensual talents of all five to break through her shields and convince her that he's the Master who can love her--body, heart, and soul.

"...an outstanding series...if you love romance, if you are part of the BDSM lifestyle or dream you could live in [that] world, or if you just yearn for a really good book, buy a copy ..."

--Riverina Romantics

The Knights of the Board Room Series
Board Resolution
Controlled Response
Honor Bound
Afterlife
Hostile Takeover
Willing Sacrifice
Soul Rest

CPSIA information can be obtained at www.ICGtesting.com
Printed in the USA
LVOW04s2003030415

433207LV00024B/1075/P